Triple Beat

Book 2 Rule of Three

Ann Grech

Edited by: Hot Tree Editing
Cover design: CT Cover Creations
ISBN: 978-0-6451500-1-8

Blurb

Single dad Mike must make a choice.

A second chance with a holiday lover torn away before either man admitted they wanted more?

Or the woman who'd become his best friend and stolen his heart?

Different from him in so many ways, both are the loves of his life.

But Mike's got secrets.

One could destroy a relationship. The other, his life.

Triple Beat is Ann Grech's long-awaited second MMF in the Rule of Three series. Featuring a doctor who has the cure for what ails his former lover, a lawyer rewriting the laws of love, a personal trainer working out just who he is, and two sassy kids, you'll fall head over heels for all of them.

*To Dr Hunt, for saving hubby's life.
And to hubby for saving mine.*

ACKNOWLEDGEMENTS AND AUTHOR NOTE

This story is incredibly personal to me as you can see from the dedication.

THIS PARA HAS A SPOILER SO SKIP TO THE NEXT ONE IF YOU WANT TO MISS IT! WPW Syndrome is a real medical condition that my hubby suffered from. Dr Hunt changed his life. His deterioration was quick and terrifying. Watching the man who could carry the world on his shoulders struggle to do the everyday basics was humbling. The medical scenes in this story are told from my personal experience as the spouse of a sufferer. WPW Syndrome affects people differently, and I have taken artistic licence in the story. Any errors are my own and I am not qualified in any way, shape or form to give medical advice, so do not take this work of fiction as such. If you or a loved one have any health issues (especially heart-related) please immediately see a doctor.

I've wanted to tell Mike's story for a long time. He's a special character to me, but he well and truly held out. Finally though, I stopped trying to tell him how things were going to go and started listening to him (I know, I really should have figured out by now that it's a waste of time trying to do things my way). Triple Beat is the result. I hope you love these three as much as I do.

I have a long list of people to thank for this book. Gianni Homes read an early version of the story and provided me with invaluable guidance. And then there was Liv Ventura! Your input and suggestions took Triple Beat to a whole new level that I'm so proud of. I couldn't have done it without you, hon. Thank you. Cheryl Riddell, your eyes captured those pesky errors that made it through the fifteen thousand reviews of this story. Thank you for picking them up!

My beautiful friends who make up the MM DreaMMers authors (Viva Gold, LJ Harris, JJ Harper, Angelique Jurd, Tracy McKay and Megs Pritchard), thank you for being the best friends I could ask for. We live spread out over the corners of the globe and yet I know I'll wake up to your messages, daily inspirational pics, advice, more inspirational pics, motivation and most of all, your friendship. I'm grateful every day for you being in my life.

Clarise Tan from CT Cover Creations, your talent is incredible. I love the artwork for Triple Beat. Thank you!

I also need to give a special thank you to Linda Russell and the team from Foreword PR too. Your advice, the laughs and constant cheerleading has made me brave enough to step this author gig up a level. Thank you for all the work you've done behind the scenes to get Mike, Robyn and Ezio's story out into the wild. It's truly appreciated. Cheers to working together for many more releases.

To my hubby, my rock, I couldn't do this without you. You're always there when I need you. You'd give me the world if you could. And you have. This year everything came crumbling down and you were there when I really needed you. You held my hand, and you gave me an opportunity to get back to myself. You've given me my mental health back, my happiness and definitely smoothed out the WTF frown on my forehead. I love you always. And to my kiddos, B and J, thank you for loving me. I love you all to the moon and back infinity times.

Last and most certainly not least, thank you to you, the readers and bloggers, for your unending love and support. Sharing, reviews, general shout outs and, importantly, reading our words means the world to every author. I never dreamed writing one novel would be possible, never mind a whole collection. But you've made that a reality and for that – the realization of a childhood dream – I'll forever be grateful.

Ann xx

GLOSSARY

This story is set in South-East Queensland, Australia. It uses Australian English. There are some terms that you might not have heard before, so I have set out a few for you. If you come across more, please let me know and I'll try to explain our slang. You might also want to take a peek at my website too – I'll add more there as they come up.

AFL – Australian Football League. A brand of football played in Australia similar to Gaelic Football. It is a full contact sport played between two teams for four sixteen minute quarters where the objective is to score more than the other team by kicking the ball between the goal posts for a goal, or between the behind posts on either side.

Arvo – afternoon.

Boardies –board shorts (quick dry shorts).

Brekkie – breakfast.

Buckley's and none – slang for two choices, one with only a very small probability and the other with virtually no chance.

Capsicum – bell pepper.

Carpark – parking lot.

Clubbie – a lifesaver belonging to a club.

Footpath – sidewalk.

Fridge – refrigerator.

G-string – thong.

Jack or jack shit – nothing.

Kitchen bench – kitchen counter.

Nipper – a trainee lifesaver who is a child.

NRL – National Rugby League. A second brand of football played in Australia. It is a full contact sport played between two teams for two forty minute halves where the objective is to score more than the other team by carrying the ball over the 'try line' and, after making a try, kicking the ball between the posts to add an extra two points to the score (called a conversion).

Rashie – a rash vest and includes sun protective shirts worn as swimwear.

Rubbish – trash.

Schooner (of beer) – In Queensland, a schooner is 425ml or 15fl oz.

State of Origin – an NRL match between New South Wales and the almighty Queensland Maroons (or Cane Toads) in which Queensland kicks New South Wales arses regularly (because we're that much better ;-)). With every year's competition, the entire state of New South Wales whinges about how the referees unfairly gave away too many pen-alties to Queensland (they don't—we're just better).

Sunnies – sunglasses.

Swimmers – swimwear.

Telly – television.

Thongs – flip flops (what kind of name is flip flop for a pair of thongs, seriously?)

Uni – university.

Vegemite – a dark brown spread made from brewer's yeast extract. It's sour and you definitely don't eat it like you would peanut butter or Nutella. Best eaten on toast with lots of melted butter, you apply it sparingly. Only the experts have an even spread of it.

Whinges – complains.

Part One

A year ago...

ONE

Mike

Paradise. He was in paradise. The warm breeze caressed his skin, the heat of the tropical sun warming him. The sky was an unbroken blue, beautiful from Mike's position on the deck of the MV Dreamcatcher. He slid his sunnies in place and lay back on the daybed as the heat dried the drops of water pooling on his skin from his dip in the pool. Crossing his legs at his ankles, Mike rested his head back on his entwined hands and sighed happily. The smell of the coconut sunscreen he'd applied still lingered, and Mike breathed deep. It was the scent of summer.

Mike resisted the urge to adjust the tiny white Speedos barely cupping the important bits. He worked hard to be able to wear them—exercising every day both with his clients and alone—but he was acutely aware of the few centimetres of exposed skin that he'd never normally show peeking above the low waistline. So low cut that he'd had to run a razor over much of his trimmed pubes. The white Lycra was almost see-through too, but the sales assistant had insisted that he take the pair. After he'd begged Mike model them for him. He hadn't had a chance to ask for a bigger pair that covered a little more—the man had shamelessly licked his lips, adjusted himself, and followed Mike into the change room. Mike had choked out an embarrassed laugh at his boldness, heat flooding his cheeks as the assistant let the curtain fall closed behind them and slipped his number down the front of the barely-there swimwear. With that kind of reaction, Mike hadn't been able to say no.

He did, however, have a pair of boardies that were much more appropriate for the family-friendly pool he took his kids in.

Mike slipped his earbuds in and played around with the volume on his phone until the sounds of old-school rock filled his consciousness. The low hum of conversation continued around him, but Mike tuned it out. He slid his eyes closed and smiled. It was heaven. He reached for the cocktail sitting next to him, the condensation sliding down the glass, wetting his fingers. The icy-cold drink was a contrast to the heat of the sun curling around Mike, the humidity making the air thick. He sipped the sweet pina colada through the paper straw, enjoying the kick from the double shot of rum.

The adults-only deck was called Serenity, and that's exactly what it was. Ordinarily, he loved being around kids. Their laughter and playful squeals as they splashed in the pool, ran through the water park, and exited the slides like a bullet was his idea of a great time. Mike's two—Alexis and Jaxson—were always the loudest, and the best fun too. But today… today was "me time" for Mike. And he wasn't going to move from this lap of luxurious relaxation until he absolutely needed to.

They were on day two of a ten-day cruise around the South Pacific. It had only taken a day for the kids to get adjusted and want to check out the kids' club. They were in different areas, Lexi, his seven-year-old, with the school-aged kids and four-year-old Jax with the younger ones. It made Mike nervous, but the kids had practically pushed him out the door. He didn't know how long they'd last there, but even if it was just a few hours, that was more free time than Mike had managed to steal in months.

Their mum and his ex-wife, Wani, was amazing. She was a great influence on them, especially their daughter. But she'd been home in the Philippines for a few months. Both her parents were ailing, and she'd been caring for them. While she was there, Mike had cared for the kids full-time. He had no idea when she was returning—she'd already extended her trip twice—but he knew she wanted to come home. He was almost going to cancel their family cruise and take the kids to see her instead, but she insisted that they go ahead without her. Mike was grateful—he'd needed the break, and he wouldn't have had that in the Philippines.

Taking another sip left him wanting, his empty glass a surprise. Cocktails apparently went down easily while on holiday. Cracking open his eyes, Mike looked around, only to see the waiter on the other side of the deck. He wasn't used to sitting still for too long, his restlessness a side effect of being constantly on the go. But it was all good. He didn't mind bar service anyway. Snagging his charge card, Mike eased himself off the daybed and headed to the bar.

Glass bottles lined the back wall, and small refrigerators sat below holding cans of every soda on the ship's menu. People lined the bar, some parts a few people deep where groups stood.

His gaze travelled over the guests, none of them really snagging his attention. He saw a lot of beautiful bodies in his line of work. Owning a gym that backed onto the beach in the centre of Surfers Paradise meant that he saw everyone who wanted to be seen, and a few locals like him who frequented the gym purely for its convenience.

But then Mike saw him.

Dressed in navy blue knee-length tailored shorts, a white linen shirt untucked at the waist, and brown boat shoes, he looked effortlessly refined. Classy without being snobby. Confident without arrogance, he looked just laid back enough to be approachable. Of average build, he wasn't muscly but not quite slim either. Black hair cut in a perfectly trimmed short back and sides style with a bit more length on the top and olive skin told Mike he had a Mediterranean heritage, but from his spot facing the bar, Mike couldn't tell whether the front looked as good as the back. He waited for a space to open up next to him and made his move, sliding in until they were shoulder to shoulder.

Resting his forearms on the timber railing running the length of the bar, Mike checked out their offering of spirits, despite knowing what he was drinking. The temptation to look sideways was too great, and what he saw made him bite back a groan. The man next to him had stepped back and was eying him up and down, his aviators pulled down as he bit down on pouty lips that Mike had the insane urge to feast on. His smoulder stole Mike's breath.

A touch older than him—mid-thirties at a guess—the man was gorgeous. Long, thick eyelashes that hid the colour of his eyes, hair sticking up in a messy quiff that was either effortless or took hours to get just right, and the perfect amount of stubble to artfully decorate his face. The chest hair peeking above the v in his shirt made Mike want to do dirty things to him.

The other man's gaze was like a caress, and Mike revelled in the shiver of desire rippling just below the surface of his skin. He waited with bated breath for the man's eyes to travel back up to meet his. His insides clenched tight from the zing that shot through him when they did. He couldn't help the tilt of his lips upward when the sexy stranger's nostrils flared as he sucked in a breath. Mr Suave pushed his glasses up his nose and cleared his throat quietly before tilting his chin up as if he was challenging Mike to call him out on his perusal.

But the joke was on him.

Mike wouldn't discourage him. Not in a million years. Not someone as sexy as him, and certainly not when Mike had picked his tiny swimsuit with the hopes of that very reaction in someone as beautiful as him.

"Mike." He leaned in a little closer to the man and held out his hand. The stranger was taller than him by an inch or two, but with a slimmer build—that was normal though.

There weren't many men who were as thickly muscled as he was. The man shifted slightly, turning toward Mike. He used his body as a barrier, sheltering them from the crowd gathered around them, and Mike's knees went weak. Was it crazy that he understood exactly why cats rubbed themselves along certain people? He understood the purring too. Wavering closer, Mike held his breath and waited for the other man to reach out and shake his hand. He'd never wanted to touch someone more, even if it was such a simple point of contact.

"Ezio," he replied, his deep voice rumbling over Mike in waves and wrapping around him just like the sun had earlier. The rich baritone warmed him from inside out and pulled a happy sigh from him. Ezio joined their hands and shook. Unlike Mike's callused ones, Ezio's were long and smooth, and his fingers curled around Mike's palm. It wasn't a quick handshake and Mike didn't want to let him go. But the other man hadn't pulled back either. The warmth of his lingering touch communicated as much to Mike as the man's slow perusal had a moment earlier.

"Can I get you a drink?" Mike offered a little breathlessly, his cool dissipating in a puff of smoke at Ezio's touch.

Ezio hesitated a moment, as if his decision was a whole lot more complicated than a simple yes or no, then gave a firm nod. He shifted closer, crowding him, and Mike sucked in a breath. He loved the show of dominance. "A cocktail," Ezio replied, his voice a low rasp, breathed more into Mike's ear than spoken out loud. They were chest to chest, their heads together. All Mike had to do was tilt his face at the right angle and their lips would brush, but his gut told him not to push.

He tried to stand still, but the temptation was far too strong. Mike shifted his weight and looked up at the handsome man in front of him. But Ezio had already moved, brushing a whisper-soft kiss against Mike's throat. Mike shuddered, the tiny contact like a bolt of electricity to his system.

"What are you drinking, Mike?" Ezio asked, his breath like a heated balm against Mike's skin. His breath caught when Ezio licked his throat, and he moaned when Ezio's arms surrounded him.

Mike reached for him, curling his hands into Ezio's shirt and holding on for dear life as Ezio sucked on his pulse point. "Pina coladas." His voice wasn't recognizable even to his own ears, filled with want and need. Desperation.

Ezio's lips turned up in a smile, curving against his throat. "Sounds just about perfect." He slipped his hands down to Mike's hips, splaying his fingers wide before pulling his face back and gazing down at Mike. He licked his lips, and Ezio tracked his tongue, his nostrils flaring at the move. "You like to work out?"

"I own a gym. It comes with the territory." Mike looked after himself not because he had to, but because he loved it. Exercise was in his blood. He surfed as often as he could, and healthy eating was the norm for him. "What about you? What do you do?"

"Doctor." He didn't expand, but he didn't need to. It explained a lot—the suave dress, the manicured hands. But not in a bad way. He was sophisticated, and his smarts gave him a quiet confidence that had Mike wanting to jump him.

They were served, and Mike motioned to the day bed his towel was resting on. "Care to join me?"

Ezio regarded him, his face serious, and after a hesitating a moment, he nodded. Mike didn't understand why he was reluctant. They were just two men sitting next to each other. Whatever they did wouldn't be any more forward than Ezio sucking on his neck a moment earlier.

Mike showed him the way and tossed his towel to the side before stretching out on the daybed. This time, he wasn't self-conscious about his tiny swimwear. It was doing him a favour of sorts by keeping his package contained as his semi strained against the material.

Ezio leisurely ran his gaze down Mike's body before he lifted a knee to the cushion and crawled onto it. Instinct had Mike shifting, letting his legs fall open in a blatant invitation. Mike watched Ezio closely. On his knees, his chest rose and fell quickly, his breathing harsh. With hands curled into fists, Ezio's stature was rigid, his lips drawn into a tight line. Ezio's intensity was a complete turn-on.

"I don't bite," Mike whispered, his voice rough. Clearing his throat, he added, "Unless you want me to." He patted the cushion next to him, and it seemed to snap Ezio out of whatever it was that had him frozen. The man smiled a slow grin that made him even more attractive, if it were possible, and eased himself further onto the cushion. Mirroring Mike's pose, Ezio reached for his cocktail before he turned to Mike and clinked their glasses together.

"To white Speedos." Ezio focussed his concentration on Mike again, and his breath caught, a buzzing white noise surrounding Mike. The other man's stare was potent, his gaze like a caress. Mike opened his mouth to respond, but nothing came out except a ragged moan. Ezio hummed and lifted the wedge of pineapple from his glass to Mike's lips. He opened instantly, and Ezio ran it teasingly along his bottom lip, waiting until Mike tried to bite it before pulling it back. His eyes darkened when Mike didn't chase a taste of the fruit, licking his lip instead. The sweet pineapple burst onto his tongue, and it was as if Mike had been struck by a live wire. He gripped the cushions surrounding him, arching into Ezio while at the same time trying to stop himself from reaching out.

Ezio's moves were slow. Exaggerated. He licked the spot where the pineapple had touched Mike's mouth, his eyes slowly falling closed and he hummed.

When he looked at Mike through lowered lashes, Mike sucked in a breath. He wanted nothing more than to have Ezio pressed against him, their naked bodies writhing together. But instead Ezio brushed the pineapple over Mike's lips again, giving him another barely-there taste. Mike closed his hand around Ezio's wrist and licked the pineapple, flattening his tongue against the flesh of the fruit. He lapped at it, the creamy white froth coating its end a sweet treat.

He plucked the pineapple from Ezio's fingers and dropped it into the empty glass to his side without releasing his grip on Ezio's wrist. Mike leaned closer and shifted Ezio's hand so he could suck on each finger. The other man's jaw clenched, and a hitch sounded in his breath when Mike licked his lips and hummed.

He watched Ezio watch him, Mike cataloguing every one of Ezio's reactions. He was still resisting the pull between them, even though the simmering heat that was building was more intense than anything Mike had ever experienced.

Mike captured Ezio's finger in his mouth, biting down teasingly and closing his lips around his second knuckle. He ran his tongue over the underside of Ezio's finger and let his cheeks hollow out as he sucked gently on the digit. Eyes locked and lips just parted, Ezio's expression spoke of heat and desire, and an intensity borne of having the man's undivided attention. Mike loved it. He wanted Ezio on top of him, pushing him into the mattress and grinding down. It would never pass for acceptable—not even in the adults only area—but at that moment, he didn't care. He needed more contact with the man. To be closer. To touch him. Pulled under him. Mike hadn't had sex in far too long, but he wasn't imagining the strength of their chemistry. If he had his way, they'd be leaving for his stateroom, but he hesitated, reluctant to propose it when Ezio had only moments earlier been shying away from him.

"Do you have any privacy in your room?" Ezio asked, his voice like gravel as he licked another finger. Mike nodded, and Ezio slipped his finger free before hooking it under Mike's chin and lifting his face toward his own. With their lips only a hair's breadth apart, Ezio whispered, "I'd really like to make use of it."

Mike wanted to smooth the line in his forehead, but settled on his own whispered reply, "So would I."

Ezio nudged their noses together and ran his thumb over Mike's bottom lip. He instinctively opened, and Ezio pressed the tip of his thumb in, slipping it in and out like he would do to stretch Mike's hole. He moaned, the sound filled with wanton abandon, and his eyelids slid closed. Mike closed his lips around the digit and sucked. Ezio's choked moan spurred him on, and he spun out of control, already flying high despite Ezio having barely touched him. Knowing he could get the gorgeous man before him this worked up went straight to Mike's head. And his cock.

"Let's go," Ezio rasped, his tone somewhere between a command and a plea. Not needing to be told twice, Mike pulled his mouth away with a pop and looked down at his groin. His erection was nowhere near contained in his swimwear anymore. The waistband of the tiny Speedos had pulled away from his body, his glans peeking out from the top. He was indecent and should have been embarrassed, but the appreciation in Ezio's gaze washed away any self-consciousness.

Ezio hummed. "Nice to know you're evenly proportioned."

Mike dropped his head back and groaned as his dick twitched, hardening even further and exposing more of him.

"Come," Ezio ordered. Those words struck Mike like a match to kindling, lighting him up and sending a wave of painless fire through his body. He gasped with the vibration against his back. His body was humming, hands shaking with anticipation.

Ezio frowned.

Reality intruded.

"Oh shit," Mike groaned, realizing what it was. He plucked his phone from between the cushions. The call was from the ship-board app.

"Hello," he answered, then cleared his throat. "This is Mike."

"Hello, Mike. It's Sarah from the kids' club. Lexi and Jax have both asked me a few times when you're picking them up. Jax has been crying for a little while now, and he's pretty worked up. He fell over—he's not hurt—but I think it rattled him. We've also had a busy morning, so he's likely tired too."

"Oh. Oh, sure. Um. Give me a few minutes and I'll come and grab them. Yeah, um. Just a few. Thanks," he stuttered and looked to Ezio apologetically. "Kids' Club. My kiddos are upset. Sorry—"

"You don't need to apologize. They come first. You here with them?" he asked, but it wasn't really a question. He'd shifted back a fraction, putting space between them that hadn't been there before. Mike hated it. He wanted them close again, pressed against each other. The smoulder from his eyes was gone too, replaced with wariness. He didn't ask the question Mike needed to answer—the one that had the potential to end what was between them before it started.

"It's just the three of us—my two kids and me. Their mum and I split years ago."

He nodded and Mike saw a flash of something in his eyes. Understanding? Disappointment? Was it that Mike was a parent? Because he was bi? Or was it that he didn't get off? If it were the latter, Mike could sympathize. Anything else was too bad. "Will I see you again? Perhaps later in the cruise?" Before Ezio could answer, Mike waved down the nearby waiter.

"How can I help you, sir?" he asked as he came to a stop near the cabana.

"Can I borrow your pen for a minute, please?" Mike asked, holding out his hand until he passed it over. He wrote his room number—8308—on Ezio's palm and passed the pen back to the waiter, waiting until he walked away to speak again.

"That's my room number. Leave me a message so I know how to contact you." Mike ran his fingers over the numbers he'd scrawled on Ezio's hand, and their eyes met. "I don't know if the kids will want back in kids' club this afternoon. Or any other times when we're not on one of the islands, but I'd like to see you again."

Ezio nodded and smiled, but it didn't reach his eyes. "We will."

Mike adjusted himself as discreetly as he could and slid his boardies up his legs to below his arse before standing.

Once dressed, he pushed his feet into his thongs and pulled his faded ball cap on.

He ran his gaze over Ezio's back. He'd sat up and turned away from Mike, his shoulders slumped and head hanging low. Mike walked around and stood between his legs, hooking a finger under his chin and lifting his face. "I want to see you again." His smile was more genuine this time, and Mike grinned, excitement pulsing through him. "I'll speak to you soon then."

"Yes." He nodded, and Mike wanted to lean down and kiss him. But he needed to go, and if he started, he wouldn't stop. He wished the call hadn't come in.

Then the guilt hit him.

He was disappointed because he'd missed out on a hook-up when his kids needed him. There was a perpetual guilt associated with being a parent, and as a single dad, he had it in spades. Every time Mike did something for himself, the voice in the back of his head said he should be putting the kids first. Mike always tried to do that—everything he did was for Lexi and Jax, but it was never enough. He wanted to be the best parent he could—help them grow and learn, inspire a love of learning and get out and experience the world with them. He hadn't yet figured out how to balance all that with running the gym, cooking, and keeping the apartment in a moderately liveable state, so taking any time for himself was riddled with guilt. What a bitch.

Mike walked backwards away from Ezio, hating the distance he was putting between them. But his kids needed him. Ezio stood and pushed one hand into his pocket. He smiled encouragingly and looked down at his free hand, the corner of his mouth turning up in a grin. Seeing him standing there and watching him push his sunnies further up his nose, Mike realized he didn't know what colour Ezio's eyes were. He was determined to find out.

The ball was in Ezio's court now. If he wanted to see Mike again, all he had to do was call his room.

TWO

Ezio

He watched as Mike walked away. Ezio could kick himself. Timing had never been so shitty. But in thirty minutes his world had been tossed on its head. He'd had a revelation standing there at the bar when he'd laid eyes on him. Ezio had only intended on getting a drink of water and sitting down for a quiet moment in the sun. Instead, he'd been blindsided. His heart had skipped a beat when the man stood next to him in line. He'd never seen perfection until he'd laid eyes on Mike. The man was too flawless to be real. Like the *Vitruvian Man* or *Discobolus*, his proportions were exquisite. Ezio was unable to resist the temptation to touch all that smooth skin and see whether it was warm and pliable or sculpted from marble. But Mike was real, and he was warm and responsive and needy. His smooth skin overlaid ripples and valleys that trembled when Ezio had touched him, and Ezio had liked it far too much.

Ezio wanted him. More than he'd wanted anyone or anything in a long time. But the phone call had saved his arse too. He couldn't go down that path with Mike. Not there. Not then. God, he wanted to, though.

In the space of half an hour with the man, Ezio had re-evaluated his whole life. Work was killing him, but he hadn't wanted to admit it to himself. He'd spent the better part of five years working three months on, before having a few weeks off. His rostered shifts were long and gruelling, and they always bled into what little free time he had. Long shifts, far too much overtime, and not enough sleep was wearing on him. Ezio felt like Vegemite spread so thin over burnt toast that it couldn't even be tasted.

That morning was the first break he'd had in a week. He was drowning in paperwork; it bled into overtime, and add that to the times he was on call and he barely had a chance to catch his breath before his next shift started. That conversation, right there, was the first time he'd done something for himself in months non-work related. He loved his job, but he was reconsidering the benefits when the hours consumed months of his life. It was beginning to drone into monotony while life seemed to flash by before him. Whole weeks could go by without Ezio even seeing daylight.

He shook off his melancholy as the door slid closed, separating Mike from him, and ignored the curious stares of the few people who were watching, with disapproval or otherwise. Ezio didn't care what they thought. They didn't know him.

Ezio's realization made the funk turn into a heaviness that pressed down around him. He wandered the ship aimlessly, trying to get his head straight. He couldn't relax though, even after a lap of the top deck where guests rarely went in the middle of the day. He stopped at the rear of the ship and gazed at the vista before him. Endless blue ocean stretched as far as the eye could see. The unblemished cerulean of the summer sky met the rich blue of the ocean at the horizon. The only other colour in that one-eighty degree view was the white wash off the ship's propellors. It was something he didn't do often enough; stopping to appreciate the view was a luxury he'd forgotten about. He hadn't realized how much he was missing out on by failing to stop and smell the roses—or the salt off the ocean in his case—until now. Maybe he should, if only to get another look at Mike, no matter how brief or innocent.

* * * * *

Two days had passed, and he hadn't called Mike. He couldn't. But it didn't mean Ezio hadn't thought of him. The man was on his mind constantly, his amused grin at Ezio checking him out lighting up his dreams almost as much as he imagined running his tongue over every inch of Mike's sculpted body. There was no doubt he was beautiful, but the way their bodies had instinctively gravitated to each other's was what had his thoughts circling like an endless loop.

Ezio had failed to tell Mike he couldn't call, and the lie of omission burned in his gut. He should at least have explained why. He could have told him how much he really wanted to see him again. But he hadn't.

Their goodbye should have been the end of things between them—he should never have started it to begin with—but Ezio was grasping at straws, wishing he'd see Mike again like in one of those Hallmark movies where the love interests bump into each other by happenstance.

If they did see each other again, it wouldn't be an accident. He'd been spending an inordinate amount of time on the pool deck sitting at the high-topped tables. The area was designed to overlook the pool so parents could watch their kids while sipping a cocktail. Laughter and the squeals of delighted children surrounded him, and the DJ played from a booth overlooking them, announcing dance competition winners. There were people all around Ezio, but he was lost in a bubble of thought. All he could focus on was a group of three people in the swimming pool—a man and his two kids.

The rock of the ship sloshed the water from one end of the pool to the other, making the people in it bob like a buoy on the ocean. He wasn't close enough to get a good look at them. People on the deck cut off his line of sight when they walked past, but he was fascinated by the way the man moved. Captivated by him. With incredible strength and a feline-like grace, he picked up the bigger of the two kids—a girl—and tossed her up in the air. She scream-giggled and landed with a splash as the younger one climbed into his arms. Over and over he tossed them, giving each a high five before picking them up again. Ezio didn't know how long he watched the family for, but when he fi-nally dragged his gaze away and looked around, the sun had set and the movie on the big screen was starting.

He flicked his eyes back to the pool and watched the man lift himself out of the water. Ezio had known before, but seeing the ripple of his muscle and the way he held him-self left him in no doubt. It was unmistakeably Mike. With broad shoulders and a trim waist, he wore the same ridicu-lous yellow board shorts he'd slipped on when he was called away. It was impossible not to recognize the shorts or the man in them.

Longing zinged through him, and Ezio wished he could have called. He would do anything for one more moment.

Instead, Ezio watched as Mike wrapped towels around his kids' shoulders, oblivious to the desire whipping a storm through Ezio. Mike snagged a towel for himself and ran it over his short-cropped hair. It was a touch too dark to be called blond, but not dark enough to be brown either. Car-amel perhaps? Whatever colour it was, it didn't match his kids'. Both had straight, dark hair. They must have gotten that trait from their mother.

When Mike wrapped the towel tightly around his hips, Ezio's dick perked up at the curve of his bubble butt. Meaty, it was more than a handful, but when he'd seen it the first time, it had been framed so beautifully in those itty-bitty white Speedos that Ezio wanted to bury his face there, then slide between those cheeks and never leave. The visual of Mike standing at the bar watching Ezio as he'd checked him out him had stuck with him. But it was Mike's reaction when

Ezio had crowded him that had truly turned Ezio on. He'd melted into Ezio, letting him use his height as an advantage. Ezio had expected him to push back, use his bulk to shove him away. Instead, Mike had almost purred when Ezio's inner control freak had poked its head out to play.

He watched as the trio walked to the door, Mike with his hand cupping the little boy's head and holding his daughter's hand. He smiled at the tenderness in their father's touch and wished time would pause just for a moment longer. Ezio could watch the other man's form for hours. They reached the heavy timber door leading away from the deck, and Mike hauled it open, ushering his kids through before he paused and looked over his shoulder.

He scanned the deck.

Their eyes met.

Ezio sucked in a breath. The electricity between them sparked, a sizzle between them arcing.

Their moment was fleeting. Mike tore his gaze away and looked inside before flicking his eyes back to Ezio's.

The ache that struck at his chest was like a physical blow. He wanted to chase after him. Without thinking, he ran, dodging between people mingling at the bar. He shouldn't have. It was a bad idea. But Ezio's body had overruled his common sense. He couldn't stop. He picked up his pace, sidestepping kids and apologizing to put-out elderly folk.

Ezio didn't hesitate when he reached the doors. He pushed through them. Mike had disappeared only moments earlier, but there was no sign of him. Through the doors, down the stairs and along the corridor, he sprinted to deck eight. He'd memorized their room number—8303—and had stopped in front of Mike's cabin door more often than Ezio had a reasonable excuse for. But unlike every other time, Ezio rapped on the door.

His heart in his throat, he waited.

A chorus of "Dad" rang out in a child's sing-song voice, but there was no reply.

The door opened, and Mike ordered over his shoulder, "Scoot. Go, shower. Now," before looking at him. When his dark brown eyes met Ezio's, they widened for a split second. He lifted his chin and regarded Ezio, those sweet lips pursing into a straight line. "One second," he muttered before closing the door again.

Ezio heard murmuring behind the closed door and it opened again. Mike slipped out and let the door click closed behind him. "So—"

"I'm sorry," they said at the same time. Ezio would normally stop, let Mike finish, but he knew if he didn't say the words then, he never would. So he barrelled on, words flowing with barely a pause. "Things are complicated for me at the moment, but that's on me, not you. We had a spark, at least I thought we did. If you thought so too, I'd like to maybe see you again."

Mike raised an eyebrow and regarded him for a moment. Ezio held his breath, his heart hammering a rapid tempo. His palms sweated, and he shifted his weight from foot to foot as nerves jittered through him. "You're nervous?" Mike asked, surprise lilting his voice an octave higher.

Ezio nodded quickly. Mike chuckled and reached out, tugging on Ezio's shirt and hauling him closer. Ezio took the cue and pressed against him, Mike's body hard against Ezio's softer one. Hands pressed against the wall, Ezio caged him in, and his mouth hovered only millimetres away from the plump lips Ezio wanted to taste so badly. "This better?" Mike murmured.

Ezio sucked in a breath and nodded again, his words dying in his throat as Mike ran calloused hands down his front and over Ezio's waist, curling around his sides. "Good," he continued. "I need you to be honest with me. Can you do that?"

"Yeah," Ezio choked out. He nodded, reinforcing his promise.

"Are you single? I don't do cheating."

Ezio didn't hesitate. His sex life had become pathetic at best—he hadn't had a partner in over a year. "I'm single."

"Those complications you've got. Are they my kids? Because if we were talking relationship, I'd say it's not negotiable. But you won't even meet them."

Ezio's brow furrowed as what Mike said sank in. "Your kids? No. Why would I have a problem with them?"

He shrugged, and it was the first sign of insecurity Ezio had seen on the beautiful man before him. "Most guys—"

"I'm not most guys." Ezio left the rest unsaid—that he loved kids, that he wanted some of his own. Ezio wasn't naïve enough to think he'd get that from Mike or his kids, but the thought was... a dream.

Ezio froze. Shock lit him up like a lightning bolt had hit him. He did want that. He really did. Why had it only just occurred to him, when he was standing right there in this man's arms, what he was missing out on? Ezio sucked in a breath and fought down a wave of emotion. Mike ran his hands up his back and held him tighter, and Ezio found himself trembling in Mike's arms. Overwhelmed and reeling, his emotions were completely out of control. What had begun as a case of lust at first sight was quickly making Ezio realize things he'd pushed down into the depths.

"C'mere," Mike whispered and turned Ezio's face towards his. They hovered there, staring each other down. It was less of a test of wills than a realization that Ezio would be forever changed by the man before him when he leaped. And he would leap. Ezio couldn't—wouldn't—deny the connection between them.

He shook himself out of his thoughts. He was being ridiculous. Mike's life may be picture perfect, but it wasn't Ezio's to live. It wasn't as if they were falling in love. Sure, he wanted to roll around on a big bed with him, preferably for more than one go, but thinking about anything more than that with Mike was ridiculous.

Ezio huffed and ran his nose up Mike's cheek, inhaling deep. He was disappointed to smell the lingering chlorine on his skin, but it wasn't as if Ezio had given him a chance to shower. He nipped Mike's earlobe and licked the shell of his ear before exhaling gently and making him shiver. Blunt fingers dug into Ezio's back, and he hummed. Ezio liked the reactions he got from Mike. He would be fun. "Can you be free tomorrow afternoon? After two?"

"I can try," Mike rasped. It was a bad idea for Ezio to put his hands on the man. Once he did, he knew he wouldn't want to stop. But he did it anyway. He ran his hand down Mike's side, delighting at the way his ropey latissimus dorsi muscle quivered under Ezio's touch. The towel around Mike's waist was wet, but Ezio ignored the dampness and grasped the meaty globe of his arse, squeezing and grinding against him. They were both sporting bulges; not yet hard, but definitely interested.

"I'll be here." Ezio pulled back and ran his eyes down Mike's shirtless torso, and bit down on his bottom lip. He reached out and ran his fingertips over Mike's abs. "Tomorrow."

Mike nodded, and a whiny "Dad" sounded from inside the stateroom. Mike rolled his eyes and hooked a thumb over his shoulder. "That's my cue." He gave Ezio an apologetic smile. "Tomorrow."

Ezio forced himself to walk away. But he knew he would be back. Nothing was going to keep him away.

* * * * *

He'd stood in exactly the same spot the day before, facing a closed door and gathering the courage to knock. He'd knocked on instinct then. Would he do it again? He knew taking that step would change him. Or had he already been fundamentally altered? Ezio flattened his hand against the door as if to feel Mike's essence on the other side and sucked in a breath.

He wanted this.

Before his common sense could kick in and force him to walk away, he rapped on the door. Ezio squared his shoulders and stepped back, pretending to play it cool. Mike might not even be there. He had kids, and they were on a family holiday. It wasn't as if—

The door opened to the man who hadn't left his thoughts in days standing in much the same as he'd been wearing the day before. A towel—a white one this time—was wrapped low on his hips. Drops of water dotted his shoulders and ran slow tracks down his chest. His hair was wet, part of it flattened against his skull and the other part standing on end like he'd haphazardly run the towel over it. He looked like he'd literally jumped out of the shower, tied the towel around his waist, and dashed to the door.

A slow smile spread across Mike's face, and Ezio nearly swallowed his tongue. The man before Ezio was more handsome than his dreams had painted him. In fact, handsome was the understatement of the century; he was stunning. "You made it."

"I didn't want to be anywhere else."

Mike grinned, and colour tinted his cheeks. "Come in." He held the door wide, and Ezio sucked in a breath. This was it. One step over the threshold and there was no going back. There was no question of what he wanted once he entered, and once he'd made that decision, his life would irrevocably change direction. He gazed at Mike. The man was undoubtedly beautiful, but there was more to Mike than that. When he'd been playing with his kids, Ezio had witnessed what a good man—a good father—Mike was. Then he'd followed him to that very spot, and his emotions had run into him with the force of a freight train. He hadn't uttered a word. He wasn't even sure he could put the sentiments into a form that made sense without Mike thinking he was nuts. But it hadn't mattered. Mike comforted him. Cared for him and bathed him in affection. That was who he was really coming back to see—the man who was behind the beauty. Ezio didn't hesitate to step into Mike's arms.

"Hi." He smiled as Mike let go of the door, allowing it to swing closed behind him and click shut. He flicked the lock and grinned at Ezio. "Trapped in here with me now."

"Such a hardship."

Mike tilted his face up and bit down on his lip. The same lips that Ezio wanted to kiss. He gently gripped Mike's chin and ran his thumb over his lip, prising it free. Ezio leaned down and nuzzled their noses together. "Hi," he whispered, breathing in Mike's clean scent. There was no chlorine from the pool this time, just the ocean, fresh and crisp. It was body wash, but Ezio couldn't get enough. He could get high off Mike's scent.

"Can I kiss you?" Ezio's voice was breathy, full of need and raw desire. Mike's response was a groan in the back of his throat as his eyes slipped closed. Ezio closed the sliver of distance between them and pressed their lips together.

This time it was Ezio who moaned when Mike gripped his T-shirt and hauled him closer. He opened to Ezio's seeking kiss, and no more words were necessary.

Ezio fell into his man—even if he was his for only one afternoon. He wanted to pause time and bask in the moment. It was the discovery of something new and wonderful. The excitement and the wonder. He ran his fingertips down Mike's muscled back, along the dip of his spine, and hummed as those muscles shifted, bunching at his gentle touch. The rough fabric of the low-slung towel met his hand, and as much as Ezio wanted to rip it off Mike and devour him, he hesitated. He wanted to savour Mike, to catalogue every moan and twitch, every gasp he dragged from him and every time he arched into Ezio's touch. Ezio wanted to sip slowly and delight in every taste like he would a fine wine.

Mike smoothed his hands down Ezio's chest, and the long hours of sedentary work, oversized portions, and easy access to far too many sweets suddenly caught up to him. Ezio was softening around the middle already. He no longer had the swimmer's body he'd had in his twenties. Compared to Mike, he was downright ordinary. Why was Mike even entertaining him in his room?

"What happened? Where'd you go?" Mike pulled back and asked, concerned lines marring his forehead. He was perceptive as well as gorgeous, especially with his lips glistening and his pupils blown with desire.

"Nothing. It's okay." Ezio smiled and cupped Mike's cheek.

"No, don't do that." Mike threaded his fingers through the hand Ezio held to his face and lowered it to Mike's chest. He could feel the strong steady beat of his heart, and Ezio splayed his fingers, absorbing the potent zest for life that Mike so obviously held. "You stiffened as soon as I ran my hands down to your waist. Do you not want me to touch you there, or at all?"

"No, nothing like that." Ezio shook his head and looked down, embarrassed at the admission he was about to make. It wasn't because he was vain, but because he should know better. Mike, as the owner of a gym, would know that too. Ezio lifted their entwined hands to his lips and kissed the back of Mike's. "I'm so plain compared to you. I got a little self-conscious. I'm getting a belly from sitting down and treating patients for so long. I eat too much shit and don't keep myself as healthy as I should. It's embarrassing how I look compared to you."

"There's always someone who'll say there's room to be healthier, to do more exercise or eat better. But we all do what we can. I'm fit, but there are so many areas where I fail miserably. We each have our strengths and weaknesses."

"What's your weakness?" Ezio asked, half joking and half needing the reassurance. His voice gave his hesitance away, the tone quiet and uncertain.

Mike ran his free hand down Ezio's chest to his stomach and around to the small of his back, holding him tight before he kissed his throat and up to his mouth. "Wanting sexy men in preppy outfits at a bar who are far too sophisticated for a schmuck like me. Wanting you inside me. A man who's real and honest and smart, not plastic-fantastic perfection. I can go to work to see that." Mike was being earnest, the warmth in his voice encouraging. They weren't in a relationship by any stretch of the imagination, but the knowledge that Mike was attracted to him nudged him beyond self-consciousness back into sweet desire.

Ezio pressed a kiss to Mike's knuckles, then another and another until he couldn't resist the distance between them and pulled Mike in for a deep kiss. Cupping his nape, Ezio pressed forward and fell into the man before him. His mind whited out and zeroed in on his touch. When Mike's hands went under his shirt, Ezio gasped. He followed blindly when Mike walked them over to the perfectly made bed and haphazardly yanked the covers down. Then when Mike inched Ezio's shirt up, Ezio held his gaze and nodded his encouragement. He let this man, who could easily be his dream lover, slowly undress him, remove his polo shirt, his boat shoes, and undo the belt on his tailored shorts.

Once the leather strap joined the other items tossed carelessly to the side, Ezio took over. He kissed a line along Mike's jaw and down his throat to the spot he'd been desperate to taste again ever since he'd laid eyes again on Mike. Sucking on the skin beneath his ear, Ezio tugged on Mike's towel and let it drop to the floor. He couldn't resist moving his hands down Mike's spine once more, not stopping until he had two handfuls of the man's firm arse in his hands. Mike's arousal was pressed up against his own, the barrier of a few layers of material too much. But Ezio didn't want to rush. He wanted to savour and enjoy, appreciate every moment they had together. Even more because of how limited it was. They were already moving at light speed, farther along the hook-up path than he'd ever travelled in such a short time.

Ezio skimmed his hand up Mike's back and splayed his fingers across his shoulder blades. Pressing Mike's chest to his mouth as he nibbled and sucked on the tanned skin against his lips, Ezio moaned. With his other hand, he kneaded Mike's smooth, muscled arse cheek and encouraged him to rock his hips, grinding on the leg Ezio had pressed between his.

The taste of his skin was addictive. A hint of body wash and the unique scent of the man before him made Ezio ravenous. "Lie down. I want to lick every inch of you," Ezio murmured against the valley between his abs.

Mike's breath hitched, and he untangled his fingers from Ezio's hair, smoothing down the dark strands before stepping back, one pace at a time. Ezio took him in, admiring him from the now dry tips of his messy caramel-coloured hair to the perfectly trimmed toenails on his feet.

Smooth, tanned skin stretched over sculpted muscle. Thick arms and a hairless chest with perfect handfuls of rounded pectorals tempted Ezio. Mike's chest rose and fell as he breathed, and his six-pack shifted, pulling taut when his lover looked over his shoulder to the bed. The neatly trimmed thatch at the base of his erect cock and balls was the only visible hair on his body apart from a fine dusting of light fur over his legs. The muscles in his quadriceps bulged and flexed as he moved, and Ezio had to resist the urge to crowd him. He wanted to plaster their bodies together from top to toe and slake the lust that was spiralling out of control within.

"You're wearing too many clothes," Mike rasped from the edge of the bed as he sank down onto the mattress, lying back and spreading his legs shoulder-width apart in invitation. At least that's how Ezio took it, and he would gladly climb between those legs and leave Mike quivering, satisfied, and boneless.

Ezio stripped his shorts off, stepping out of them where they fell, but left his underwear on. He still needed it between them for the moment—a physical restraint to temper Ezio's desire.

Mike hummed as Ezio stalked him and reached down to touch himself. The man's cock was as beautifully proportioned as the rest of him. Thick and veiny, the foreskin pulled the rest of the way back as he gripped himself and stroked downwards. "You're beautiful," Mike uttered on a sigh as he twisted his fist over the head of his cock and spread the pre-cum down his shaft.

Ezio straddled Mike's leg, and Mike lifted his other knee, stopping him from climbing on top. The man was in no doubt about where he wanted Ezio, and Ezio loved it. They were compatible in so many ways. He shifted until he was kneeling between Mike's spread legs and hitched his lover's other knee up, showing the muscled god in front of him he knew exactly what Mike wanted. Entwining their fingers together, Ezio lifted his free arm until their knuckles were touching the padded headboard and watched as Mike worked his cock. He held himself up, hovering over the beautiful man below, and joined their lips together when he couldn't wait any longer. Exploring the other man's mouth in a slow caress and grinding on him would have been enough for Ezio. There was a lot to be said for make-out sessions. But Mike wasn't having it. He wrapped his legs around Ezio's waist and pulled him down, eliminating the space between their bodies with sheer brute strength. It flipped a switch in Ezio. The slowing himself down, the resisting he'd talked himself into doing all went up in a puff of smoke. Mike wanted this as much as Ezio did.

He let his weight press Mike into the mattress, licking and sucking every square millimetre of skin he could touch. He buried his face in Mike's pit and breathed in his natural scent, licking at the still damp hairs from his shower. Ezio tucked the moment away as he sucked on the discs of Mike's flat nipples and licked a path straight down his stomach. He circled his tongue around Mike's belly button, and every muscle in his torso quivered, his hands clutching the sheets in a white-knuckled grip. He ran his hands down Mike's sides to his narrow waist, then followed the path with his tongue.

How had he been lucky enough to catch Mike's eye?

He licked over the tan line at his hips and rubbed his stubbled chin on Mike's cock. The other man gasped and tried to arch into his touch, but Ezio's hands on Mike's hips held him still. His transverse abdominus was so defined that it looked like a fold in paper. Ezio didn't even know what exercises to do to create the perfect cum gutters that Mike had, but he suddenly had a hankering to watch the man work out.

Naked.

A shudder passed through Ezio, and Mike hummed. Ezio skipped over Mike's cock and nuzzled his balls, running his nose over the tight wrinkled skin of his sac. He licked him, spreading Mike's legs and reaching back to run his fingertips teasingly over the man's perineum. Mike choked out a gasp and moaned, his cock flexing.

"Mmm, you like that?" Ezio asked, but it wasn't really a question.

"Yes," he hissed. "More." Mike gripped his cock and lifted his legs off the bed, presenting his hole to Ezio's gaze. Pretty and pink, tight, and with the slightest smattering of longer curlier hairs that Ezio could tell were completely un-trimmed and unwaxed, Mike's hole was, like the rest of him, perfection. "I'm clean," he moaned.

That pulled Ezio up short. As a medical professional, he didn't like the connotations of those two words. "Negative, you mean?"

Mike laughed, the sound more like a moan. "I'm nega-tive too, but I meant that I'm clean. Like, I douched."

"Oh." Ezio huffed out a surprised and very pleased laugh. *Hell yeah.* He licked him, tasting Mike's skin and the flavour that was uniquely him. The soft skin of his upper thigh and over his taint to his other leg. Up a bit, to his sac and up his shaft, licking him like a lollipop, then closing his lips over that divine cock, down until he was lodged deep in

Ezio's throat. Mike's tangy pre-cum washed over his senses, and Ezio's eyes rolled back in his head. Cradling Mike's arse, he lifted him to his searching tongue and feasted. There was too much perfect skin to taste, so much to touch, and Mike's moans and quivering muscles under his hands and his mouth sent Ezio wild. He kissed and licked, nipped and teased with gentle fingertips until Mike was an incoherent mess, begging with gasps and moans for Ezio to fuck him.

But he couldn't. He wouldn't. Ezio wasn't a stranger to hook-ups. He was careful. Safe. He made sure that the men and women he went home with knew the score—he wasn't in it for a relationship. Work hadn't really allowed him to do it. But Mike was different. A hook-up, yes, but he already knew that once wouldn't be enough.

A foil packet and a sachet of lube landed next to him, but Ezio pushed them away, not having had his fill of the man spread out invitingly before him. He licked, prodding his entry gently with his tongue and circling him with drenched fingers. Mike cried out, tensing, and a fine thread of pre-cum dripped down onto his flat belly. "Ez," he cried impatiently, desperation colouring his tone. "Please."

Ezio moved up and licked the drip off his six pack and slurped down his dick, veiny and thick. Ezio delighted in the bringing Mike to the edge of sanity. His fingertips, whisper soft against his ring, were driving Mike wild. He growled, and Ezio knew. He was ready, pushed to a point where it was painful. Now was the time to take him to nirvana.

Ezio tore at the sachet of lube and coated his fingers before pressing a digit inside him. He withdrew and repeated the motion, giving Mike the lube he needed. A second finger, then a third, tagging Mike's prostate each time he thrust forward, his cock pressing against the back of Ezio's throat. He was riding a high—the beautiful man before him was coming apart from his touch.

"Oh fuck, I'm gonna come."

Ezio pulled off Mike's cock and eased his fingers from his channel, and Mike groaned, a pained sound that sent a shiver through Ezio, on his knees between Mike's legs. The man lying wanting and desperate before him was the epitome of temptation, chest heaving, neck arched, and his bottom lip pressed between his teeth. Ezio had never wanted another person more.

He slipped out of the underwear he was wearing and kicked it aside before he tore the rubber open and rolled it down his aching dick. "Don't move," Mike rasped, and Ezio froze, a hand still on his cock. Mike sat up and ran his hands down Ezio's sides, pulling him in for a kiss. "Fuck, you're sexy."

Ezio moaned as Mike slicked up his cock and pulled him down until they were chest to chest, his legs wrapped around Ezio's waist. "Come inside of me, Ez. I want you."

He did, pressing the blunt head of his cock to Mike's opening and gasping when tight heat surrounded him. "Oh, fuck," he breathed, waiting for Mike to adjust to his intrusion and relax under him. Mentally cataloguing bones within the human body to pull himself from the edge didn't work, so he massaged Mike's leg, rubbing soothing circles along the thick muscles. Mike hummed, and Ezio shifted forward gently, slipping further inside.

Mike's reaction was instantaneous, his eyes rolling back in his head as he moaned long and low. Ezio loved the sounds he made. He wanted to pull more like that out of him.

Cupping Mike's face with one hand, he held himself up on his elbow and plastered their bodies together from shoulder to hip. He leaned down, joining their mouths, and started a slow grind, rolling his hips sensuously. They broke apart for breath, and Mike's gaze clashed with his and held. He couldn't look away. Mike's eyes were the darkest of browns he'd ever seen, rich and warm. Ezio could read the emotion in them. He was spellbound, looking over every inch of the man's beautiful face. Sex-mussed hair and flushed cheeks, swollen lips and a voice rough with desire; he was a picture Ezio never wanted to forget.

Mike came first, his hand wrapped around his cock as he stroked roughly. Ezio kept up the slow thrusts, moving deep inside him until the contractions around his dick pushed him to the precipice. Mike's choked cry, and Ezio's name a whisper on his lips, sent him over the edge. He buried his face in the crook of Mike's neck and cried out, the other man holding him as he quaked with the force of the orgasm that rolled through him.

Sweaty and exhausted, Mike rolled them to the side, and Ezio pulled back, taking care of the condom. When Mike's eyes slipped closed, he shifted further, backing away from the satisfied noodle-like state Mike was in. "Don't go."

"I'll get a washcloth." Ezio slipped into the bathroom and, with shaking hands, warmed the water and wet a cloth. He checked the mirror and was shocked to see he still looked the same. He sure as hell didn't feel the same. Something fundamental had shifted within him, and it had everything to do with the man in the other room. But he'd known going into this that the experience would change his life. Or rather the man would. Stepping over the threshold had been a watershed moment for Ezio, and the extent of that truth terrified him.

When he returned to the double bed, Mike was curled on his side in precisely the same position he'd left him in. He smiled and wiped his stomach before hitching his leg up and cleaning off the lube. "Any pain? Sensitivity?"

"No and yes, but in a good way, Doc." Mike opened his eyes, and his shrewd gaze regarded Ezio. He sympathized with the insects pinned to display boards in museums. Mike seemed to see far too deep into him. "Get over here and cuddle me. Let's just forget about everything outside of that door for a few more hours."

Ezio smiled. "I can do that." He slipped back into bed, and Mike rested his head on Ezio's shoulder, wrapped an arm around his waist, and tangled their legs together. Ezio curled into him, running a hand through Mike's hair and caressing his forearm, watching as the muscle bunched and flexed against his hand as Mike drew lazy circles in the dark hair decorating Ezio's chest. He sighed, a satisfied sound, and was content for the first time in years if he was being truly honest. They talked quietly about everything and nothing—food, definitely sweet for Ezio and too healthy for Mike; football codes, rugby for Mike and AFL for Ezio; their mutual dislike of golf; the degrees they studied; and their families. When Mike asked him if he was out, Ezio stiffened. He usually needed a drink to go there.

"It's okay if you aren't. It's a personal thing."

"I'm out, but it's a sensitive topic. My mother and father are… old-fashioned. Dad told me that it's a man's duty to sow my oats and have fun, then find a nice girl and get married. Mum wants grandkids, so it's on me to deliver," he said by way of explanation with more than a hint of derision. "I derailed their plans when I came out. I had a boyfriend in uni, and I took him home. I thought if they just met him, they'd change their minds. They didn't even acknowledge him the whole weekend we were there. He left early, and I heard the speech about him disrespecting them." He huffed and shook his head, and Mike kissed his chest, the move giving him more comfort than he cared to admit. "I broke their hearts, but they've crushed mine. When I took a girlfriend home during my residency, I thought it would be different. But then they lectured me about not being able to make up my mind. When they found out she was also a doctor, they were disappointed because I picked a woman who wouldn't look after me like they think I deserved. I can't win with them, so I don't try anymore."

"You bi or pan?" Mike asked, resting his chin on Ezio's chest so they were gazing at each other once more.

"I spend my days labelling everything and finding ways to treat illnesses. I didn't want to diagnose myself, you know?"

"Yeah, I get it." Mike smiled and kissed his chest again. "This okay?" he asked hesitantly. Ezio gripped his head gently and held him there, humming as Mike grinned against his nipple and licked him.

THREE

Mike

He hadn't expected Ezio to agree to get back into bed with him, or to open up and share things that Mike was sure he didn't dredge up often. He hadn't expected to have so much in common with the man, or for the second round of sex to be even hotter than the first. They'd said goodbye when Mike had to get his kids for their dinner, and Mike watched him walk backwards down the hallway with a smile, not breaking their gaze until the corridor turned.

Ezio hadn't mentioned anything about who he was travelling with, but like Mike, he had people to see and things to do until much later in the evening. Almost sheepishly, Ezio had asked if he could meet back at Mike's room after midnight. They'd get a few hours of alone time—the kids would be fast asleep—but privacy was non-existent in the stateroom. Mike had made it clear that nothing could happen; no blow jobs, no hand jobs, nothing more than making out. Ezio had smiled fondly and peppered his face with kisses until they were both laughing, which had turned into

Ezio climbing between his legs and cradling him, kissing him long and slow until Mike couldn't think straight. For a hook-up, he was oddly okay with spending time together without having sex. Mike wasn't complaining. It had been a long time since he'd done something for himself. The guilt he perpetually carried around with him couldn't hold a candle to the happy vibe that Ezio left him basking in. Mike was energized after those few hours. Buzzing. He was grinning like a fool and had a giddiness coursing through him that had nothing to do with how hard he'd come.

Grumbling greeted him when he picked the kids up, but it soon turned into Jaxson's excited ramblings about their activities and Lexi explaining the games she'd played.

"Dad, are you listening?" Lexi demanded as he lost himself in thought again at the table. Jax tugged on his sleeve and huffed out an annoyed breath when Mike stilled his hand.

"Sorry, Lexi, I completely spaced out. What were you saying?"

"Not me. Jax. He said he wants the nuggets. I want the pink fish."

"Jax, you aren't having nuggets again. They're processed, and anyway, you already had nuggets for lunch. What about the…" Mike quickly scanned the menu and pursed his lips. "Prawns and salad? It's got cucumber and spinach leaves. You like those."

"Yeah, okay." He sighed, like he was hard done by eating gourmet meals on a cruise ship. "As long as I get ice cream for dessert."

"If you eat all the salad, deal." He shook Jax's hand and moved to Lexi. "Salmon with veggies or salad?"

"Mashed potato and salad. And chocolate cake."

"Done." Everything was a negotiation with his kids. He had to remember that while he wanted them eating healthy for the most part, they were kids too. Sugar-filled everything was part of growing up, whether he liked it or not. The conversation stalled when the waiters were at their table, and Jax jumped up, hugging both. They had the same two servers for the whole cruise, and they'd lucked out with Christopher and Adriana. They'd quickly become the kids' favourites, mainly because they came prepared with magic tricks, dances, and could fold napkins into whatever animal the kids could think of.

Dinner didn't end in any meltdowns, most of their plates were cleaned, and the kids were still hopping with energy when they'd finished. It was early too, so a movie then baths were on the cards before Mike would tuck them into their beds and read a chapter from their book—this week it was *The Lion, The Witch and The Wardrobe.*

He smiled, watching his kids race ahead playing tag as they giggled and dodged around people. "Slow down," he cautioned, giving them the eye when they raced around a man with a walking frame. They stopped when they reached the heavy doors at the top of the stairs. Neither one could open it. Mike reached over their heads and pushed open the door, allowing them to scoot out before he shifted and let another couple through.

Lexi held his hand after Jax insisted on climbing onto his shoulders. Knees into his back and toes digging into his ribs, his four-year-old scrambled up Mike's body seemingly without any effort. He wouldn't let Mike lift him up, even though it would have been easier. Instead, Mike had to kneel and let Jax get on himself. Mike shook his head, grinning up at his little boy. "You right?"

"Yeah. Dad, come on, we're gonna miss the start," Jax whined.

"We're plenty early, bud."

Lexi spotted two free chairs first and dragged Mike there by the hand. Jogging with Jax on his shoulders and carrying a bag of the kids' tracksuits wasn't easy, but there was no way she was missing out on the prime position right in front of the screen.

His little girl launched herself onto the seat and glared at the couple who'd paused in front of the lounger next to Lexi. Mike excused himself and fell backwards on the seat, dropping Jax onto it with a squeal. He hadn't even had a chance to kick off his shoes when two brightly coloured bodies launched themselves onto him. With an "oomph," he reached out blindly, a leg across his face, to tickle whatever he could grab hold of as they squirmed on top of him, trying to wrestle him into submission. High-pitched fits of giggles sounded until Mike sat up and twisted the kids so Lexi was draped over one arm and Jax the other. Shuffling to the edge of the seat, Mike stood, and the kids squealed happily. They were light as feathers, but it was still awkward to shift their bag and shoes across both loungers so they would still be there when they got back. Mike nodded at the waiter balancing a tray of cocktails and dodged a girl about Jax's age as she darted between them, sprinting across the deck.

It was a mild night, the warmth of the tropical air cooled only by the ocean breeze, but the open deck was sheltered by the floor-to-ceiling wall of windows that surrounded it, the walking track above providing some shade around the edges on a sunny day. He carried the kids upside down to the drink machines and flipped them over, keeping a hold of them until they weren't red in the face anymore. He made them hot chocolates loaded with marshmallows and carried the tray back to their chairs, directing the way with a hand on Lexi's shoulder as Jax held on to his shorts.

He wrapped them up, and they got comfortable before the movie started—Lexi on her own chair, and Jax on his lap. He was fast asleep before the halfway point, something Mike hadn't expected. When he saw Lexi nodding off, Mike nudged her. "Lexi, honey. Come on, let's get you into bed."

"Nooo," she grumbled. "I'm still watching."

"I've got it on my laptop. You can keep watching it in bed if you like. I can't carry you both though, so we need to go, yeah?"

A soft snore and a sigh. "Okay, Daddy."

Mike packed up his gear and loaded the bag, slinging it over his shoulder before lifting Jax into his arms. Lexi stood, swaying on her feet, and followed him, rubbing her eyes. She was flagging by the time they got to the lift, and Mike relented, picking her up too. The kids were dead weights in his arms, and his biceps burned.

"Where are you headed?" a lady asked him.

"Eighth floor."

"Me too. I can help." She hit the button for him and took the lanyard from around his neck with his room key. When they got to his room, she swiped the card and held open the door, popping it on the shelf just inside as she closed it for him. He flicked the lock and stumbled sideways to the double bed, sinking down onto his knees so he could gently lay the kids down. The bed had been neatened since his session with Ezio, the covers folded down and chocolates placed on the pillows.

He stripped Jax out of his tracksuit, leaving only his t-shirt and undies on, and laid him on the top bunk. Lexi wouldn't be happy with Jax taking her bed, but she was curled up fast asleep and he couldn't get purchase on the slim aluminium ladder to lift her up that high.

He took Lexi's shoes and socks off, and she slid under the sheet, tracksuit and all. Her long dark hair swept out behind her on the pillow, and her long eyelashes fanned out over her cheeks. She was beautiful—an exact replica of her mother. Mike kissed her goodnight, turned on her ladybug night light, and stood, adjusting Jaxson's covers before kissing him too.

He turned the TV on its stand, closed the privacy curtain between the bunks and his bed, and settled in. It was difficult not to count the minutes until Ezio arrived. He failed miserably, looking far too often as the hands of his watch crawled by.

Finally though, the soft knock at the door came. Mike jumped up, the bed creaking in protest, and almost tripped over his own feet to get to the door. He expected Ezio, but his breath still caught when he opened it.

Ezio gave a quick look up and down the corridor and he stepped in. Letting the door slip closed quietly behind him, he flipped the lock and cupped Mike's face, bringing him close. He gazed at Mike, his eyes full of something that looked like wonder and affection. Mike needed to get closer to the man, especially when his expression was so loving. He'd never been treasured like that by a lover. When he was with women, he was the one doing that, and his hook-ups with men had him bending over for them when they progressed past BJs or hand jobs. They were always quick. They fulfilled a physical need for release and very little else. This was so much more than that. Mike couldn't explain it. He didn't know whether it was Ezio's way. Did he do that with everyone he was with? Or did he genuinely feel every emotion glittering in his eyes, visible in the low light?

He wrapped his arms around Ezio's waist and slipped his hands under the man's polo shirt. Mike hummed at all the warm skin against his palms and the solid body pressed against his own. They didn't speak a single word, but the nudge to his nose and Ezio's soft kiss that lingered against his lips said enough. I like you. I want you. He drew Ezio backwards past the kids' bunks, but Ezio stopped and smiled gently at the two children cuddling their teddies. "They're beautiful, Mike."

"They are pretty great." Mike nodded in the direction of the bed, and Ezio stripped off Mike's shirt, tossing it on the floor before doing the same to his shorts. Mike wore only a jock—his normal underwear. Ezio swallowed hard, and his eyes flicked up to Mike's. Pupils blown, they were full of heat and told him just how dirty Ezio wanted to get with him. It was like a physical caress, one Mike could have spontaneously combusted from.

"Jesus fucking Christ," Ezio muttered. "You get sexier every time I see you. One day, I want to make love to you while you're wearing these. They're as hot as Hades."

Mike chuckled and undressed Ezio down to his tighty-whiteys. He didn't understand the obsession with white underwear—unless you were always wearing white pants, there really was no purpose, and Mike's electric green were definitely more fun. He pulled him onto the bed, on top of Mike, and they settled like that, kissing and petting while they whispered together. The credits rolled on the movie, casting the room in near darkness, and Ezio nuzzled his throat, getting comfortable and letting all his weight finally drop onto Mike. Cocooned there in Ezio's arms, he never wanted the moment to end. Mike wrapped his arms and legs around Ezio and held him close, touching him everywhere he could reach. The chemistry between them was off the charts, but it wasn't sex either one of them was reaching for. It was comfort and affection. Ezio's touch that afternoon had been incendiary. He instinctively knew how to draw the bone-melting pleasure from Mike. But there had been as many quiet moments between them. Ones like this where they held each other and learned how their bodies slotted together perfectly, or how Ezio practically purred when Mike ran his fingers through his hair. Mike wished he could ask Ezio to keep things going between them after the cruise. It had only been one day, and Mike already knew he was in store for a serious case of blue balls when the trip ended and he had to mentally move past the man in his arms.

The rocking of the ship was lulling him to sleep, the wash against the hull as the captain powered the MV Dreamcatcher through the calm blue waters of the Pacific a soothing melody.

* * * * *

The sun on the horizon was an annoying bright light in his eyes. Mike startled and sat up, dislodging Ezio from the spot on Mike's shoulder he was using as a pillow. Breathing hard and wide-eyed, Mike strained to see whether the kids were waking.

"Shit," Ezio whispered. "I'm sorry." Mike shut him up with a kiss and breathed his reply rather than spoke it.

"I want to see you again. How can I get in contact with you?"

"Leave me a note in the mail holder outside your door. Let me know when you're free, and I'll see if I can make it." Ezio silently slipped on his clothes and waited for Mike to peer around the curtain to see if the kids were still asleep. They were, but not for long. Lexi was already stirring.

Ezio crept past their beds with Mike. He pressed a hand on top of Mike's when he went to open the door for him and leaned in for another of those toe-curling, lingering kisses that Mike couldn't get enough of. "Soon."

Mike nodded and smiled, his heart beating triple time when Ezio pressed another kiss to the corner of his lips and slipped out the door.

He heard "Good morning, Doctor," as he closed it. He'd obviously charmed the room attendants too. Not for the first time, Mike wondered where Ezio's room was—it must have been close by if they had the same crew looking after them.

He turned and leaned back against the door, grinning like a fool. He was happy. There was no denying it. The man he'd spied at the pool was something else. Someone wonderful.

The floor creaked as Lexi stumbled out of bed and rubbed her eyes, blinking up at Mike. She wrapped her arms around him and snuggled into his waist. "Hi, Daddy. Did I finish the movie last night?"

"You feel asleep, sweetness. Maybe we can watch it later. We've got a big day today. Breakfast, then we're going for a trip on a boat to an island so we can go snorkelling."

"Will I get to see turtles?"

"Maybe." Lexi's eyes lit up at the possibility before her brow was marred by a scowl.

"Jellyfish or sharks?"

He didn't want to lie to her, but he had to reassure Lexi too. She was terrified of getting stung by jellyfish, and Jax had a morbid fascination with sharks. "Sharks are possible, but unlikely. The water is quite shallow there, so any sharks that come in will only be little ones, and I'll punch them in the face if they get too close."

She raised her eyebrows at him. "You wouldn't do that!" Mike held his hand up and smacked his fist against it, narrowing his eyes and pursing his lips together in an exaggerated snarl sending Lexi into a fit of giggles.

"Watch me." He chucked her on the chin and grinned at her. "Hopefully the wind and currents won't bring the jellyfish into the bay. You'll be wearing a full rashie anyway, so you won't have anything for the jellyfish to sting."

"Why can't I wear my Transformers swimmers?" She'd worn the same swimmers all week—a red one-piece and bright blue boardshorts. It was the closest he could get in girl's swimwear. Everything else for her age was Disney princess, and that was not his daughter's style.

"We'll be out in the sun, so you have to wear a rashie, but I brought the red one to wear with your blue shorts."

"Awesome!" Lexi did a little dance and popped into the bathroom while Mike made his way over to Jaxson's bunk.

"Hey, buddy. Good morning." Jax groaned and rolled over, kicking a leg out over the side of the bed and covering his face with his arm. Mike chuckled and patted him. "Wake up when you're ready, grumpy pants."

"Leave me alone," his I-hate-mornings four-year-old grumbled.

"We're going snorkelling today." Mike stood back to wait for his reaction. In one move, Jax whipped around and sat up and slid down the ladder. Wide-eyed and completely alert, he darted over to the cupboard with their gear in it and started pulling it all out. Flippers, goggles, and face masks were tossed behind him as well as the strap for Mike's underwater Go-Pro. "Just your shorts and a tee will be fine, mate. We've got to get brekkie first."

"Oh." Jax sighed, and in a move reminiscent of a deflating balloon, he crumpled to the floor, his spine bent and his head down.

Mike laughed and picked him up, hauling him over his shoulder as he grabbed some clothes for his youngster before tossing him playfully onto his bed. "Go on, buddy. Get dressed, and I'll pack our things. We can go straight to the island after breakfast."

"What's the island called, Dad?" Jax asked.

"This one's Lifou."

Lexi came out, and Jax replaced her in the bathroom while she got dressed. Backpack filled, Mike now dressed, and the kids pushing and shoving each other, he herded them into the corridor. With smiles at the crew who were beginning to wheel their trolleys around, they headed to breakfast.

"Oh, sugar. Wait, kids." He turned and dashed back into the room and scrawled a note for Ezio, inviting him over any night after the kids' bedtime. He guessed that Lexi and Jax would also want to be in kids' club anytime they weren't on an island or on the waterslides so he wrote those times down too.

Mike slipped it into the plastic notice holder where the day's activity mail was placed and caught back up to his kids.

"Are you having a good day, Dad? You're smiling a lot." Lexi's words pulled him up short.

"Do I not smile enough?"

"No, you do. You smile at us all the time, but this smile is when you're looking away. It's like you're happy on the inside."

"Oh, honey." He wrapped his arm around her shoulders and squeezed her. "I am happy on the inside, but even if I'm not smiling, I'm not sad. How could I be when I have you?"

"Dad, can I have ice cream for breakfast?"

Mike laughed. "No, Jax. No ice cream. But you can have a piece of fruit after you eat some eggs."

"Urgh." Mike bit down on his lip to stop his snort of laughter at his son's disgust. If Jax was good at anything, it was expressing his feelings.

* * * * *

The snorkelling was amazing even with having to constantly empty Jax's mouthpiece. He kept trying to speak underwater, and frequently ended up with mouthfuls of seawater. Lexi mastered snorkelling a little easier—the lessons he'd given them in his best mate's pool were paying off.

Brightly coloured fish swum around coral so vivid, it was hard to believe it was real. The sounds were incredible too. Blue fish with sharp beaks seemingly chewed on the coral, the crunch echoing through the water. Turtles swam right up to them, and Lexi had reached out to touch, only snatching her hand away at the last moment. They'd spent hours in the water, exploring every nook and cranny of the bay. Toward its opening, the reef dived deeper, the coral decorating the sea floor changing in colour and shape. Larger, sleeker fish lurked in darkened holes, and the odd sea snake darted in and out of the rocky outcrops. Mike didn't hang around when he saw them. He wasn't a fan of snakes at the best of times, never mind when he had two kids in tow and couldn't get them to emergency care if one was bitten.

He took the kids back into the shallows and over to the ladders along the edge of the bay. There was no beach there. Trees grew to the rocky ledge that plunged into the water. At only knee deep, it was easy to get in and out of, but manoeuvring Jax and Lexi with flippers on was a challenge. Mike helped them up and followed, slipping his own flippers off once he was on the timber boardwalk jutting out over the water. Mike stepped off the path onto the grassy area under the canopy of palms and hardy salt-resistant trees that towered above them. The same passenger who'd helped him get the kids into their room the evening before was there. "Oh, hey. Thanks for last night."

"I see they're bright-eyed and bushy-tailed today." She smiled at the kids, and Jax grinned at her, always ready to talk a stranger's ear off.

"Did you meet my dad last night?" Lexi asked.

"Yes, honey. This nice lady opened our door for us when I was carrying both of you."

"Okay." Satisfied with the answer, Lexi walked away and sat down on the grass. Mike nudged Jax to follow and smiled again, ready to say goodbye.

"Did you know, my dad has the biggest doodle ever?" Jax asked, wide-eyed and perfectly innocent.

The woman's eyes grew impossibly large, and Mike froze, mouth open. Bloody hell, he wanted the ground to open and swallow him whole. A sink hole, volcanic fissure, piece of the earth's crust breaking off and him falling into it. A meteor. Rogue bolt of lightning. Jaws jumping out of the water. Anything. A fierce flush crept up his neck and over his cheeks, the burning sensation igniting his nerve endings. He tried to say something, but his mind had blanked and his words had scampered away, hiding like he wanted to do. Jax opened his mouth as if he hadn't finished talking, and Mike lunged for him, clamping a hand over his mouth before he could blurt out anything else. Mike smiled sheepishly at the woman and lifted his son, his hand still covering his mouth.

"Maybe we could get a drink one night when the kids are asleep."

Visions of Ezio above him, inside him, filled his mind, and Mike instantly got all melty, the smile spreading involuntarily. "Thanks, but I'm seeing someone." His answer was automatic, but it probably shouldn't have been. He and Ezio were supposed to have been a one-off thing. If they could time it right, he'd make sure it happened again, but they were hardly in a committed relationship. There was one thing for certain though; Mike would never leave his kids alone in their stateroom.

He said his goodbyes quickly then and carried Jax over to the spot where Lexi sat. "Jaxson," he chastised. "You can't say that stuff, mate. It's embarrassing as hell—"

"You swore!" Lexi helpfully pointed out.

"Sorry," he responded without thinking. "Jax, seriously, why did you say that?"

He shrugged. "I saw you in your undies this morning."

"Okay. But why did you say that to her?"

Jax shrugged again, this time with his bottom lip quivering. "I dunno. I'm sorry, Daddy."

Mike hugged his son and shook his head. "I'm not angry, buddy. Just embarrassed. It's not something you would normally tell a stranger." Jax nodded, and Mike pushed away the mortification so he could focus on the funny side. He couldn't help his smile when he dug the sunscreen out of his bag. "Come on then, let's get this on you and we'll walk back. Maybe we can get some lunch here on the island and go for another swim."

FOUR

Ezio

Ezio compared the note from Mike to his schedule. He couldn't make most of the afternoons and evenings Mike had listed, but there was one late night he had four hours and another afternoon with six hours free. It would be on the second-last day of the cruise—a sea day. Mike's kids would hopefully be in care. That made him a horrible person. Any parent would want to spend quality time with their kids on holidays. He shouldn't wish that they would want time apart. But if Mike was free, they could see each other again.

The back and forth, the should he or shouldn't he, was making him dizzy. It wasn't as straightforward as he wanted it to be though. Morality and duty warred with everything he wanted. But Mike had captured his attention and swallowed him into his orbit. Ezio was hooked. Entirely enraptured. So much so that the thought of not seeing him again before they parted ways was too painful to comprehend. Should he want to see Mike again? Absolutely not. It was bad enough that it'd happened once. Twice was unforgivable, but a third and fourth time? He was setting himself up for serious trouble.

He closed his eyes and sent up a wish into the universe. *Please let me see him again, damn the consequences.*

A quick knock on the door sounded before it opened, and the nurse stuck her head in. "Your next appointment is in the infirmary. Contusions from a fall." He stuffed the papers in his desk drawer and tried not to look guilty. He probably failed miserably.

"Stitches?" he asked as he stood.

"No, it's just scrapes. Nothing too serious. They didn't have anything to clean it with, so they came down. I've washed the wound and have all the plasters there ready to go. I just wanted you to sign off on it." Ezio nodded and followed her into the treatment room. With two beds side by side and a curtain that could be pulled between them to section off each area, the infirmary was more like an ambulance than an emergency room—his facilities were designed to treat injuries and stabilise major cases until they could be transported to urgent care facilities. Anything from rashes and burns to heart attack, stroke, broken bones, drug overdoses and the like occurred. Whenever there was an emergency that needed outside intervention, the captain, William Preston, had to be notified. They'd developed a close working relationship since his time as ship doctor began, and they'd become friends. The thought of the captain made Ezio's gut sink. What kind of person was he to ignore the cruise liner's rules?

The weight of that question sat heavy in his gut. He was disappointed in himself, but he hadn't broken them lightly. It wasn't for just anyone. Mike was important. He was the kind of man who tempted Ezio to walk away from everything just for another night together. Mike looked at him like he never wanted to let Ezio go. Ezio smiled. That look—the affection and heat between them, the quiet moments and the perfect way he fell asleep in Mike's arms and woke up still curled into him—made everything worth it. Ezio may be a shitty friend, and an employee with a death wish for their career, but Mike was worth it.

Ezio's shift passed in a blur. He had one thing on his mind its entire duration. The door to the infirmary hadn't even closed behind him before he was racing up through the belly of the ship to the eighth floor staterooms. The numbers on the stairwell doors grew until he reached it. With a hand on the doorknob, he sucked in a breath to steady his racing heart. He closed his eyes and blew it out slowly. When he opened them again, he pushed through to the guest quarters. He was no longer hesitating. It was a risk being seen there, especially in uniform, but he had to deliver the message to Mike's room above anything else. The need to have Mike in his arms again was overwhelming. It drove him. Pushed him. But it also gave him purpose. It calmed a part of him that he hadn't realized was wandering aimlessly.

He didn't stop walking until stateroom 8303 was before him. He rested his palm on the door and let the tension seep from his shoulders. Ezio doubted whether Mike would be inside—he certainly couldn't hear any chatter from his kids. But just knowing it was his space, albeit a temporary one, calmed him. It centred him. Ezio wasn't nervous anymore. He wasn't debating the righteousness of his actions. He was taking Mike and giving himself in return. Ezio fished out the note from his shirt pocket and slipped it into the message stand for the room. It might not seem like the right thing to do—perhaps not for his friendship with the captain or his career—but within himself, Ezio knew he was meant to take that path.

Ezio walked away with a smile, calmly heading toward the staff-only areas of the ship. He shouldn't have been on the deck where he'd seen Mike in the first place; there were rules about where staff and crew could socialise and relax. As the on-board doctor, he had certain privileges, including being able to access everywhere onboard in case of an emergency. But he'd been abusing those privileges of late.

He couldn't bring himself to regret it for a moment.

* * * * *

The corridors in the guest quarters were surprisingly busy at 9:00 PM. Ezio was on a break between shifts. Out of uniform, but on call for the rest of the evening after having a four-hour break. He couldn't stay with Mike the entire time. They'd come too close to getting busted by his kids the last time, but Ezio needed Mike in his arms. He was desperate to touch him and kiss him, like he'd been starved of oxygen and Mike was his lifeblood.

He knocked quietly, and a moment later the door opened. One-handed, Mike gripped his shirt and hauled Ezio over the threshold, pinning him against the wall as he swung the door closed. Mike didn't look at him; his eyes were focussed on the carpet. Nerves jostled in Ezio. Mike had a tense set to his shoulders, and his movements were jerky.

Mike stopped the door from slamming at the last moment and laid a palm on it when it clicked into place, still not letting go of Ezio's shirt. He flicked the lock and finally turned his gaze to Ezio. When he did, Ezio's heart lurched and his dick pulsed. Need blazed in Mike's eyes, his pupils blown, and his bottom lip was swollen like he'd been biting on it.

Ezio gasped and reached for the man, gathering him in his arms. Mike went willingly and moaned quietly as Ezio tilted his face up, pressing a whisper-soft kiss to his lips. One after another, he kissed Mike until the other man opened to him and their tongues touched.

Ezio's breath caught and Mike melted against him. The need to touch him wasn't even sexual—he wouldn't cross the line that Mike had drawn—but he was overwhelmed by the desperation to feel Mike's naked body against his own.

He slowed their kiss until Mike pulled away. But he didn't go far, nuzzling Ezio's smooth cheek with his stubbled one. "Hi," he whispered.

Ezio beamed, sunshine lighting up his world at Mike's shy greeting. "Hi, Moo." He laughed at Mike's puzzled look and shrugged. "Mike and Boo—Moo."

Mike snorted out a quiet laugh and shook his head. "Take me to bed, Ez."

"Will the kids be okay if we have a shower instead?"

Mike bit down on his lip and moaned quietly, his eyes slipping closed in the sexiest of moves. He unclenched his hands from Ezio's shirt and smoothed it down gently, sending ripples of awareness through Ezio at his reverent touch. He tilted Mike's face and kissed him again. "It's okay if your answer is no. I have you for four hours. I don't care whether that's naked in a shower or cuddling in a bed together. As long as I can be near you, I don't care what we're doing."

"I need you." Ezio paused when Mike didn't elaborate, waiting for him to speak again. He ran his thumb over his cheekbone and smiled gently, encouraging him. When Mike spoke again, it was in a whisper. He laid himself bare. "I don't know. I just need… you." His vulnerability and honesty, and the trust he put in Ezio to meet those needs, were humbling. Ezio slipped his hand into Mike's, clasping their fingers together, and tugged him into the bathroom. Mike barely had the door closed before Ezio had Mike's T-shirt on the floor and his shorts and jock around his ankles. He couldn't get out of his own clothes fast enough, kicking off his shoes and tossing his polo over his shoulder. Shorts undone and underwear off, he was blessedly naked with Mike, and they came together with a ferocity that left him gasping for breath. Mike spun him, pressing Ezio back against the timber door, and grasped his hips, grinding on him. Their semis hardened at the contact, and Mike dominated their kiss, taking exactly what he needed from Ezio.

Ezio loved it.

But then he was gone. Pulling back and turning on the water in the bath and shower combo, leaving Ezio shaking and needy. He sucked in a breath and moved forward on unsteady legs, his cock as hard as a fence paling. He'd never been so turned on in his life.

Mike stepped into the shower, and Ezio paused, watching the rivulets of water running down his body, trailing over paths that Ezio wanted to lick. The beautiful man before him held out his hand, and Ezio moved, crashing into him and taking Mike's mouth in a hungry kiss.

Ezio soaped up his hands and ran them over all the smooth skin and sculpted muscles on the man before him. Washing Mike's body was a privilege. Something like a religious experience. He wanted to worship him, revere the commitment and hard work he put into achieving perfection. Ezio traced each corded muscle and watched every one of Mike's reactions. A sigh and a bite on his lip with one move, and his eyes rolling back and a groan with another. He avoided Mike's generous cock and balls, leaving them until he'd finished his job. Falling to his knees, Ezio ran soapy hands over strong legs, marvelling at the soft hairs and veins that ran over his feet. When he stood, he added a dash of shampoo to Mike's hair and massaged his scalp, taking his time when Mike fell against him, turning boneless. Ezio smiled. He loved being able to make this man happy. To satisfy him.

It said a lot about where he was at with this supposed hook-up. It had gone beyond a one-night stand days earlier and was looking more like a holiday fling that had the potential to quickly turn serious. Ezio fought down the disappointment of their inevitable ending. The cruise would continue for only a few more days. A future that extended beyond it was impossible. How could they have one when he was doing everything wrong? He was lying to Mike, and it wasn't just a little white lie either. When the man found out who Ezio was, he'd probably lodge a formal complaint. Mike deserved more too. He deserved someone who would come home to him every night. He deserved love and affection and not a fly-by-nighter who'd pop in for a few weeks and dash back off to work for months at a time. No, Mike deserved the world. He deserved a love that the universe itself couldn't match. One that Ezio would gladly front up for but be ill-equipped to live up to.

He directed Mike under the spray and rinsed the shampoo out of his hair, making sure none of the suds washed into his eyes. Then he repeated the process with the conditioner.

It wasn't long before Mike was spinning Ezio around, repaying the favour. "Brace your hands against the wall, Ez." He obeyed, and his knees nearly bucked when Mike traced his tongue over every part of him before soaping him up and taking his fill. Mike did the same as Ezio, lingering on spots that provoked a reaction, and it was a sweet torture.

The man's hands were magic. Calloused and rough from the weights Ezio knew he lifted, they were soft and tender at the same time. Intimate, gentle swipes of his thumb against the dips in Ezio's back, a brush of knuckles down his spine. A whisper-soft kiss with the rasp of stubble against his shoulder.

Ezio choked out a muffled cry when Mike slid his hand between his cheeks and soaped up his hole before teasing his perineum. Down his legs and around behind his knees, where he lingered, licking the inside crease and tickling the sensitive spot there. Ezio's knees nearly buckled, but strong hands kept him steady and then resumed their push into ecstasy as Mike moved down his calves to his ankles.

Mike turned him again and pressed a hand to his belly, pushing him back against the tiled wall. Ezio shivered at the shock of cold on his heated skin, but he was grateful for the support when Mike traced a line up his body with his tongue. His mouth was sinful and sweet and utterly addictive. Mike wrapped his fingers around Ezio's cock and licked him. Water streamed down over them both, drops catching on Mike's eyelashes as he looked up at Ezio and curled his tongue around the head of his cock. He wasn't going to last long with Mike's talented tongue doing crazy things to him. But he indulged in the moment, never wanting it to end.

The tingling in his spine had Ezio pausing. He pulled back, not wanting to come yet, and Mike got the hint. He tugged him directly under the spray and rinsed off Ezio before turning off the water and snaking out a hand to grasp one of the towels hanging on the racks. Mike ran it over

Ezio's hair, using it to pull him closer and kiss him. His body pressed against Ezio's was incendiary. Within a split second, the kiss turned ravenous as Mike ground against his leg, his cock leaving a sticky trail of pre-cum along Ezio's hip.

Ezio hugged Mike to him as he abandoned his attempt to dry Ezio's hair and tossed the towel aside. Ezio bent his knees, lining up their cocks, and closed his hand around Mike's shaft, pressing them together. With fingers intertwined, they worked each other together, and Ezio saw stars. Panting breaths filled the steamy shower, and Ezio nuzzled Mike's neck, sucking softly on the skin there. "Oh God, don't stop," his lover breathed as Ezio bit down on the tendon, letting his teeth scrape over it and his lips caress the sting. Ezio shifted his hand, grasping Mike's arse cheek and squeezing tight, urging him to thrust. Together they moved, pumping their cocks into each other's tight fist and locking their lips together. Mike's movements stuttered first, his cock growing impossibly hard next to Ezio's. That was all it took to tip him over. They came one after another, capturing each other's moans in their kiss.

Ezio looked down, seeing the evidence of their combined release, and lifted their entwined hands to his lips. As he sucked each one clean, Mike's cock twitched and made a valiant attempt to give it another go. When he let go of Mike's fingers, Ezio wrapped his arms around his broad back and pulled him in for a kiss. It was long and lazy, but warm and filled with affection too.

"I should get you cleaned up and tucked into bed," Ezio whispered between kisses.

"Are you staying?"

"For a bit. I've got to get back to my stateroom by one."

Mike studied him for a moment, and Ezio looked away. He didn't want to deceive Mike—the omission that he was working not holidaying was bad enough, but he never wanted to openly lie. Finally, Mike nodded, seemingly resisting the urge to question him further. The relief that coursed through him was like a tsunami, but Ezio's rebounding emotions made him dizzy. How could he be relieved and disappointed at the same time? He wanted to know everything about Mike. It was stupid of him to think that Mike would want to reciprocate. But then he was also glad that Mike had let Ezio's cryptic answer go. It was better that he didn't know. Ezio had crossed the line so many moral miles ago, but he didn't want to drag Mike into his unethical behaviour. Ezio may have been prepared to risk his career by breaking the cruise liner's rules, but he wouldn't lie. It was a line Ezio refused to cross.

They rinsed off again, dried, and dressed before climbing under the sheet. Mike turned away from him but grasped Ezio's hand and dragged him close until they were spooning. Ezio couldn't help his smile against his lover's back. "Did you and the kids enjoy the island?"

Mike hummed. "We did. Took them to see the aquarium. Lexi has a thing for turtles; she loved it. But Jax was disappointed. He wanted to see sharks." Mike huffed out a laugh. "He's a little morbid—he wanted to watch them feed."

"I swam with whale sharks in the Philippines. They're spectacular. Absolutely fascinating. It's good that Jax is curious about them."

"Nah, he just wants to see blood and gore." Mike rolled to his back and blushed a pretty shade of red and shook his head. "He's bloody embarrassing too."

"What happened?" Ezio couldn't help his grin when Mike rolled his eyes.

"Apparently I have—and I quote—the biggest doodle ever." Ezio snorted out a laugh and buried his mouth against Mike's shoulder, stifling the noise.

"What? How? I have so many questions."

"There was a lady who helped me with the kids a few nights ago. Both of them fell asleep, so I was carrying them and didn't have a free hand to open the door. She did it for me. We ran into her on Lifou, and Jax just blurted it out."

Ezio moved so he was propped up on his elbow, leaning over Mike, grinning down at the man. He ran his nose down Mike's cheek and pressed a kiss to his jaw, chuckling softly again.

Mike poked him in his side, and Ezio laughed harder. He turned his face away, and Ezio nuzzled him, half lying on him as he kissed along his throat and up to Mike's mouth. "Have to say, I like your proportions too."

"Do you want me to top you?" Mike asked, his brow furrowed.

"I don't usually bottom. It's not really my thing, but if you want to—"

"No." He shook his head vehemently. "I'm good. I can't really…" He blew out a breath, and Mike thumbed Ezio's nipple, sending a zing of sensation straight through him. "It doesn't matter."

Ezio pulled back and slid his hand into Mike's, wanting to ease whatever it was that had panic flashing in Mike's eyes. "You can tell me." Mike shook his head, but Ezio was undeterred. "You told me not to shut you out before. I'm telling you the same."

"I hate topping. I can't do it. It's never felt right. I just can't get off. I'm lucky if I can even keep it up." He closed his eyes and buried as much of his face in the pillow as he could. But Ezio saw the colour blazing in his cheeks. The look on Mike's face was anything but shy embarrassment. It was shame.

Ezio lifted up onto his elbow and ran his fingers through Mike's hair, before turning his chin until he was facing him again. "Mike, look at me." He took a moment before he blinked open his eyes and when he did, Ezio leaned down and kissed his forehead. "Wanting to bottom isn't anything to be ashamed of. It's simply what your body demands." He peppered Mike's face with more soft kisses. "I love that you'll share your body with me like that."

They lay there together, kissing and petting, their whispered conversation filling the quiet in their bubble of existence. He'd missed this more than he ever could have admitted. Maybe Ezio was tempting fate by breaching his contract. Or maybe he'd had enough of life on the ship.

Ezio had his eyes closed, caressing Mike's side, when the bed shifted and a small arm slid in alongside his. Mike froze, going rigid and Ezio pulled back, stifling the squeak of surprise. Jax, who'd been asleep on the bottom bunk, had climbed out of bed and into Mike's. "Daddy, I'm thirsty," he mumbled, still looking as if he was asleep.

"Okay, honey. Hop back into your bed, and I'll get you a drink."

Jax sat up and rubbed his eyes, looking at them with his brow furrowed. "Who are you?"

Ezio's heart beat hard, inexplicably wanting to leave a good impression on this little boy. "Ah—"

"He's my friend. Now go on, back into your bed." Mike's voice was soothing, but Ezio could hear the tightness in his words.

"Why is he in your bed, Dad?"

"Shh, lie back down or you won't get back to sleep." Mike herded him back over to the bunks and winced apologetically at Ezio. They'd had three hours of uninterrupted time together. It was more than he should have hoped for. Mike rummaged around in the bar fridge and pulled out a water bottle, handing it to Jax. Ezio waited until he'd had his fill and rolled over, facing the wall, before he eased himself out of the bed and motioned for Mike to follow him into the bathroom.

"Will Jax remember that in the morning?"

He shook his head. "No, he was still asleep."

Ezio nodded and stood there awkwardly, searching for the words he desperately wanted to say. *See me again. I want to keep this going. I don't want the end of the cruise to be goodbye.* But instead he said, "I should go. In case either one of them wake up again. I don't want you to have to explain…"

"Yeah," Mike agreed. "Probably best." He watched as Ezio slipped on his shorts and cringed as he wrung out his polo, soaked from the water that had escaped from behind the shower curtain. He had his shoes on before Mike spoke again.

"So, the day at sea… I can see you again?" Ezio nodded, and Mike gifted him with a smile. "Good. I'm looking forward to it. I'm sorry about—" He motioned over his shoulder.

"Don't apologize, Mike. Your first responsibility is to your kids. I'd never stand in the way of that." Mike stepped into his arms and kissed him, deep and slow. It was a kiss goodbye, and Mike took a piece of Ezio's heart with him when they finally pulled apart and Ezio slipped out the door. He leaned against the wall and closed his eyes. How was he ever going to go back to his old normal when he and Mike parted ways?

FIVE

Mike

The cruise had been magical. Every single day. Every part of it. It was exactly what Mike and the kids had needed. Ten days of sun, sea, and sand with no work, no running around or schedules to keep. No telephone calls, no billing reports or complaining customers or staff. No homework and no bringing work home. He'd been able to relax for the first time in far too long. Unwind.

His time with Ezio had been a bonus. Something that he'd idly entertained the thought of when he was on dry land before dismissing it as impossible. But Ezio was very real—his tender arse attested to it after three rounds of mind-blowing sex that morning. Getting on the waterslides with Jax that afternoon perhaps wasn't the smartest idea either, but his youngest was persistent and Lexi had wanted to record them coming down together.

He was glad she had too. Mike wore a carefree smile in the shots that he hadn't seen in a long time. It was Ezio who'd given it to him too. He'd had a blast with his kids, but Ezio had been there for him, gifting him something immensely personal. Mike hadn't experienced anything like it in years. It wasn't just the sex. They were a perfect match in bed, but they were more than that too. It hadn't been a one and done like so many of his other hook-ups had been. Ezio had hung around and given Mike more affection than any other lover before him. Mike had fallen hard and fast. He was madly in lust with the man and crushing even harder.

Their goodbye was brutal. Mike forced himself not to ask how to contact Ezio after the cruise ended. The man he'd shared his body with had been hiding something, and Mike didn't want to remember his rejection. He'd left the words unspoken so he could walk away without knowing whether there could have been more between them.

But Ezio's actions had given Mike that spark of illogical hope. He didn't think the man was that good an actor to completely fabricate his reactions. Mike would bet anything that Ezio had treasured their time together. If given half the chance, he was sure they could have amounted to more than a holiday fling. Knowing that was some kind of warped closure. But it had given him confidence in himself. After Ezio, he believed that someone could fall for him. Was he reading too much into Ezio's soft touches and lingering kisses? Did the shine in his eyes attest to a deeper feeling as he walked backwards, not breaking sight of each other until he'd run out of corridor? Maybe, maybe not. But the interpretation he adopted was Mike's choice. It was also the only way that he could stop himself from banging on every door of the ship until he found him to beg him for more.

Lost in his thoughts, he watched Lexi and Jax play in the water park. Spouts of water shot up from jets on the spongey floor. Kids manning the water cannons mounted on turrets sprayed anyone that dared cross the threshold to storm the pirate ship. Giant buckets dropped a waterfall onto those unlucky enough to be standing below them, and smaller showers switched on and off in a random pattern that was impossible to predict. Jax was having fun, but Lexi caught his watchful eye. She looked like she was flagging. They'd had a big day. Kids' club, then lunch, the pools, waterslides, dinner, and now the water park. It was way past their bedtime, but Mike wanted to indulge them on their last day. They had plenty of time to sleep on the plane and at home the next day once they got back. But they only had a few more hours on board.

Reality was intruding too fast. The list of things he had to tend to was growing already—unpacking and washing clothes, checking in at the gym and resolving any disasters that had befallen them this week. Mike groaned, not wanting to go back just yet. He wanted to laze about in the post-sex happy vibe he had going on. Maybe even extend his cruise and stay for the next one.

Mike shifted his weight to his other butt cheek and smiled watching his kids. But something was wrong. Lexi crumpled, dropping like a stone to the ground.

Jax screamed.

Mike leaped up from his deck chair and ran, sprinting toward his baby girl. "Lexi!"

He hurdled the low concrete step bordering the water park and skidded to his knees, reaching for his unmoving daughter. Mike's heart thumped hard, adrenaline raging through his system as panic clawed at him. He picked her up, and her arm flopped like a ragdoll's, completely limp.

Terror filled him.

Mike carried her away from the water, laying her down on the step he'd just jumped. He checked her pulse, its beat thready under his fingers. Her breathing was even, but shallower than normal. What do I do? How do I fix her? Mike's years of first aid training were gone in a puff of smoke, his mind completely blanking. All he could see was his baby girl lying there motionless. "Oh, Jesus, wake up, Lexi. I don't know what to do."

"Dad," Jax cried frantically, fear lacing his voice.

Mike sucked in a breath and tried to steady himself. "She'll be okay, Jax." He shook Lexi's shoulders helplessly, and Lexi stirred.

"Move," boomed a voice behind him. Familiar, yet different too. Authoritative, and with none of the warmth that he'd heard it whisper countless times in his ear over the last few days. Mike closed his eyes, grateful that Ezio had seen him.

Ezio dropped to his knees and without a word to Mike, took charge, checking Lexi's pulse and breathing as she blinked open her eyes and squinted. He didn't know when he'd reached for Jax, but the little boy was clinging tight to him—another thing Mike was grateful for.

"Has this happened before?" Ezio asked as he held a bottle of water up to Lexi's lips to take a sip from.

"No, never. She was a little tired and then just fell."

Ezio turned to Mike, and their eyes connected. Mike saw so much being communicated in Ezio's gaze—care, concern, and something else underlying it. Fear, perhaps. "Did she hit her head?"

"I don't think so." Mike shook his head and smoothed his hand down Jax's back needing to comfort himself. "She was standing still and then... crumpled to the ground."

"She's fainted. How much water has she had today?" Ezio's words didn't hold any judgement, merely professional concern. But hearing her diagnosis, Mike knew that the blame was squarely on him. He should have realized Lexi was dehydrated. It was a beginner mistake, one that he had no excuse to get wrong.

Mike rubbed his forehead and wanted to kick himself. "I don't know. Not much since we've been here, I guess. She had a glass with dinner, maybe. I think probably another glass or two while we were swimming this afternoon."

"That's not enough in this heat," Ezio said gently. "She's likely dehydrated. It's best to get her into the infirmary so I can administer a drip." It was only then that Mike really looked at Ezio. He was dressed in a uniform, nothing like the casual clothing Mike had seen him in and out of. White pants, white officers' shirt, a white lab coat with a stethoscope hanging around his neck, and a name tag that proclaimed him as the ship's doctor. He looked good; professional and smart. Was that the secret he'd been keeping from Mike? What was the big deal? He could have just told him; Mike would have understood that he had to fit any time for the two of them between his shifts. Ezio's words broke him out of his musing. "Let's get Lexi downstairs into my treatment rooms. I want to make sure that she's okay to travel tomorrow. Can you carry her?"

"Of course—"

"Dad," Lexi whined weekly. "I can walk." His daughter was fiercely independent and insisted on doing things herself. Mike loved that she was growing into someone who knew her own mind and would stand up and make her voice count, but right at that moment, he needed to be her daddy. He needed to care for her like she was his baby—something that no matter how old she was would always be true.

"I know you can, honey. But let your old dad pamper you for a moment." He waited for her nod and lifted her into his arms. Jax tugged on his shorts and looked up to him. "You're coming too, buddy. Can you walk next to me? I need you to stay close."

Ezio led the way, holding open the heavy deck doors and pointing to the button for Jax to press. Lexi was heavy in his arms, still limp as she rested her head against his shoulder. As the doors to the lift closed, encapsulating them in chrome and timber panelling, Mike's heart rate skyrocketed. His breathing shallowed and light-headedness stole over him. Suddenly woozy, he needed to lean against the mirrored back wall of the lift as it descended into the bowels of the ship. A sweat broke out on his brow as his pulse screamed through his veins. Mike's lungs squeezed tight, and he struggled against the weakness in his limbs as his heart beat like the flutter of a hummingbird's wings. He closed his eyes and calmed his mind, focusing only on slowing his heart. It wasn't the first time something like this had happened, but it was the most inopportune. "Ezio," he wheezed, "I need—"

"Bloody hell, Mike! Don't pass out on me." Ezio took Lexi from his arms, jostling her out of her comfortable snooze and making her grumble. "Deep breath, open your eyes, focus on me. Jax, I need you to hold your dad's hand. Mike, you squeeze it. Jax, if you feel Daddy's hand go loose, I need you to tell me straight away, okay?" Jax nodded and Mike wiped the sweat away from his forehead with his free hand, still trying to get his heartbeat under control.

"Give me a minute, I'm okay." Mike's voice was slurred even to his own ears. He sounded like he was stumbling around drunk. Concentration split between squeezing Jaxson's hand and slowing his breathing and runaway pulse, it took longer than normal for Mike to feel like his heart wasn't beating out of his chest. Exhaustion slipped over him. He struggled to stay upright.

He hated these episodes, especially when his kids needed him to be strong. He didn't even know what brought them on; he'd had them exercising, at random times during the day, and when he was stressed or overly excited. The doctor thought they were anxiety attacks, but they weren't like other people's. They didn't leave him crippled with fear or in a downward spiral. They came on quick, and usually stopped after a minute, leaving him a spent and sweaty mess. It was more like he'd run a hundred-metre sprint with a lion on his tail. The anti-anxiety medication he'd been prescribed did absolutely nothing, so for the most part, it was just something he lived with, and he did.

Mike took back Lexi when his strength slowly returned, but by that time they were outside the infirmary door. Ezio unlocked it and it slid open to a reception desk and four chairs decorated in calming blue fabric, clean white walls, and another door that Ezio headed straight for.

"Wait here for a second." Ezio slipped through the door quietly, and a moment later held it open for them. Jax passed through, with Mike and Lexi bringing up the rear. His thongs squeaked on the linoleum floor as Mike walked past a green curtain pulled across part of the treatment room. He laid Lexi down on a bed with fresh green sheets tucked tightly in and bathed in white light from an overhead lamp.

She looked so small in the clinical bed, her still-wet hair splayed out beside her pale face. Dark circles shadowed her eyes, and her lips had none of the rosy pink colouring Mike was used to seeing.

"You, sit," Ezio demanded of Mike, patting the bed at Lexi's feet. "Jax, my man, you get the armchair." Ezio opened and closed cupboards, setting up what Mike could see was an IV line and drip. "This is purely to rehydrate Lexi. You won't want her travelling any real distance unless she is properly hydrated, or her headache will be unbearable. Do I have your consent to administer it?"

Mike didn't hesitate. He trusted Ezio, both the man and the medical professional. "Yes, one hundred percent. How long will Lexi need to be hooked up to it?"

"It will only take about thirty minutes to be administered, but I'd like to keep her here overnight for observation. I have a patient in the other bed too."

"What were you doing up on deck?"

"I was called up, but it was resolved by the time I got there, so I didn't need to do anything. Then I saw you." Ezio rested his hand on Mike's shoulder and tipped his chin up to look in his eyes. "Had anything to drink?"

"No alcohol, if that's what you're talking about." Mike's tone was clipped, and he didn't mean it to be. He knew Ezio was just looking out for him. He blew out a breath and continued quietly, "My doc said that I get anxiety attacks sometimes, but they go away quickly. They leave me tired, but I'm okay."

"Hmmm," Ezio pondered, his brow furrowed.

They waited then, as the drip did its magic. Jax fell asleep, curled up on the armchair, and Ezio took his stethoscope and stood between Mike's legs. His warmth and scent surrounded Mike, and he resisted the urge to melt into the alluring doctor. It was hardly professional in Ezio's place of work, but the temptation was strong. Ezio's voice held that same affection Mike had heard many times during the cruise, and especially that morning. "How often do the anxiety attacks happen?"

"They're starting to come on more. But they're not too serious. They aren't debilitating like so many other people have."

Ezio smoothed his hands down Mike's shoulders, and he gave up any pretence of resistance. Resting his head on Ezio's chest, he soaked up the man's calm and warmth. He felt more than heard Ezio's question. "Did the doctor give you medication?"

"It does jack. I don't bother taking it anymore."

"Good." Mike pulled back to look at the man before him, the one who'd held him tight as he rocked slowly into him for the final time that day. The same man he'd ridden and who'd uttered, "love, love, love," until Mike had closed his eyes and imagined it was him Ezio was talking about, not what they were doing. The one who'd kissed him with such passion as they'd said goodbye at Mike's doorway that he'd stolen Mike's breath. Ezio's comment was the opposite of what he'd anticipated he would say after their morning together. "That didn't look like an anxiety attack to me. Can I check you over?"

Mike acquiesced, and Ezio slipped his hands up Mike's sides, lifting his singlet slowly, and pulling it off his body. Mike's breath hitched and his eyes fluttered closed as he tilted his face up to Ezio's. Warm lips met his forehead and Mike moaned softly. "I wish—"

"I know." Ezio nuzzled his face and kissed his temple softly. He fitted the earpiece of the stethoscope and breathed on the metal, warming it before touching it to Mike's chest. The cold was still a shock, but Mike didn't flinch too much. Still, it was enough that Ezio's lips tilted up in a smirk and he moved the stethoscope around in different places over Mike's heart. The look of concentration he wore was as sexy as when his focus was directed to making Mike's eyes roll back in his head.

"What's the verdict, Doc?"

"I don't know. Your heart sounds pretty good to me, but I'd like you to talk to your doctor about it again. Can I take your blood pressure?" Mike nodded and Ezio fitted the cuff, pressing the button to inflate it. He saw the numbers counting, reaching higher than they normally were. "It's elevated, but that's to be expected after what's happened." Mike yawned, his body losing its fight against the exhaustion that always overcame him when he had an attack. Ezio cupped Mike's face and caressed his cheek with his thumb. "Why don't you take Jax back to your room and have a sleep? I'll sit with Lexi the whole night in case she wakes up."

"I don't want to leave her," Mike whispered, torn in half. Ezio wrapped an arm around his shoulders, and Mike leaned in close, cuddling into the taller man's chest. It was comfort and warmth. Affection. Something Mike needed at that moment more than anything else.

"I know, but both of you need some sleep or you'll feel awful tomorrow. You already look like you're ready to pass out." Mike hummed, sleep already starting to overcome him, the vibrations from Ezio's voice calming him even more. "I know I don't deserve your trust, but please. Trust me to look after your little girl. I'll call you as soon as she wakes up, and you can come straight back." Mike didn't know what Ezio was talking about, but he was too tired to process it. Was it just because Ezio hadn't told him that he was the ship's doctor? So what? At least it wasn't that he was going back to his husband or wife between their hook-ups.

"I trust you," Mike mumbled.

"Then go." Ezio ran his fingers through Mike's hair and pulled away. He instantly missed the other man's heat and solid presence. Mike wanted to stay like that. He would have been perfectly happy to doze, leaning into Ezio. But the doctor had a point. He was on shift and couldn't hold Mike up while he slept. At the brush of a kiss against his forehead, Mike blinked open his eyes. He nodded, and Ezio helped him off the bed before bending over and scooping Jax up off the armchair. He waited for Mike to brush Lexi's hair off her face and drop a soft kiss to her forehead. Ezio placed Jax gently into Mike's arms, hardly jostling him, and pressed his forehead against Mike's.

He knew from the depths of his soul that Lexi was in good hands. It was the only reason he could force himself to turn and head to their stateroom.

Mike had to pack. He had to get their things organized so he could have them transported off the ship rather than having to look after them himself. But he didn't have it in him. His energy was sapped dry, his worry combined with the attack leaving him hollowed out and empty. Jax hadn't woken when he placed him in his bed, and Mike eyed the detritus scattered around the room—days' of activities and dashing in and out and hours of making love on the double bed. He'd have to pack it sooner or later, but now wasn't the time. He kicked off his shorts and faceplanted the pillow. Sleep took him before he could even exhale the pent-up breath he held.

* * * * *

Mike woke in a panic, his eyes popping open and his breaths coming quickly. Darkness surrounded him, but he could make out the outline of his sleeping son on the lower bunk. He searched out the top bunk, and memories of earlier that night slammed into him. Lexi was in the infirmary. He needed to get there.

He searched blindly in the cupboard for a pair of shorts and found the soft material of his tracksuit pants instead. They would do. He pulled them on sans underwear and lifted Jax into his arms. Thankfully, his little boy slept like the dead. Until he was ready to wake up, nothing would make him stir.

Pulling his pillow off the bed and slipping it under his arm, Mike hustled out of his stateroom and headed straight for the infirmary. The trip was quick. Either no one was awake in the dead of night, or they were all occupied in the clubs and bars and not catching the lift anywhere. Mike was grateful for it. He was raw. Tired and overwhelmed. In two places at once—a reality that seemed to be cracking apart and a dream world that had him and Ezio holding his kids' hands as they walked off the ship together. He'd held out asking to see him after he left the ship during their first goodbye, but he couldn't do it during their second. He wanted this man more than anything he'd ever had for himself. Years of fumbling through relationships, of trying to make them work was exhausting. He'd been continually forced into a box that he just couldn't fit into. But now he knew. He'd known it all along really, except he hadn't been willing to admit it. Yet he'd been left without a doubt with Ezio.

He steeled himself as he knocked on the still-locked door of the infirmary and it opened a moment later. Ezio stood there, blinking. He was exhausted—his hazel eyes were flat, and a five o'clock shadow dusted his cheeks. But he looked good too. "You didn't sleep?"

"I did, but I had to come back. It's not that I don't trust you, but I couldn't have her waking up without me."

"You're a good dad, Mike. Come in." Ezio held the door to the treatment room open and took the pillow from him. With a hand on the small of his back, they walked together to Lexi's bed. The IV line was no longer attached to her, and even the cannula that Ezio had inserted into her hand had been removed.

"Did she wake up when you took it out?" Mike motioned to the cotton wool taped onto her hand as Ezio reclined the armchair and fluffed the pillow up. Mike laid Jax down, and Ezio passed him a soft blanket to drape over his little boy. He was still wearing his quick-dry boardies and his rashie, so it didn't surprise him when he immediately kicked off the blanket.

"She spoke to me, but I think she was still asleep."

Mike nodded. She probably was—he could hold an entire conversation with both his kids, and they wouldn't remember a thing the next day. "What did she say?"

"Said hi and asked where you were. I told her you were sleeping, and she nodded straight off again. She was knackered after yesterday." Ezio motioned to the door. "Can we have a word?"

"Yeah."

Mike ran his hand over Lexi's hair and smiled. Ezio motioned for him to go first and he did, pulling open the door to the waiting room as Ezio tugged the curtain across Lexi's treatment space.

Alone together, the electricity sparked between them again, and Mike stepped into his arms, hauling Ezio close by the lapels of his lab coat. Their mouths crashed together, and Mike moaned into the connection as their tongues delved and duelled, not for dominance, but in rediscovery. A whispered possibility of more. Mike wanted it. Wanted everything he could get. He was under no delusions. Ezio would be away for months at a time—he knew cruise ship staff and crew worked for long periods at sea—but he'd make it work. They had something special; Mike was sure of it.

Ezio's hands were doing crazy things to him, but he was only running his fingertips down his spine. Mike pulled him closer, needing to touch every part of Ezio.

After long moments, Ezio pulled back, gasping for air. When he whispered words of how perfect Mike was, of how much he wished for a future with him, Mike believed him. He closed his eyes and basked in the dream that this could become his life.

"Oh shit, sorry."

Ezio wrenched himself away from Mike and looked around wide-eyed. Mike followed his gaze and spotted a man in a white uniform. Dishevelled but undoubtedly someone important, judging by the stripes on the wrinkled jacket in his hand. Ezio paled, and when Mike took a step forward, he shot him a look that stopped him in his tracks.

His heart sank. The rejection stung, fierce and strong.

"C-Cap… Captain," the doctor stuttered, wide-eyed with shock. The other man's gaze bounced between him and Ezio, assessing them, and he held his hand up to silence Ezio. His lover's face blanked, shutters snapping into place. Any hope Mike had was snuffed out instantaneously, like a power outage plunging him into immediate darkness. If Ezio couldn't even bear to be seen with him, what kind of future could they possibly have? The memories of the times they'd met all came crashing down around Mike. They hadn't been together in public once except for their initial meeting. Ezio had been reticent at getting too close.

He huffed and shook his head, stalking away from the man he'd put his hope in. He was an idiot. He should have known their relationship was too good to be true. Mike opened the door to the treatment room, the snick as it closed echoing through the silence that descended around him. He went to his kids then, determined to be ready to get off the ship the moment he could.

SIX

Ezio

"I'm not awake enough to deal with this now, but you need to come and see me after we've docked," the captain ordered.

"Yeah," Ezio rasped, then cleared his throat, nodded, and spoke again. "Yes, Captain."

What have I done? The thought rattled around in Ezio's brain, and it took everything in him to stay put and continue the stilted conversation with Captain Preston. Will was his friend, but Ezio knew he was going to be speaking with him as his boss, not as his buddy. Ezio was prepared for the consequences he'd wrought upon himself from his actions. He knew, without a doubt, that he'd lose the job he'd once loved—the number-one rule of working on a cruise ship was to never have an inappropriate relationship with a passenger. Even hugging Mike was out of line, never mind what they'd done. But he was oddly okay with everything if the trade meant having been with Mike. If only it could have continued. He realized that his spirit and his heart were both in the treatment room next door, and even if he could change how things had turned out, he wouldn't. Every instinct screamed at him to chase Mike and beg him to understand. To plead for his forgiveness. Ezio hadn't been forthright with Mike, and his worlds had collided, exploding like a flaming pile of dog shit in his face. He had no one but himself to blame, but it was Mike who'd been hurt.

He would never forget the flash of pain in Mike's eyes, realization and betrayal dawning.

Ezio didn't regret his time with Mike. How could he? But he'd tried to keep their relationship hidden, as if his lover was a dirty little secret. In his world, however, he was exactly that. Ezio had rebelled the moment he'd seen him. He'd wanted a taste of the man who'd piqued his interest at first sight, but once was never going to be enough. He'd caved to his body's demands that he get close to Mike and stay glued to his side. The sex was incredible, but that wasn't the only thing compelling his return to stateroom 8303. He wanted to be in Mike's presence. To talk to him and kiss and caress him. He wanted the man with rippling muscles to curl into him and let his guard down. He wanted to be Mike's pillar of strength, if only for a moment. In the short time they'd known each other, Ezio was awed by the way Mike handled everything with a minimum of fuss and an ever-present patience and good humour.

It had taken all but a moment for Ezio to fall in lust with him. His job—the one that prohibited him from having any kind of relationship with the guest other than a purely professional one—became an annoying detail. Ezio realized that he was prepared to bend rules that he'd thought were hard and fast to have it all. But it had failed spectacularly.

He should have explained everything to Mike during their first conversation; before Mike's impact on him had taken effect. In fact, he should never have been at the bar at all. Once he'd gotten close to Mike, there was a seismic shift in Ezio. The tectonic plates he'd based his entire hard-earned career on shifted, and he was on new ground. Ezio should have been upfront; there was no doubt about it. He should have told Mike he was the ship's doctor. He should have explained the rules by which he was supposed to abide. But it would have meant that they couldn't date. They couldn't even be seen together in a social setting. If Mike had known that being caught together would be the end of Ezio's career, would he have experienced their time together? The answer had to be no, and that was something Ezio wasn't prepared to agree to. So, he hadn't told Mike anything about the rules or the restrictions imposed on him by the cruise ship company. Ezio had winged it, only to get caught in the act by the captain. Despite the way Ezio's heart beat faster when he looked at Mike and the sense of absolute rightness that swept over him when Mike was in his arms, his knee-jerk reaction was to push him away. To make it worse, he shot Mike a look that Ezio was sure was filled with horror when Mike stepped forward to introduce himself to Captain Preston. It wouldn't be a great leap for Ezio to fall in love with the man; he was easy to love. But Ezio's selfishness and his reaction when caught in the act showed just how unworthy of having a man like Mike he truly was.

After what felt like an insufferably long time, but in reality was less than a couple of minutes, Captain Preston staggered out of the reception area to begin his shift. Ezio ordered him a coffee; he knew just how desperately the captain would need it. Getting in his good graces wouldn't make the captain forget, but it couldn't hurt his case for a simple dismissal without receiving the writeup for a breach of ethics.

The long night was catching up with Ezio too. His other patient was the captain's boyfriend. Eddie had an anaphylactic reaction to a peanut-eating fan getting too close. Ezio was already in the infirmary looking after him. If it wasn't for Lexi being in there too, he would likely have closed his eyes for at least a few minutes. But he'd sat by her bedside all night just like he'd promised Mike. The hours crawling by without interruption was good for one thing. He'd identified all the little parts of Mike in his daughter's features. There were a precious few of them too. Lexi's nose, the shape of her bottom lip, and the line of her chin were all Mike. He'd never wanted to see himself in another human being. Looking like his father was enough for Ezio. But seeing Mike in Lexi and getting to know the kids was something that Ezio could easily have pictured for his future.

He'd never really spoken with either Lexi or Jax, but he'd been privileged enough to hear a story or two from Mike. Caring for his lover's little girl and being the person that

Mike, as a parent, had placed his innate trust in made Ezio want to prove himself worthy.

Instead, he'd pushed the other man away. He hated himself in that moment. Hated how he reacted, how he'd remained quiet, and hated that he hadn't fought harder for the one thing that Ezio never knew he wanted but now wasn't sure he wanted to live without. He didn't have a right to wish for the things that had played on the loop through his mind since the moment he'd finally managed to tear himself away from Mike that afternoon. The man had an inexplicable hold on him, and if he wasn't careful, he could easily fall under the same dazzling spell Mike's kids would no doubt effortlessly weave over him.

He understood now though. He could see what it all meant. Resolution steeled Ezio's spine. The hurt on Mike's face when Ezio had pushed him away had crushed his own heart. Fear had driven his knee-jerk reaction, but it had only taken a moment for Ezio to realize that the fear of losing Mike was far worse than any reprimand he'd receive.

He was already moving toward the door separating them. His strides ate the distance between himself and the man who had the potential to hold Ezio's happiness in his hands.

The shrill ring of the phone shattered the silence.

Ezio hesitated.

Ignore it and go to Mike, or fulfil his calling? The timing was terrible, but despite his otherwise easy dismissal of the rules, his professional responsibilities were ones he took seriously. "Dr Dimitriades," he answered, repressing the sigh that threatened to escape.

"Doctor, there's an emergency." He closed his eyes and forced the lump in his throat down. His chest squeezed tight. The words being spoken over the phone only half registered in his preoccupied brain. It didn't matter though. He'd been trained to multitask, and his subconscious took note of the key words the other staff member was delivering in a rush. "Blood everywhere," "bone sticking out."

His gut sank.

Ezio nodded, only realizing he hadn't spoken when the person on the other end of the phone prompted him for a response. "I'm on my way." He hung up and stepped over to the door which separated him from Mike. He pressed his forehead against it, his fingers curling against the cold surface. Time wasn't on his side. He couldn't have the conversation he needed to have with Mike right now. He left his future in the hands of fate, trusting that they were destined for more. But he couldn't leave without asking Mike to wait for him so he could explain. Determined, Ezio inhaled, pulled his shoulders back, and pushed through the door.

He looked into Lexi's treatment area and his heart tripped over itself. Mike was there with Lexi curled into his chest. Jax hadn't moved from his perch on the armchair, and all three of them were fast asleep. Ezio's chest squeezed, and his feet carried him to Mike without hesitation. He ran his fingers through Mike's hair, brushing it back before leaning down and pressing his lips to his love's forehead. The smell of the ocean, salt air and pristine white sand, and the sweetness of coconuts filled his senses. "Wait for me, please."

As much as he wanted to, he didn't linger. Ezio spun on his heels and dashed out to the waiting gurney, stopping only to toss his medical bag on top of it. He steered it one-handed as he sprinted down the corridor to the lift, on the phone with his nurse giving her a rundown of the patients in the infirmary and the emergency he'd been called to.

He hoped that whoever had called in the emergency was exaggerating.

But they weren't. It was worse.

* * * * *

Mike

Mike pushed through the door to find Jax stirring. "Shh, buddy. Go back to sleep." He brushed his fingers through Jax's hair, settling him again. But his little boy sat up.

Wide eyed, he asked, "Dad, do you know why we can't play outside?"

Mike shook his head, biting back his smile. Jax asked the most random questions, especially when he was asleep. "No, Jax, I have no idea."

"Killer clowns." He nodded, yawned, and laid his head back down on the pillow, curling up on the recliner. Mike wrapped the thin blanket Ezio had tossed over the back of the armchair over him and smiled at his son.

Lexi blinked open her eyes and smiled when he moved closer to check on her. "Hi, Daddy. Can I cuddle you?" She reached for him, arms up in the air, and Mike didn't hesitate.

"Let me get up, honey." He climbed onto the bed and pulled her into his arms, letting her sleep on his chest.

There was warmth and lips pressing against his forehead, but his eyes were heavy and exhaustion overwhelmed him. Whispered words tickled at his consciousness. He hated goodbyes, but this didn't feel like one. This gave him hope, even in his groggy half-awake state.

He smiled and stretched, seeking those lips against him again.

A gust of cold air. A sense of being bereft. Loss.

Mike gasped and opened his eyes, sitting up and jostling Lexi awake. He patted her head, his heart racing as she grumbled.

He stumbled off the narrow bed and staggered out the door. Where was Ezio? Mike needed to see him. He called for him but was met with silence. There was no one around. Mike's heart thudded in his chest, an unreasonable panic winding its way around him. What if they'd left them there? Logically he knew that even if all the passengers left, new ones would board within a matter of hours and all the staff would remain onboard. They weren't on some ghost ship floating through mist-covered oceans.

Mike shook off the sleep weighing him down and pressed the assistance button. A moment later, a woman dressed in a cruise ship uniform greeted him with a smile. "Good morning, sir. I have instructions from Dr Dimitriades that you and your family may leave and ready yourselves for disembarkation. We're already in the harbour, so it will only be another twenty minutes or so to dock and an hour until you can depart."

"I need to see the doctor. Where is he?" Mike's chest heaved as his heart raced, urgency squeezing his gut into a knot.

Her expression was unmoving, not giving away any hint of surprise. But when she spoke, a small furrow appeared between her brow—concern. "Is there something wrong, sir? If it's a medical emergency I can try him, but he's on an urgent call out that he really can't leave."

"Can I leave my number for him? I need to speak with him."

"Your doctor can request your medical records to be sent through. The cruise company will be able to do that on the doctor's behalf." She smiled serenely, apparently unde-terred by Mike's increasing agitation.

"It's... I need to speak with him. It's important." Mike was begging. Desperation filled him, and the panic which seized him earlier returned with a vengeance. He didn't want to get off the ship without speaking to Ezio one last time. Their parting had been less than stellar, and Mike needed to fix that. But how? How could he when he had to leave the ship in mere moments? With the staff member acting as gatekeeper between them, he'd never get any-where.

The lady straightened her posture, and the smile fell from her face. With a tilt of her chin upwards, she repeated her earlier comment that if he had a medical emergency, she'd be happy to call the doctor. Mike sagged into the clos-est chair in defeat and shook his head. "It's not an emer-gency. Not a medical one at least. I just need to speak with him. It's personal."

"I'm sorry, sir, it would be highly inappropriate for me to even pass him a message from you. Now, given the time, I recommend that you and your children head on back to your stateroom and ready for disembarkation."

"Yeah." He scrubbed his forehead and sighed. "Yeah, sure."

When he arrived back at his cabin, he couldn't help but check the place where Ezio had left his prior messages. But there were none.

The kids sensed the dip in his mood, but it didn't dim their excitement in seeing Sydney's sights. The Harbour Bridge and Opera House awed them. For Mike, they were the knife cutting him open. He was leaving a piece of his heart on the ship. He'd gained so much more than a holiday in paradise.

Part Two

Six months ago...

SEVEN

Robyn

The academic's report sat on her desk, dog-eared from how many times she'd read it. Post-it Notes tagged most of the pages, Robyn's scrawled handwriting highlighting the important passages. Photos of the cave drawings lay next to it. Tens of thousands of years of cultural heritage on the line; millions of dollars to be made by destroying it. Robyn was in the middle, the lawyer employed by the mining giant charged with securing the permits for the exploration. Yet she was desperate to save the caves. Her bosses could only see one thing—the dollar signs. She couldn't get past the sick feeling in the pit of her stomach.

She'd trusted them at first. The board had given her a report prepared by an expert who boasted qualifications and impressive client lists. Robyn had checked his credentials out, looking for a way to pre-emptively overcome any discrediting of his opinion. She'd prepared the application for the exploration and blasting permit, and it was solid. The expert's report looked thorough too.

Soon enough though—during the court-ordered mediation—she found out the truth. The report had more holes in it than Swiss cheese. The so-called expert had manipulated history to suit Western Mineral Exploration's agenda. He'd whitewashed the First Nation's cultural heritage, downplaying the significance of the area to both them and the world.

The mediation hadn't resulted in an agreement. The Elders were seeking to stop the mining exploration. Her job was to talk them out of pursuing legal action so the permit could be issued. She hadn't; she couldn't. Robyn wasn't as morally bankrupt as the board she reported to.

Robyn's trust in the organisation she worked for had been destroyed in that moment, as had her future in the company. The toll it took on her to continue working there was shredding her very soul, but it was the price she had to pay. Robyn couldn't leave; she wouldn't. Not when there was a chance that she could help bring about a refusal of the permit. As long as she was there, she still had a modicum of control over the process.

It was a naïve view though; one that was destroying her sanity. The months she'd remained there and fought from the inside to bring about change dragged out, the journey getting more difficult with every passing day. Robyn had never felt like a number, but soon realized she wasn't even that. No, she was barely even a cog in a wheel powered by capitalism and corporate greed which could and would operate with only the slightest hiccup if she fell out of the machinery. Singlehandedly, the mining giant would destroy anything in its path. Political donations to friendly candidates to promote them into positions of power and influence were daily occurrences. The populace was bribed with the promise of jobs and prosperity, and the fancy marketing campaigns won over the moderates with the illusion of the company's community-minded spirit, giving nature, and awareness of environmental concerns. The reality was much more tarnished.

But Robyn took the responsibility placed on her shoulders seriously. The oath she made upon admission as a lawyer required her to represent her employer to the best of her ability. Her overriding obligation to the courts was the only thing that kept her going in her darkest days. She wasn't protected as a whistle-blower—what the company was doing wasn't strictly illegal. Rather, the laws were too weak to protect the site. It was why the refusal was so difficult to achieve, and the very reason why Robyn couldn't sit back and let the legal system run its course. She needed to act. Doing so, though, put her in the realm of professional misconduct. She was acting unethically. If she was found out, it would be the end of her career, not just her job.

She'd tread lightly, pushing back against the board at every opportunity under the guise of compliance. Robyn made her employer jump through more hoops than necessary, telling them that it was important to dot the i's and cross the t's. She'd stalled the issue of the licence for longer than she ever dreamed was possible by asking for more evidence, more expert confirmation that the site was not as significant as the Elders claimed. With every report she commissioned, she nudged the experts, hoping that they would express the value of the caves as strongly as the First Nation's people had. Some were better than others, but all of them tailored their advice to favour Western Mineral Exploration. Without fail, they underestimated the significance of the caves. She would have believed them too, if it wasn't for her visit to the site. She was one of the privileged few to walk among tens of thousands of years of history. The caves were evidence of continuous habitation for forty-six thousand years—since the last ice age. Robyn sensed the ghosts of the past with her during her visit to the sacred site with the Elders. None of the experts approved by the company went there, and they certainly didn't consult with the First Nation's people when preparing their reports, despite Robyn explaining how important it was for full and open discussion with stakeholders.

Robyn's stalling tactics and misdirection enabled her to gather a mass of evidence of her own. It started with taking statements from the Elders, getting the site photographed, and paying for anthropologists and archaeologists who'd refused a retainer by the mining giant to walk through the site and give their opinion. What she discovered horrified her. Through her actions—submitting the application and initially giving it the best chance to succeed—something vitally important to a people who'd already lost so much was going to be destroyed. Literally obliterated.

Now they'd run out of options. Robyn was now utterly powerless to stop the caves' imminent destruction. The permit had been approved the day before. The Elders had begged her to make one last-ditch effort to prevent it, but she'd run out of hope. Explosives would blast through the site within hours.

She was still trying though. Robyn had gone back to square one, looking for something, anything, that would help. Every piece of possibly relevant legislation sat open on her computer screen. Jumping between international treaties, federal and state laws, government policy and expert and academic reports, she'd read and re-read the archaic provisions more times than she could count. Robyn considered every case on the topic in every country that had similar systems to Australia. But her search for relevance, for anything even remotely pertinent to hang an argument off, was at an end. She'd checked and re-checked the interpretation of every word in legislation and judgements alike to see if she could piece together an argument that gave the Elders a chance.

But there was nothing.

Robyn rubbed her temples, long since beyond the point of exhaustion. It was late, or early depending on how one interpreted doing an all-nighter in the office. Her office phone was on speaker. Emma, her closest friend, and her husband, Nick, were on the line, talking to her from across the country. The two lawyers had worked just as hard on this as she had, dedicating every spare moment to a cause that had consumed her despite having a toddler crawling around their ankles.

"They didn't listen," she hissed, furious at the mining executives who were enjoying their comfortable beds at three in the morning. The First Nations people near the mine site were protesting, a last-ditch effort to stop the trucks carrying the explosives into the sacred area. The charges would be laid that morning and detonated in the afternoon. The resulting blast would tear through the caves and leave nothing but a gaping hole and a dust cloud. Twelve hours, and it would be all over. The caves and the drawings on their walls would be obliterated. Incinerated. All in the name of the almighty dollar.

Robyn was disgusted. At herself as much as at her bosses.

"I've tried everything. I've got nothing left. Nowhere else to go. It's my fault. I failed."

"You've done everything you could do. Being powerless to stop this isn't on your shoulders, Robyn," Nick counselled. "You did your job. You trusted the expert when you lodged the application. It wasn't your fault that he downplayed the significance of the site. You've done more than anyone else would have done to stop it."

"The laws are fucked-up," Emma added. "And that's not your fault either. If I was in your shoes, I'd have left long ago. Protested the exploration, yes, but I also would have left. You didn't. You stayed there, all because you took it upon yourself to fix a mess you weren't responsible for. It's on the company's shoulders, not yours. You've made a difference, even if you can't save the caves."

Robyn huffed and wiped the tears from her eyes. Anger, frustration, heartbreak, and hopelessness all warred for prime position in her exhausted psyche. "Still a bitter pill to swallow."

"I get it, I do. But, Robyn, I'm worried about you." Emma's voice was barely a whisper through the phone. She knew that Robyn was barely hanging on. Emma sighed when she didn't answer, the line quiet apart from that noise. After a time, when she must have realized Robyn couldn't say anything back, she added, "What about the media? Is there some way we can speak to them without breaching your employment agreement?" Emma asked.

"Or, you know, getting you disbarred?" Nick added sardonically.

She shook her head. "I don't know." She cried in earnest then, her hot tears tracking down her cheeks. It was as if she was standing on a precipice, waiting for someone to push her in. The sensation of slipping, knowing she was about to fall into the depths of darkness and despair, was terrifying. "I want to, but I'm scared," she uttered, the confession one she was no longer able to deny. "I think it's the last chance, but even then, it's a pinprick of hope at best."

"Robyn," Nick began. "We'll support you no matter what you decide. If you think fronting up to the media is the right thing to do, do it. We'll be there with you." She did know. Emma was loyal to a fault, and Nick was the love of her life. He could have been a playboy, flitting around on a yacht never working a day in his life. Family money made him rich beyond anything she could imagine. But he was down to earth and kind. He went to work every day like the rest of them, fought cases like the rest of them too, and had fallen madly in love with her best friend. Both were lawyers. Both were environmentalists. Both would be behind her one hundred percent.

"I got onto the Minister again," Emma segued. "He basically disregarded everything the First Nations people gave him. He said he had no power under the Act to consider it, but that's rubbish. He'd made his mind up before anything else was given to him."

"So, our last hope is the judge declaring that the Minister wasn't fit to make a decision because of the political donations he received."

"Nope." Robyn sighed. "He dismissed that line of argument before I'd even finished the sentence, and I don't have standing to lodge a sealed application to challenge the licence approval. I got a caution yesterday that I was playing with fire. His Honour reminded me of my duty to my client. I reminded him of my duty to the court and to ethical conduct. He wouldn't listen." Robyn's shoulders sagged under the weight of failure. Her legacy was going to be the obliteration of the caves and the destruction of tens of thousands of years of cultural heritage. She hated her whiteness at that moment and the systemic racism inherent in the laws devaluing anything that wasn't built by white man. "They're going to be obliterated, and I can't stop them. Short of going onto that picket line myself, I can't do anything." Tears tracked down her cheeks, rage and impotence stealing over her. "Goddammit." She slammed her fist down against the desk, her world crashing around her like molten lava hailing down and threatening to burn her to ash. "I can't do this anymore. I can't."

"Leave," Nick commanded her gently. "You've given everything you can. Get out now before you have nothing left inside of you. You have a position with my firm. Take it."

"In mining?"

"No. Planning and environment law. Working with me."

She knew he was serious but walking away from her responsibilities was a big deal—not because she was dedicated to her job, but because she couldn't bear to think about what other cultural genocide the company would commit without someone intervening.

"I'll book us some tickets so we can help you pack," Emma said, her mind made up. It was a five-hour flight from the Gold Coast to Perth. They were on opposite sides of the country, but they were willing to drop everything to come to her aid when she needed it.

"There's a signing bonus and relocation package available for you," Nick added, and Robyn choked out a disbelieving laugh. Then she breathed deep and closed her gritty eyes. Exhaustion washed over her, the pull into a deep sleep palpable. Before all she could see was darkness and despair. Hopelessness. But now, with the support of her friends, there was a hint of something else. Maybe she'd done everything she could. It wasn't enough. It would never be enough if the explosives were detonated. But she'd given everything she had to give. She had nothing left. Her life was a hamster wheel, one she needed to get off or find herself catapulted away, unable to dust herself down and start again. She was already sensing the fracture in the depths of her mind getting deeper. Wider. Walking away was a failure, but maybe it would rescue her too. Maybe it would give her back that part of herself she'd given away and didn't know how to get back.

The constant pressure she was under was a chain around her neck weighing her down. She carried it with her no matter what she did, and it was only getting worse. Those last few months had pushed her to the edge of what her body and mind were capable of. Guilt and failure would rot in her soul forever. She would carry the burden of knowing she wasn't innocent for the rest of her life, but Robyn was only human. She'd placed her naïve trust in the people she'd worked with. The people who'd said hello to her every morning and who'd lived and breathed the corporate bullshit just as much as she had.

"Nick, thank you—"

"But…"

"But I need to reassess. I need to find myself again. I don't like what I see when I look in the mirror anymore. I don't even know who I am." She sighed and shook her head, knowing they couldn't see. "I'm burnt out. I'm at the end of my rope, and I need to think about whether I can keep doing it day in and day out."

"Write your resignation letter, Robyn," Emma coached her. "Pack a bag and get on the next plane. Stay with us until you're ready to decide. The sun and sand will do you good. So will having friends around you." Emma knew her too well. If she stayed in Perth, Robyn would bury herself in guilt and rage.

"Yeah," Robyn choked out. "Yeah, okay."

"Good. Now that that's settled, if we've reached the end of the line and there's no hope left, we go big. I've got a contact in Sydney. I'll send you her details. She'll want to hear from the Elders. She may not be able to do anything to stop the exploration, but she'll make so much noise that the government will order a Royal Commission just to shut her up." Robyn's phone chimed with a text from Emma. "Tell them to call her."

Things happened quickly after that. She made the phone call she'd been dreading for weeks. She couldn't stop the blasting, but it might be some small solace to give them this—the direct phone line to one of Australia's most respected journalists. When she spoke, people listened. Robyn hoped that it would be enough to ease the anguish of endless generations of souls.

Her resignation letter was in the CEO's pigeonhole and emailed to each director on the board. She'd pulled no punches. It was cathartic to be able to voice her honest opinion on their attitudes and her inability to follow them any longer. They wouldn't care—she would be replaced by the end of the week—but Robyn refused to be the fall guy. She'd hesitated only for a moment before sending out a copy of her resignation letter to Uncle Graham too, the Elder she'd spoken to the most. Western Mineral Explorations' board would gladly throw her under the bus to save their reputation. At least that way, her actual resignation letter—with its objections to the company's actions—was held by someone independent.

The front door to her apartment building closed behind her, shutting out the only sound at that time of night—the ocean waves crashing against the shoreline at Cottesloe Beach. She was a block away from the water, a thirty-minute motorbike ride from work. It was further than convenient sometimes, but when she'd seen her first sunset over the ocean, she was desperate to watch them every night. Disappointed that she hadn't seen nearly enough, Robyn shook her head at her stupidity. Taking the final few stairs to the first floor, Robyn yawned. She needed sleep. She also knew it would evade her. The double shot espresso had taken care of her immediate exhaustion and would wear off soon enough, but the anxious adrenaline running through her system would continue until she managed to purge the last few weeks from her memory.

The day's events were ones she would never forget.

Robyn dodged her neighbours as they wrangled two fluffy dogs into the stairwell for their early morning walk. Dawn was breaking as she opened her front door and stepped into her apartment, the night sky turning into a light grey as the sun rose from behind the building.

News must have broken only a few minutes later. Robyn's phone began pinging with texts and calls. She ignored them all, except the text from Emma. Within an hour of a thirty-second clip about the approval being broadcast, the petition Emma had set up gathered a hundred thousand signatures. The government minister who'd rejected their pleas and supporting evidence had also changed his tune, agreeing that the treatment of the First Nation's cultural heritage was akin to extermination. Ironic when it was the stroke of his pen that allowed it to occur.

Robyn turned on the TV, unable to look away from the chaos unfolding before her. It was like a train wreck, except instead of innocent victims, she hoped it was the careers and reputations of every board member caught in the smouldering wreckage.

The CEO's media conference was set up in the lobby of the CBD office building she'd walked in and out of every day for the better part of ten years. Money talked, and it spoke loudly. Standing at a lectern like the bloody Prime Minister would, Aurelius Branigan's raspy smoker's voice filled the speakers. Bile curdled in her stomach at the stone-cold tone he projected. "We are committed to the generation of economic prosperity in Australia. The exploration of this site is critical to the continued development of Australia's iron ore supplies and the employment of hundreds of thousands of hard-working members of our local communities. We at Western Mineral Explorations are respectful of all laws and government directives that we operate under. We have secured all permits necessary to conduct the exploration, and none of the spurious cases challenging those permits have been successful. Exploration will begin at 3:00 PM Australian Western Standard Time. Thank you."

Robyn turned off the TV with a disgusted huff and tossed the remote across the bed. Exploration was such a benign word for what would happen. Explosives would tear through the rock, splintering it into a trillion pieces. Robyn's heart rate spiked, and her palms grew clammy. Chest tight when she thought about what the detonation would do, she tried to breathe through the bile clawing its way up her throat.

She had to get out of there. Tossing open her balcony door, Robyn leaned over the railing and gulped in breaths of the salty sea air. Her suitcase was half packed, and her plane left in a few hours. Robyn's neighbour would collect her mail and look after her potted plants. It was pathetic that those two insignificant things were the only ties she'd built on this side of the country. Nothing else held her there. She wasn't sure whether that was good or bad—the last decade of her life had been ended with the stroke of a pen on a single-page letter.

Thank God.

EIGHT

Mike

Mike pulled his SUV up to the curb in front of Nick and Emma's house, directly behind Connor's classic Mustang. They were all spending the morning there—the five adults, himself, and the kids. He was the odd man out. The only single one. It was precisely why he'd been avoiding his best mate and working himself into the ground. Seeing Nick and Emma so ridiculously happy, as well as Katy, Levi, and Connor, who were just as in love, never usually affected him, but since he'd returned from his cruise—since he'd realized exactly what was missing in his life—he ached with longing when he saw them together.

Using work as an excuse was easy, but he wouldn't be able to get away with it forever. Nick wasn't a pushover; nor was he stupid. It didn't take a genius to figure out why Mike was staying away, and when they did, he'd either be pitied or read the Riot Act. Emma asked him if he was ready to start dating again, but he'd waved her off. He wasn't ready then—he wasn't sure if he was ready now either—but as the days stretched into months, the realization that he'd never again see Ezio had settled in like an anvil. The knowledge had been difficult to come to terms with, and it still left a bitter taste in his mouth.

He was beyond grateful for his family. His kids gave him more happiness than he could ever have dreamed of, and yet, he still yearned for more. Was he selfish? Undoubtedly. His life was blessed, but it was times like this—Sunday morning get-togethers—that the loneliness was infinitely multiplied. The quiet nights, when he wanted to feel the warmth of someone lying next to him to have whispered conversations with and laugh at inside jokes, were the worst. He'd had it twice before, once with Wani, but they were better friends than lovers, and once with Ezio, so he was already beyond lucky. But he wanted it again, and this time he wanted it to last. It wasn't so much to ask for someone to share his life with, was it? For someone who'd love his kids like he did? Apparently, it wasn't meant to be.

Looking to the rear-view mirror, Mike's heart filled. He may be single and a little starved for adult company, but he was happy. No, he was blessed. "Lexi, can you grab the beach bag, and Jax, I need you to take your body board. Both of you hop out of Jax's side, please." They did, and he ruffled their hair after passing them the things he needed help with.

Jax was already inside the sprawling mansion by the time Mike reached the front step. "Hi, Uncle Nick," Jax called in his too loud voice when Mike crossed the threshold. "Lena!" he cried, no doubt hugging Helena, Nick and Emma's toddler.

"G'day," Mike called out as he headed straight through the garage into the storage room where he placed their gear with the other surfboards, bodyboards, and diving equipment neatly stacked in the room. When he headed back, joining the others, his shoulders unclenched. Seeing the ocean crashing in rolling waves on the white sand from the wide-open doors was his happy place.

Jax asked, "Who are you?" as Mike entered the room, and he looked over to the voices.

"My name's Robyn." He didn't recognize the woman who answered. She was beautiful, yes, but something else about her captured his attention. Was it the sadness that she couldn't hide? Her smile didn't quite reach her eyes. Or was it the weary circles darkening her smooth skin? She seemed to be holding herself back. Arms crossed against her body like a shield, she was protecting herself. Mike was certain that there was more to the lady in the cut-off jean shorts and red bikini than he could see at first glance, but his first impression was good. She was focussing on his kids and Helena, talking with them at the expense of the adult conversations going on around her. They were the centre of her attention.

"Do we call you Aunty Robyn too?" Mike wasn't related to Nick and Emma, but he and Nick had been inseparable since they were kids. They'd grown up at the same surf club as nippers and attended the same local school. Nick had gone to university an hour away, and Mike had chosen the local training college for his PT qualifications, but their separation hadn't mattered. They'd always been tighter than Mike even was with his own siblings. His kids had grown up around Uncle Nick, and when he'd met Emma, they'd immediately adopted her as an aunt too. When Helena could finally pronounce "uncle," he'd have that moniker with her too.

"No," she said with a smile. "I'm just Emma's friend."

"My dad and Uncle Nick are just friends, but we call him uncle," Lexi patiently explained, assessing her reaction.

"Oh, okay." Robyn nodded. "I understand. What are your names?"

Lexi hitched her thumb in Jaxson's direction. "He's Jax, and I'm Lexi, and my dad is Mike."

Mike stepped forward then and smiled. He extended his hand, and her shake was firm. No nonsense.

"Nice to meet you, Mike. I'm Robyn."

"Good to meet you." Their gazes held, and Mike found himself running his hand through his short hair and laughing self-consciously. She was beautiful, and he was flustered, an experience he hadn't had since Ezio had stolen his heart. He immediately sobered, a longing for the impossible snuffing out the simple joy of meeting a beautiful woman.

"Dad, can we go for a swim?" Jax asked impatiently while they milled around the table outdoors. As the only two single people in the group, it seemed the other adults were content to leave him and Robyn to talk—a blatant attempt at partnering them up that didn't go unnoticed by either of them.

Mike gratefully jumped at the interruption before the silence between him and Robyn became too awkward. "Beach or pool?"

His son's eyebrows pulled down in almost comical exaggeration, and his mouth popped open. "Beach, Dad," he drawled, with an eye roll for added impact.

Mike held up his hands and laughed. "Just checking, dude. You know the drill." Rashies on and zinc applied, the kids had their body boards from the storeroom out before Mike had even applied all of his own sunscreen. "Anyone else coming in?" he asked before pulling his ball cap on. The kids were already through the back gate, so he jogged to catch up with them as everyone else finished drinks or stripped off to their swimmers.

Mike would never get sick of where Nick and Emma lived. Directly on the beach, it was prime waterfront. Literally a multi-million-dollar view. But even though the white two-storey house topped with a third-floor penthouse apartment with its manicured gardens and display home interior design was beautiful, it was what stretched out before him that always took his breath away. The majesty of nature's force and the play of the moon to control the tides, the sun to leave the water glittering like it was decorated with a billion tiny diamonds, and the wind and water creating a perfect wave always captivated Mike.

Even during summer there were few tourists who ventured along this part of Surfers Paradise beach, but in winter it was almost empty. The people lying on the sand, running, or swimming were locals. They lived in the apartment building next door to Nick and Emma, or were visiting Mrs Preston, the old lady who lived in the 1970s cottage on the other side of his best friend.

The kids rushed forward, not hesitating to throw their boards down and stand on them, surfing the couple of centimetre deep water along the shoreline. The white water washed around them as more waves rolled in, and the sounds and smells of the beach enveloped Mike. Seagulls and salt air always made him happy.

He was across the road from the beach himself only one suburb over in Broadbeach. His fourteenth-floor apartment had pretty spectacular views too, but there was nothing like being able to walk straight onto the sand from your back door. This was where Mike was most at home. Breathing in the air, crisp with the morning chill, he laughed as Jax shrieked when he hit waist-deep water.

He joined them out there, and the chill of the water had Mike holding his breath as he sank down to his armpits. His skin prickled with the cold, but it didn't last long.

The kids were already setting up to catch a wave by the time Mike managed to get past the shock of the chill and called out his encouragement. "Kick, Jax! That's it, buddy."

Jax missed the wave, but Lexi caught it, and he whooped his joy. Mike lined Jax up on his board and watched for a decent wave for his son to catch. "Okay, mate. This one coming is yours. When I tell you to kick, kick as hard and fast as you can. I'll give you a push too. Don't stop kicking until you feel it take you, but you've gotta get yourself to the bottom of the wave before you stop, yeah?"

"Yeah, Dad."

"Get ready." Mike waited for a second more and called, "Kick!" Jax's little legs moved, and Mike gave him a push. Jax took off. He couldn't see his little boy from the back of the wave, but he could hear the cheering from the shallows and Jax's celebrations. When his head popped up, Mike caught a wave in, body surfing until his knees hit the sand.

"Dad, did you see me?" Lexi asked.

"I did, honey. You did great." He ruffled her hair and helped her get back on for another paddle out, doing the same for Jax. He swam out again, getting closer to the deeper water where Nick, who was holding Helena, Emma, Robyn, Levi, and Katy, who was piggybacking a much taller and heavier Connor, were swimming.

Mike didn't catch much of the conversation; he kept his eyes on his kids in the waves and could see Jax struggling to get another one. With Mike's help, Jax caught it, and Robyn joined him in the shallower water.

"They're great swimmers."

"They were in the water swimming before they could even crawl, and they love the beach. We're here pretty often."

"I don't blame you. It's beautiful."

"Where are you from?" he asked, watching the way she tilted her face up to the sun soaking up the warm rays.

"Perth. Originally Sydney like Emma, but I've been in Perth since I graduated uni."

"How long are you here for?"

"Not sure." She smiled, but the tension in her expression was obvious. "I quit my job, so I'm having a bit of a break. Reconsidering where I want to be." Her eyes slipped closed, and she sighed happily. "But have to say, the Gold Coast is lovely. Perth is too, but I didn't see much sun when I was there."

It was a strange comment to make—Perth was known for its warm weather—but understanding soon dawned on Mike. Robyn and Emma must have studied the same degree. "You're a lawyer."

She huffed out a laugh, but it held no humour. "That obvious, huh?"

"I've seen how long the hours can be for you all." Nick had worked double what he did now during the first decade of his career. It was right where Robyn would be, and where Emma was sitting too. It was better for Nick these days. He could work from home and was able to manage his hours because of the team he'd built around himself, but the early years had been hard on his best friend.

"What do you do?" Robyn asked.

"Personal trainer. I own a gym here on the beach." He motioned north to the towering buildings less than a kilometre away. "It's in the touristy part of town, so we cater to a lot of one-off visitors, but we've got a good stable of locals who come in too. I've only been operating for a couple of years now, so we're still growing and finding our feet."

The truth was that he'd dived into work like a man desperate to forget the moment Wani had arrived home from the Philippines a month after they'd arrived back from their cruise. Still raw from losing Ezio, it had been excruciating watching the kids greet her and eagerly leave for a two-week visit. Mike had nosedived straight into the gym, picking up shifts so he had no spare time. He was starting to see the benefits of the last six months of gruelling work—he was more profitable—but he'd also put his life on hold. Their days had become routine, and apart from the kids' after-school activities and Nick's house, he hadn't really ventured out. His social life was non-existent, but that was okay with Mike too.

Robyn spoke about the training she'd done at university, blowing off steam in kickboxing classes, and he commiserated with her lack of routine now. Once they were past those awkward first introductions, their conversation flowed easily. She was interesting, and it seemed like she'd been starved of company, much the same as him. He could see them becoming friends.

Time passed quickly, and before Mike realized, the sun was high in the sky and his stomach was rumbling. The kids had been building sandcastles on the beach for a while, and when Mike looked around, he couldn't see the others. Surprise shocked a laugh out of him. "I think we're the only two still out here."

"We are?" Robyn looked around before turning to him wide-eyed. "At least the kids are still having fun."

"Yeah, although I should get them in the shade. Their sunscreen will be wearing off by now." Robyn nodded and started to swim toward the shore, a lot of hard work on an outgoing tide. "You don't know how to body surf?"

"No." She shrugged. "But it's okay, I can swim."

"Wait for a second. We'll be able to catch this set coming in." He gave her the same instructions as he did Jax. It was a simple concept, but much more difficult to achieve in practice, especially if you couldn't kick hard enough. Mike looked over his shoulder. "Okay, get ready… start swimming now."

Robyn took off, swimming hard. Her freestyle stroke was smooth and powerful. Mike watched as the wave picked her up. "Torpedo arms!" he yelled, and lost sight of her as the wave washed over him. He waited until she popped up closer to the shoreline and whooped. Mike laughed and caught a wave in after her. He managed to surf a lot further than she did, but he had to hand it to Robyn for a good effort on her first go.

The thought of Ezio almost knocked him sideways. It struck him like a bolt of electricity. Did he know how to body surf? Surf? Was he a swimmer, or did he prefer to stay on the sand? Had he improved his diet and started doing more exercise? Mike wished he knew.

"Oh my God, how much fun is that!" Robyn exclaimed excitedly with a broad smile. It lit up her entire face, taking the weight from her shoulders and making her look radiant. Mike couldn't help but grin at her enthusiasm.

She pulled the elastic out of her hair, and the long strands fell around her shoulders in a wet and messy heap. Robyn arched her back, her mane dipping into the water behind her, and she stood again, her dark locks falling as smooth as silk almost down to her waist. Mike swallowed hard. Damn.

His dick twitched, and he instantly looked down, as if it were ready to tell him something. Not much had happened in the last six months—he certainly hadn't been with anyone else since disembarking the cruise. He woke with morning wood, but that was purely physical. More often than not, the immediate all-consuming thoughts of Ezio and the longing spearing through his heart as strong as a physical blow to the chest worked wonders to deflate him. Mike hesitated, then walked out of the water, needing a moment to get his scattered thoughts in order. He called out to the kids as he rushed past them, "Lexi, Jax, time to head in for breakfast."

He refused to turn around as Robyn complimented them on their sandcastle efforts, but instinctively checked as he heard their retreating voices. Instead of coming up the beach to the house, they ran back to the water, rinsing off the sand coating their bodies from head to toe. As soon as they were clean, they raced up the beach again, covering themselves in the fine white powder once more. Mike leaned against the low post-and-rail fence, the white-painted timber matching the rest of the fresh modern look of the beachside mansion, and shook his head at them. Robyn was the first person through the gate that he held open, and his kids soon followed. "Go shower and get that sand off you."

They moaned, and Nick ordered them into the shower before they went near his food. Mike's self-imposed distance from his friends and family was an ill-thought-out attempt to avoid the hurt of watching them together. But the joke was on him. He'd missed this. Missed being part of a family that stuck together through thick and thin. He missed their company and missed having someone to back him up with his kids. He missed seeing happy people who were in love. Instead, he'd moped for months, and in doing so dragged his kids along for the ride. He wanted Lexi and Jax to see examples of what successful relationships were. Nick and Emma and Katy, Levi, and Connor were the perfect depictions of that. Even if he was a ring-in—although not as bad with Robyn around—Mike shouldn't have stayed away.

He resolved to do better, even if the loving touches and private glances carved his heart out.

Sunday mornings were Nick at the barbecue grilling sausages and bacon while wearing the ridiculous chef's hat and apron that Emma had bought him. They were the brightly coloured juice concoctions he usually experimented with and fluffiest pancakes and cupcakes that were Katy's speciality. Guilt ate at him, and he tried to push it aside when he saw his kids happily dashing over to Helena, dripping wet after their rinse off under the outside shower.

Mike's heart hammered in his chest with the realization that he'd been punishing himself as much as he was retreating from the hurt. The steady thrum of his pulse sped up until it was racing. Beating faster and faster like a stampede thundering through his veins. Mike closed his eyes, light-headed from the sensation. He wavered and staggered over to the lounger as his knees gave out. With his elbows resting on his thighs, Mike sucked in a breath and tried to steady his heart.

"Mike, mate, you right?" Nick asked.

He couldn't answer verbally. Not yet. Instead, he gave him a thumbs up and breathed out slowly, resting his head in his hands. He sucked in another breath and held it. Mike concentrated, narrowed his focus down to his heart. He visualized the muscle pumping blood around his arteries and pictured it slowing down. Thud... thud... thud...

Slowly, after what felt like an age, he blinked open his eyes and breathed. Inhaled, then exhaled. Mike wiped the sweat off his brow and pulled off his cap. He ran his hands through his sweaty hair and breathed again.

His throat was raw, and his limbs heavy. Mike sagged into the low chair and struggled to keep his eyes open. Exhaustion washed over him as his heart rate returned to normal. The urge to sleep overcame him. God, he hated when that happened.

"Get some food into you, mate." Nick patted Mike's shoulder and rested a plate with a bit of everything on the table next to him. "Kids are already eating." Mike tore his eyes open and looked around, and sure enough, everyone was over at the outdoor table on the wide patio. Nick had slipped onto the lounger next to him under the palm trees in the backyard. "Didn't get much sleep?"

"Mustn't have." Mike groaned when he moved. He might as well have just run a marathon. His body was filled with lactic acid weighing down his limbs, and his energy levels were zapped to zero. He yawned, and Nick handed him the plate.

"Eat." Nick turned on his chair and watched Mike swallow a forkful of eggs. "I haven't said anything, because I'm hardly one to talk about working excessive hours, but Mike, I've watched you work yourself into the ground these last few months. Talk to us. If we can help, we will."

"There's nothing—"

"Then what's going on?" Nick demanded, his voice a low growl. "We're worried about you."

Mike sighed and scrubbed his forehead. "I've just been doing it tough."

"Is the gym not turning a profit yet? Because you know I don't care if you repay the loan. If you need the money you transferred, you can have it back." Nick was a solid mate. The best he could ask for. Mike had entertained the idea of opening a gym years earlier. It'd been a dream, one that had been dismissed when he worked out just how much money he would need. Then Nick found his notes and insisted on being part of it. Mike fobbed him off, refusing the cash. It was the right decision at the time—his marriage was on rocky ground, and starting a business wasn't what he needed. But once the divorce went through and everything had settled, Mike had run out of excuses. Then, as serendipity worked sometimes, he'd driven along the Esplanade to meet a client and saw the beachfront site. It was perfect. Exactly what he'd dreamed of. Literally on its own patch of sand, the gym had easy access to the street front, great signage spaces, change rooms already built in, and was just the right size. He'd known instantly it was the one. Nick jumped on board, wanting to give him the money, but Mike wouldn't accept it unless it was a loan to be repaid with interest.

"No, it's not that. It's doing well." Mike smiled a small smile. A proud one. "It's making more money than I thought we would be at this stage."

"So why are you working such long hours?"

"Avoidance." Mike huffed and put his plate to the side, turning to face Nick when the other man furrowed his brow and opened his mouth to interrupt. "I'm lonely." Mike motioned to the others sitting around the table. "You're all so happily coupled up, and I'm perpetually single. I haven't been on a date in six months. Watching you…"

"Oh." Nick paused, the weight of Mike's words hanging between them. "I'm sorry. We can tone it down—"

"No. Don't even think about it. You and Em, and those three"—he motioned to Levi who was resting his head on Connor's shoulder while Connor stroked his fingers through Katy's hair—"are what I want the kids to see. You're what a real relationship looks like."

"You know Robyn's single?" Nick grinned at him and wiggled his eyebrows. Mike huffed out a laugh and shook his head. "I mean, you two seemed to get along well."

"She's nice."

"Oh fuck, don't let her hear you say that." Nick laughed, and Mike joined him, rolling his eyes.

"You know what I mean. She's cool. Pretty too. But right now I think I need a friend more than I need a relationship." Nick opened his mouth, and Mike held up his hand. "Don't you dare suggest a friends-with-bennies arrangement—there's no way I'd put you and Emma in that position."

Nick reluctantly nodded and sighed. "You said six months. Was that the cruise?"

"Yeah, but nothing came of it. Holidays, you know?" Memories of intimate moments bombarded him at the most inopportune times, and now was no exception. Ezio had been on his mind a lot that morning. He hated that they'd ended the way they did, and his powerlessness to change it ate away at him.

He and Nick didn't talk much after that, instead finishing their breakfast. Mike took Nick's plate when it was empty and collected the others too. When Robyn joined him in the kitchen to load the dishwasher, he smiled at her and passed over the plates he'd scraped clean. They washed and dried the rest, and their conversation flowed the whole time. They didn't speak about anything important, just favourite movies and music, sports they'd played and enjoyed watching, and favourite football teams. Robyn had been on the opposite side of the country but hadn't fallen prey to the kind of football they played over there. She was still an NRL supporter through and through, despite supporting the wrong team. He'd teased her about it, and Robyn had bantered back, giving him as good as he gave.

The dishes were done, and Mike found himself lingering in the kitchen with her. The others were outside, the kids happily the centre of attention with all five adults hanging off every word they said. Mike smiled at them before turning his attention back to the woman before him. She met his gaze and breathed in slowly, her chest rising as she did. He watched her blink, her long eyelashes fanning out over her cheeks.

She dropped her gaze and licked her lips, and he felt the motion like it was against his skin.

He swallowed. Hard.

Robyn shivered, gooseflesh breaking out over her arms. She pressed her legs together, and Mike, realizing that he'd been staring at her, dragged his gaze back up to her face. His nostrils flared when he sucked in a breath, and her breath hitched. Robyn's lips were parted, and she stared at him from beneath lowered lashes.

Mike found himself stepping forward, his body screaming at him to eliminate the gap between them. He didn't know what the hell he was doing. It was insanity. He'd just told Nick he wanted a friend; now he was crowding her as if he was going to kiss her. He didn't even want that. Did he? He wanted someone he could talk to and have fun with. And yet, his body moved without conscious permission. Robyn reached for him—

"Dad, can you help me with my rashie? I need to pee." Lexi's words were like a bucket of iced water being tossed over him. Mike shook himself out of his stupor and blew out a breath.

"Sure, honey." Mike turned to her and tugged the stretchy fabric over her head, then rested both fists on the kitchen bench. The marble was cool to the touch, dousing whatever the hell it was swirling through him.

He couldn't deny being affected by Robyn, but there was no way he'd go there. Not the first time they'd met, and certainly not in Nick and Emma's house. He mentally slapped himself. He was being an idiot. Mike needed to remember how much easier it was if he just remained friends with the women he met. Ezio's words floated back to him: "Wanting to bottom isn't anything to be ashamed of. It's simply what your body demands." That's what caused the problems. Stumbling through a physical relationship with a woman was always a nightmare when it came to penetrative sex. At least if he kept a hook-up off the table, he wouldn't have to deal with his defective dick.

Robyn cleared her throat quietly and Mike snapped his attention to her. "I haven't heard you mention your kids' mum. Is she in the picture?"

"No. Well, we share custody, but we're not together. The kids are actually going back to her house tonight ready for school and kindy tomorrow."

"What about you? You at work?" Robyn asked the question casually, but it had Mike pausing. Was she asking him on a date?

Mike hesitated. "Ah, yeah."

"Cool. I might check out the gym. I want to get back into exercise. I'll come for a walk and get a program."

"I'll set you up with a free pass if you want to join."

Robyn smiled. "Thanks." She folded the towel and hung it over the drying rack on the sink. "I should head back out."

Mike knew Emma would want a cuppa, and he was still craving an energy boost. He'd downed a juice, which Levi had taken over making that morning, and while it had helped, he was desperate for caffeine. It was a luxury he didn't indulge in much—Mike avoided any kind of stimulant—but his guilt trip earlier that morning had left him spent. It gave him the perfect opportunity to have some space, delaying walking out with Robyn. He fixed up a round and doctored everyone's drinks before taking them out on a tray.

NINE

Robyn

The first few weeks of being on leave were surreal. Actually, scratch that. The first few weeks of being free, of not having to compulsively check emails and take calls from the board at any time of the day or night, were surreal. Robyn still woke up with a start each day. Her alarm had buzzed for the first few, and she'd rolled out of bed, stumbling into the bathroom to shower and dress. It hit her when she turned the water on that she wasn't at home. But she'd done enough all-nighters that showering at the office had become second nature. The guest bathroom at Nick and Emma's was much more plush—stunning white marble instead of plain tiles—but white nevertheless. At four thirty in the morning, her overstressed brain hadn't differentiated between the two.

Reaching into the unfamiliar wardrobe for her suits was another jolt to her system. She'd left them all in Perth. It was the longest Robyn had gone without dressing for work in years—aside from the forced holidays that stressed her more than the short times away she could manage.

After a few days, Robyn had turned her alarm off, but her body clock was trained to wake up well before dawn. Even if she could doze for a while, as soon as the sun deigned to peek above the horizon over the darkened water just outside her bedroom, she was awake. Although groggy, she couldn't relax enough to go back to sleep. Years of early starts had taken their toll. So instead of lying in and staring at the ceiling, she took to walking along the beach. She hadn't made it to Mike's gym to check it out, but the kilometres she walked each day were more exercise than she'd managed in years.

The winter breeze was crisp that early in the morning, but in the subtropics, winter wasn't exactly cold. Robyn stepped onto the sand and stared out at the water. With her back to the buildings and the city behind her still slumbering, there was absolute silence except for the crashing waves. The constant undulation of the tide before her, the push of it up the beach as the waves tumbled over the hard-packed sand, and the pull as the ocean sucked the water back into its depths was a sight to behold. Even so early in the morning while the Pacific was still dark and the creatures lurking in its inky expanse made it intimidating and uninviting, Robyn was bewitched by it. This was what she'd hoped for when she'd rented her little apartment in Cottesloe Beach, but she'd never really taken the initiative to enjoy it. The pressures of work had gotten too much, and she'd begun living to work rather than working to live. It was a distinction that Robyn was realizing a little too late made all the difference to actually enjoying life.

She strolled along the hard sand just above the water-line, her thongs in her hand, and watched the sky change from the grey of pre-dawn to hues of pale pinks and purples before Mother Nature in all her glory painted the heavens a crystalline blue. Energized, the kilometres passed quickly underfoot, and Robyn noticed the drop in height of the buildings and the distinctly residential feel to the area before she approached another set of towers. These ones weren't as tightly packed together, but the twin buildings with a great curve along their facades were unmistakeably Broadbeach. Emma had taken her out to dinner in a Turkish restaurant under those towers the first night she'd been there.

Peace washed over her as Robyn turned her attention back to the water. The motion of the waves calmed her. She breathed deep, the salt air filling her lungs and flowing through her veins like a shot of tranquillity.

The beach was livelier than it had been an hour earlier at the beginning of her walk. The faint hum of traffic between the crashing waves and the sharp rap of jackhammers and nail guns on the nearby construction sites also intruded into her thoughts. The city was waking up and getting to work. Robyn didn't envy any of them.

She blocked out the invasion on her senses and watched a gorgeous man jog down the sand with a surfboard tucked under his arm. He was wearing the most ridiculously loud bright yellow board shorts she'd ever seen. But if anything, the clothing highlighted his assets. Tanned muscles flexing and bulging as he moved, he was fit and utterly perfectly proportioned. The man paused at the edge of the dry sand, dropped his towel, and surveyed the water. He wandered forward, bending and strapping on his leg rope, before picking something up from the sand and tucking it into his pocket.

Then he surged forward into the water, shifting the board in front of him and pulling himself onto it before ducking beneath an oncoming wave. The strength and grace he displayed doing the deceptively simple duck dive was enthralling. She couldn't help but ogle him as he powered through the whitewash and beyond with thick arms. The waves crashed around him, and the man simply rolled the board over, pulling himself underwater, before popping up again on the other side righted once more. A few more strokes and he sat up, straddling the board and looking toward the horizon. He sat out a few of the incoming waves, but then seemed to spy something. Robyn couldn't decipher what; the waves all looked the same to her, but he clearly knew.

Paddling hard, the man took off, and Robyn watched in fascination as the wave picked him up in precisely the way Mike had coached her on her first body surfing session. It crested behind him and began curling over as he leaped to a crouch in one smooth move. The wave nearly engulfed him in the tube, foaming and rolling behind him as he surged forward. When it dropped off, petering out behind him, he slowed and gracefully toppled backward into the water. He stood in the shallows and wiped the salt from his eyes, his arms flexing as he did. It gave her a show of pure sexiness as he mussed his hair up, spraying the water from it.

The suspicion that Robyn knew the man was confirmed. She watched with a smile as Mike reached for his board, still bobbing in the foaming sea around him, and turned his face to the sky. He paused for a moment, seeming to let go of all the weight on his shoulders. Standing straighter and with a small smile, he opened his eyes and looked straight over to Robyn.

Busted. He'd caught her staring, but Robyn wasn't even remotely sorry. As far as she was concerned it should be illegal to be that gorgeous. They'd been saved—or perhaps thwarted—by his daughter the day they'd met. If she hadn't interrupted, Robyn wouldn't have been responsible for her actions. Mike would have been naked under her in only a few minutes. At least this way, in public and with a bit of distance between them, she could watch him unimpeded. It probably made her one of those people who stared in morbid fascination at car crashes seeking a glimpse of the carnage, but with Mike as her eye candy, she couldn't deny the appeal of being unable to tear her eyes away.

Robyn waved awkwardly, and Mike grinned before tucking the sleek surfboard under his arm and jogging effortlessly out of the water. She picked up the towel he'd dropped on the sand and shook it out, passing it over when he laid his board down.

"G'day."

"Hi," she greeted, smiling and willing the heat in her cheeks to dissipate. "Early morning surf?" Oh. My. God. Robyn shook her head at herself, mortified.

"Thank you." He motioned to the towel and rubbed it over his face and hair. "Yeah, it's nice out there once you get used to the chill. Enjoy your morning walk?"

"I did." Robyn nodded, words escaping her. She'd been so comfortable around Mike up until their moment in the kitchen. Then they'd avoided each other for the rest of the day. "How are the kids?"

Mike smiled. "With their mum for the week. We've gone back to week on, week off, otherwise"—Mike looked at his watch—"I'd be getting them up for school." Robyn nodded and rocked on her heels. Mike hesitated for a moment and motioned to the surf club. "You want to get some breakfast with me?"

Robyn opened her mouth, ready to turn him down. Ready to rush off and get on with her day of... blissful nothingness. She was still getting used to the idea that she didn't have anywhere to be and didn't have to cut her social life short because it would get in the way of her job. The freedom was exhilarating, and getting over the awkwardness with Mike was even better. "I'd love to."

Mike grinned, pulled a pebble from his pocket and tossed it on the sand, then wrapped the towel around his waist. Robyn looked at the simple, smooth stone and couldn't for the life of her think why he'd have it in his shorts. She could feel Mike's eyes on her, and when she met his gaze, he hesitated again before speaking. "You'll probably think I'm crazy, but I always take something from the beach when I go surfing. A shell or a rock. I put it in my pocket and then return it when I'm back on the sand." He shrugged and looked away, but Robyn wanted to hear more.

"Is it something you've always done?"

"Yeah, kind of." He looked out to the water and his lips turned down. "We've lost three clubbies during lifesaving competitions at this beach. They were just kids. Teenagers doing what they loved. I was competing in two of the competitions, and I helped search for them when they went missing. The waves here can get pretty gnarly..." He blinked a few times and rubbed at his chest as if relieving an ache behind his breastbone. Robyn wanted to reach out and comfort him, but she didn't know whether it would be welcomed. "It kind of became a habit from then. Another reason to make it back in." He blew out a breath and shook his head. "If I've taken something from nature, I have to put it back where I got it from. Back on the beach safe and sound."

"Oh, Mike." This time she didn't hesitate to reach for him. Hooking her arm through his, she squeezed his bicep and leaned into him. They stood there, looking at the ocean rolling in. It wasn't rough. Each wave was clean, and the light breeze barely raised a ripple in the otherwise smooth swell further out. Robyn could see the gutter where the waves weren't as high. A few weeks ago—before she'd arrived on the coast—she would have swum in that precise spot. But Nick had schooled her on the permanent rip near his house. He'd explained how the waves weren't as high because the force of the water being dragged out was stronger than the incoming waves. Lifesavers would know that—they trained to save people from it—but anything could go wrong in rough surf and bad conditions.

Mike's stomach growled, and Robyn smiled softly. "Do you need to be dressed to eat at the surf club?"

"Mmm, yeah. But I live just there." He pointed to the white high-rise with yellow features on it directly behind them. "If you want to grab us a table, I'll run up and get dressed. I'll be back in five."

"Sure." They turned away from the water and walked off the beach. As Robyn headed to the surf club, Mike jogged back to the road.

The club was a typical pub-style eatery, except it had the most spectacular view of the beach. Bifold doors opened to a large balcony right over the sand, the white tables and chairs spaced out so each had a little privacy. The morning sun was bright but not yet hot, so Robyn found a spot along the railing at a table for two. She'd only had time to order her coffee before Mike loped over to the table.

"Perfect spot."

Mike ordered a decaf, and Robyn stared at him in horror before managing to place her breakfast order with the waiter. When they were alone again, she asked, "Okay, what gives? You run your own business and you're up early to exercise, which is insane in and of itself. Don't tell me you're one of these freaks who actually get enough sleep and don't need coffee to survive?"

Mike laughed, a full-bellied chuckle. "I usually don't have caffeine, and I limit sugar too so I'm not up and down."

"Oh, okay. So, you're on speed. Makes sense." She nodded and kept a straight face for barely a second after Mike looked at her shocked, his jaw slack. "Jesus, that was too easy. But seriously, you don't live on caffeine? How?"

"I watch what I eat, so I've got plenty of energy, and yeah, I try to get enough sleep most nights. I've also learned the hard way that I can't do everything with my business, so I delegate. Otherwise, I'd never see the kids, and that's not fair to them or to my ex."

"How long were you two together?"

"Wani fell pregnant with Lexi only a few weeks after we'd started dating. We stayed together, and it was good for the most part, but we worked better as friends. We'd decided to split when she found out she was pregnant with Jax. We broke up but stayed living together until after he was born and Wani was ready to go back to work. Once she had some money saved up, we decided to get separate places close to each other and share custody. She's only a few streets away." Mike sipped his poor excuse for a coffee and grinned when Robyn shuddered. Their breakfast was placed on the table, and Robyn smiled her thanks, only to sober when Mike asked his next question. "What about you? Anyone special?"

"Between working the hours I did, and working some more, I didn't get time to meet anyone. I've been single for years. Pretty pathetic actually."

"Nah, just doing what you had to do. But you're re-evaluating yeah? Maybe now's the time to enjoy life a bit." Mike smiled warmly, but his eyes were sad. He pitied her, and that ate at her even more. "We've all been there. If it wasn't for Nick, I'd still be a broke PT working as many hours as I could to make ends meet. At one stage, I had three jobs just to pay the rent. I barely saw Lexi and missed most of Wani's pregnancy with Jax. We weren't together, but she was still carrying my baby." He pursed his lips before continuing. "I wanted to be there, but with her not working, it fell on me."

"You were doing it for your family. I was doing it for other people's money." Robyn huffed and shook her head and pushed away her half-eaten breakfast. Clenching her teeth, she blinked back the tears burning her eyes. She would never forgive herself for her role in obliterating the caves. "What I did was inexcusable."

"Hey." Mike reached out and grasped her hand, his warmth and strength comforting. "You won't find judgement from me. But I will call you out if you're being too hard on yourself, and right now, you're being too harsh."

Robyn shook her head and, with her eyes downcast, explained to Mike what had happened. She tried to pull back, ashamed and wanting to curl into a ball, but he didn't let her. He held her hand as she spoke, squeezing her fingers when her voice wobbled, and he stroked his thumb over her knuckles when she wiped an errant tear from her cheek. She told him everything, confessing her role in making the application and in trying for months to stop the blasting. It didn't absolve her, but at least he knew what she'd been a part of.

"You were doing what you were asked by your bosses. Then when you realized what was wrong, you tried to stop it." Robyn shook her head, disgusted with herself, and Mike reached across the table, tilting her chin up, his voice serious as he spoke. "It was on the experts to get their advice right when the company hired them. You trusted their judgement. It wasn't your fault they were telling you what your bosses wanted to hear. You did what you could to protect the site with a set of laws that are outdated and unfair." He squeezed her hand again, and the warmth in his voice made her close her eyes and bask in the comfort of his presence. "Hell, I would have quit well before the point you did. It probably wasn't healthy you staying as long as you did. You weren't responsible, but yet you wanted to help. That tells me you're dedicated. You made a difference." Then as if he'd read her mind, he added, "You're a good person, Robyn. Don't ever think you're not."

She huffed out a teary sigh. "You and Nick are a lot alike. He said almost the same thing to me."

Mike grinned, and Robyn's lips tilted up in a small smile. Another round of coffees ordered, they sat back and talked about lighter topics until their parents were mentioned. Mike rolled his eyes and huffed out a laugh. "Mine are happy they have grandkids, but the world almost ended when I got a divorce. Now they're insisting that the kids need a mum—"

"Ah."

Mike laughed and held up his hands. "See, you get it! On top of that, I'm bi, so I might end up with a man." Becoming serious, he added, "They'll never understand that, unfortunately."

His news surprised her, not because she was judging based on stereotypes, but because she couldn't understand how love and acceptance didn't extend to sexuality. It was much the same as someone's eye colour as far as she was concerned—something important about a person, but certainly not a choice. Now it was her time to squeeze his hand and give him some of the support he'd just shown her. "It must be hard not having their understanding."

He shrugged noncommittally. "It's not so bad. They're not openly hostile or even really intolerant. They just don't get it. They think it's because I can't make up my mind. What hurts the most is that they said they thought I'd grown up and matured when Wani and I got together. Then when we split, they kept asking if I'd cheated on her with a man." He shook his head and looked her in the eye. There was only truth there. "I've never done that; I never would. They equate being bi with promiscuity and indecision. I can't get through to them, so I've stopped trying. They love the kids. That's enough."

"Still, it's not too much to ask that your parents believe you. If they don't understand, surely they can learn about it. It's not exactly rocket science." Robyn huffed, annoyed for him.

He grinned. "Now you sound like Nick and Em. They're always telling me that I give them too much leeway.

Apparently, I need to hold Mum and Dad accountable for their prejudices."

She nodded and grimaced. "But I can see why you try to keep the peace. Having a falling out with them doesn't just affect you. It impacts the kids too." Mike hummed in agreement and ordered a fresh carafe of water for their table. People came and went, and the two of them talked, laughing together as they wiled the morning away. It wasn't until Robyn's phone beeped with a message that she realized the time. "Bloody hell, I've kept you nearly all morning. Were you supposed to go to work today?"

"I was, but I'm only doing paperwork. I can do that anytime." He dismissed her concerns with a wave of his hand. "You're giving me a good excuse to ignore it." Robyn flipped her phone back over, ignoring the message, and Mike raised an eyebrow in question.

"Work. Well, my old boss. I'm kind of scared to speak with him. I'm not ready yet."

Mike spoke, but her attention was focussed on his actions. He stretched an arm over the chair next to him, his bicep and shoulder flexing as he moved. She swallowed hard as she visually mapped the bulge of muscle and wished she had the right to trace her fingertips—or maybe her tongue—over his tanned skin. When Mike cleared his throat discreetly, Robyn's attention snapped back to his face, and hers flushed with embarrassment. "Sorry?"

Mike smirked and asked, "Are you worried he'll ask you to go back?"

"Not likely, given what I wrote in my resignation letter, but as much as I needed to get out of there, I loved working with him. I still don't want to disappoint him." She shrugged. "I kind of feel like leaving was failure on my part—I couldn't hack it in the hot seat. But there's no way I could go back. Not now that I know what they're capable of."

They left the café when people started filing in for lunch, and Mike walked her back to Nick and Emma's. He insisted, and even though she really didn't need him to, Robyn couldn't help but smile at his chivalry. They strolled along the sand in a comfortable silence while the waves washed over their feet. It was easy being with him. The man was sweet and genuinely great. He was the sort of person her parents had been begging her to find and marry for years—ironic that they were both under pressure to settle down, despite the very different reasons cited by their parents and the completely different stages of their lives.

Mike stopped and latched the waist-height white-picket gate after Robyn stepped through it. "I'll leave you here," he said. "Thanks for joining me for breakfast."

"I had fun. Maybe we can run into each other again soon."

He nodded and smiled. "I'd like that. Maybe next time we can do dinner or drinks. I'll dress in something a little more appropriate too."

"Sounds great." Robyn took a step backwards and grinned before she nodded to the house. "I'd better go. Look after yourself."

"You too, Robyn."

TEN

Mike

Robyn took a sip of the water she was drinking and unconsciously went back to playing with the plastic rim of the bottle. She was in a better place than she had been a few months earlier when they'd met. She'd regained her strength, no longer beaten down by carrying the weight of a responsibility she'd never asked for but had taken on because it was the right thing to do. The noble thing to do. She was smart, strong, and fun, and Mike adored her. They'd become fast friends in the months since she'd been staying on the Gold Coast. She was the light he'd needed in his life when he'd been struggling.

The springtime sun beamed down around them, the humidity making the air sticky. A storm would roll in that night, judging from the clouds gathering to the east along the horizon. Mike's loose singlet stuck to him, wet from the rivulets of sweat running down his back from chasing his overzealous kids. Lexi had planned their entire day at Sea World, picking which of the shows they would see—all of them—the timing of visits to every one of the animal encounters—

all but one—and where to eat lunch. His daughter was precise, demanding, and had an expectation that everyone would fall into line and conform. Thankfully, she'd announced that it was time for some fun after getting the serious stuff out of the way and had ordered them over to Castaway Bay.

The umbrella in the centre of the table provided some much-needed shade, and the ocean breeze was stronger at this end of the park. Even though it was sticky, it was a perfect spring day. Mike leaned back in his chair and relaxed, watching the kids climb. He opened his mouth to warn Jax about the height but thought better of it. He was having fun, and Mike didn't want to scare him unnecessarily.

Jax was at the top of the rope bridge before he hesitated, having climbed it so fast he must have forgotten to be scared of its height. Mike saw the moment panic set in. Jax's mouth popped open, and he looked around wide-eyed. The wobble in his voice when he called, "Daaad," was almost comical, except for the very real fear in it. Mike heaved himself out of the chair, readying to go to him, but Lexi waved him off. She was already halfway up, going to save her little brother. She reached him before Mike had even walked over to the bridge and guided Jax down with ease. Mike ruffled his hair, and Jax dashed off before he could even ask if he was okay. Shrugging, Mike returned to the table and sat down, rolling his eyes at Robyn's grin.

"Aw, such a good dad."

"It's a skill." He took another drink and stretched out his legs, watching the kids as they shot streams of water at the passing pirate ship and all the kids on board.

Despite all the noise—exhausted kids crying, screams from the rides, and the MCs from the show being performed in one of the nearby stadiums—he and Robyn had a moment of peace. Mike sighed happily and basked in the heat. He loved the warmer weather.

"So, what do you think?" Robyn asked, jolting him out of his reverie. His brow furrowed, and Robyn shot him a small smile. "Sorry, I forget sometimes that you can't read my thoughts. The conversation running in my head makes sense," she explained. "I'm talking about Nick's job offer."

"It's a great opportunity," he hedged. Mike would love for her to settle on the Gold Coast permanently. She was living between two states, still staying at Nick and Emma's while all her possessions were on the opposite side of the country in Perth. It left open the possibility that she'd return, and Mike hated the thought. He didn't want her to leave, and not only for his own selfish desire to have his friend nearby, but also because Robyn had changed since she'd been living there. She wasn't as closed off. She smiled more and was genuinely happy. She'd discovered a love for life that he was worried would be sucked back out of her if she moved back.

But taking a job with a friend—especially the one she was living with—was a big step too. Nick's offer was genuine. He'd needed someone for at least six months. There didn't seem to be a downside as far as Mike could see, as long as she could keep work separate from their home life and she didn't work herself to the bone like she had in her last job.

"But?" she prompted when he didn't continue.

"Not so much a but as a question. Are you ready to go back to work? Do you think you can have more of a balance with this job?" Mike grasped her hand. "Don't get me wrong, Nick's my mate, but I don't want you to lose yourself in work again just when you seem to be finding the real you again. I think it's a great opportunity for you if you'll be okay. And you can stay here with all of us then."

"Aw, you want me to stay with you?" she teased.

"Ah—" he hedged, laughing.

Raising her brows and trying to keep a straight face, she chastised him. "Don't change your mind now, Mike. You said you wanted me to stay here with all of you." She wasn't going to let him back out of his gaffe. Not that it really was one—he really did want her to stay.

"I do," he quickly reassured her, then huffing out an embarrassed laugh, he added, "but I didn't realize I'd said that out loud." Robyn's chuckle was warm and rich, and she squeezed his hand.

"Thank you for worrying about me. I've been scared to dive into a high-pressure job again too." She rubbed her forehead with her free hand and sighed. "I'm not scared of hard work, but I haven't been good at balancing it in the past. All I've done for the last few years is work. I never took days off, and even when I was sick, I'd work from home. I've had more fun in these last couple of months than I've had in all the years since I finished uni combined." Mike saw a spark of excitement in her eyes, and it warmed him, making him smile with the knowledge that she was happy spending time together. "I mean, it's a hell of a shift, going from working in a company to working for clients, but if I can make it work, it'll be a great career move. Then I could get my own place, and maybe even get a dog to keep me company."

"The kids would never leave if you did that."

She shrugged and grinned shamelessly. "They're fun. They can stay whenever they want. So could you, you know?"

Mike took in Robyn's features. A cheeky smile had her lips tilting up, lighting up her face. Her blue eyes sparkled with mischievousness, and her cheeks flushed an adorable pink. The few years age gap between them was nothing, but Robyn acted so much more mature than he ever had in his twenties, even as a father. It was wonderful to see her so carefree and happy now.

He smiled, knowing she was still teasing him. "I think you know what you want."

"I know I do." Her words were quiet, and he knew that they were no longer talking about her job. She met his gaze head on, looking at him through lowered lashes, and Mike's gut coiled with something unfamiliar. Desire? Want? A healthy dose of guilt and disappointment in himself too.

He'd still thought of Ezio every day over the last couple of months, but Mike was finally accepting that he'd never see the man again. The sharpness of the pain had dulled to a throb that lived behind his heart, and with every passing day he spent with Robyn, he was realizing that maybe he didn't need to find "the one." Maybe he already had. He was attracted to Robyn, and every time they were together, he smiled. But he'd been hurt before, and taking that step worried him more than he was prepared to admit.

Mike looked away and clenched his jaw, trying to convince himself that that's all there was between them. Disappointment at how weak he was bloomed like a cloud of noxious gas choking him. Frustration and anger at himself warred with each other, vying for dominance. He wanted to move on and get over Ezio. But at the same time, he couldn't get over the feeling that he was betraying their memory too, and that notion was as utterly ridiculous as it was fanciful. Ezio had probably already forgotten about him. After all, the man lived on a cruise ship in paradise where most of the guests strutted around half-naked—exactly the same way he'd picked Ezio up. The man could get any person he wanted into his bed. Mike wasn't as lucky—his limitations in the bedroom meant that he couldn't just love the one he was with, even if that one was Robyn and she was amazing in every way.

He pulled away from her, balling his fist and shaking his head before huffing out his frustration. Maybe if he was better at moving on, he would have been able to forget Ezio. He wasn't an idiot. He knew Robyn wanted him. She'd laid it out pretty clearly before but had left it to him to make the first move. If he were different—if he could move on, if he could... perform, maybe he and Robyn could give it a go. She could be the woman of his dreams, but even if she was, fear held him hostage. It didn't help that he still couldn't get Ezio out of his head either. How did he deal with that? Robyn deserved someone who could love her completely, not someone still hung up on a man eight months after they'd last seen each other. But his heart was a fucking idiot, and his head probably more so. He could fall head over heels in love with Robyn, but for as long as he couldn't get Ezio out of his head, he'd be alone.

"Mike," Robyn started, sighing when he shook his head and refused to look at her.

"I can't, Robyn."

"Why?" she asked gently. "Please tell me."

"I just... I can't, okay?" he replied, still not looking at her. If he did, he'd snap, and he wasn't sure who would be hurt worse by the inevitable fallout.

* * * * *

Mike sat at the mismatched collection of chairs and outdoor couches they'd reserved, waiting for the others to join him. They were out celebrating after Robyn's first week working with Nick. She'd been riding a high. Every time they'd spoken, she was bubbly and excited about one case in particular she was working on. He didn't know the specifics, but apparently her mining expertise was being put to good use. This time, though, she was convinced she was acting on the right side of the fence, making a genuine difference to the potential outcome of an attempt to protect land occupied by an endangered species of frog.

Mike couldn't wait to let his hair down. He'd had the kids all week, and God love them, but they'd been a pain in his rear end. And not the fun kind. Jax was throwing temper tantrums, and Lexi was argumentative and stubborn, neither one of them cooperating when he tried to get them out the door each morning or into bed at night. He needed a breather, then a few days of quiet time at home so he could get the house back in order.

Their table was in the middle of the gentle grassy slope. Halfway across the open-air pub, he watched Connor setting up, readying for his performance. Levi was with him, rearranging the equipment on the stage. Katy was on her way, as were Nick, Emma, and Robyn. Until then, Mike sat back and people watched. The venue was about as casual as they came on the Gold Coast—a lawn with a stage at one end under a Bali hut, a bar at the other, and picnic tables, outdoor couches, swing chairs, and cabanas dotted around the place. Some were full, others with empty seats. But the bar had a queue, and more people were arriving through the gates and via the water taxis waiting to dock.

To the west of where Mike was sitting, the river meandered towards the ocean, boats puttering in and out while others were moored. The sun had nearly set, the sky a mixture of pinks and oranges behind the towers. The lights strung between the palm trees and along the paths winked on as staff wandered around lighting the tiki torches. The light reflected off the water, its surface glassy except for the ripples caused by the boats slowly motoring along the waterway.

He relaxed back on the padded seat and sighed happily, watching the sun sink below the mountains.

Katy arrived first, greeting him with a kiss on the cheek and a smile. "How are you?"

"Glad it's Friday." Mike laughed and shook his head. "It's been a week. How are you?"

"Commiserating with you. Every day has been awfully busy." She stretched her neck, and the vertebrae cracked, making her wince before looking around, no doubt searching for her men.

"The boys are near the stage. Connor was getting ready to go on." Mike motioned to them, and Katy squeezed his arm and smiled.

"If you'll excuse me, I'm gonna say hi and get a drink. Can I get you another one?"

"I'm good for the moment, thanks." He tipped his glass to her and took another swig. The juice was perfectly chilled and smooth going down.

"Okay, I'll be back." Katy hurried off and brought both Connor and Levi back with her. It didn't take long for a few other friends to join them. Mike didn't recognize any of them, but from the gist of their conversation he understood they'd worked with Levi when he was a TV presenter. Soon, the only people they were waiting on were Nick, Emma, and the guest of honour—Robyn.

She showed up last, making an entrance like no other. In a red dress that followed the shape of her curves perfectly, tied with a black belt around her waist and matching pointy-toed flats, she stood out like a ray of sunshine on a cloudy day. Her glossy dark hair fell over her shoulders in waves and fluttered in the breeze as she picked her way over to the bar. Mike smiled at the sight of her, excited that his friend had arrived.

"When are you gonna ask her out, man?" Connor asked him with a nudge to his arm. "You undress her with your eyes every time you see her, and she's into you too."

"Nah, we're just friends."

Connor snorted and shook his head. "Keep telling yourself that. I know what unrequited love looks like, believe me."

It dawned on Mike that Connor knew exactly what he was going through. "There's a bit of a difference between our situations though."

"Seems pretty straightforward from where I'm sitting. You like her, she likes you..."

Mike ran his fingers through his hair and tugged on the ends, groaning in frustration. "It's not as easy as that though. It's all kinds of fucked-up, in fact."

"I know Nick's your man, but I'm always here if you want to talk. It helped me to be able to confide in someone who could see the forest for the trees, if you get what I mean."

"Me too," Levi said, coming to stand behind Connor and resting his hands on his shoulders. "Whatever it is that you guys were talking about, I'm here too if you want to talk. I know what you and Nick did for Connor when he needed someone. So, you know…" He shrugged as if it was no big deal, but to Mike, it meant the world.

"Thanks, mate. I appreciate both of you saying that. I'm a bit of a mess, but I'll sort it out."

Connor clapped him on the shoulder and stood, pressed a kiss to Levi's lips, and excused himself. Levi grinned happily and watched him walk over to Katy and kiss her a little less chastely before shaking himself off and turning his attention back to Mike. Mike couldn't help but laugh. "You are so totally gone for him."

"One hundred percent. He's our missing piece."

Mike sighed and nodded. "In some ways, I think it'd be easier to navigate if two of you—"

"This seat free?" Robyn's sweet voice, husky from a long day's work, curled around him, and he bit back a happy sigh at having her near him.

"For you? Always." He smiled and she grinned back, slipping into the seat and turning to Levi.

"Sorry, I've just interrupted your conversation, haven't I?"

"Nah." Levi shook his head. "I was just telling Mike that I'm completely gone for both Connor and Katy. I'll let you two catch up."

Robyn opened her mouth to object, but Mike waved off her worry. "You look beautiful tonight. No one else here even compares."

She smiled shyly and hooked her arm through his. "Flattery will get you everywhere, you know." She took a sip of the cocktail in her hand, something clear with crushed blueberries in it, and sighed happily. Before long, their group was seated on the couches, and they were buying rounds for each other. Cocktails, beers, and bottles of wine went down too easily, and before Mike knew it, he'd downed a schooner of beer and had a happy buzz going on. Robyn was laughing next to him, and the warmth from her body pressed against his was a welcome presence.

"I feel like dancing. Come dance with me." She tugged on the sleeve of his button-down shirt and nodded to the dance floor, an open section of grass immediately in front of the stage.

"I don't know if that's a good idea. I think I'm tipsy." Mike laughed, lightness surrounding him, but Robyn wasn't taking no for an answer. Truthfully, Mike didn't want to resist too much either. The thought of letting loose and having some fun after his week was a temptation he couldn't easily pass up.

She stood and held her hand out to him, and much to his chagrin their group whistled, cheered, and catcalled until Mike gave the others the finger and hurried them to the stage. Levi and Katy followed on their heels and begin swaying to Connor's smooth voice as he strummed his guitar and sang about dancing by the water, Mexican skies, and Mariachi bands. Mike breathed deep, salt air filling his lungs, and his heartbeat kicked up a notch. He wrapped an arm around Robyn and pulled her against him until she straddled his leg. Her breasts pressed against his chest, and he revelled in the touch of another person. It was a sensation he'd denied himself for far too long. Missing Ezio was one thing, but he'd been punishing himself too, depriving himself of any close contact except hugs from his kids.

Grasping Robyn's petite hand in his bigger, rougher one, he moved his hips, leading her in more of a grind than a dance. Her pupils dilated, and her lips parted as she traced a pattern with deft fingertips on his chest.

Mike sucked in a breath and the subtle hint of a light perfume, and the musky scent of her skin after a day at work had him reeling. He was hard, his cock flexing against her belly. Robyn groaned, a pained mumble from deep within. He should have resisted. He shouldn't have let his tipsy brain egg him on. But common sense had checked out for the night. Mike leaned forward, his lips only a hair's breadth from hers when she looked at him through lowered eyelashes. Mike's body pulsed like he'd been struck by electricity at her reaction. She wet her lips, tempting him to taste her, and her cheeks flushed a rosy red. Desire looked damn good on her, and Mike couldn't help but run his nose along the soft skin of her throat. He breathed her in and flexed his fingers involuntarily at her back. Every part of him demanded he get closer to her. It was as if Robyn had a tractor beam, and he was firmly within its grasp. He wavered closer and closer, the gap between them getting smaller with every roll of his hips and sway of their bodies together. Mike bit back a moan when Robyn slipped her delicate fingers inside the back pocket of his jeans, palming his arse.

He spun her, pulling her against his body again, and this time his rigid cock fit snugly between her arse cheeks. Splaying his hand against her abdomen, his moves mimicked making love. He dropped kisses along her exposed shoulder, and she tilted her head, giving him more access. She was intoxicating, her skin soft and supple against his rough stubble. Robyn threw her arm around his neck and held him there while she ground against him, his dick rigid and throbbing. He grunted, staving off an imminent explosion of epic proportions by slowing her moves. Curling his fingers around her hips only served to pull her closer to him.

He groaned as his dick pulsed and he shot to the edge of bliss. The sounds of the people around them—laughter and conversations—the music and the clinking of glasses all faded away. Mike could have been alone on a desert island with Robyn for all the notice he took of people around them. His body screamed for relief. For attention. To give in to the desire and need coursing through his system to make love for endless hours.

His heart rate picked up speed, racing as they moved. His breathing sharpened, and the world lost focus. A wave of light-headedness washed over him, and he understood what it was like to be high on someone. Robyn spun in his arms and pressed her body against his again. Her eyes were dark, her pupils blown. Her lips were parted, the gloss she wore tempting him to kiss them. He leaned in and swayed on his feet, his pulse hammering through his veins. Robyn ran her hands up his front but stopped short when she reached his chest.

"Shit, Mike, are you okay?"

"Mmm," he hummed, but swayed on his feet again. He couldn't catch his breath. Why was he so puffed? Mike didn't feel so good. He could hear his own heartbeat hammering against his chest. Was that supposed to happen? Blood thundered through his veins, making his fingertips throb and his lips tingle. Mike sucked in a breath and staggered when Robyn guided him off the makeshift dance floor and onto a nearby chair.

Noise sounded like it was heightened, then muffled as if he had cotton wool in his ears. Colours were the same—saturated then muted. His vision blurred then snapped into focus, and all the while he couldn't catch his breath. He was fitter than this. Dancing shouldn't wind him like it had.

Something wasn't right.

Mike remembered the drink. He didn't normally have more than one. Had he had more? He must have. That had to be it. Or maybe it was because he hadn't eaten much. The kids had been difficult too, and he'd spent a few sleepless nights after finding it hard to wind down.

Robyn's cool hands on his sweaty cheeks snapped him back into the moment. "I'm okay," he rasped, his voice sounding like he'd swallowed nails after running straight up the side of a mountain.

"No, I don't think you are. You're too pale. Your heart's beating a mile a minute too."

"'S alright. I'll be right. Just gimme a sec," he slurred, exhaustion overcoming him. Damn it. This was what happened when he drank too much. He needed to sleep off the excess alcohol. He'd only had one, hadn't he? It didn't make sense. Mike rested his elbows on his knees and concentrated on slowing down his heart. He pictured the valves opening and closing, the muscle contracting to push blood through his arteries, and the rush of blood moving at the pace of a lazy river rather than the plummet down Niagara Falls. His eyes were heavy, his blinks slowing. Sweat beaded on his forehead and dripped down his nose. Robyn was there. Others were too. Someone passed him a glass of iced water, closing his hand around it. The cold of the glass gave him something to focus on. He gulped it down and swayed in the seat.

"We're getting you home, mate. You're in no state to be here," Levi announced. "I'll stay with you."

"Nah," Mike protested, but was grateful when Levi helped him to his feet, and they staggered out of the bar. No sooner than his arse hit the seat in the ride share, he was fast asleep.

ELEVEN

Robyn

Robyn paced. Levi had taken Mike home an hour earlier. He'd messaged to say Mike was in bed. She should have been there with him. She'd wanted to, but Levi had insisted. It was her night, he'd said, and yes it was, but she never would have organized it if she'd known Mike would end up sick. It was unlike him to drink, and she didn't think he'd had too many, but he'd mumbled about not eating anything. Whatever he'd drunk must have gone straight to his head.

She nodded at Emma and tried to smile when she nudged her and asked under her breath, "You okay?" With a raised eyebrow, Emma added, "You want to go to Mike's place and check on him?" It was a rhetorical question. She could always read Robyn like an open book, but hearing the words out loud made her feel like a stalker. Or Mike's mother. She didn't know which was worse.

"No," Robyn hedged. She shrugged, trying to play down how much she'd looked forward to his being here. The plan was to get tipsy, flirt, have some fun, and hopefully push their relationship past the friend zone.

Emma laughed. "You're a shitty liar."

All eyes turned to Levi when he arrived with a blond giant of a man. "Look who I found."

While Katy cocked her head to one side, her brow furrowed as she thought for a moment, Levi moved over to Robyn, gently squeezed her shoulder, and spoke in a low whisper. "He's okay. Went straight to bed when we got to his place. He was asleep before I even turned out the light. Talk about a cheap drunk." He smiled, and Robyn nodded her thanks when Katy's animated gasp had her turning.

Katy's reaction to the good-looking stranger had the table laughing. With her mouth comically open and her eyes wide, she uttered a surprised, "Will? My God, it's been years. How the hell are you?"

"I'm really well." He reached out to shake her hand, but she brushed him off and hugged him instead. "It's good to see you again. How are you?"

"Great! Everyone, this is Will Preston. He's the captain of a cruise ship. I baked the cake celebrating his promotion and then Levi interviewed him for his podcast." She was rambling, an excited smile on her face. As a ship captain, Will fit in with the high-profile guest list for Levi's podcast. He was a few seasons in, interviewing inspirational and successful LGBTQIA+ figures, seeking advice from professionals, giving support, and raising awareness on community issues. Levi started it when he lost his job as a children's TV presenter. Being outed as both bisexual and in a poly relationship on national telly—care of a tip-off from Katy's brother no less, and some explicit footage of him and Connor together—had ended his career and the show that he presented on. But it hadn't stopped Levi. He'd picked himself up and transformed himself into a local superstar for the rainbow community. He emceed fundraising events, dedicated time volunteering at charities as well as producing the podcast. A few months earlier, he'd gone back to his first love too—youth fitness—and started training groups of teens at Mike's gym.

Nick spoke up. "You aren't related to Lynn Preston, are you? She lives in Surfers."

"Right on the beach?" Nick nodded, and Will laughed. "Yeah, she's my nan. How do you know her?"

"She's my next-door neighbour. Nick Daniels, and this is my wife, Emma, and Robyn Stevens, who's staying with us." They all shook hands and motioned for Will to pull up a seat at the table. "It's a small world. Can't believe that."

"It's crazy; six degrees of separation in this town. How is the grumpy old bat? I haven't had a chance to see her since I got back onshore."

Nick laughed and nodded his head in acknowledgement. "Spoke to her yesterday. She's good. She was having coffee with your mum or aunt, maybe. Lady with tattoos."

"My stepmum."

"Cruise ship captain is cool," Emma commented. "What company?"

"Dream Liner. My ship is the MV Dreamcatcher."

"Isn't that the same one Mike went on?" Emma asked her.

Robyn shook her head, unsure. "I have no clue, but pretty sure it had an MV in its name."

"Depending on the size of the ship he was on and where he departed from, it could have been mine," Will replied. "Hope he enjoyed it."

"He loved it. So did his kids," Robyn answered confidently.

Connor joined the table a moment later and chugged the glass of water that Katy held out for him. With a smile, he asked Will, "Mate, how are you?"

"Good!" They gave each other a one-armed hug.

"Who you here with?"

"Brother and sister and a few friends." He motioned a few tables away and added, "I was supposed to be getting a round of drinks, so I'd better head back."

"Good to see you. We'll have to catch up another time." Connor shook his hand, and Levi stood and did the same before taking Connor's hand in his. Robyn waved goodbye, as did the others around the table before Nick stood again and reached over to shake his hand.

"Next time you visit your nan, stick your head over the fence. We'd love to have you over for a beer."

"I'll be there soon actually. Once my boyfriend finishes his spell at sea, we'll go and see her. I want to introduce them. If we need an escape plan, I'll give you a shout out."

"There's always someone around so pop by anytime, but I'm sure she'll love him."

"Everybody does." Will blushed and coughed out an embarrassed laugh. "And on that note, great seeing you all. I'm sure we'll run into each other again soon."

The conversation continued, and Robyn's mind wandered. She upended the glass of wine, discovering it was empty, and pursed her lips together. "Anyone want anything from the bar?"

* * * * *

How are you feeling? The text to Mike was still unanswered at 7:00 AM. It was unlike him. He always woke early. He made the dawn look like it slept late. Robyn had been obsessively checking her phone for at least an hour, and she nearly dropped it in fright when it vibrated with a response. Self-consciously, and glad no one could see her pacing the bedroom, she huffed and checked it.

I'm okay. I feel worse that I missed being there for your celebration. Can I make it up to you?

Robyn smiled sadly at the phone. He hadn't done anything wrong. Having one too many drinks wasn't a sin, and before then, it had never happened before. *I missed hanging with you too. Maybe we can catch up sometime in the next few days. House hunting this weekend!*

Now that she was working, Robyn wanted to get a place of her own. Living with Nick and Emma was great, but it was only ever going to be temporary, and it was time to move on.

* * * * *

Two weeks had passed with absolutely no luck. Properties for rent came and went so quickly that she struggled to book an appointment to see them. It used up all her free time, and Robyn was getting frustrated. She hadn't even had a chance to catch up with Mike. They'd spoken every day, but she missed him.

Robyn regretted not taking one of the apartments she'd seen the weekend before, but she really wanted to be able to walk outside and feel the grass under her feet, then walk to the beach. There was something to be said about being close to the ground. It was the one thing she was really looking for; she didn't much care what the inside looked like, but ground or first-floor apartments were as rare as hens' teeth.

Trolling the real estate websites was painful, even more so when she'd call and the place was already rented. But she didn't have a choice. She needed to find something. Robyn fixed herself a sandwich, poured a cup of tea, and sat outside in the shade. It was hot. The spring sun was merciless—just like a baby snake pumped out toxic amounts of venom with every bite, the sun's strength was intensified at the beginning of the season. Except that she knew it would get stronger as the year progressed. The ocean breeze kept her cool though while she searched for a rental.

Then she found it. A flat above the garage of a Main Beach house. The house was an old Queenslander, but the flat looked more modern. Still though, it had loads of personality and charm. Rich timber floors throughout, a crisp white bathroom that looked new, and a decent-sized kitchenette. The bedroom had an inbuilt wardrobe, albeit a small one, and the lounge room overlooked the front garden and the poinciana trees along the street beyond. It made for a lovely outlook. Sandwich forgotten, she telephoned the lady whose name was listed. Within minutes, she had an appointment and had booked a ride share.

The car pulled up at the curb of the dark blue house with white trim, and Robyn couldn't help her smile. One block in from the Broadwater, it was prime real estate, but far enough away from the main roads to avoid most of the traffic noise. The street was lined on both sides with flowering poincianas and pandanus palms, and even though every house had a front fence, there was an open, community feel about the place. The neighbours across the street were talking, and pedestrians meandered along the footpath heading toward the beach. Laughter rang out, a couple of kids riding their bikes on the road, and Robyn immediately wanted to live there. This was what her apartment in Perth had been missing.

She pushed open the front gate and found a lady in a broad-brimmed white hat, cut-off jean shorts, and a bikini top with garden gloves up to her elbows digging in the dirt. "Hi," Robyn greeted her. "Are you Cassie?"

"Yes. Robyn?" She smiled warmly and took off her gloves.

"I am." Robyn shook her hand and looked around the yard, enchanted. It was beautiful. A jacaranda tree that stood higher than the roof of the house, resplendent with purple blooms, branched out to create a wide canopy covering most of the yard in shade. A brick pathway cut the yard in half, diverting around the tree in its centre. At the base of the tree's trunk, flowers bloomed in every colour, and vines with pink and white roses grew along the fences, enclosing the yard in complete sweet-scented privacy. A calmness immediately washed over her, but at the same time, filled with life, it was vibrant. Robyn could picture herself sitting in the swing to the left-hand side of the stairs welcoming guests onto the wide veranda.

Along the same side as the swing, a red climbing rose perfumed the air, growing along lattice mounted in the garden bed. The stairs above led to the structure above the garage, and hopefully, her apartment. The place was magical; she already wanted to live there and hadn't even seen the inside of it.

A fancy navy-blue BMW pulled up as they were halfway up the stairs. Cassie introduced her husband, Jacob, who after shaking her hand and flashing her a pearly white smile, left them to it, taking a couple of shopping bags inside with a wave. They both seemed like good people. Down to earth, despite clearly having money.

When Cassie opened the door, Robyn didn't even need to step fully inside before she blurted the words, "I'll take it. Can I take it? I love it. It's beautiful." Dappled sunlight shone in through the wide windows, the gauzy curtains billowing in the breeze. The wicker fan would provide more circulation, but it wasn't needed that afternoon. The rich timber floors were a burnished caramel colour, and the walls a crisp white. The white kitchen sparkled, and brand-new stainless-steel appliances made it modern, while all the timber gave it a traditional feel, full of etched details. The room wasn't large—just big enough to fit her couch, the papasan chair she'd always wanted, and a desk under the window—but it was perfect. The bathroom matched the kitchen—white, modern but with period details and a handy cupboard that housed a washing machine—and the bedroom was simple but would be cosy with her bed in it.

"It's just lovely," Robyn uttered.

"I'm glad you like it." Cassie smiled and patted the timber-framed glass front door as she closed it after them. "We were going to use it as our office, but Jake and I don't take up too much room, and our assistant works from his place, so we didn't end up needing the space. By that stage though, we had the approvals through for the construction." She shrugged. "It wasn't hard to get it changed to a granny flat."

"It's got such a great feel, and it's so quiet here. I expected it to be noisier with all the busy roads and bars nearby."

"We're very lucky to be in this part of the street. Up the other end it's noisier," she explained as they descended the stairs into the picture-perfect yard. "I baked some scones earlier. Let's have a cuppa and we can chat some more."

So that's what they did. Sitting on the front veranda, overlooking the garden, they got to know each other. For the next hour, Robyn told them about how she had friends who lived on the Gold Coast and had decided to relocate from the west. How she'd recently started working at a firm in Brisbane but would only be commuting a couple of days a week and working from home the others. She explained that she had a motorbike but didn't mind parking it on the street and promised not to rev it too loudly or early, given the tram station was walking distance away. Jake insisted that a carpark was included with the rent; there was plenty of room in the oversized double garage when they only had one car. They asked about whether she drank or smoked and were happy when she answered no. The only disappointing thing was their insistence of no pets—Cassie's passions were gardening and baking, so anything that could or would destroy the yard or pose a threat to the native wildlife was out. That was fine with Robyn, albeit a little disappointing.

Both Cassie and Jake were real estate agents who'd moved up from Sydney to start their own business. In their early thirties, they worked just as long hours as she did, except they both operated from home.

Before the afternoon was up, the paperwork was signed, and Robyn had transferred payment to them. She had the keys and wore a undiminishable smile. It was even better when she set down the dainty teacup and her phone vibrated. The message from Mike made her cheeks heat, and a goofy smile lit up her face. *How's the house hunting going? Can we celebrate yet or are we still commiserating? Was thinking I could cook you dinner tonight. Just the two of us.*

"I have a date." She laughed happily, then looked up and saw Cassie and Jacob grinning at her. "He's pretty special. Single dad, great guy. We've been friends for a few months." Robyn typed out a quick response, then looked at her watch and frowned. "I'm so sorry, but I have to get my butt into gear if I'm going to make it to his place on time."

"Not a problem. Let us know when you're moving in, and we'll make sure we're here to lend you a hand."

"Thank you. I'm so excited. The apartment is perfect. It's exactly what I wanted and so much more."

Cassie hugged her quickly and smiled. "We're looking forward to having you here."

Robyn waved as she climbed into the ride share, her belly flip flopping with excitement. Their date was really happening. Finally. She'd been open with Mike about wanting more with him than friendship, but she hadn't pushed the matter. She knew he was divorced, and although he and his ex were friends, having his marriage fall apart couldn't have been easy on him. She also knew he hadn't dated a lot since he'd become single. So Robyn was prepared to be patient. She liked him too much for things between them to be a one-night only affair. And now that patience had paid off.

Unless it was dinner as friends.

But why would he have said that it was just the two of them? She sighed and crossed her fingers that they were finally on the same page before she rushed inside to get ready.

TWELVE

Mike

A nervous energy swirled around his chest. He was finally doing it. He was having Robyn over for dinner. Just the two of them.

He'd been unable to get her out of his head since they'd danced together. Reliving each and every swivel of their hips in synchronicity and the sweet scent he'd breathed in while holding her close. Confusion had reigned supreme over the last few weeks, his brain a mess of longing, desire, and guilt. He could no longer deny that he liked Robyn. Like, *like* like her.

And now he sounded like a teenager.

He'd moved past wanting to be friends with her, but he couldn't. Not with thoughts of Ezio still swirling around in his head. How the hell did that even happen? How did he end up wanting two people? He wasn't like Levi, Connor, and Katy—his situation was hopeless. Ezio was out of his life, but the feelings he still harboured for the man were real. And now he had to admit he was falling for Robyn too.

He had to get his head around it, but he also had to set things straight with her. He knew Robyn wanted more with him, but he'd never treat her like a consolation prize. So, the solution was simple—stay friends. Don't take their date further. Don't date her at all.

It's not a date.

If he kept telling himself that, hopefully his head would rein in his over-amorous heart. He would make sure their night together wasn't any different than when they'd caught up as a group or with his kids. They were still friends, except now they'd be two friends eating food and relaxing after a busy week at work and house hunting.

It wasn't a big deal for him to cook rather than order in. Showering and dressing a little nicer than his normal boardies and singlet only meant that he wanted to make it special.

It's. Not. A. Date!

Shit.

It was a date.

No, it wasn't. This was an apology and a way of making up for the mess he'd made of himself at her party. But he wouldn't let himself get carried away with the fluttery excitement of having her here now swirling around inside him. Her friendship was important to Mike. Robyn was exactly what he'd needed after Ezio. She brought sunshine back into his life. He was perfectly happy with being friends. He had to be. It didn't matter that his dreams of late had been filled with threading his fingers into the dark strands of her silky hair and kissing her until they were both breathless.

Maybe tonight… Not a date, Mike.

Two friends. That's it.

Even if he had the right to reach out and kiss her, he couldn't. He always circled back to the fact that she deserved so much more than he could give her. He wasn't talking about material wealth—he knew she wasn't focussed on that—but she did deserve someone who could love her without exception. Without limitation.

He was her friend. That had to be enough.

He needed to think about his kids too. They were another reason he couldn't risk their friendship. They loved having Robyn around as much as he did. Lexi was in awe of her, and Jax had hearts in his eyes whenever her name was mentioned. When Robyn and Jax spent the few-hour trip back from Australia Zoo talking crocodiles, dinosaurs, and every lizard species from Komodo dragons to frill necks, it was inevitable she'd become his favourite person.

Mike sighed, resigned to having to mentally castigate himself all night, and smoothed down his black button-down shirt.

The reflection staring back at him in the mirror was wary. His hair was messy like usual, except that the product in it gave it some kind of style. His cheeks were stubbled, and his tan was deepening now that the weather was warm again, but he could see the fear and weakness in his eyes too. Mike rolled up the sleeves on his shirt, his thick forearms straining the open cuff, and washed his hands ready to set the table.

The chicken and potatoes were roasting. The tomato sauce, made from a puree of charred capsicum and vine-ripened and semi-dried tomatoes simmered on low on the cooktop. The salad was in the fridge ready to go. He couldn't take credit for the dessert—that was Katy's doing—and the petite cakes looked delicious.

Mike was kidding himself. This wasn't what he'd do for dinner with friends. If he was doing that, he'd order in or he'd barbecue. He sighed and rubbed his temples, wondering if it was too late to cancel. He didn't want to make a fool of himself.

The lobby buzzer sounded. *Too late.*

"Hello," he answered.

"Hey, it's me," Robyn replied and with a teasing lilt to her tone added, "Feel like letting me in?"

"Nah, I'm good for company tonight," he joked as he pressed the button to open the doors and unlock the lift. There was a knock at his door a few minutes later, and Mike steeled himself for the embarrassment and hurt he was going to inflict when he had to clarify that, despite all appearances, it couldn't be a date.

Pulling open the door, his mouth popped open, and he was lucky not to choke on his tongue. Robyn stood before him dressed in an off-the-shoulder coffee-coloured dress. The three-quarter-length sleeves ended just above her wrists, revealing her delicate bone structure, and the loose top hinted at her sensuous curves without being too revealing. It was fitted from her hips to just above her knees, showing the length of her smooth legs down to a pair of tiny-heeled shoes with a cute bow that covered most of the black satin shoe.

"You look… wow," Mike stuttered.

"You scrub up pretty well yourself." Robyn smiled and ran a hand down the front of his shirt, smoothing the ripples in it.

"Come in." He shifted to the side and motioned for her to enter. Robyn handed him a bottle of sparkling apple juice and inhaled before humming. Mike couldn't help running his gaze down her body, getting stuck on her arse, perfectly framed by the form-fitting dress. Mechanically, he placed the bottle down and turned to her.

She leaned against the table and gave him a shy smile. "So, I got a place."

"You did?" he asked, excitement bubbling over. Even after she'd accepted the job, he hadn't dared hope she'd make the move permanent. He certainly didn't have a right to wish she did. He found himself closing the distance between them, wrapping her in his arms and holding her close. She held him tight too, her hands splayed on his back, and every soft curve in her body slotted against his harder muscles. He breathed her in and got dizzy from the high. Mike nuzzled her face with his scruff and his lips ghosted over her cheek. Everything in him screamed to put the brakes on this madness but at the same time egged him on. The devil and angel on his shoulders encouraging him and cautioning him simultaneously.

"Are we finally on the same wavelength, Mike?" Her voice was husky, filled with something akin to desire, and his gaze snapped to meet hers. Unable to speak, his voice stolen by a frightening mix of anticipation and hesitance, he remained silent. "You know I've been wanting to ask you out for a while. I haven't because I didn't want to push you. But your reaction is different now. Was it because you didn't know if I was staying? Was that holding you back?"

Mike opened his mouth to deny it, but he couldn't. "Maybe." He winced. "Subconsciously at least. I didn't know how scared of you leaving I was until just now."

"I'm staying, Mike." She rested her palms on his chest, her hands curving around his pecs. "I wasn't sure whether we'd just be ordering a pizza and hanging out like we usually do as a group, or whether this was going to be more of a date."

He wrapped his hands around her hips and stepped closer still. "I know you want to—"

"No more buts, Mike." She gave him a small, hesitant smile. "I'd really like it if there were no more buts." Her eyes flicked down, and her shoulders unclenched, seeming to unknot. "I've waited for you. I want more."

He fingered a lock of her hair, wonderstruck by how silky smooth it was. "When we met, I needed a friend, and you were there. Now you're here too. There are so many reasons why this shouldn't be a date and so many reasons why we shouldn't be together, but I want it to be a date too." He closed his eyes, ashamed by his weakness in resisting the pull growing steadily stronger between them.

He opened his eyes when Robyn's gentle fingertips brushed his lips, and the air shifted, sparking with electricity. Instinctively he leaned closer, almost bridging the gap between them. He hovered there, only a hair's breadth from her lips. Wanting. Denying himself. Instinctively, his eyes flicked to her lips as her tongue darted out and wet them. Mike sucked in a ragged breath and held it as Robyn wavered closer still.

He wasn't sure who finally closed the distance between them, but it didn't really matter. The touch of their lips in a soft, sweet caress left him breathless, like energy passing through a conduit. Robyn gasped and this time touched her fingertips to her lips. A blush stole over her cheeks, and Mike's body reacted, heat flaring through him. He kissed her again, harder this time. Longer. He pressed her up against the table, and his tongue delved in, tasting and teasing her. Losing himself in the moment, Mike reached behind him to shove the table settings out of the way, but Robyn still had her wits about her. She pulled back, breaking the sizzling connection between them, and patted his chest before blowing out a breath and fanning herself exaggeratedly. It broke the tension between them, and Mike laughed at himself.

Robyn moved around the table, her hips swaying gently as she collected the wine glasses from the two place settings. Mike peeled the foil from the bottle and popped the cork, pouring in the sparkling juice when she returned. They toasted Robyn's new place, and she spent the next twenty minutes telling him about it. It sounded like she'd found exactly what she was after—not living in a high-rise was her dream. He'd love a house too, but affording one was another story. None of that mattered though. Robyn was staying, and she'd found somewhere idyllic. Best of all, she was close by.

Mike served their dinner, and it went off without a hitch. The food was great and the company better. There was something so much deeper humming between them, but he needed to set Robyn straight. They needed to talk.

He led them to the two-seater lounge on the balcony overlooking the darkened beach. The waves crashing below provided the musical score for a romantic serenade. Darkness as far as the eye could see stretched before them, tiny pinpricks of light and the barest sliver of the moon twinkling above. It was magnificent during the day; blue ocean stretched to the horizon to meet a sky so vivid, Mike often wondered whether the saturation of the colours had been turned up to full volume. But at night, when the traffic noise and construction work died down and the sound of those waves dominated, this slice of heaven gave Mike the sense of peace he needed. The balcony was his place to come and capture a moment of calm in his crazy-busy life.

Now, here with Robyn, something new washed over him. Nervousness tinged with anticipation, desire, and a bone-deep contentment. Mike had a hard time denying how well they fit together.

He sat and motioned for Robyn to join him. After laying the blanket over her bare legs, he wrapped an arm around her shoulders to keep her warm. He was stalling, trying to come up with a way to explain what was in his heart and his head. They were at war with one another, and he needed to be completely honest. He needed to tell Robyn everything before he could even think about taking another step with her, despite the devil on his shoulder telling him to keep his mouth shut unless his lips were pressed to hers.

Robyn seemed to sense his restlessness and took hold of his fingers, threading hers with them. "What is it? You can talk to me. We're friends first, remember?"

"Yeah, this is difficult to admit though. I'm a bit of a basket case." He looked away from her, staring out over the open ocean, wishing the words would come easily. That he wouldn't hurt her with his admission.

She squeezed his hand. "I know you, Mike. Whatever you have to say isn't going to scare me off."

"This probably should though." He took a breath and steeled his spine. "I said I needed a friend earlier and that you were there for me. Nick is the only person who knows any of this, but even he doesn't know the full story."

"I'm good at keeping secrets. What happened, Mike?"

"When I met you, I was getting over a breakup. But I don't even know that you'd call it that. Our relationship ended. It ran its natural course and was over." He huffed and shook his head, thoughts of Ezio bombarding him. "The thing is, it's ridiculous. I met a man on the cruise I took the kids on, and we clicked. He was everything I wanted in a partner." He squeezed her hand and ran his thumb over the soft skin there. It was as much to reassure Robyn as it was to calm himself.

"In my head I saw us as a once-off hook-up, but we couldn't stay away. We had a week together, and I fell head over heels in love with him. Then the cruise ended and so did we. I was miserable for months. I kept thinking if I'd done something differently, we might have had a chance. I waited too long to try to give him my number. Maybe if I'd done it sooner, or even if I'd told him I wanted more, we might have worked something out. Or not—I don't even know which part of the country he was from." He swallowed, stopping the flow of words that were spewing out of him. In almost a whisper, he added, "The kicker is that I'm still in love with him."

"How do you feel about me?" Robyn asked softly, her voice unsure.

Mike let out a soft sigh, the pain of losing Ezio a raw wound in his chest. "When you came along, you lit up my world again. I don't know that I'll ever stop loving him, but I'm falling for you too." He shook his head, unsure how to explain the swirling feelings that bombarded him with the soft warmth of happiness when he thought of Robyn.

Robyn nodded slowly and pursed her lips in thought. Fear of hurting her churned in his belly. He hadn't been open with her in the past for fear of losing her. He valued her friendship too much. But they'd reached a crossroads now. This was the point where he needed to step up and tell her before anything more than a kiss happened. Mike had proven to himself that he was too weak to resist the pull between them, but the ball had to be in Robyn's court. She had to decide whether she was comfortable with Mike's heart still pining for Ezio, despite the odds of Mike even seeing him again being Buckley's and none.

Never in a million years did Mike expect that Robyn would give him a sympathetic smile. "I can't imagine walking away from someone you love. I'm sorry you got hurt. I wish you didn't have to experience it." She paused and threaded their fingers together. "I appreciate you being honest with me."

Mike nodded, waiting for the rest of what she had to say. He couldn't help but fill in the pause, anxiousness getting the better of him. "As trite as it is to say, it's... You deserve better than a man who's already given away part of his heart."

He sucked in a breath, waiting for the slashing pain in his chest to subside. Losing Ezio had been agony, but losing Robyn—her friendship and the chance at more with her—would be worse. He didn't want to scare her away, but he had to be honest. There was no way he'd ever hurt her by not being truthful. Sharing his confession hadn't lessened the weight on his shoulders though.

Robyn hooked a finger under his chin and turned his face to hers. Shifting so she was sitting sideways on the lounge, she tucked her foot under her leg and swung the other one over his. She waited until his gaze met hers before she spoke. Her words were quiet, but sure. They left Mike with no doubt about the strength of her conviction. "The capacity for love in human beings is endless. It's not pie. Giving a piece of your heart to someone special doesn't mean that there is less for you to give to others. For you to give to me." Mike furrowed his brow, a little confused and beyond surprised that she would say that, and she smiled gently at him. "Look at your kids. Did you love Lexi any less when Jax came along? What about your friends? Do you love them any less when you make new ones? We all have pasts, some of which leave us a little more battered and bruised than others. This man you met—"

"Ezio."

She smiled. "Ezio gave you a piece of his heart too, I'm sure of it. You're someone special, Mike. You're a beautiful human being, inside and out. If I'm lucky enough to be someone you fall for, I'll treasure that, especially knowing you've loved and lost and you're still brave enough to try again."

"Rob," he whispered, his voice full of longing and awe for this amazing woman. He'd been scared she'd walk away from him, never to speak to him again. Instead, she'd embraced his past and spoken about treasuring him? He fell a little more in love with her right then and there. Leaning down, he pressed their lips together, threading his fingers through her hair. The shiny strands were thick and silken between his fingers. Mike groaned, and she opened to him when he touched the tip of his tongue against her lower lip. He gently explored her mouth, slowly tasting the sweetness of dessert on her tongue and the hint of peppermint from her tea. The soft notes of her perfume and the underlying scent of her skin made him dizzy in the best possible way. He wanted to get lost in her, to breathe her in and make her come undone from his touch. He wanted to explore every inch of her delicate body and map her curves with his tongue. He wanted to make love to her like his mind's eye had played out in vivid detail to him in so many of his dreams.

But she pulled back, resting her forehead against his. With her eyes still closed, she murmured, "You were there for me at my low point too, Mike. You helped to open my eyes and see things I didn't know I even wanted."

"Tell me," he breathed, his voice a ragged rasp.

"A family. Fun. A life that didn't revolve around working twelve, fifteen, even twenty-hour days. I don't need to be your first love, Mike." She ran her thumb over his stubble, her eyes full of affection and her soft touch like a balm to his soul. "But I do need you to be with me—I don't want to be second-best to Ezio."

"Never. I'll always cherish you."

She pressed a kiss to his cheek and lingered there. "Life is beautiful with you, and love is kind of wonderful. We should all aspire to do more of both, and if that means holding Ezio in your heart, then I'll help you remember him. I'll help you celebrate the short time that you got together while building memories of our own."

"I don't know what I did in a past life to deserve someone like you, Robyn, but—"

She shifted then, pressing their lips together and diving in to taste him. Robyn cupped his face, manoeuvring him into position as she took control of their kiss. Shifting, she leaned closer while Mike wrapped his arm around her narrow waist. He slid his hand up her back. The material of her dress was soft, a kind of knit, but it was coarse and scratchy compared to the silkiness of her skin. She pressed her leg up against his groin, giving his cock some much-needed friction, and Mike's restraint snapped. He pulled her tight to him and delved deeper, sliding his hand down to her waist and over her arse. He kept going, down to her thigh where he gripped her gently and pressed her leg harder against his cock. The heat between them was incendiary, threatening to combust him on the spot. Her scent, her taste, and the touch of her body against his were driving Mike wild.

"Mike," she pleaded, her words getting lost on a moan when he kissed a line down her throat and over her collarbone. He flicked his tongue over the pulse point at the column of her neck, the thrum of her heartbeat pounding against his lips.

She was light as a feather compared to the heavy weights he lifted at the gym, and he picked her up easily, shifting her until she straddled his hips. Mike slid his hands up underneath her dress to palm her arse, the silky G-string plunging between her cheeks tempting him to follow. He resisted. Barely. But he needed more. He needed to touch and caress Robyn, to show her exactly how drawn to her he was. He nudged down the neckline of her dress with his nose and laid a trail of soft kisses between her pert breasts. She gasped when he blew against the wet trail and whispered his request against her skin. "Yes," she breathed, her consent sounding like a plea.

Mike eased the material down, revealing her breasts to him. She'd gone sans bra, and when cool night air kissed her skin, her nipples pebbled before him. If sensual and erotic had a physical form, it would be the sight of the beautiful woman straddling his lap and making his cock hard enough to hammer nails. He couldn't believe that they'd gotten to this point. "Pinch me," he whispered.

"Hmm?" Her surprise was dulled by the lust clouding her features.

"I can't believe this is real." Mike shook his head and huffed out a laugh. "I have the most beautiful woman half naked and writhing in my lap. When did this become my life?"

She grinned against his lips and delved in for a quick kiss before she pulled back and cupped her breasts, her thumbs brushing over her nipples in a sensual tease. She was a firecracker, and he wanted her more than he had any right to. "Yeah? Better get back to it then."

Mike laughed and pulled her forward again, and licking her skin, he tasted her, getting intoxicated from every swipe of his tongue. Her fingers threaded through his hair, and she gripped him hard, telling him without words what she needed. The heat from her core pressed against his stomach, and he wanted to sink his fingers inside her tightness more than anything on earth.

He wondered what colour her underwear was and how wet she would be for him. Trailing a hand down her back, he used the other to massage her breast as he nibbled on her nipple with his lips, swiping away the sting with a flick of his tongue. He reached her leg and snuck his thumb up under the hemline of her dress, brushing the sensitive skin of her inner thigh.

"Can I?" he asked, his lips pressed against the cleft between her breasts.

"Yes," she hissed. "Need to touch you too." Her fingers were shaking when she undid the buttons of his shirt, pulling it open and running her hands over his chest. He brushed his fingers over her pussy and hummed at the heat pooling there. Robyn's breath hitched when he slid two fingers deep into her core, moving slowly in and out and pressing his thumb down on her clit. He circled the sensitive nub, and her soft walls gripped his fingers tight, clenching around him as he returned to laving her nipples with his tongue.

It didn't take long for Robyn's breathing to become choppy as she rode his fingers. Swivelling her hips and rocking back and forth, she moaned and tossed her head back, the soft waves of her hair brushing over his knuckles as he held her to him. Mike's cock was fit to burst, probably with a permanent indent from the zip it pressed against, but he ignored it, completely lost in Robyn. He splayed his big hand across her back and sucked a mark into the skin on the side of her breast as he concentrated on her G-spot and clit. "Fuuuck," she uttered. "Oh, God."

Then she was coming.

Her choked cry sounded as a full body shudder passed through her, her pussy clamping down tightly on his fingers. Sensation rippled through her, gooseflesh breaking out over her skin as she flushed hot then cold. When she flinched, Mike lifted his thumb from her clit and slowly slid his fingers from her. She shivered, and he went to lift her dress back up, trying to cover her from the chill of the night air. "No," she rasped. "Want you to be able to see me when you come."

With shaking hands, Robyn popped the button on his jeans and wrapped her fist around his cock before easing the zip down. He kissed her, then pulled back and licked the fingers he'd had within her, savouring her taste on his tongue.

"Oh shit," she gasped. "So hot." Robyn pulled his cock out, trying to tug his jock out of the way. He lifted his hips, shoving his jeans down over his thighs until his cock slapped against his belly. Robyn curled her hand around him again, easing her fist up and twisting her wrist so she brushed over his sensitive head on her way down. "Damn, you're well proportioned."

Mike grunted and tried not to come right there and then, wishing he could savour the moment longer than he was sure to last. The tingle at the base of his spine was already radiating outwards, his orgasm an unstoppable force. She was using the perfect amount of pressure, his pre-cum slicking the way as she shuttled her hand over his shaft unhurriedly, but fast enough that he was hurtling toward the edge. The knuckles of one hand brushed against his abs as she moved the other to his balls and rolled them in her palm. When she leaned down to whisper in his ear, he saw the picture in his mind's eye as clear as if he was replaying a dream. He probably was. "I want to taste you now, too. Wrap my lips around your cock and lick you like a lollipop. Want to see you come, Mike."

That was it. Her words sent him over the proverbial cliff into ecstasy. Sensation zapped through his body, frying his nerve endings and whiting out his vision. Words that he couldn't make out were whispered in his ear, but he caught the gist of them—she was encouraging him to let go, to come, to show her how much he wanted her. It was all true. It had been for months, and he was done fighting the desire coursing through him. He heard the hoarse cry that left his lips and felt the thrust of his hips into her fist as he chased more of her touch. It was if he was having an out-of-body experience, levitating on an otherworldly plane of existence.

Robyn licked at a bead of sweat that had broken out on his temple. Out of breath and floating in happy hormones, he barely had the strength to open his eyes, never mind reach for her when she swiped up a bead of cum and licked her finger. It was indecent. Dirty and so fucking sexy. His cock gave a valiant attempt at showing interest again, bucking at her touch, but he was well and truly spent. The effect of edging for so long when he'd been focussed on Robyn had taken its toll.

She climbed off him on unsteady feet when Mike had caught his breath and he could lift his hand to help balance her. He didn't bother pulling up his jeans or doing up his shirt—he was covered in cum, and a shower for both of them was on the cards. Mike led Robyn directly into his attached bathroom, and she smiled and nodded when he asked, "Stay the night?"

Stripping the beautiful woman before him naked was no hardship. Just seeing her body revealed had Mike's spent cock thickening with interest. He ignored it to adjust the water temperature and tugged Robyn into the shower with him when it was perfect. Mike squirted body wash into the palm of his hand and embraced her from behind, rubbing the soap all over her body. He dropped to his knees and playfully bit her arse before cleaning her legs down to her toes. When he stood again, his erection fit snugly between her cheeks, and she moaned, rocking back against him and sliding his cock into the cleft of her arse. The sounds she made went straight to his dick. He couldn't help but pull her closer and reach for both her breast and her clit with his soapy hands. One touch and she was ready to go again. She thrust against his hand, taking her pleasure in the way she needed. With an arm thrown over her shoulder, anchoring him to her, Robyn rode his fingers. She pushed harder against him when he let up the pressure against her clit and shook her head when he shifted in a way she didn't like. Mike loved that she was demanding. Assertive enough to chase what she wanted until she had it.

He wasn't used to the friction against his cock being a warm, wet body. It was incredible. It'd been a long time since he'd been pressed against anything except his fist, and he found himself edging closer as Robyn's breaths became choppy and she slipped and slid against him. The sob hitched in her throat, and she cried out, bucking against him. Mike had no hope of resisting the sight. He came again, shooting ropes of thick cum from his cock and painting her back and arse. His chest heaving and his legs about to buckle, he eased his fingers from her pussy and directed Robyn under the spray of the water, rinsing his seed from her back. She turned in his arms and pulled him forward so they were pressed together again and brought his face down to hers with a hand at his nape.

"Take me to bed, Mike," she murmured sleepily when he'd turned off the water. "My legs feel like jelly." He grinned against her lips and wrapped a towel around her shoulders before picking her up. He carried her like a bride out of his bathroom and deposited her gently on his bed.

THIRTEEN

Robyn

Robyn came back to herself slowly. The warm body pressed against her back, snuggling into her was new. The night before flashed behind her still-closed eyes, and she smiled. Mike. He'd been resisting the pull between them even harder than her, but for a very different reason. It'd been wearing on her, making her wonder whether the attraction was completely one-sided, but Mike's confession made all the pieces slot into place. He hadn't wanted to pursue any kind of relationship because he was still hung up on Ezio.

She processed that for a moment—Mike was still in love with another person. Surprisingly enough, the thought didn't upset her. She meant what she said the night before. The capacity for love was endless, and Mike was a good man. She knew he'd treat her with respect, and although she wouldn't be the only person he loved, she knew he would adore her. Their friendship had taught Robyn what kind of man he was, and the night before had left her with no doubts. If anyone else had confessed a secret love to her right before they hooked up, Robyn's reaction would undoubtedly have been different.

Her thoughts shifted when a sleepy kiss dropped on the nape of her neck reignited the desire to get closer to the man behind her. His morning wood was making an appearance, and Robyn hadn't tasted him properly the night before. She slid out of his arms, and Mike blinked open his eyes, a smile as radiant as sunshine lighting up his face. "Good mornin'," he rasped.

"Mmm, will be." She pecked him on the lips and slithered down his body, dropping open-mouthed kisses as she went. Over the lines in his abs, down the v framing his cock, and to the totem pole he had between his legs. Thick and erect, his dick throbbed in her grip as she angled it into her mouth. The body wash from their shower the night before lingered, but she was able to smell more of his scent after a night wrapped around each other, and she loved it. Musky and masculine, he was addictive. His salty taste burst onto her tongue, and she hummed, making Mike white-knuckle the sheets. She sucked him until he was panting and incoherent. He wound his fingers into her hair, making shallow thrusts into her mouth, and chased his orgasm. He was close too. A burst of pre-cum bloomed on her tongue, and he hardened even more. Mike was on the edge, but Robyn wanted to feel that monster inside her when he came. She pulled off with a lascivious pop and reached for his bedside table drawer, figuring she was likely to find rubbers in there.

Mike snagged her wrist and stopped her. "Not yet," he rasped, his voice thick with desire. "Need to taste you." He rolled her onto her back effortlessly, pressing her into the sheets as he blanketed her body and ran his tongue down her throat, sampling every sensitive spot. The combination of sensual licks, his soft stubble, and the nips of his teeth lit up every one of her nerve endings like a New Year's Eve fireworks display. When he reached the apex of her thighs, he feasted, and Robyn was catapulted into sensory overload. He was relentless, not stopping until he'd wrung her third orgasm out and she was lying boneless on the bed.

"I don't think I can move." Robyn huffed out an exhausted laugh as Mike shifted, lying next to her on his belly, his knee bent toward her. Her extremities were still tingling, and the ache in her pussy would last for hours. She hadn't ever felt this well used before and couldn't get over Mike's attentiveness. It was the first time she'd been with a lover who focussed on her so completely. Still out of breath, she added, "I can't even feel my legs anymore."

"Glad I could help." Mike grinned and threaded their fingers together, bringing Robyn's hand to his mouth and kissing her knuckles gently. Robyn swooned. Just a little.

"If you want to straddle my shoulders I can—"

"Oh, ah… no need." Mike lifted one shoulder in a shrug and flushed, his cheeks turning a rosy red. Enunciating his words as if he were embarrassed by the confession, Mike explained, "I kinda get off doing that. I love your responsiveness."

Robyn blinked, took in his words, and blinked again. She was speechless. It was another first for her. Admittedly Robyn's list of relationships wasn't long, but she'd hooked up with enough men to see a pattern—and there weren't many who even liked it, never mind got off on it. Robyn laughed, her happiness bubbling over. "Well, I for one think that's fuckin' fantastic, because I love it. Anytime you want to do that, feel free."

Mike grinned and rolled to his side, pulling her into his arms. "I'll take you up on that."

* * * * *

It was four hours later that the knock on the door sounded. Mike had already buzzed Wani and the kids into the building. Robyn was meeting her for the first time, and nerves hummed through her veins like ants scurrying over the ground. Holding her mug with both hands and hiding in the kitchen, Robyn waited with bated breath until the stampede of two young kids charging in and dumping their bags in their bedroom had subsided. Mike and Wani were talking, catching up on their weeks, when Mike said the words that made Robyn's gut swoop with nerves. "I have someone I'd like you to meet."

"Sure, when?"

Robyn swallowed hard and closed her eyes, wishing that Mike would have chosen to wait until she was at least dressed in fresh clothes. But he'd insisted. Robyn looked down at herself. Dressed in the day before's getup, it was obvious that she'd had stayed the night. There was no doubt she was dressed more for an evening out than a lazy Sunday.

"Love, this is Wani, Lexi and Jax's mum. Wani, this is Robyn. Robyn works for Nick now, but she's been friends with Emma for years...." He trailed off, his gaze snagging on Robyn's. She was shocked still, her mouth open and her head tilted to the side, trying to process the pet name he'd given her. Love. His brow furrowed, and Robyn gently placed the mug down on the bench and moved over to him. Her smile was slow spreading, but she couldn't stop it even if she'd wanted to. Love. The concern etched on his features disappeared, and he grinned back at her, both of them beaming like giddy teenagers. Mike reached for her hand and threaded their fingers together. She squeezed as the silence stretched between them and electricity sparked.

Robyn had almost forgotten Wani was there until the other woman cleared her throat. Mike snapped his eyes toward her, and Robyn followed when she saw the colour drain from Mike's face. Wani looked thunderous.

The awkward silence stretched on, and Mike tried to break it, saying, "Ah... Yeah."

Robyn didn't want there to be any animosity between them so she pulled away from Mike and held out her hand to shake. Wani looked at her with distaste before crossing her arms and glaring. It had happened at work before, but it was a first for her personal life. Robyn took a deep breath and plastered on a smile, determined to be the bigger person. "It's nice to meet you, Wani."

"Why now, Mike? Why do this when the kids have just arrived home and they need to transition back to your house? You couldn't have waited?" Wani whisper shouted.

"No, Wani, I couldn't. The kids know Robyn. They love her. We've been friends for months, and now that we're dating, I wanted to pay you the courtesy of introducing you rather than hearing it from the kids. That would have been worse, don't you think?" Mike asked, his tone defiant.

"How about you two discuss this alone?" Robyn cut in urgently as Lexi and Jax came bounding towards their dad, babbling at a million miles a minute about what they'd done over the last few days and asking what was to eat. While Mike was caught up in their whirlwind, Robyn stepped over to Wani. "I'm sorry to cut in, but I didn't think you'd want to have that kind of discussion in front of the kids. I'll leave if you want to talk to him. If you need me to take the kids, I can do that too."

"You're not taking my kids anywhere," she hissed. "I don't know you."

"Fair enough." Robyn didn't need to say the kids knew her, because Jax, holding a banana in his hand, rushed over. Robyn kneeled to give him a proper cuddle. "I missed you, little man."

"Hi, Robyn," he whispered shyly, a rosy tint colouring his cheeks.

"Want to show me the dinosaur you got for your birthday again? I found a cool YouTube channel that has all these facts about dinos. Maybe we can watch it with Lexi while your mum and dad catch up."

"Hi, Robyn." Lexi rocked back on the balls of her feet, her hands in the pockets of her jean shorts. Her tee had a purple dragon on it, with silver and black flames made from sequins that wrapped around her side and over her shoulder.

"Hi, sweetheart. Want to watch that YouTube channel with us?"

Lexi shrugged, her eyes moving to her mum, then her dad. She was only seven, but then again, anyone would feel the tension between the adults in the room. Robyn stood and held out her hands to both kids. She figured the rule about no food in their bedroom could be relaxed for once and led the way there. She shut the door while Jax pulled out his iPad, and they got comfortable on the floor. Robyn launched the app and cranked the volume up, hoping that any yelling wouldn't be too loud.

After a few minutes, Lexi paused the clip, much to Jax's annoyance, and asked, "Robyn, are Mum and Dad fighting?" She sounded so unsure and worried that she couldn't help but hug the little girl to her side.

"No, sweetheart. They were just talking."

"Why didn't you want us in there then?" Robyn thought Lexi was observant, but she'd underestimated Jax's attentiveness. Like always, he asked the difficult questions. The answer stumped Robyn for a moment, until she realized the simple truth was the best answer.

"You walked in on the middle of a conversation, and you could have misunderstood what they were talking about. They weren't fighting, but you might have thought they were because you don't know the full story." She wrapped an arm around Jax's shoulders too and looked from one to the other. It was uncanny how they both looked so much like their mother but had inherited so much of their dad too. "They aren't fighting, but they do need to talk, and sometimes adults get frustrated with each other like you two do. Sometimes they yell. The most important thing to remember is that they both love you very much."

"Okay." Lexi nodded thoughtfully, and Jax shrugged, no longer interested. He pressed play again on the episode, and they watched YouTube together for what felt like hours, until a knock on the door sounded and Wani opened it.

"I have to go, kids. Can I get a cuddle before I leave?" Both kids scrambled to their feet and launched themselves at their mum. With her arms full, Wani looked over at Robyn and nodded. She gave her a small smile in acknowledgement and placed the iPad on Jax's bed before standing up too. "I'll speak to you tonight before bed, okay. I love you both."

Robyn motioned up the hallway and followed Wani out when she let go of the kids. "I'm sorry if it felt like Mike and I were springing our relationship on you. I didn't expect him to want to introduce us so quickly."

Wani crossed her arms over her chest, an impenetrable wall around her. She looked fierce, her expression going from happy and open with the kids to "don't fuck with me" with Robyn. She ran her fingers through her dark hair, and the electric blue streaks glinted in the sunlight. Tucking the strands to the side highlighted the choppy layers and high undercut. The whole look was edgy and daring. Robyn loved it, envying her ability to express herself in a way that didn't fit within a corporate box.

Wani looked at the wall where photos of the kids were framed, and her features softened once more. But then she sighed loudly, and Robyn winced. The kids could hear, and no doubt they were listening. Wani asked her, "What do you want?"

Robyn wanted to bite back and tell her she and Mike were together and Wani would just have to get used to it. She would happily have added that Wani was risking damaging her own relationship with her kids with her petulance. But she didn't say either. Robyn wanted to build bridges. Mend fences. She wanted the woman to respect her—or at least acknowledge the inevitability of her being in the kids' lives—because Robyn was in awe of her. She was a brilliant parent and such a great influence on both Lexi and Jax. If Robyn could be half the role model their mother was, she'd be ecstatic.

"I know you don't know me, but I've had the chance to spend a lot of time with Lexi and Jax over the last few months. They're incredible kids. You and Mike have done an amazing job raising them."

"And what, you're here to take over now?" Her words were sharp and full of warning. But it was more than that too. Robyn saw the hurt still simmering below the surface. The fear that made offence her defence. It took all the wind out of Robyn's sails.

"I'm not trying to do that at all. They were worried the two of you were fighting. I told them you weren't, you were just talking."

Wani leaned back, resting her head against the wall and blew out a breath. "I don't like change, especially when it affects the kids."

"I get it. I'd feel the same way if I were in your position. I hope one day we can be friends and that you and Mike don't fight. Whatever happens though, please make sure the kids know how much you both love them."

"Yeah." Wani nodded and walked away, pausing at the door before letting it click closed behind her as she left. Robyn turned and saw Mike watching their interaction. He looked frustrated, a deep crease running between his eyebrows. Robyn didn't hesitate, slipping her arms around him. He held her tight, and she breathed him in, finding comfort in his embrace.

"You okay?" Robyn whispered against his throat before turning his face to hers and kissing him slowly. Mike hummed as he pressed his lips to hers again.

"Ew, gross! You're kissing," Jax remarked, and Robyn pulled back, embarrassed at getting caught the moment they were alone. She and Mike hadn't spoken about whether they'd be telling the kids about the change in their relationship. It hadn't even crossed her mind. She'd assumed they'd keep things under wraps until they were a little more settled; Mike wouldn't just announce every date to his kids as his girlfriend, but even she acknowledged they were a little different to what either one of them had experienced before. Robyn wanted to shout about it from the rooftops, but they were still new. Who knew whether they would last in the long term. Maybe it would have been better for the kids if she'd left before they arrived. That way she and Mike wouldn't reveal themselves before they were sure and the run-in with Wani could have been avoided. Dating Mike was a minefield of these little things that were a whole lot bigger than Robyn anticipated. He didn't have baggage; that wasn't at all what she was thinking. Both his kids had to be the stars of the show. They had to be front and centre of Mike's mind, and Robyn wanted to support him in every way she could to make that happen. But Mike didn't seem to have any of her hesitation.

"Yes, Jax." Mike chuckled. "We were. That's what adults who really like each other do."

"But you never used to kiss her before." Jax scrunched his lips and nose, and Robyn couldn't help but laugh. He was trying to act all grossed out, but Jax was simply adorable. A hellion, but totally adorable too.

"I want to kiss Robyn, and she wanted to kiss me too. Jax, I need you to understand that Robyn and I are going to hold hands and hug each other, and we'll even kiss." Mike waited until Jax nodded before he continued, "But you'll always get the first kiss and cuddle from her."

Jax blushed and smiled but groaned another, "Ew!" He ran back into the bedroom before popping his head back out and adding, "You coming, Robyn? We have to finish watching NewTube."

"NewTube—that's so adorable." She shook her head and smiled before kissing Mike on his stubbled cheek. "Hey, Jax? Lexi? Want your dad to watch it with us?" Mike grinned and stepped back as the kids tore out of their bedroom and launched themselves onto the couch. With a few cushions being used in a pillow fight, the kids were soon on the floor, patting the space between them and calling her name. Mike took Jax's iPad, did something to the TV mounted on the wall, and before they knew it, the YouTube episode was playing on the flat screen. Mike had his hands in her hair, threading his fingers through the strands while they learned about the dragon-like dinosaur found in central west Queensland, the Australotitan cooperensis.

"Robyn, are you going to live here with us now?" Lexi asked as the video ended.

Robyn looked to Mike and answered with a smile, "No, honey. I am moving though. I have a cool little place near the beach that has lots of flowers in the yard. You can come and visit when I've moved in."

"Can you keep coming over, but?" Jax asked.

"I'd love to." Robyn looked at the time and nodded to the door. Mike dipped his head in understanding. It was Sunday afternoon, and the kids needed to have some semblance of routine before returning to school the next day. Mike had mentioned having paperwork to do too, and she had work of her own that she wanted to look at before her Monday meetings. "But for the moment, I need to head home. Can I come over this week and see you?"

Jax protested her leaving, while Lexi wanted to know which day.

"I'm not sure yet, honey, but we'll work it out."

"I know you're disappointed that Robyn's leaving, but she's spent half the day here, and we both have to get some work done."

A lot of grumbles and two moping kids later, Mike was rolling his eyes while they stomped off into their bedroom. Robyn staved off a broken heart seeing them walk away. She didn't want to disappoint them, but she needed to give both herself and the three of them a chance to get used to the idea that she and Mike were together. Mike should be the one to answer their questions, and they were speaking with their mum in a few hours. She didn't want to have just walked out when that happened.

Mike led her to the front door and pressed her against it, trapping her with his big body. "I feel bad," Robyn started, motioning to the kids' bedroom.

"Mmm, if I tell you I don't want you to leave either, will that change your mind?" He nudged her nose with his and kissed her. Slow and demanding, he teased her tongue with his before nipping a line down her throat to her collarbone. He sucked on the sensitive skin there, and when she moaned quietly, he pressed his fingers gently against her mouth. She shifted and sucked them in, making Mike punch his hips forward. He was as hard as iron, and she could just picture him picking her up and fucking her against the door. If the kids weren't there...

The ache in her pussy intensified, and she slipped her hand around his front, palming his cock. "Fuck," he hissed. "Want you."

"Need you."

"Da-ad," Jax shouted, and they froze, not daring to move an inch. "Can I have a packet of chips?"

Mike cleared his throat and answered, "Sure, bud. Ask your sister if she wants one—"

"I don't" came the reply from Lexi before Mike had even finished his sentence.

"I should go." Robyn pulled her hand free and brushed her lips across his, loving the rasp of his stubble against her mouth.

"When can I see you again?"

"I'll try to get here on Tuesday, but it'll be after the kids go to bed. I won't be back from the city until at least eight."

"Can't wait."

* * * * *

"So, how did the date go?" Emma asked coyly as Robyn closed the door and leaned back against it with a smile. Emma wore a smirk and a blue bikini with a lacy sarong tied around her waist, her blonde hair tied in a messy bun atop her head. Her friend looked as happy as Robyn was. No, scratch that, Robyn was giddy. So excited that she wanted to jump up and down and squeal. "Earth to Robyn?" Emma called, and she laughed.

"I'm apparently doing the walk of shame at two in the afternoon, so…"

Emma grinned and lifted one of the two glasses of wine she was carrying. "To long nights of making love." Nick followed closely in a pair of navy board shorts, with a bottle and a platter of cheese and crackers. The adorable sight of Helena wrapped around his leg like a koala while she sat on his foot had Robyn smiling even wider.

"Hear, hear," he added. "Want to join us?"

Robyn smiled and motioned to the guest bedroom. "I'm gonna have a shower, then I have some work to do."

"That's what we're doing, and Helena's eating. Feel free to bring what you need onto the deck."

Her shower was quick, the hot water soothing as she washed her hair. The delicious licks of heat shooting through her body as she soaped up her stubble-sensitive skin reminded her of Mike's roving hands and mouth. She wanted him in there with her, but logically she knew she shouldn't get carried away. They were new, but they'd clicked in bed. They hadn't faltered in making the adjustment from friends to lovers so far, and she was excited about that. Managing the kids' expectations was going to be as important as managing their own. She was glad it was out in the open with them though—there was no way they would have been able to keep it a secret. Wani, though, was going to be a challenge. The last thing she wanted was to put a wedge between Mike and the mother of his children, but Robyn couldn't bear the thought of backing off either. It was going to be a tricky tightrope to walk until they all got used to this new relationship.

She absently brushed her hair and got dressed before joining Nick and Emma at the table outdoors. They were sitting opposite each other, Helena in her high chair sucking on a stick of cheese, while her parents concentrated on whatever was on their laptops. A couple of open files sat on the table, and Nick flicked between pages before going back to typing. Emma patted the seat next to her, and Robyn slid in.

"You and Mike, huh? For what it's worth, I'm glad you've finally stopped dancing around each other."

"Me too." Robyn opened her laptop but paused before she dived into work. "I met Wani today."

Nick stopped typing mid-stroke. "Did Mike tell her you're together? How'd she react?"

"She was pissed. She didn't appreciate Mike introducing me when the kids were there."

"What's the problem? You've been friends for months," Emma said, disbelief colouring her tone.

Nick was thoughtful for a moment. "If she thought you'd only just started seeing each other and didn't have the history you do, I can understand why she'd be upset about Mike introducing you."

"That's a hell of an assumption to make though," Robyn challenged.

"It is, but she's on the receiving end of news that she probably wasn't expecting. Mike introduced you because he's serious about you, and given she'll always be in his life, I'm sure it'll be important to him that you each give the other a chance." Nick filled the empty wine glass in front of her. "Don't be offended by how she acted. She'll come around."

FOURTEEN

Mike

TWO MONTHS LATER

He knocked on the door and leaned against the railing.

"Hey, mate," Jacob called up in a friendly voice as he walked across the yard carrying a rubbish bag. Mike had met him when Robyn moved into the flat. Jake helped unload Robyn's belongings, shifting the furniture into place and re-assembling the bed with him. That was a pretty great thing to do as far as Mike was concerned—he was good people.

"G'day." Mike smiled just as the door to Robyn's apartment opened. She was dressed in an ankle-length black dress that fell loosely over her body and flowed when she stepped forward and grabbed him by the shirt, hauling him inside. Mike laughed and nudged the door closed behind him as Robyn wordlessly walked backward, taking him straight into her bedroom.

Sunlight streamed in, and when Robyn fell onto the bed, it bracketed her like a halo. Mike stopped in his tracks, his mouth going dry and his heart expanding in his chest. The sensuous smile she wore slipped a fraction. That wouldn't do. He crawled over her, straddling her legs and lowering himself down so his lips were a hair's breadth away from her cheek. "Hi, beautiful," he whispered.

She flushed and smiled slowly, her eyes lighting up in delight. "Hi yourself."

"I've missed you this week." He ran his nose up her throat and laid a line of kisses along the sensitive skin there, humming when gooseflesh broke out. He looked down to her pebbled nipples, and his cock gave an appreciative flex in his jock.

"Me too. I hated not seeing you." Robyn reached up, sliding her hands underneath his shirt and running fingertips gently over his chest and abs. He shivered, moaning quietly against her throat.

"I'm here now," he rasped. "And I don't have to be home until tomorrow afternoon. We've got a full twenty-four hours to fill in."

"No idea what we could do with all that time." She laughed, then gasped as Mike ran his thumb over her peaked nipple and let his weight press down onto her. His heavy erection fit snugly in the valley between her closed legs, and he bucked his hips forward, grinding down on her. His gym uniform—a red polo shirt and loose black shorts—

lasted ten more seconds on his body, his neon-green-and-white jock the only thing remaining when Robyn had yanked his clothes off. She was ravenous, but Mike took his time, slowly lifting her dress and kissing every inch of her body from her delicate ankles to her pretty pink lips.

When she was wearing nothing except a tiny black G-string, he lifted her legs over his shoulders and feasted. Rubbing his stubbled chin over the thin material covering her sensitive flesh made her moan. He ran his fingertips over Robyn's slick opening and hummed. He was so turned on with her responsiveness to his touch that he was almost going cross-eyed.

The first two orgasms he pulled out of her were hard and fast. The third crept up on her when he playfully trapped her hands above her head and thrust again. She'd laughed, but when it turned into a moan and she'd stiffened, Mike knew to stop playing and give her what her body demanded. He ground his material-clad cock against her clit until she cried out and shuddered, pushing Mike to the edge of sanity. The wet spot on his jock had grown, not only from Robyn's essence painting him, but from the steady flow of pre-cum leaking from his neglected dick.

Robyn was spent; completely boneless. Ignoring his own need, he rolled her to the side, wrapped her in his arms, and kissed her forehead as she recovered. But she hadn't had enough. Peeling down the front of his jock, she fisted him, and Mike's eyes rolled back in his head. Pre-cum slicked her way, and she uttered the sexiest words he'd ever heard. "Feed your dick to me, Mike. I want you to taste you."

He waited while she rolled onto her back before he straddled her shoulders, gripped the headboard, and angled his dick into her willing mouth. Heat and suction surrounded him, her tongue doing things that were probably illegal in a few countries. When she ran a finger over the seam of his sac and beyond to press against his perineum, his hips stuttered in their movement. Mike sucked in a breath as she gripped his arse cheek and kneaded the muscle there, pushing him to the edge faster than he'd ever gone with her before. "Oh, fuck," he breathed as his cock flexed and his orgasm barrelled through him, whiting out his vision and electrifying his nerve endings.

Jelly-legged, Mike fell to the side and hissed as Robyn leaned over him, licking up the drops she'd missed. She crawled up his body and lay down next to him, curling into his side. He pulled her close, and they kissed, lazily making out until both their lips were kiss swollen.

He needed to be close to her. Needed the connection. Neither of them pushed to take it further—the sexual energy between them had built to exploding point with their sexy bantering and the teasing pictures they'd shared while apart. Now, after working it out of their systems, they were reconnecting. With tender swipes of tongues and fingertips, Mike showed her just how long the week had been without her there.

Robyn held him just as tight as he did her, despite their size difference and the way she was curled into him as they lay together. The security of being in her arms was something he hadn't realized he'd needed after the week he'd had. Robyn laced their fingers together and spoke softly, her voice barely a whisper. "I'm glad you're here, and not just for the orgasms."

"Me too." Mike kissed her hair and sighed happily. "It's been a hell of a week."

"Did the trainer seriously resign without notice?"

"Yeah," Mike huffed. "I sent him a message asking him where he was, and he told me he'd started another job. He asked me to pay out his notice in annual leave. But there were two classes I was short staffed for as well as four PT sessions because of him. That was just on Tuesday, mind you. I'm now down a staff member, and I had to pick up the extra sessions he was supposed to take for Kathy while she was on leave."

"What a mess."

"Yeah." He nodded, then huffed again and shook his head in disbelief. "I'm advertising for two more trainers though, so hopefully I'll be able to spread the work more and not be as reliant on a couple of full-timers."

Robyn hummed and ran her fingers over his chest, and they talked, telling each other about the big things and the little ones. Mike let his fingers wander over the expanse of Robyn's back and arse, her soft skin captivating him. Robyn's touches turned more insistent too, and he rolled, capturing her underneath him. Mike intertwined their fingers and kissed her. She arched into his touch, wrapping her legs around him and urging him to thrust. "I want you inside me," she rasped. "Make love to me, Mike."

He closed his eyes and, for the first time in his life, prayed.

A cloud of dread rolled in like a storm front. Looming dark and threatening, Mike kicked himself for being so cowardly. Now, the lightning strikes would be sure to land with pinpoint accuracy, destroying him. Destroying what he'd built with Robyn.

Mike kissed her, needing the connection and the grounding that it gave him. He wanted to share this next step with her—she'd waited long enough for him to make the move. Too long. She shouldn't have had to. Mike should have spoken to her about this already. He'd lost his marriage over his inability to hold an erection when he was topping his partner. He didn't want to lose Robyn too.

But he was scared.

She reached under the pillow and pulled out a foil packet, and Mike coughed out a nervous laugh. "So confident."

"Wishful thinking." She pressed the condom into his palm, and he gave her a small smile, one he was sure looked as brittle as his nerves suddenly were. Like ice cracking under an immense weight, Mike was on tenterhooks, hoping that when the inevitable happened, he wouldn't end up drowning.

It happened in every relationship where he'd been the one doing the penetrating. He just couldn't make it happen. Couldn't follow it through to the end. This time though, he was desperate for the outcome to be different.

He ripped open the foil with shaking hands. Slid the rubber out. *Inhale.* He pinched the tip. Held it as steady as he could. *Exhale.* Rolled it down his shaft.

He concentrated on his breathing, drawing air into his lungs and expelling it. Numbness had set in already, a tingling that began in his chest and spread over his body to his extremities. He sucked in another breath and held it. *Please, stop. Enjoy this. Do it for her.*

Ants crawled under his skin, and he flushed hot. A sweat broke out, beading on his brow. Mike clenched his teeth, willing the anxiety attack—or whatever the hell his doctors had diagnosed his racing heart as—away. He shivered, suddenly cold.

He wanted to run. Hide. But he'd never do that to Robyn.

Even when things were at their worst with Wani, he'd never done that. Avoided and segued, absolutely. But he'd never run. And he loved Robyn more than anything he'd experienced for Wani.

Why was he like this? Broken? Screwed up? Why didn't he love it? He loved sex in every other form. Why not like this? Why did his body have to hate it? He was bisexual. He should love being with women. Making love to them. No, that wasn't right. He did love being with women in exactly the same way he loved being with men. He just... didn't like penetrative sex. That wasn't right either—he loved it when he was on the receiving end with a cock or a dildo buried inside him.

Fuck. He was a mess, and no matter how much he tried to talk himself out of it, deny that this part of him existed, he would never be able to do it.

He was doomed to fuck up another relationship. Again.

Robyn ran her hand down his chest, and he flicked his eyes to hers, not brave enough to meet her stare for any length of time. Her brow was furrowed, concern in her eyes. "You okay?" she asked. He nodded quickly, unable to speak. His voice would crack under the pressure, making him sound even weaker than he was.

Nausea rolled over him, and he swallowed hard. His chest tightened. He floated, untethered to his body. This disconnect within himself wasn't supposed to happen. He hated it. Was terrified when it happened. Would he come back to himself again? How long would it take? For the first time in his life, Mike truly wished he was somewhere else. Doing something else. The notion was ridiculous.

Sex wasn't supposed to be something he'd suffered through like some kind of punishment—he loved every other experience, so why was this his Achilles heel? The idea of burying himself in another person was like some kind of ridiculous kryptonite to him. Mike understood how the human body worked. Understood that testosterone drove his desire for sex—that was fine. The oxytocin in his system could trigger an orgasm, and he got the release of dopamine too. But when he got to penetrative sex—where he did the penetrating—something went wrong. The wiring or the chemicals stroked out, going haywire. All he had to do was think about it and fear and loathing ran rampant through his system. He'd always known what it was. Doctors and even marriage counsellors had confirmed it. It didn't make things easier to deal with.

How couldn't he enjoy it?

The moving in and out of his lover, the tight clasp of a channel wrapped around his slicked-up cock should have sent him to heaven. Instead, it made him want to rock in a foetal position, hiding away. He loved everything else, every precursor to that final act, but the part that so many men salivated over—being buried inside another person—was terrifying to him. Being with men was easier—blowjobs and hand jobs were as far as things progressed most of the time for him, but when he did hook-up with someone for long enough to get naked between the sheets, he'd only once found himself with another exclusive bottom. Most of the men he'd been with loved the idea of topping the big burly guy. But women? The fallout from the implosion of his secret in the past had been as devastating as a nuclear bomb.

He hadn't wanted to risk it with Robyn. He was at the precipice now. Just about to step off the cliff into the deep, dark void. He either confessed his damage, or he tried to overcome it.

He'd told Wani everything. Then she'd walked away. This time he was going to work through it. He had to, because if he didn't overcome it, his relationship with Robyn was going to be next into the rubbish pile. For Robyn, he'd do anything. He'd be what she needed. Or at least try.

Mike shook off the dark clouds as best he could. Concentrating on Robyn always put him in the right frame of mind. He loved touching and tasting her. His dick might be defective, but making love to her with his fingers and tongue was something he could do for hours. Mike ignored the elephant in the room and sank down onto her, kissing and licking his way to her core. He'd learned how to get around his limitations. Taking her to the edge first would get her there when he finally entered her. Even if he couldn't perform, Robyn would get her orgasm.

When her fingers tightened in his hair and her body was rigid, her toes curled and her legs shaking, he knew she was on edge. "Mike, fuck," she gasped, and he reached for his cock, pumping it. He was rigid. Hard and wanting. Having a warm, wet mouth around him would be heaven.

He gritted his teeth, hating that he was so uncomfortable in his own skin. Despising himself for being unable to enjoy this moment.

Mike lined his cock up at her entrance and slid inside the beautiful woman underneath him. Tight heat surrounded him, and Mike groaned, the sound a pained one. Her breath caught, and he paused, waiting for her to adjust.

"Don't stop," she breathed, urging him to keep going. He found her clit with his thumb and rubbed, holding himself up with his other hand and thrusting slowly. Deep, until his hips were flush with hers, he forced his mind to stay focussed on the task—in and out.

His vision tunnelled down to a pinpoint focus, and his heart beat faster. The tightness in his chest squeezed the air out of his lungs. He gasped. Tried to suck in much-needed oxygen as his world tilted. He was in freefall, spinning out of control. *No. No, no, no!*

He was going soft.

He wouldn't be able to finish. Again.

History was repeating itself, except this time it was more than a comfortable friendship on the line. It was everything. It was love.

He'd known he was falling for her, but now faced with his world collapsing in on itself, Mike understood. Blinking back tears, he looked at his lover—the woman he was in love with—and begged the universe to change him.

He looked away, but Robyn wrapped a hand around his nape and urged him closer. He knew she wanted a kiss, but he couldn't give it to her. His mind had turned sluggish, fighting against his body. Cotton wool filled his ears, and his vision was hazy. It was as if he was drowning, liquid filling his lungs and making every inhale as painful as glass in his lungs.

"Mike," she whispered. "Mike, what's wrong?" He scrunched his eyes closed and shook his head. "Talk to me. Stop," she said more forcefully.

He froze.

Opened his eyes and forced his gaze to hers. Was he hurting her? Was she hating this as much as him? Some twisted part of him hoped so, but he couldn't bear to think that he'd done something—anything—she didn't like. He gripped the condom, stopping it from slipping off his nearly flaccid cock, and withdrew from her, sitting back on his knees. He'd been naked with her countless times before, but the concern etched on her face in the furrow between her brows and the downwards tilt of her lips left Mike exposed like never before. She shifted to her knees and cupped his face.

"Mike, what's wrong? Talk to me."

He shook his head not knowing how to put the words together. He hated this. Hated himself. Hated the powerlessness and the betrayal by his body. It was a place he'd sworn he never wanted to go to again, but falling for Robyn had sealed his fate. His stomach lurched, and he clenched his jaw, breathing through his nose as he forced himself not to puke everywhere.

Robyn ran her fingers along his cheek and searched his eyes. It was as if she could see into his soul, and her concern tore at him. "Can I hug you?" she asked, her voice barely a whisper. When Mike nodded, she wrapped him up in her arms and held him tight. She was comfort and love, and Mike clung to her with desperation. "Talk to me," she begged.

"I can't," he choked out and drew back from her, stumbling off the bed, unshed tears stinging his eyes.

"Mike, wait."

"I'll get a cloth to clean you up." He speed-walked to the bathroom and shut the door behind him. Leaning against it, he slid until his bare arse hit the tiled floor and looked down at himself in disgust. His flaccid cock lay against his hip, the empty condom hanging off him. He tugged at it and the unlubricated rubber slid uncomfortably against his skin until it was off. Mike dropped it into the bin and ran his hands through his hair, gripping the ends and tugging violently.

His scalp stung, and his eyes burned. Tears he had no right crying fell, and Mike curled in on himself. His chest was tight, a vice squeezing him until every breath was a mammoth effort. He shuddered, the cold from the tiles stealing the warmth of the woman waiting for him away as he cried.

Robyn would ask him to leave soon. When she did, he would go home and try to pick up the pieces, putting himself back together, but like Humpty Dumpty, he was a broken man. Losing Ezio had been torture, but he'd only spent a week with his lover. In the months he'd known Robyn, she'd become his best friend. He talked to her every day, texting and messaging throughout the day, and they spoke every night after the kids went to sleep. How would he survive without her in his life? He cursed his traitorous dick, self-hatred filling him. It spilled over until he wanted to punch something. Shatter the tiles beneath him, the wall or the mirror. He wanted to destroy himself. Tear the reflection of the dejected man that would stare back at him off the wall and burn it.

But he didn't.

Like a man facing the executioner, he picked himself up off the floor and mechanically wiped his eyes with the backs of his hands. Mike exhaled, the sound heavy even to his own ears and leaned against the sink. His head held low; he didn't look at his reflection—he couldn't bear to. Instead, he plucked a washcloth off the shelf and ran the water, the cold liquid falling over his hands. He pressed it to his swollen eyes, the chill permeating his body. The detachment that left him operating like a zombie was dissipating now. Clearing from his head and leaving him fragile.

He wet the cloth under the running water again now that it had warmed and closed his eyes. Sucked in a breath. He walked out and found Robyn sitting on the edge of the mattress, wrapped in the sheet off the bed. "I got…"

She looked up at him, and his heart shattered. Robyn had been crying. Her eyes were red and swollen too.

"Love, what's wrong?" he asked, rushing to her and wrapping her up in his arms. His own issues forgotten, he wanted to be there for the woman he adored.

"I'm worried about you. Something's happened, and I want to try to fix it, but I don't know what's wrong. I can't make it right for you. Please talk to me."

"I'm sorry. I'm so sorry," he rasped and Robyn curled into him, holding him tighter. Guilt ate at Mike. He'd been so wrapped up in his own head, in the effort it took to hold himself together, that he'd ignored the woman who meant the world to him. "I fucked up, Robyn. I'm sorry."

"No, no, no, I'm not upset with you." She ran her fingers through his hair, soothing him. It tore at him. He was supposed to be comforting her. She was upset, and yet she was holding him. He was a failure. "I hate seeing you upset, especially like this. What happened? What do you need? I want to help."

He shook his head. "You won't like my answer."

"Let me decide that. I promise you I'll listen. Whatever it is, we can deal with it together."

"Together." Mike huffed out a bitter laugh. "Yeah, that's what Wani said too."

"I'm not Wani, Mike." Robyn cupped his face in her hands and rested their foreheads together. "We'll never work unless we can talk to each other."

"Is that what you want? For us to work?" Mike looked at her through lowered lashes, scared out of his mind. Vulnerable und unsure, his self-confidence at an all-time low, he didn't dare hope.

"Yes, I want this. I want us." Pulling back a little, she looked him, wanting him to understand just how serious she was. "That's not going to change. But please, talk to me."

"I'm scared, Robyn. I want us to work too, but Wani and I had this conversation, and it was all downhill from there. We split up because of it. I don't want that to happen to us. I don't want to change what we have."

"I can't promise this won't change us, but change is good. I want us to be happy together. You can't carry whatever this is around with you in the fear that I'll react the same way Wani did. We'll never work if that happens. Please Mike, let me share the load with you. Trust me enough to tell me."

He nodded and sucked in a breath. "It's like some kind of mental block. I've had every test and tried all the medicines, and I still can't do it."

"Do what?" she asked gently, rubbing his back.

"Enjoy having penetrative sex when I'm doing the penetrating." It took everything in him to get the words out. They were quiet. Strained.

Robyn froze. Cocked her head to the side and furrowed her brows.

The oxygen whooshed out of his lungs like he'd been sucker punched. Mike pulled away. He needed space. He needed to breathe. He was off the bed in a flash and strode over to the window, sucking in a lungful of ocean air blowing in. He stared out over the neighbour's overgrown yard, his back to the woman who held his heart in her hands. Hands braced against the windowsill, he dropped his head and willed his heart not to shatter. "You don't have to pretend this is okay with you. I'll understand if you want to walk away now."

Robyn growled behind him, her voice coming out low and steady. "I'm not going anywhere, Mike. It took me a second to understand what you meant, and honestly, I'm still not sure. But that's it. There's no judgement." She wrapped her arms around his middle and held tight, kissing his back. "If what we did… If anything we do makes you uncomfortable or you don't enjoy it, we won't do it again. It's as simple as that. I'll never ask you to do something you don't like."

Mike turned his gaze to hers slowly and with furrowed brows gazed at her. Was she serious? Did he dare hope? When Robyn smiled at him, his heart unclenched and it left a trail of tingles that radiated outward until his whole body was light and fluttery. "You'd be okay with that?"

A spark of adoration flared in her eyes, and his chest warmed. His heart thudded harder, and the butterflies in his belly went nuts. "I love you, Mike. I want to see you happy. I want both of us to be happy."

"I love you too." His eyes slipped closed, and he rested his cheek against her forehead. "I've been so bloody scared of losing you. I don't want that to happen."

Robyn ran her hand up to his nape and pulled him down to kiss her. When their lips met, he opened to her, his tongue searching hers out and teasing and tasting her. Mike wound his arms around her, and Robyn snuggled close, sheltering against him. "You have me, Mike. I'm not going anywhere." She nudged him, and he shifted until he was leaning against the wall and she was standing between his spread legs. Robyn cupped his face in her hands. "I'm not Wani."

"No. No you aren't." He wrapped his arms around her and held tight. He swallowed hard, his hands still shaking from the fear and self-loathing.

"Are you okay?" she asked, her lips against his skin. He nodded, but then sighed. "Should we get dressed? Maybe go for a walk and clear our heads?"

"Yeah. Yeah, okay."

FIFTEEN

Robyn

Seeing Mike dash into the bathroom had broken her heart. She'd wanted them to take things to the next level. To make love like they'd done countless times before when he'd made her come with his fingers and his tongue. Every time they'd joined together like that, he looked after her, treasured her. He'd shown her with every touch just how adored she was. He hadn't said the words, but she knew he loved her.

Now he needed her love and support, and she was determined to give it to him. They hadn't spoken much since they'd left her flat, the short walk to the beach passing in silence. It was a lot to get her head around, but she was genuine when she'd said that she wanted Mike happy. He deserved every moment of joy he could eke out of their relationship—as did she—especially when his marriage to Wani seemed to have been less than stellar.

Robyn didn't wish things with Wani had been different, if only for entirely selfish reasons. If Wani had been understanding, she and Mike could have still been together. All in all, she was grateful, both for Wani's decision to walk away, and for every moment she could have with Mike.

White sand squeaked under her toes and the warm breeze tossed her hair about her face. Robyn lifted the front of her dress and left the back of it to drag behind her as they walked along the base of the dune. The waves crashed against the hard-packed sand, the music they created soothing. The blue of the sky and the sparkle in the ocean was dazzlingly beautiful, but the only thing she concentrated on was the warmth of Mike's hand in hers. The intermittent squeeze he'd give her. They'd walked for a good thirty minutes before Mike motioned back in the direction they'd come, silently asking her whether she wanted to return. "Yeah, if you want to." She nodded.

She didn't expect to see Cassie waiting for her on the bottom step when they returned, but Robyn could tell at first sight that she needed a friend. "I'll go." Mike motioned to his four-by-four parked on the curb, and Robyn was torn. She knew her friend needed her, but Mike had to be her first priority, especially after the devastation that had just been wrought on his emotions.

"You sure? I don't want you to be alone if you'd prefer company."

He gave her a small smile and nodded. "Actually… I could do with some time alone to process, if that's okay."

"Yeah." She cupped his face and kissed him gently. "Of course. Whatever you need. But I'm here if you need me. I can come over later if you want, or tomorrow?"

"Tomorrow. Morning." He rested his forehead against hers and squeezed her waist affectionately. "Thank you. For listening and understanding. For everything."

"Always." Robyn smiled as he backed away and slipped out the gate before she turned to Cassie and smiled. "Is that cake for us?"

"Sure is." She pointed to Mike. "He didn't have to leave. I didn't mean to interrupt your time together."

"That's okay. Come on up."

When she opened the door and motioned for Cassie to go first, the other woman placed her package on the kitchen benchtop and heaved out a sigh, her shoulders sagging. "Hey, what's going on?" Robyn asked gently. Cassie shot her a brittle smile, and Robyn knew exactly what she needed. Her friend was a hugger. She opened her arms, inviting Cassie into her embrace, and she didn't hesitate, stepping up to Robyn and holding her tight.

"You okay, honey?" Robyn asked, and Cassie pulled back and gave her a small smile.

"Yeah. I don't want to talk about me. What's new in your world?"

Robyn tilted her head to the side and raised her brow at her landlord and friend. "I'm not a bad listener, and anything you say is between us. I'll never tell anyone, not even Mike."

"You've been dating him since you moved in, haven't you?"

"Yeah. He's pretty amazing." She paused and voiced the question concerning her. "Are you and Jacob okay?"

A shadow passed over Cassie's face, sadness radiating from her. "Yeah, just going through a rough patch—we're not fighting or anything," she rushed to add. "But we're kind of alone up here. We had a whole community of friends in Sydney, and since we moved, we've been a bit... rudderless."

"Is it homesickness? Do you miss your folks?"

She laughed, but it held no humour. "It's more our friends. My family visit all the time, and we speak often too."

"You can't go back to Sydney to visit your friends?"

"No. If we stepped back into Sydney, his dad would be ordering us to leave before we'd even collected our bags."

"You don't get along with Jacob's dad?" Cassie shook her head, and Robyn changed the subject. "Well, next time we go out you should join us. You'd get along with all our friends."

"Thank you. We'd love to tag along." Cassie smiled, but the air of sadness still lingered. "I still hate him for what he did, you know? And his mum." Cassie shook her head. Stomping over to where Robyn kept her knives, she gritted her teeth and wielded the one of the larger knives like a sword, adding with a vehemence Robyn hadn't heard from her before, "God, she's no more than a trophy by his side. She has no opinions of her own and has the emotional range of a wet fish. I hate them for what they did to him. To us. If they just understood... or not even understood, but were at least tolerant, Jake's and my life together would look very different." She angrily cut two large slices out of the cake and plated them up, huffing out a breath. She gently placed the knife down and closed her eyes for a moment, calming herself. "But let's not go there. It's a whole other story that you don't want to hear."

"I'm here if you want to talk about it."

"One day, perhaps." Robyn boiled the kettle and got out some cups, then accepted a plate of cake from Cassie. The scent of rich vanilla and passionfruit filled her senses, and Robyn breathed deep. "So, when are you seeing Mike again?" Cassie asked.

"Tomorrow morning." Robyn's heart flip-flopped in her chest, and her smile turned goofy. They hadn't been dating long, but Robyn cared deeply for him. She could see them moving forward together. Finding a little house near the beach, and the four of them living happily in it. They could get a puppy or a kitten too. Growing old with Mike was a dream that hadn't changed with the news he'd shared that afternoon. If anything, she respected him more—she would treasure the gift of his trust and the bravery he showed in coming out to her for all time.

* * * * *

Robyn slipped her high-top Chucks on and pulled the door closed behind her before she jogged down the stairs. Her motorbike gleamed white where it sat in the garage next to Jacob's dark BMW. Her matching helmet balanced on the seat. Slipping it on, Robyn did up the strap, slung her leg over the seat, and gripped the handlebars. She shook her hands out, trying to get in the zone so she could concentrate on the ride before her.

She eased out of the garage and onto the quiet residential street. Her instinct was to gun the engine, revving as she took off and tearing out of the drive onto open road where the wind would blow through her hair. But she wouldn't. There were no open roads nearby. No deserted country lanes or winding mountainous trails where she could let her hair down and nudge how far she could push her bike into its top end capacity. But even sedate riding on traffic-laden streets would be enough to turn her focus outward. The roar of her powerful Yamaha and the vibration under her centred Robyn, settling the mix of excitement and nervousness coursing through her veins.

The trip to Mike's building was far faster than she was prepared for. Pulling into the visitor park, Robyn hesitated. She didn't want to seem too anxious or overenthusiastic, like a date who calls straight after you exchange numbers. But... she couldn't wait to see him. Her man was inside the building, and he'd shared a piece of himself. Robyn needed to know that he was okay, and she had to show him that she loved him more than ever. As much as Robyn hated that he'd gone home—even though she understood his need for space to decompress—it was probably a good thing for them. Coming at their conversation with fresh heads and knowing where they stood meant that Robyn could work to undo some of the damage Wani had caused when she'd pushed Mike away. As much as she admired the woman's parenting skills, she hated the hurt she'd inflicted on Mike. She strode through the lobby, entered the lift, then double timed it along the corridor until she stood at his front door. Nervous energy swirled around her gut when Robyn knocked.

She held her breath and waited. Moments stretched on interminably, the silence ricocheting around her like the echo of a gunshot until, finally, the door swung open. Mike looked surprised to see her even though he'd just buzzed her in. His eyebrows were lifted high, and a slow smile spread over his lips as she stepped forward. "Hi," he whispered. "Come in."

She grinned and wrapped her arms around his neck before pressing her lips to his in a chaste kiss. "Hi to you too."

He pulled away, still looking at her with a mixture of awe and adoration before he motioned to the kitchen. "Can I get you a water? Tea, coffee?" Mike didn't give her a chance to respond. Instead, he walked over there and flicked the kettle on.

"Mike," Robyn said, following him into the compact area and reaching for him. She threaded their fingers together and smiled at the warmth of his big hands and the thrill that went through her. "Let's sit."

Her man nodded and blew out a breath, then followed her to the couch. He sat rigidly, his back straight and his hands clasped in his lap. She turned to face him and grasped his hands again, running her thumbs over his knuckles.

"Are you okay after yesterday?" Mike nodded, but avoided eye contact with her. Robyn forged ahead, desperate to give him the reassurance he seemed to need. She was determined that Mike understand she loved him no matter what. She wouldn't walk away from the relationship they'd been building over the last few months like Wani had. "I want to reiterate that you can tell me anything. I don't want you to ever feel like you did yesterday, so if there's something that you don't want, I need you to tell me. It's never something I'll be upset about, because if we talk, maybe we can skip to the things you like, yeah?"

Mike nodded once, and Robyn leaned forward, resting her forehead against his shoulder, and continued, "I love everything we do. Everything we have done. Every time we've been together, you share a part of yourself with me, and I love that. You're loving and gentle when you need to be. You care about everything you do, and you watch me to make sure I'm enjoying it. You know how I'm going to react before even I do. But even if the sex between us wasn't the greatest, it wouldn't matter to me, because when we get naked together it's more than just getting off. The connection we have grows, and I love feeling that with you. I want you to have the same experience every time too."

Mike pulled back and smiled shyly, looking at her through lowered lashes. His cheeks flushed pink, and he bit his lip. "You were serious yesterday, weren't you?"

She nodded vigorously. "Absolutely serious."

The relief that passed through Mike was palpable. His shoulders relaxed, and it was as if a weight had been lifted from them. His smile turned broad and he launched himself at her, laughing as he tackled her until she was lying under him. "I was nervous this morning. Even after we spoke yesterday, I was scared you were going to come here and tell me it's over. I don't want my issues to take away from what we share, Robyn—"

"Hush. I told you yesterday that I'm not Wani. I'm going to prove it to you, Mike. One day you'll look back at this conversation and smile. You'll tell me that it was the beginning of something even more incredible than what we already have."

He laughed, the chuckle vibrating through her body, and Robyn grinned, wrapping both her arms and legs around him. She planted a wet kiss on his forehead as Mike replied, "You're right—what we have is incredible. The connection between us is... I don't even know how to describe it. I've never had that with anyone else before. No one except you."

"So now you need to tell me what you do like."

"Everything else is good—great, in fact. I love all of it, except... except the using-my-dick part." Robyn smiled at his bluntness, and Mike huffed out a laugh. "It sounds ridiculous saying it, doesn't it?"

"It's like we're teenagers talking about what base we got up to." She nudged him with her shoulder. "I scored with this cute guy yesterday. He kisses like a god and uses his fingers and tongue like the devil."

"I don't kiss and tell." Mike nudged her chin with his nose and she gave him the room he needed to trail gentle kisses down her throat.

"We could do everything except sex of the use-your-dick kind," Robyn suggested.

Mike turned his gaze to hers slowly and assessed her with those dark brown eyes she could get lost in. "You sure you're okay with that?"

"Were you not listening before? Kisses like a god and uses his fingers and tongue like the devil." She smiled and ran her hand over his chest. His heart beat steadily under her palm. "I love you, Mike. I want us to be happy."

"I love you too. I may just need to be reminded a few more times. Can you be patient with me?"

"I'll remind you every day."

He touched the spot below her ear, the one that sent tingles firing through her nerve endings, and she moaned. Mike's grip on her tightened, pulling her against his body, and suddenly there were far too many clothes between them. "Take me to bed, Mike," she breathed.

He shifted to his knees, taking her with him. With hands under her arse, he lifted her as if she weighed nothing. His lips never broke from her throat as he jogged to his bedroom. Robyn laughed, the joy fit to burst out of her. He laid her gently on the bed, treating her like a delicate blossom. Something to be cherished. Robyn couldn't tear her gaze away from him. The smoulder in his eyes had her pussy clenching. She wished he'd touch her.

He used his big hands to slowly spread her legs. Robyn arched into his touch, and her breath hitched, a shiver tearing through her. She loved him, and he loved her, and that made every touch between them so much sweeter.

Mike leaned over her, holding his weight up until Robyn once again hooked a hand around his nape and her legs around his hips. She grinned and pulled him down until he was pressed against her from chest to ankle. He chuckled and rolled his hips. His hard-as-steel cock rubbed against her sensitive core and sparks lit up her vision. Robyn cried out and scrambled to get even closer to him.

She tugged at his shirt, pulling it up until the smooth expanse of his back was against her palms. Rippling muscle under warm skin. Needing to touch everywhere she could, she slid her hands under the waistband of his jeans, grasping his thick arse cheeks in her hands. Robyn followed the line of his jockstrap with her fingertips reaching for the junction between his legs and traced her finger up the crease of his arse. When she followed the cleft back down, Mike's breaths sped up and he clenched, his entire arse going tight.

"Like that?" she whispered. He nodded frantically and cried out when she slid her finger between his cheeks and tapped his hole. His dick pulsed against her, and Robyn shuddered. Knowing she was turning Mike on, that he was finally able to express his desires to her, was a hell of a thrill, and even more of a turn-on. She wanted him writhing under her. Coming apart at the seams so she could piece him back together with her love. She wanted him screaming her name as he came with a cock buried in his arse. Robyn closed her eyes and the scene unfolding in her mind's eye made her clit pulse, on the verge of coming herself.

Mike ground down on her and Robyn gasped, "Oh, God. Do that again." She pressed her finger against his hole, breaching Mike with her fingertip. He sobbed and arched into her, dragging his achingly hard cock against her clit again. Stars lit up behind her eyes, and Robyn was coming. She cried out. Rocked her hips against Mike and rode the waves of blinding ecstasy crashing over her.

"Fuck, you're gonna make me come," he ground out.

"Not until I'm inside you," she gasped. "Do you have toys? I want to watch you. I want to fucking claim you." Mike went rigid above her before he shivered, his nostrils flaring as he seemingly struggled for control. "Get naked, Mike. Show me what you like."

He rolled off her and gripped his cock through his jeans. "I'm riding the fucking edge here, love. Fuck," he uttered, his breathing ragged.

She slid over to his nightstand and opened it, rummaging around in his things. Under the pyjamas stuffed in the bottom drawer, she found it. A long, thick dildo, veiny and rigid. Robyn slapped it against her palm and grinned, wiggling her eyebrows. "This is even bigger than you. You're a bit of a size queen, aren't you?" He huffed out a laugh but still hadn't moved. That wouldn't do. "Mike. Get. Your. Pants. Off. Hands and knees. Spread your legs. Give me that hole."

He bit down on his lip and groaned as if her words pained him. But Robyn could see that it was desire driving him wild. His eyes, glazed over with lust, were hooded, and he white-knuckled his cock, staving off his orgasm. "Yeah. Yeah," he breathed. Mike's movements were jerky, his hands shaking as he tried repeatedly to flick open the zip on his jeans and kick them off when he eventually got it.

He shifted into position, and Robyn moaned. Thick legs supported him, and his back arched beautifully, presenting his arse to her. The straps on his jock framed those muscular cheeks like a freaking Monet, and the front supporting his cock and balls hung tight against his body. His muscles were straining, rippling with tension. His tee rode up, exposing his back to her too. Robyn laid her hand on his spine and petted him, soothing the shake in his body.

He reached for the jock, readying to pull it down "Leave the jockstrap on. I like that." It was electric blue—one she hadn't seen before—but it was the perfect contrast to his tanned back and creamy white arse.

Mike shifted, resting his forehead on his crossed forearms, his core muscles pulling tight and he balanced himself. His moan was muted, muffled by the mattress under him. "Need lube. Same drawer." Robyn followed his direction and pulled out the half-full bottle and hummed.

She licked the shell of his ear before whispering, "Do you use this on yourself when you're alone, Mike? When you're thinking of me?" Mike nodded slowly, his body tense. Robyn hated that he might have been unsure of her reaction. If this was the way they had sex now and in the future, she was absolutely along for the ride. Robyn eased her hand down his flank, soothing the tense muscles, and cupped his balls, rubbing her hand up and over the head of his cock, which was now protruding out the side of his jock. The precum leaking from his slit was such a damn turn-on.

"Need you," he begged as Robyn moved her hand back over his balls to his hole.

Robyn paused. She didn't have the first clue of what she was supposed to do. Mike's ring was tight. Clenched. She couldn't just shove the dildo in there, even with lube. "Show me how," she urged him.

Mike shifted, pulling a hand free and holding three fingers out straight. "Lube." Robyn did as he asked, and Mike painted his hole with it before using his middle finger to breach the ring of muscle. The moan he let loose was guttural, full of need and pent-up desire. He pumped his finger in and out, reaching to his second knuckle before pulling out and adding a second finger. Watching his hole stretch around his digits was hot as hell. Robyn kicked off her clothes, getting naked before licking a line up his hamstring. She shifted the jockstrap out of the way and jacked him, sucking on his crown as Mike worked a third finger into himself. Scissoring his fingers and curling them over, Mike gasped and shuddered. Pre-cum leaked onto her tongue. She'd heard about a guy's magic button—just like her own super-sensitive clit, Mike's prostate could send him into orbit. Robyn loved the possibility that she'd be able to send him there.

"I'm ready," he rasped, his voice sounding like his throat was coated in sandpaper. Robyn drizzled lube over the dildo and nudged his fingers out of the way. She positioned herself between his legs and reached around to grip his cock. Tapping the dildo against his still-relaxed hole and lightly gripping his cock set Mike arching into her, thrusting back and forth, trying to impale himself and grind into her fist at the same time. Robyn pressed herself as close as she could to his legs and gripped the base of the dildo near her pussy. Then she breached him. Going slowly at first, she watched as his arse swallowed the skin-coloured dildo. He cried out, his dick softening in her hold. "Gimme a sec," he gasped. Robyn froze, but after a moment, Mike pushed back, taking more of the fleshy cock into him. She slid her fist over his dick and worked the dildo deep into him, thrusting her hips forward.

Mike went rigid. "Fuck," he swore as a full body shiver rocked through him. Robyn pulled back and thrust forward again, holding the dildo against her body, repeating her move a handful of times. Mike cried out again, the sound more like a sob, and he was coming.

Thick, milky ropes of cum painted the sheet below him as he shuddered and moaned, pushing back and then thrusting into her fist. Him taking what he needed, finally showing Robyn what that was, was the most perfect thing she'd ever witnessed. Mike was beautiful, his body a work of art, but it was more than that. His honesty, his vulnerability, his willingness to trust her word not to judge him and to work through the difficulties, made Robyn fall harder.

Mike collapsed forward, Robyn guiding him down so that the dildo was still lodged deep inside him. He rolled to his side and pulled her into his arms. She went willingly, needing the connection after what they'd just shared. It had rocked her world. Absolutely and utterly changed her forever.

"I had no idea it could be like that," Robyn breathed against Mike's mouth. She ran her hand down his side and over his arse, her fingertips brushing over the dildo still protruding from his hole. He groaned and twitched in her arms and laid a kiss on her lips. Slow and sensuous, Mike explored her mouth with his tongue, his hands cupping her face. Robyn's heart filled and she whispered the words to him that were only growing stronger by the moment. "I love you."

"And I love you." Mike pulled her tighter against him, and Robyn hitched his knee over her hip. Mike's breath left him in a rush when Robyn eased the dildo out to its crown and slowly slid it back in.

"Are you too sensitive?" Mike arched into her touch, and that was all the encouragement Robyn needed. Slowly working him over, she kissed him and used both her hands to bring him to the edge again and send him over. When Mike was panting, sweaty, shaking mass of noodle–like limbs, Robyn kissed him again.

Mike tensed when the knock at the door sounded. The only people who could come straight up without being announced were his kids. That meant one thing—Wani was dropping them off. Robyn lurched upward, dislodging Mike's heavy leg from her, and rolled out of bed. Dragging her T-shirt on, she hopped from one foot to the other as she tugged her jeans up her legs. Crashing into the wall, Robyn was anything but elegant. But it didn't matter. The last thing she wanted was Wani having ammunition against them. Keeping her waiting, then answering the door with sex-mussed hair and reeking of cum would do exactly that, but the alternative was Mike answering the door still shaking from his last orgasm. She pulled her hair back and knotted it, tying it into a bun as she stumbled into the lounge room and yanked open the door. Still breathing hard, Robyn felt the colour in her cheeks rise as the kids stared at her in shock.

"Ah, Robyn, your T-shirt is inside out." Jax rolled his eyes and shook his head as if it was the most obvious thing in the world. It was tragic that it was.

"Oh goodness, I've been wearing it like this all morning." Robyn stepped aside and resisted the urge to wipe her still-sticky fingers on her jeans. "I'll just go and flip it the right way round."

"Where's Dad?" Lexi asked.

"Bathroom. He'll be out in just a minute." Robyn didn't dare look Wani in the eye. Instead, she hastened a retreat into the bedroom and closed the door quietly, the snick of the handle echoing in her mind. Robyn was flustered, com-pletely out of sorts at having been busted in the act. She should have planned better. She should have made sure they were at least dressed when the kids came back. What sort of example was she setting for them when she couldn't even put her clothes on right?

Robyn washed her hands and looked at herself in the mirror. Apart from the disastrous last five minutes, the morning had been near perfection. Mike wrapped his arms around her waist and dropped a kiss on her neck.

"The kids were wondering where you were."

"It's okay for them to wait a minute or two." Mike tugged her hair out of the bun and ran his fingers through it, tousling her long locks. Then he lifted the hem of her tee over her head and turned it the right way round before kissing a line up her neck. Breathing against her skin, he whispered, "I didn't get to say thank you for understanding what I needed and for not pushing me to change." Their eyes met in the mirror, and the vulnerability in them wrecked Robyn. "I've seen doctors, marriage counsellors, and sex therapists all to make someone else happy. The Viagra worked, but it left a gaping crevice in me that would swallow me whole every time I went there. You looked after me. You didn't judge, you didn't laugh, and you weren't horrified."

"Mike," Robyn cried softly. She turned in his arms and held him close while he buried his face in the crook of her shoulder and breathed her in. "I really want to do violent things to her." She ran her fingers through Mike's short hair and kissed his temple. "If something is within my power, I will always give it to you. Whether that's my love, acceptance, or encouragement, you'll always have it."

"I love you too." Mike kissed her slowly, then pulled back and ran his fingertips over her collarbone. "We should get out there." Robyn nodded and followed him out once she was properly dressed. Wani hadn't moved from the front door, glaring at them as Mike walked over to greet her.

"The house stinks of sex. At least make sure it's fit for the kids when I bring them back." She spun on her heel and walked straight out, slamming the door as she went. Mike sighed and shook his head, while Robyn opened up the sliding doors to the balcony. Instantly, the warm sea breeze blew through the apartment.

"Have you eaten, kids?" Mike didn't wait for their answer. "I was thinking of a barbecue down the beach."

"Yes!" The kids thundered into the room like elephants, jumping and squealing.

"Go on then, get yourselves ready." Mike wrapped his arm around Robyn's waist and slid his fingers into her hair, tugging Robyn closer to him. He kissed her slowly, pulling back only to whisper against her lips, "I hope that was okay."

"Always."

Sixteen

Mike

Robyn stayed that night. Lying naked in each other's arms with the truth no longer hidden, the secret he'd borne for so long no longer weighed him down. Mike was floating. But it soon turned to shock.

"What would you say to me getting a strap-on?" Robyn kissed his pec, sliding her hand around his waist and snuggling back into his shoulder as if she hadn't dropped a bombshell on him. One that rocked his world and excited him beyond any reasonable measure. Mike choked out a cough and looked down at her, tilting Robyn's chin up until they were gazing at each other in the moonlight filtering in from the open blinds in his bedroom.

"Are you serious? I mean… I'd love that, but I don't want you to feel uncomfortable. It's not a role that is typical for a relationship like ours. A hetero one, I mean."

"The fact that you're a man and I'm a woman in this relationship doesn't change who you are. It doesn't change your sexuality, or your needs, and I promised you if I could give it to you, I would. That includes giving it to you." Robyn sniggered, biting down on her lip to unsuccessfully stifle her giggle, and Mike couldn't help the bark of laughter that erupted from deep inside his chest. He never imagined in a million years having this kind of conversation with his female lover. But he never in a million years imagined he'd find the love of such an amazing woman either. He kissed her, rolling on top of her until his forearms bracketed her face and he could show her just how much he adored her.

"Yeah, yeah I'd like that." Mike's voice was rough with emotion and a healthy dose of desire, but even though in his mind's eye he was picturing exactly what he would love to have happen, this moment was more than sex. "Maybe one with a vibrator or a dildo that could fit inside you. You need to enjoy this as much as I do."

"I will, especially if we get one with a vibrator." Mike nodded and rolled back off pulling Robyn into his arms again. When he closed his eyes, he couldn't help the smile that lit up his face. He was blessed. Two beautiful kids and the love of his life in his arms. He wanted this forever.

* * * * *

A week after he'd come clean to Robyn, Mike was still on a high, despite having had no sleep and very little to eat since the morning before. Jax was vomiting, and Lexi had the same headache Jax suffered with for a couple of days before getting sick. Having both kids down for the count was the last thing he needed when he had staff out on leave, new clients, and classes running solid. Thank God for Wani—she'd saved his arse, going straight over there when he'd called for help.

A few hours into his day, and Mike was in the thick of it, finishing the cooldown with a spinning class and about to move on to an appointment with a new client. Through the glass wall, he saw his manager hold up a protein bar and a fresh bottle of water for him. Mike could have kissed her. He'd been flagging in the second half of the spin class but was determined to push through—the advanced students were all fitness fanatics, and he'd never live it down if he didn't finish as strongly as them.

The end of the class couldn't come soon enough.

The music wound down, and he gingerly lifted himself off the bike and fist bumped a few patrons on his way to the door. They'd outdone him, but he was still upright, and Mike was counting it as a win. Shaking out his legs, he plucked the bar out of Meiko's hand and demolished it before she could even say, "There you go." She handed over the iPad with his next client's completed questionnaire open as he chugged the water.

"Anything I need to know in advance?"

"No, no injuries or medical conditions. He's a doctor at the University Hospital. He wants to get rid of the dad bod before it gets worse."

Mike smiled, feeling for the man. They had a lot of clients like that—professionals who worked long hours and struggled to maintain a healthy level of exercise. "Not a problem. I'll go through all this with him, then run a session."

"You've got a break after him. I'll order you some lunch so you can eat before your next class. What do you feel like?"

Mike shrugged. "Chicken and salad from the usual place would be great. Thank you."

He walked out into the patio area, a shaded patch just off the sand where they had a few tables and chairs set up. A window opened into the reception area so that people could buy a bottle of water or a snack and rest for a moment after their workout. They were sheltered from the full force of the gale that often blew in off the sea, but enough of a breeze existed to always keep the area cool. Mike met all his new clients there. It was away from the clanking machinery and free weights, and the music pumping through the speaker system was quieter, so they could talk without shouting. Gym-shy clients tended not to be as intimidated to talk honestly about what they wanted to achieve too, no mean feat in an environment where people went to be seen. Every oiled-up, overly tanned muscle man and every Insta fitness model and their dog made an appearance at the gym.

Mike stepped onto the Astroturf and eyed the man waiting with his back to him. His midnight-black hair was streaked with flecks of grey, and his olive skin contrasted against the light grey tee and charcoal shorts he wore. Clean sneakers completed his outfit, and a new gym bag lay by his feet. At least he was kitted out, if not experienced in a gym.

He scrolled back up to the top of the completed questionnaire and stopped short, nearly tripping over his own feet.

No. Surely not.

Title: Dr

First name: Ezio

Family Name: Dimitriades

Mike's heart stuttered. His breath caught. His vision spun, and his gut swooped like a bird riding the currents. It was him. After all this time, and yet, after no time at all, he was there.

Ezio, the man he'd fallen hopelessly in love with, who he'd pined over for months, was right there. Back in his life.

* * * * *

Mike's mind whirred like particles being fired in the Large Hadron Collider. His thoughts circled, round and round on an endless loop while he waited for Robyn to get there. He'd called her, and she'd known something was up the moment she answered. He was exhausted; his thoughts completely frazzled and his emotions numb after being overloaded. At least the kids were fast asleep. Wani had looked after them at his place, cleaning their sheets and filling their bellies with clear chicken soup while he was at work.

Robyn buzzed, and Mike waited, the door propped open on his hip. Seeing her step out of the lift was everything he needed in that moment. She was like a warm summer's day breezing in and shaking some life into him. The smile Robyn shot him was sad as she took his face in her hands and kissed him gently. He held her close, burying his face in the crook of her neck, and breathed her in. Took solace from her touch.

"Hi," she whispered when he pulled back. Mike smiled, warmth flushing across his face, and he looked down, mumbling his reply. Robyn chuckled and added, "You look exhausted. Let me help." She led him to the couch and sat him down, grasping both his hands. "Tell me what needs to be done."

"The kids are asleep. Jax finally stopped vomiting late this afternoon, and Lexi has had some painkillers. I'm hoping she doesn't catch the vomiting part of this bug, but I'm pretty sure the headache is how it starts. They both usually get sick, with the shared bedroom." Mike rubbed his eyes and sighed. "I'm tired."

"Why don't you go to bed? I can stay up and listen out for the kids in case they need someone." Robyn laid a hand on his leg and squeezed, encouraging him to listen.

"I haven't eaten anything yet. I should probably eat."

"Stay there. I'll whip up something for you." Mike was only going to rest his eyes for a moment, close them just for a second before joining Robyn in the kitchen and cooking with her. He loved those domestic moments, the quiet times where they did the little things together—cooking, washing and drying the dishes, setting the table and eating with just the sound of the ocean in the background and the lights dimmed down. But before he knew it, he was being gently shaken awake, and a delicious aroma permeated the air. "Here, have some dinner, then off to bed with you."

Mike gratefully accepted the bowl of stir-fry and rice and shovelled down the first few chopsticks full. "This is good, thank you," he said around bites. Their conversation waxed and waned, Robyn filling him in on her day and asking Mike about his. He stalled, not knowing how to break the news to her. How did he tell her that he'd seen Ezio? How did he tell her what happened in the first few moments after they laid eyes on each other again? And the two hours after that?

Bowls empty, he took Robyn's and placed it on the coffee table next to his, resting back against the couch and sighing happily. For a moment he forgot what had been on his mind, but it all came crashing back when Robyn squeezed his knee and said, "Before you go to bed, I have something for you."

Robyn opened her bag and pulled out a box wrapped in brown paper with a love heart scrawled on it. "This came today." She handed it to Mike with a smile, and he slipped his finger under the fold. He hesitated. His hands were shaking, and his heart beat faster. Sweat broke out on his brow, and Mike took a steadying breath. He couldn't explain why he was so damn nervous except that it was a gift Robyn had bought him when he was about to deliver news that would break her heart. He swallowed hard, and Robyn laughed, playfully shoving him. "Open it. It won't bite."

Mike nodded, and with clammy hands, he tore the paper. He slid the box out and held his breath. When he saw the image on the front, his gaze snapped up to Robyn's. The wicked grin on her face made an anvil settle in his stomach, weighing him down. The gift was a purple strap-on dildo with a smooth bulbous head and ribbed pad where it would rub Robyn in all the right places. The straps were designed to fit around her waist and legs, and it came with a small remote. The vibrations that rolled through the toy would stimulate both of them. Mike was holding his dream sex toy in his hands. The strap-on was the first one he'd seen in real life. He'd never actually ventured into an adult store to shop for himself, despite having his size-queen dildo. Before Robyn, he'd never had a partner who'd even consider wearing one, but his beautiful girlfriend was one of a kind. She'd just given him the ultimate gift, and it wasn't the strap-on, despite how much he would enjoy it. Her unconditional acceptance and embracing what he'd always considered a defect meant the world to him.

And now he was going to hurt her. Guilt and shame assailed him. He wanted this, he really did, but everything had changed now too.

"I'm not suggesting tonight, but next time..." Robyn furrowed her brow and took the box off him, placing it on the coffee table. "Mike, talk to me. What's going on?"

He pointed to the box before wiping his sweaty palms on his shorts. "I don't know what to say. It's everything. You accepted me when no one else has, and you were so keen to change things up to make me comfortable. I have no idea how to react." Robyn grasped his hand and squeezed it.

"It's just sex, Mike. There's no point doing it if we're not both enjoying it." Her voice was gentle, giving him the option of just agreeing with her and letting it go. She wasn't dismissing him. Instead, she was letting him get his hang-ups off his chest without making a big deal of it, and Mike adored her for giving him even more.

"My whole life sex has been a different kind of experience for me. In school, my mates raved about what it was like sinking into a woman. I was coming to terms with my attraction to both men and women, and it threw me for a loop. But because I was bi and not gay, it was also easier to hide." He shook his head and huffed out a laugh that held no humour. "Then when others were talking up how amazing their sex life was, all I could think about was how I couldn't even keep it up during penetrative sex. I was so terrified of girls finding out I'd gone soft inside them that I basically turned celibate." Mike rested his elbows on his spread knees and hung his head in shame. "I got to my training college, and there was this cute guy. He was out and proud and took me under his wing. He showed me the ropes. It was the first time sex clicked for me; the first time I understood what everyone was raving about."

"Were you together for very long?"

Mike shook his head with a fond smile. "Nah, we were just casual. Neither of us wanted a relationship. When I met Wani, I thought everything would be sweet. She fell pregnant the first time we'd actually had penetrative sex. We were young and stupid, not careful, and even though I never came inside her, it was enough. I don't think Wani ever really understood what I was going through until it got really bad between us. We fell apart because I couldn't perform."

"It wasn't your fault, Mike. There are two people in every relationship, and each one has a responsibility to the other. Wani failed you just as much as she feels like you failed her."

"I don't regret it. I mean, it was a rough time on both of us, but I don't regret getting a divorce, because it led me to you. This," Mike picked up the box and held in both hands like the precious gift it was, "this is something I never dreamed of. You accept me in a way that no one else has ever before. You understand me. You love me unconditionally. And I feel exactly the same way about you."

"I do love you. It's stupid how much, actually. But I'm no saint; this is just as much for me as it is for you. What we've done over the last few weeks has been hottest sex I've ever had. Being able to reduce you to a whimpering, cum-splattered mess is hella hot. The idea of getting an orgasm out of it myself as well was too tempting."

He took a breath. It was now or never. He needed to tell her what had happened. "Robyn, ah…" He hesitated. "Something's happened that you need to know about. I don't want to change things, but I think it already has." He placed the box down gently and turned to her, taking each of her hands in his. He threaded their fingers together, his own shaking and clammy, and squeezed her hands, hoping that it wouldn't be the last time he got to do so.

"What is it, Mike? You're scaring me."

"I saw Ezio today. He lives here, on the Coast. He signed up to the gym. Came in for a personal training session." Once the words started, they wouldn't stop. He was rambling, his drivel filling in the dead air between them. He didn't know whether he was excited or filled with dread. The thought of Ezio being back made him dizzy with happiness, but then he thought of Robyn and his heart broke.

The colour drained from Robyn's face. Her complexion turned ashen when his words sank in. "Ezio's here? On the Gold Coast? You saw him?" Her voice trembled, increasing in pitch with every rapid-fire question she asked. Her eyes filled with tears, the emotion she was unable to suppress fighting its way out from her.

He nodded, his face solemn.

"No," she whispered, shaking her head.

Part Three

Present day...

SEVENTEEN

Ezio

The paunch of his belly was getting worse, and his arse looked saggy. He had a dad bod, and he didn't even have kids. Hell, he was single too. How had he ended up so out of shape? It wasn't a hard question to answer—taking every available shift at the hospital and not eating right was it in a nutshell. Life off the ship had been an adjustment, one that he was only just working out how to manage. It had taken a while for the sea legs to disappear, and even longer for him to come to terms that his career had taken a hit. Captain Preston—Will—had done him a solid and asked for his resignation rather than terminating his employment on the spot. It meant that head office was none the wiser about his relationship with Mike, but it also meant it didn't feel right to ask Will, or anyone else from the cruise company, for a reference. Job hunting was made so much harder when his longest employer wasn't supporting his application.

He didn't regret his actions with Mike or even telling the captain about it—not for a moment—but he did wish there was a different outcome. If he could turn back time, he never would have told Mike to wait, then dashed off. He would have exchanged numbers with him there and then. Ezio had access to Mike's contact details from the ship's records, but it also hadn't felt right snooping for it. It was an invasion of privacy, one he couldn't make himself commit on top of his other indiscretions.

But after a tumultuous year, he was turning over a new leaf. Renting an apartment in the heart of Surfers Paradise was step one. Finally getting unpacked with some semblance of order was step two. Starting to look after himself again was step three. The high-rise tower he lived in had a gym, but Ezio hadn't been there a single time in the months he'd lived in the area. He just didn't have the self-discipline to use it regularly enough to make a difference. So, he'd signed up with the gym nearby and was meeting with a personal trainer. It was time to start feeling better about himself. He wasn't interested in getting back on the dating horse, but he was at least going to get back into shape.

Ezio's knee bounced as he waited for the trainer he was supposed to meet. All he knew was that it was a man. At least their meeting was happening outside the gym. He was so out of place there it wasn't funny, so not having to speak louder than the music within hearing range of people with perfect bodies was a relief.

"Oh, fuck," a man gasped behind him. Ezio blinked, not expecting the outburst. He sat up straighter when a set of muscular legs in tight black knee-length bike shorts stepped up. Unable to help his wandering eye, Ezio slowly raked his gaze up the man's body. The red polo shirt he wore clung to every hard plane. He bit back the groan at the specimen of perfection before him who sent every one of Ezio's desires into overdrive. Trailing his eyes up slowly, he savoured the sights. But when Ezio saw the man's name tag, an unreasonable hope crashed into him. It happened every time he saw the name. Ezio didn't even know what part of the country Mike lived in, but he couldn't help it.

His eyes snapped up. His breath caught. His heart somersaulted in his chest. The same fiery passion he'd remembered mixed with a healthy punch of adrenaline surged through his veins.

"Mike?" Ezio stood on unsteady legs and stared, open mouthed, at the man before him. He was a sight for sore eyes. Gorgeous. Even better looking than he remembered him. Instinctively, Ezio reached for him. Was he hallucinating? Was Mike really there? The wall of muscle launching himself into Ezio's arms said yes. He hugged the man he'd dreamed of for months, never wanting to let go. The man who'd consumed his thoughts and unknowingly carried a piece of Ezio around with him was in his arms again.

A sense of calm and peace washed over Ezio as he held Mike close. Contentment and love and pure joy rocked through him until Ezio laughed. But he didn't let go. He couldn't. He needed to be close. Needed to reconnect with the man he'd missed with every fibre of his being. Right here, this was where he was supposed to be. Holding his lover as tight as he could.

For long moments, neither of them moved. Ezio simply breathed Mike in. Ocean and salt and love and desire—all the scents he had missed immeasurably. He mapped Mike's thick muscles under his fingertips and sighed happily.

Mike pulled back, stepping away from him. The same rush of longing and depth of want hit him like an out of control freight train. Ezio fisted his hands by his sides, barely resisting the temptation to drag Mike to him again and press their lips together. He was desperate to touch and taste the man in the ways he'd dreamed of for nigh on a year. Mike trembled and took another step back, stumbling as he did. Ezio reached for him, but Mike waved him off, slowly levering himself into the vacant chair at the table.

Having him so close and yet so far was torturous. He was bereft, his body right back at Sydney Harbour as the last of the cruise ship passengers disembarked and Ezio had cried. Mike slid the precariously placed iPad the rest of the way onto the table and rubbed his eyes before resting his elbows on his knees and hanging his head low. He inhaled, his chest expanding as he did, and held it interminably before slowly exhaling again.

"Mike—" Again he held up a hand to him, and this time it silenced Ezio. Mike inhaled again, holding it once more. Ezio couldn't keep his eyes off the love of his life. He was really there. In the flesh.

But something was wrong. Sweat had broken out on his brow, and Ezio could see the pulse point in his neck beating frenetically.

Was he having an anxiety attack? The same kind he'd had when his little girl had collapsed? He watched Mike tremble as he regulated his breathing like a seasoned pro. It clearly wasn't the first time something like that had happened to him—Ezio remembered seeing the same symptoms before. The sweating, the elevated heart rate, being unsteady on his legs. A pang of worry hit him, and he wished he had the right to take Mike home and care for him.

After long moments, Mike looked up. Ezio's heart shattered into a million pieces. Sweat was beaded on Mike's brow, one rivulet collecting and running down his temple. But it was his eyes that spoke to him. Glassy and bloodshot, it looked like he'd been crying. Was that what he'd just been doing? Crying? The dark circles spoke of exhaustion, and his lip was cut and bleeding. He'd bitten it. What was going on? Ezio reached for him, taking Mike's hand in his, but he remained silent. He didn't even know where to start. Actually, yes he did. "I missed you—"

"You're here—" Mike smiled, chuckling softly at their interrupting each other. He motioned for Ezio to speak.

"What are the odds?" Ezio shook his head and smiled at the man who'd stolen his heart. "I could have picked the gym up the road, not joined at all, not even moved to the Gold Coast, and we never would have seen each other again."

"Serendipitous for sure." Mike shook his head. "I can't believe you're here in front of me."

Ezio reached out and took Mike's chin in his hand, brushing his thumb gently over the tortured part of his lip. "You're bleeding."

"It's nothing." Mike threaded their fingers together and looked down at them before he squeezed his hand and let go. He smiled, but it was different than it had been before. Almost brittle. "Meiko said that you work at the hospital. No longer on the ship?"

"No, staff members aren't allowed to date passengers. I resigned after the captain saw us together." Mike paled, his eyes widening and his mouth opening on a silent gasp. "But I don't regret it for a moment. I would do it a hundred times over if it meant holding you one more time or seeing you again now."

"I…" Mike shook his head as if he were uncertain of what to say, brow furrowed, and his tongue tenderly swiping over the swollen spot on his lip. Ezio waited for Mike to figure out the words. "I never stopped missing you. Loving you. But I'm in a relationship."

Mike's words were spoken gently, almost with resignation, but they were firm, and as much as Ezio wanted to protest, to insist that he be the one Mike gave his heart to, he knew he didn't have the right. It was an acknowledgement that hurt him more than anything else that had happened over the last year. He blinked, willing away the stinging in his eyes, and nodded. "Oh. Okay."

"She knows about you," he offered like some kind of peace time trinket, but all it did was serve to rub salt in the wound. Mike's woman knew of their hook-up turned repeat. What was he supposed to do with that? Was it supposed to make him feel better?

"Yeah, well… it was a good time."

"No, don't do that." Mike reached for him, but Ezio pulled his hand back. He didn't think he could bear to have Mike touch him. "Ezio—"

He stood, the chair bouncing along the Astroturf with the force. "I'd better go."

"No." Mike was on his feet, grasping his forearms. His warm, strong hands trailed down his arms until he was linking their fingers together. Who was Ezio kidding? There was no way he would rebuff Mike's touch. "Please stay." He shook his head, and his exhale was more of a relieved huff. "I can't let you walk away again. I can't offer you the same as what I could before, but I need you in my life. I'm being selfish, I know, but please."

Ezio squeezed his hands, closed his eyes, and leaned forward, resting his forehead against Mike's. The moment they shared was quiet, reconnecting in a way that Ezio was unsure of. Would it break him? Would his heart be able to withstand being so close to Mike and yet so far away? Being here was a dream. He'd never imagined for a moment that it would ever be a reality, but fate was funny like that. "What you don't realize, Mike, is that I'll never be able to walk away from you."

"Tell me everything." So, he did. The hour-long consultation and workout to get his fitness in order turned into two hours of catching up. Ezio told him everything, from the meeting with Captain Preston, to his last few weeks on the ship with Eddie, the captain's boyfriend, and being so lost when he disembarked for the last time. If it wasn't for Will's generosity in letting him stay with him and Eddie for the first couple of months, Ezio would probably still be wandering around scratching his head. Will was the captain of the ship, yes, but he was also a friend, and Ezio had needed that friendship more than anything. It was Will who'd told Ezio just how ridiculous he was being by not using him as a referee, and it was Will who gave him a recommendation that made him the top candidate for the position in the hospital. He'd been working hard ever since, paying penance it seemed for not abiding by the rules. His days of long shifts had turned into weeks of them, then months. Then he woke up one day and realized life was passing him by. He got himself his apartment and signed up to a dating site. Ezio grinned ruefully and squeezed Mike's hand. "It was a disaster."

Mike laughed. "Yeah, can't say that I've ever done that. Never been brave enough."

"How did you and your lady meet?"

"Through my best mate. Robyn is his wife's best friend. She used to live in Perth but went through a rough patch at work and resigned. She came here on holiday to gain some perspective and never left. Now she works with Nick, my best mate. We became friends first. Both of us needed that. I'd just lost you, and she'd walked away from a job that was destroying her. There was sort of a shift between us and we... happened. She's a good woman, Ezio. She loves me for exactly who I am."

"Do you love her?" Ezio's question was quiet, and he hated the vulnerability in his voice. Hope was a bitch of a thing, but he couldn't help it. He wanted Mike to be happy with every fibre of his being, but God he wished Mike would be happy with him instead.

Mike traced his thumb over Ezio's hand, his moves gentle. Ezio's concentration was pulled to the point where they joined, the only part of them that touched. He almost missed Mike's words, but the tone in his voice and the love heart eyes he got when he spoke about his girlfriend were unmistakable. Mike was madly, truly, deeply in love. So why was he sitting here with Ezio, holding his hand like a lifeline?

"Ah, Mike? Sorry to interrupt, but your class starts in five minutes," the lady from the reception desk hesitantly said. Mike startled, and Ezio realized they'd stopped speaking and were simply grinning at each other like lunatics.

"Oh, damn. I didn't realize the time." He stood and picked up the iPad, handing it to his colleague. "Meiko, can you please sign Ezio up on the friends and family discount."

"Sure, boss. Would you like me to book another appointment where you two can actually get some training done?" she added with a twitch of a smile, but then sobered. "Or, you know, maybe give him to another trainer so you can go home to your girlfriend?"

"Meiko, I appreciate the concern, and I appreciate you looking after Robyn, but this doesn't involve you."

Her eyes narrowed. "Yes, boss." She spun on her heel and let the door slam behind her.

"I'm sorry, I have to go. But I'd really like to see you again. Meiko is probably right, we shouldn't do this. But I have no idea how to stop."

Ezio smiled sadly. He knew exactly what Mike meant. It didn't make it any easier though. He stepped closer and cupped Mike's face, pressing his lips to his forehead. He lingered there, not wanting to say goodbye, but it was unfair to Robyn for him to keep seeing Mike, knowing how strong the pull between them was.

"Bye, Mike." He didn't trust himself to say anything else and had to force his limbs interaction to be the one to walk away.

"This isn't goodbye, Ezio. I have your number. I'm going to call you."

Ezio smiled, ducked his head and exited the gym. Life certainly had a way of throwing curveballs.

EIGHTEEN

Robyn

It was the middle of the night when Robyn made it home. As if she was on autopilot, she parked her bike, closed the garage door, and stumbled to the steps that lead up to her flat. Holding herself up from the railing, she breathed through the physical pain that was lancing through her. It was so unfair. She whirled around and, with a roar, kicked the recycling bin. A cacophony of noise shattered the silence of the night. Glass cracked on the concrete, and aluminium cans skittered along creating a ruckus.

It wasn't fucking fair.

She and Mike didn't have a conventional relationship—and that wasn't because of the sex—they'd met and become friends first. But having that grounding before they go involved with each other sexually made their relationship picture perfect. She loved him with all her heart. Her entire being. She knew he loved her too, but how could she compete with a ghost? One that had come back to life. Robyn slumped down and sat on the bottom step, cradling her head in her hands and crying. Big, fat, ugly sobs tore out of her. She was unable to stop the inevitable. Mike would leave her for Ezio. If she were a better person, she'd be happy for him, but it hurt too much to think of her life without the man who had captured her heart and given her more than she could ever have dreamed of.

The creak of the stairs let Robyn know she wasn't alone. Cassie's familiar floral scent wrapped around her at the same time the other woman's arms pulled her into an embrace. "Shh, it's okay. You're not alone. Jacob and I are here."

"He's here, he's going to take him," Robyn said between her sobs. She knew what she was saying wouldn't make sense to Cassie, but Robyn didn't have the energy to explain everything. All she could focus on was being alone again. Of losing the three best things that had ever happened to her, because it wasn't only Mike she would lose, but Lexi and Jaxson too.

"Come upstairs, and I'll put on a pot of tea." Cassie helped her up, steadying her as Robyn ascended the stairs. She took her keys and opened the door before leading her inside and helping her curl up on the couch. Robyn felt like an invalid, unable to even piece together her thoughts well enough that she could function. She thought she had been through bad times before, that she'd suffered heartbreak. But that was nothing compared to this. Her tears started afresh, and Cassie was there for her. Two mugs of steaming tea were placed gently on the coffee table before Cassie took Robyn's hand in hers and brushed back Robyn's hair from her face. "Talk to me, honey. What's got you like this?"

Robyn took in a shuddering breath and let it out slowly, trying to calm herself enough that she could speak. After a time, the words came to her. "Before Mike and I got together, when we were just friends, he was getting over a breakup. One that neither he nor his partner wanted to happen." She closed her eyes and wiped the tears from her face. Heartbreak for Mike and Ezio and now herself assailed her. How did she get past the void in her chest? "They lost contact. They had no way of seeing each other again. Neither knew where the other lived, so when they ended, both thought it was completely over. It took so long for Mike and me to move past the friend zone because he was still in love. He still is. I was an idiot; I thought that by celebrating their relationship that maybe he'd be able to move on. I thought that there was enough room in his heart for the both of us, but now I'm not so sure."

"Why do you say that? What's happened that's changed everything?"

"He found him again." Robyn laid her head on the soft back of the couch and closed her eyes. "And they're still in love."

"Mike's last partner was a man?" Robyn opened her eyes and looked to Cassie, ready to tell her that he was no less a man because he'd fallen in love with another man. But Robyn didn't see judgement there at all. She saw understanding. She saw the same sadness she'd seen before in Cassie, and she knew, without a doubt, that Cassie knew what she was going through.

"Who was he? The one who broke your heart?"

Cassie huffed out a laugh, a tear falling down her cheek. "My father-in-law." This time Cassie laughed properly, but it was at Robyn's horrified expression. "It's not in the way you're thinking. Jake is bi too. We've had men in our bed before, but there was one in particular who we wanted to invite back. We had instant chemistry, but it went to shit. Jake's dad let himself into our townhouse and caught us in bed together. It might not have been so bad had I been the one in the middle, but I was only watching. Jake's dad lost his shit, and our lives imploded from there. We found ourselves on the Gold Coast a week later."

Robyn was unsure how to react. In one way, Cassie's story gave her hope that she and Mike would be able to move past the bump in the road. In another sense, it broke her heart because someone, one of the three of them, would end up hurt.

"What happened when Mike saw his ex?"

"They hugged, and they talked for two hours. He said that they held hands and Ezio kissed him on the forehead. Mike told him about me and said that he couldn't offer the same thing to Ezio that he had in the past, but he wanted a relationship of some sort with him. I trust Mike. I know he would never do anything to hurt me intentionally, but that's what scares me. They were together for a week. He's been in love with the man for nearly a year. How do I compete with that?"

"It seems to me that he's already made his decision. Don't you think? Who did he come home to? Who did he refuse a relationship with?"

"He has such a big heart, and I can't bear for him to give up the possibility of finding love with Ezio, but to do that I need to walk away." She shook her head, tears springing to her eyes afresh. "I can't do that either. I don't want to lose him, or his kids." The heaviness that sat around her heart at the thought of losing them hadn't lessened, but getting her deepest, darkest fears out in the open was a relief. When Mike had told her, all she could do was cling to him, never wanting to let him go. But Mike needed sleep more than anything else in that moment, so she reassured him everything was all right, tucked him into bed, checked on the kids, and let herself out. She wasn't proud of running, but being surrounded by Mike when all she could hear was the death knell of their relationship was too much to bear.

"I'm going to suggest something left of field here. It doesn't work for everyone, and unless you're one hundred percent okay with it in your own mind and heart, you can't go there, because it will end up in heartbreak for everyone." Robyn nodded, wanting to hear what her suggestion was. "Why don't you bring Ezio into your bed?"

Robyn's first instinct was to say no. To dismiss Cassie's suggestion as ridiculous. Whose relationships ever worked when there was a love triangle involved? Threesomes were for drunken uni nights. But Robyn knew that that was untrue. Katy, Connor, and Levi were proof that three people could love each other. Still, that was totally different to inviting him into their bed. Robyn wasn't sure she would ever be comfortable with that notion. She shook her head, and

Cassie added, "You need to do what's best for you and Mike."

"Thank you. I'm not asking you to leave, but I know how early you wake up for work. I'm okay. I'll be okay." Cassie hugged her, said her goodbye, and let the door click closed behind her. Whatever happened between her and Mike, Robyn knew she had the support of her friends. Emma, Katy, and Cassie would all be there for her.

* * * * *

Sleep had evaded her that night, and Robyn's mind was still too clouded to be able to function at work. She sent Nick a text in the middle of the night and explained that Mike's kids were sick. He replied straight away, telling her not to go in so she could be there for them. Robyn was back on her bike before dawn, standing at the locked foyer doors just as the sun was readying to crest the horizon. That moment when the sun appeared, the beginning of a new day, was something Robyn hadn't seen as much of since she'd moved into her flat. She needed the reminder of the perfect moment. Of the beginning that would turn into something beautiful, even if it was only temporary. The sun would return tomorrow. It was reassuring to know. Robyn wasn't going to give up. She would be there today, and she would be there tomorrow. She would show Mike just how much she loved him.

Then it dawned on her, the realization planting itself like a budding seed in her mind. With light and love, that seed could grow into something as magnificent as the huge Moreton Bay fig trees she'd first seen on the Gold Coast. Hell, maybe even one of the giant redwoods in California.

Robyn was loathe to hit the buzzer, so she sent Mike a text instead. The door buzzed open only a second later, and Robyn smiled at the love hearts he'd sent back.

He was waiting for her at the door when the lift opened, and when she saw him, Robyn raced into his arms. Wrapping her up tight, he held on for long moments. His arms were her safe place, somewhere she always knew she was loved. Adored. "Hi," he whispered, pulling back just far enough that he could kiss her temple. He ran his fingers through her mussed-up hair and kissed her again. Robyn wrapped her arms tighter around his waist and pressed a kiss to his naked chest.

"I missed you."

"I wasn't sure if you were coming back." Robyn slid her arms up his broad body to cup his face and kissed him slowly until he knew that she wasn't going anywhere.

"I got scared, but I want to be here. I love you, and that means never walking away."

"Never." Brushing sweet kisses over her face and throat, he tugged her inside and let the door fall closed behind them. He picked her up like she weighed nothing, and Robyn instinctively wrapped her legs around his waist and arms around his shoulders as he carried her into the bedroom. Laying her down on the bed like a delicate rose, Mike kissed her throat and flicked open the button on her shirt. "Can I make love to you, Robyn?"

"Always." He kissed her then, slow and sensuously, until her toes were curling, need pulsing through her. Mike stepped back, putting distance between them when Robyn wanted none, but after closing the door and flicking the lock, he was back there, crawling over her until she was surrounded by him. Tortuously slowly, he undressed her, pressing kisses to every part of freshly exposed skin. She moaned and begged him to touch her. His mouth and fingers sent her over the edge quickly, but it barely served to dampen the need. "Mike, please."

"What do you need?"

"I need you to ride me. I have so many positions I need to be in with you. I just need to be inside you." The rumbling moan that came from deep inside Mike's chest had Robyn biting her lip, desperate to reconnect with him. He reached for his nightstand and tugged open the drawer, pulling out the toy. He already had it out of the box and had figured out how each of the pieces fit together.

"On your knees for me, my love." She followed his direction until they were both kneeling on the bed. Gently, he fastened the waist and leg straps until the strap-on was in the perfect position. Robyn reached for it, gliding her fist over the smooth silicone. The nobbled pad rubbed against her still-sensitive clit, and a shock of sensation passed through her. Robyn's breath caught, and she did it again. Mike moaned, and Robyn opened her eyes, not even realizing that they had slipped closed. Watching him touch himself was a hell of a turn-on, and Robyn licked her lips, wanting a taste.

"On your back, Mike." He shuffled down and lay with his legs spread open so Robyn could crawl between them. Gripping his shaft, she angled it toward her lips to taste the salty pre-cum beading at the slit. Licking and nibbling her way down to his sac, she took her time with him in the same way he'd done to her only moments earlier. She loved his taste, the scent of his freshly washed skin with a hint of ocean freshness that seemed to linger on him. Robyn worked the dildo as if she was jacking herself. She watched Mike watch her through half lidded eyes, his pupils blown with desire.

"I need you inside me, Robyn." She nodded and reached for the lube. Mike squeezed some on his fingers and prepared himself while Robyn sucked him deep and slathered the dildo in a generous coating of the slick. His back arched, and his cock hardened in her mouth. He was already close. She pulled off, and Mike rolled onto his side, patting the bed behind him. "I'm gonna need to try this way first. I don't know if I'll be able to take that monster any other way."

"I'll be gentle."

"Not too gentle, I hope." Robyn huffed out a laugh as she guided herself into place, lining the silicone toy that was acting as an extension of her body up with his hole. Robyn hesitated, not wanting to hurt him as she pressed the bulbous head forward. But she need not have worried. Mike pressed back, lifting his leg closer to his chest and opening himself up until Robyn could see that his hole was stretched tight around the toy. It was only a little further before the broadest part of it would be inside him, but Robyn held still, letting him adjust to the intrusion.

She ran her hand from his knee to his chest, stroking his flank and reigniting the flames of desire in him. When his breathing slowed, Robyn inched forward, slowly pressing into him until their hips were flush. A lick of sensation rippled through her, the nubs of the toy stroking her bundle of nerves as she shifted. Mike's cry turned into a low groan when she pulled back slightly and nudged forward again. Her moves were tentative. She was a novice at best when it came to this role, but she knew where she wanted to take them.

Robyn pulled out further and this time thrust forward with more confidence. Mike hissed, and Robyn went to repeat the action when a low buzz began in the toy. Robyn choked on a gasp as tendrils of ecstasy wrapped around her, and she bucked forward again, chasing the sensation. Robyn curled her fingers around Mike's hip but couldn't get the purchase she needed. Instinctively, she moved him, lifting his knee and pressing his hip forward until he was almost completely on his front. She moved with him, rolling on top of him as he went, and held her weight up with her arms, using gravity to join them together. Her orgasm washed over her, deep and shaking. The ripples radiated outwards, consuming her as she kept moving, chasing another one. Never wanting it to end.

Mike keened and slid his hand down between his legs, jacking his shaft as Robyn pumped into him. "Faster," he begged. "Harder." Robyn hesitated. She plastered herself against him and rolled her hips, grinding more than thrusting against him. Her senses lit up again, synapses firing as another wall of ecstasy slammed into her. Fingertips shaking against his sides, Robyn ran them along his sweaty skin and kissed and licked his nape, needing to be closer. Needing to never let go. Mike shuddered and turned until their lips met in a sloppy, desperate kiss.

Robyn thrust her hips forward again, and Mike buried his face in the bedding. He stiffened, everything tensing, and Robyn drove forward again. It wasn't another orgasm that hit her, more like a renewal of the one that had barely stopped pulsing through her, but it was stronger too. She cried out, burying her face between Mike's shoulder blades as he trembled, choking out a cry and grasping for her. He clamped his hand around her leg, holding onto her like a lifeline.

Robyn whispered, "I love you. You were beautiful. You did so well, Mike. So perfectly." All nonsense, really, but all true at the same time. He was perfect and beautiful, and Robyn loved him more than anything.

Breathing hard, she slumped down on him, and the vibrations stopped. They rested, catching their breaths, and Mike eventually turned his face, reaching for her again. "I love you," he whispered, blissed out. Robyn shifted, trying to get close enough to reach his mouth, but she only had the energy to tilt her face. Mike grinned and kissed her anyway, a peck on the tip of her nose, before he added, "Think you can move enough to pull out? I'm kind of impaled on you."

Robyn huffed out an exhausted laugh and slid back, watching the point where they were joined. Fuck, it was hot as hell watching Mike's hole stretch wide as she withdrew the bulbous head of the dildo from him. Mike groaned, and Robyn paused. "Does it hurt?"

"I'm good," he gasped as Robyn hovered there. "Keep going." She pulled back, just the tip of the toy breaching him, and Mike's hold tensed around her, as if he wanted to keep her there. Robyn squeezed his meaty arse cheek, and Mike moaned. "Fuck, that feels... God, I want to do it again already."

When they were finally apart, Robyn rolled into him, pressing herself against his side. Mike rolled and grimaced. "Ew, wet patch." She laughed and snuggled into him, wrapping her arms around his waist. They lay there for long moments. Mike's breathing had evened out, and she thought he was asleep when he whispered, "Thank you for coming back. After last night, I wasn't sure if you believed that nothing more happened between us."

Robyn shifted to look at him. "I was scared. I thought I'd lose you. I'm trying to believe that I won't, because I know we're the real deal. But regardless, Mike, I trust you. If you said nothing more happened than you talking and holding hands, I know that's what happened. My question is whether you wanted more to happen."

"I..." He swallowed. "Honestly?" When she nodded and smiled gently, he frowned. "I wanted to kiss him." He talked faster, not allowing her to interrupt, as if he needed to get the words out to reassure her. "I never will though. I'm not a cheater, Robyn. I'll never do it. I missed him, but I'd never do that to you."

Robyn looked at the man before her, laying his battered heart on the line. Wani had done a number on him, rejecting Mike for a part of himself that was so uniquely him. For a part of him that if only she'd given him a chance, she could have felt how wonderful it could be. His parents' small-mindedness hadn't helped either, always accusing him of not being able to make up his mind and being responsible for his marriage disintegrating. Robyn knew how hard it was for Mike to be so open with her, to say the words he just had while fearing what they would mean. It reassured her. Solidified what she knew was the right thing for them. "You should date him."

Mike's eyes widened, shock and devastation making him recoil. He blinked, his eyes turning glassy. "What? No!"

"I didn't say we should break up. I said that you should date him." Mike's brow furrowed, and he looked at her like she'd grown two heads. She could understand why. But Cassie's suggestion had planted the seed, and the more she'd thought about it as she stared at her darkened ceiling, the more she knew it was the right thing for them. Mike needed Ezio in his life. He loved the man, and he deserved that love returned to him. From the moment Mike had told her about Ezio, she'd known that loving him didn't mean Mike loved her any less. The words she'd spoken to him at the time had never been truer, especially now. Robyn knew Mike loved her, and because of that she was secure in suggesting that he be with Ezio too. She'd be a hell of a hypocrite telling him he had to stop loving the man now. But more than that, Robyn knew that if Mike saw Ezio but was unable to love him openly, it would tear Mike apart. "You love him, and you said he was just as happy to see you. Even holding your hand the entire time tells me he's crazy about you too. You should explore where it could go. I'm not giving you up. I'm not walking away. I'm encouraging you to build what we have with him too."

"I don't... what?" He shook his head, completely flabbergasted and Robyn chuckled.

"Why do we need to stick with what society tells us when something might work better for us? I love you, you love me, so we're together. But that doesn't mean you should miss out on the love that Ezio can give you too. Why should you? I don't want to deny you that. Just look at Katy, Connor, and Levi. Their relationship is unconventional, but it works. Maybe the reason we found each other was to get us to this point."

"I can't cheat on you, Robyn. It wouldn't be right." Mike touched her cheek with his thumb, and the emotion in that simple gesture filled her heart to brimming.

"How is it cheating if I'm telling you to do it?"

"Because even though we've never said were exclusive, we always have been."

"And we still will be, with one exception. Your feelings for Ezio haven't dimmed in the entire time you were apart. I want you to have that love returned to you. I'm not some martyr who's sacrificing herself for you just to keep you. I'm doing it because I think it will make us stronger. I think that more love a person receives, the more they can give. You have the biggest heart of any person I know, and I want us to be the happiest we can be. If that means sharing the best of you so that it grows and strengthens, then how will I be missing out?"

"Are you asking for an open relationship, because if that's what you want—"

"No. I'm happy being with you. If that changes, we can talk. And I'm not suggesting an open relationship. I'm talking about you being in two committed, otherwise exclusive relationships, one with me and one with Ezio." Robyn paused for a moment, thinking through the logistics. "If we're open and honest with each other and we talk about anything bothering us, I can't see a downside. We just need to be mature about it. Communicate properly."

There was a soft knock on the door, and Lexi called, "Daddy." Robyn hurried to unclip the strap-on, and Mike reached for pyjama bottoms that he slid up his thick thighs, covering his still-lubed arse. Heading into the attached bathroom, she closed the door as Mike opened the one to the bedroom. She heard murmuring voices as she quickly cleaned the toy and stashed it in the bottom drawer before wrapping Mike's robe around her body. When she opened the door, her heart filled fit to burst. Lexi was curled on Mike's lap, and her father was stroking his little girl's hair. Her face was pale, dark circles under her eyes, tears running down her face. He was rocking her gently. He mouthed to Robyn, "Headache." Robyn went back into the bathroom and wet a cool face cloth.

"Let's get her back into bed. A dark room and quiet will help get rid of it." They did, and Robyn laid the face cloth on Lexi's forehead covering her eyes. She whispered, "Sweetheart, I'm going to get you some juice and something to help make the pain go away. Dad will sit with you, and I'll be back in a moment." And that's what she did, spending most of the day caring for the kids while Mike went to the gym for a few hours to run the classes he had scheduled.

NINETEEN

Mike

He couldn't believe he was about to do this. No, he couldn't believe that Robyn had suggested it. In what universe did that happen? He'd thought she was going to break up with him, but instead Robyn was trying to give him something he'd never dreamed possible. She'd encouraged him to spend time with Ezio again. He was still dumbstruck when Lexi had interrupted them. Then they'd gotten caught up and he'd had to dash off to work while Robyn had looked after the kids for the rest of the day. But when they had a moment to themselves, she'd cornered him, asking whether he'd thought about it. He had, non-stop. He'd also saved Ezio's number to his phone. Bless his gym records.

Mike wanted to see him again. More than anything. But he was scared too. What if he destroyed everything? What if, by being friends with him or taking it further, he hurt all of them? What if he couldn't be what either of them needed, like he couldn't be what Wani had needed? The truth was that if he lost either one of them, Mike would break.

It was why he hadn't gathered the courage to get in contact with Ezio yet. At least standing still—frozen to the spot in fear—meant he couldn't screw anything up. His two most important relationships, outside of his kids, were on the line, and Mike needed time to mentally prepare himself for whatever happened.

But when he'd admitted to Robyn he hadn't called yet, she'd smiled indulgently and squeezed his hand. "Come on, let's do it together." She led him into the bedroom and shut the door, nudged him until he sat on the bed, then perched herself on his knee. His head was spinning, and while he was terrified of what could go wrong, he was excited too. The possibilities, the hope that maybe things would go right, bloomed inside him.

"Unlock your phone." He did, and Robyn plucked it out of his fingers with a grin. She searched his contacts, brought up Ezio's number, and dialled, well before Mike was ready. Pressing the phone to his ear, Robyn kissed him on the temple before standing up. But Mike stopped her. He wrapped an arm around her waist and pulled her back down onto his lap resting his forehead against hers. If he was doing this, he wanted no secrets between them. This was a three-way discussion.

"Hello?"

"Ah, hey." He cleared his throat, self-consciousness making him nervous. Was it weird that he was speaking with a former lover in front of his girlfriend about hooking up again? Yeah, it was weird. "It's Mike. Are you free?" Nerves sizzled through him, and his gut flip-flopped in anticipation at the same time. He was still astounded that he'd actually run into Ezio. Again. How, in such a big world, had they crossed paths? Once was serendipitous, but twice seemed a lot like fate.

"Yeah." He sounded breathless, his voice quiet.

"Could we, maybe, catch up?"

Robyn snorted out a laugh. "You were as hopelessly tongue-tied with me too. I'm glad you're like this with everyone."

"Who was that?" Ezio asked, the puzzlement in his voice sounding through the line.

"Robyn. She, ah, suggested that I call you."

Robyn shook her head. "No, I told you to ask him out on a date." Mike opened his mouth to protest, then nodded in acquiescence. He was getting there. It might have taken him a few moments—or even a few calls to work up the courage to do it—but he was getting there. "Put the phone on speaker," she encouraged, a smile in her voice. Mike couldn't believe what was happening. His girlfriend was truly one-of-a-kind, and he wasn't sure whether to be terrified of her efficiency or in awe of her ability to drill straight down to the point. He didn't bother arguing, and she was clearly pleased with his easy assent. She continued speaking, "Hi, Ezio, I'm Robyn, Mike's girlfriend."

He exchanged a tentative greeting with her, and unperturbed, Robyn got right down to business. It was as if she was negotiating a contract. In some ways—if he took the emotion out of a situation like this—he supposed she was. That innate ability to solve a problem was one of the things he loved about her. She was a doer. She had an analytical mind that pulled apart a situation until she could find a way through it, and then she made the solution happen. She loved big and selflessly, demanding the best from both of them and he loved that too.

"I've known right from day one about you, and when Mike told me that you'd seen each other again, I suggested that you should explore what could be between you. We haven't broken up, and we're still exclusive, but I don't want Mike to walk away from you again. That means, if you are happy with the arrangement too, Mike would like to take you out on a date."

Ezio sounded like he was choking. "Sorry, I just took a mouthful of coffee and sprayed it all over the kitchen bench." There was a muffled cough, and he cleared his throat. "Do you mean like one date?" he asked hesitantly.

"No, no limits. If you both decide you want a long-term relationship together, where Mike is with both of us, I'm okay with that—"

"And if Mike chooses one of us?"

She paused, her confidence wavering. "Then I'll respect that. I'll always respect his decision."

"Robyn's genuine, Ezio." He huffed out an affectionate laugh. "Crazy, but genuine." He leaned up and she met him halfway, kissing him softly.

"I don't want you to have to choose," she murmured. "I want to give you the world." Mike smiled and kissed her again.

"And I want the same for you."

"Yeah, okay. So…," Ezio chipped in.

Robyn paused for a moment, thinking. "I do have one condition for all of us. There's nobody else. You've only just seen each other after a long time apart, I get that, and I don't want to force you into something more serious than either of you might want. But this is complicated enough as it is. It would make it a lot easier if we don't see anyone else."

"Mike?"

He could answer that without hesitation. Without even needing to think about it. "I don't want anyone else except the two of you. The three of us, exclusive."

"If we're talking the possibility of sex, I think all three of us should get tested," Ezio suggested, and Mike flushed, remembering his morning and what it had been like when he and Ezio were together. The sexy doctor continued, unaware of Mike's growing predicament. "That way we'll all know that none of us are risking the others. I'm on PrEP, but that doesn't cover everything, so I think it's only appropriate."

"Agreed." Robyn laughed, palming his groin, making Mike's breath hitch and a soft moan fall from his lips when her exploration dipped lower. "Honey, are you okay with this?"

"Ah, yeah?" he squeaked before clearing his throat and continuing. "I think so?" Mike palmed his hard dick and huffed out a laugh. "It all seems a bit surreal, especially negotiating sex like it's a deal."

"With a raging boner," she added.

"Robyn!" he huffed, mortification warming his cheeks.

She became serious and kissed his temple. "I don't want to take the romance out of it, but if we talk about this in advance, set the ground rules upfront for this relationship, or whatever it's called, then we'll all know where we stand. I just don't want any of us to get hurt," Robyn murmured.

Ezio responded, "I appreciate that, Robyn. I'm still trying to figure out why you're willing to share."

"Because I know how big he loves." Robyn smiled and gestured to the phone before mouthing silently to him, "Tell him how you feel." Mike nodded and hugged her close. She spoke to him, letting Ezio listen in on their conversation. "You make me crave things I never knew I wanted. I want you to experience the same thing with Ezio."

Ezio huffed out a soft laugh. "I was holding out hope that your relationship would fall apart so I could sweep in and save Mike from a broken heart, but this... this is even better." Then as if he were right there, face-to-face and speaking directly to him, Ezio added, "Mike, I'd love to go on a date with you. On multiple dates. I'd love to hold your hand and kiss you so the world can see. I never got to do that on the ship, and I really want to." He cleared his throat, and heat flushed over Mike's skin. He couldn't help the grin that spread over his lips.

"I love you," Mike whispered. He was looking at Robyn, but he'd spoken the words to Ezio too, and from the soft smile that spread across her face, lighting her eyes up, she knew exactly what he meant.

"And I love you."

* * * * *

Date night wasn't a typical Friday or Saturday night. Ezio's shifts at the hospital meant that his weekend was Tuesday and Wednesday. Robyn offered to look after the kids and had worked from home so she could be there earlier. He was so grateful for her support. She was wonderful, and he needed the reassurance, because as much as he loved the idea of being with Ezio again, he didn't want to screw up their relationship by doing so.

Nervous excitement raced through his veins and made him jump when the buzzer from the lobby sounded. Mike had planned to pick up Ezio, but his date had insisted on coming to him. At least it meant Robyn would have his SUV if she needed to run out somewhere, but it wasn't as if Mike was disappearing off planet. He'd booked a table at one of the steak restaurants walking distance from his apartment, a cosy place that he and Robyn had always enjoyed going to, so he was literally minutes away.

Mike's palms sweated as he answered the buzzer and Ezio announced himself. He invited his date up and questioned his sanity the moment he'd hung up the phone. Should he have gone downstairs instead? It was already going to be awkward, and he didn't want to make Robyn any more uncomfortable than she probably already was.

Robyn smiled and strode over to him, slipping her arm around his waist. She cupped his face with her free hand. "Hey, relax. Your date is going to be perfect, and even if it isn't, it doesn't matter. Not everything is riding on the next few hours. You have all the time in the world to make this relationship work." He leaned down and kissed her, getting lost in her lips until there was a knock at the door. Mike jumped, and Robyn laughed. She opened the door, and Mike's pulse did somersaults seeing the two loves of his life standing across the threshold from each other. Ezio was holding a single yellow rose in one hand, and he shook Robyn's hand with the other. Before Mike had shaken himself out of his stupor, they'd already introduced themselves.

"This is for you," Ezio said as he handed Robyn the rose. "I'm told that yellow means friendship, and I'd like that for the two of us."

"I'd like that too." She smiled at him, a faint blush staining her cheeks. It was one of the rare times Mike had seen her flustered, and it charmed him knowing that Ezio was the one to do it. Robyn turned to him and grinned. "He's a sweetheart. You can keep him." She breathed in the scent of the fragrant rose and, with a skip in her step, placed it in a small vase that Mike didn't even realize he owned.

"Hi," he murmured to Ezio, unsure of what the protocol of meeting your date in front of your girlfriend entailed. But Ezio didn't hesitate. He closed the distance between them and hooked his finger under Mike's chin, drawing him into a chaste kiss. It was like coming home. The rush of warmth and affection skittered through his veins, and Mike wavered closer. Their lips lingered, barely a hair's breadth apart until Mike couldn't stand the distance between them anymore. He wrapped his arms around Ezio's waist, pulling the man he'd adored from a distance for far too long against him, and brushed their lips together again. This time it was more than a sweet kiss. Ezio opened for him, and their tongues touched, gently exploring each other's mouths. Mike moaned softly, and Ezio swallowed the sound with his kiss. It was sweet and hot, and as far as second-chance kisses went, it was perfect. Ezio pulled back just enough to whisper against his lips, "Hi."

Inexplicably, Mike flushed, suddenly shy in front of him. He laughed self-consciously when Ezio continued, "You look dashing tonight." Mike looked down at himself wearing dark blue jeans, black Chucks, and a black button-down shirt and shrugged.

"Thank you?"

Ezio laughed at his question and brushed another kiss to his lips. His date was dressed much the same, except where Mike was in dark clothes, Ezio had gone for lighter ones. Faded blue jeans with a tan jacket that brought out the brown in his hazel eyes, and a white shirt that set off his olive skin beautifully.

"As much as I loved watching that, you guys should head off. The kids and I have a busy night planned."

Mike strode over to her, cupped her face, and pressed a soft kiss to her lips. "Have I told you today how much I love you?"

She laughed and nodded. "And I love you. Now go." She playfully slapped him on the arse, and Mike grinned before holding a finger up to Ezio asking him to wait for a moment. He ducked into the kids' bedroom and said goodnight, hugging both of them before he left. When he returned, Ezio held out his hand, and Mike threaded their fingers together. That one small move, the public acknowledgement he'd never had with him before, meant everything. He waved to Robyn and let the door click closed behind them, ready for this next step. Except that it was the first time they'd seen each other since speaking on the phone, and Mike was suddenly nervous. There was a healthy dose of excitement mixed in too. They waited for the lift, and Mike watched the tiny smile playing on Ezio's lips until their eyes met and their smirks turned into joyful grins. Ezio squeezed his hand, and Mike laughed, pulling the other man into his arms.

A few minutes later in the restaurant, Ezio motioned for him to slide into the booth first. Instead of sitting opposite, he slipped his jacket off, tossed it onto the bench across from them, and slid in, pressing his side against Mike's. A shiver ran through him, and Ezio reached over, wrapping an arm around his shoulder. He tugged Mike close and nuzzled his cheek. The skin was sensitive there after his shave, and Ezio's touch—the gentle kiss he brushed against his cheek—left him tingling. Mike exhaled, resting their heads together, taking in the moment.

They were in the back corner, tucked away from the other patrons and overlooking the small garden next to the restaurant. Fairy lights twinkled outside, and the shadows cast by the spotlights lighting the dense garden of tropical plants created a magical oasis. Inside, the lights were dimmed low, and the noise from the few other diners was muffled by the high-backed booth. Theirs was the only occupied table on this side of the restaurant, the other diners choosing to sit along the front windows to people watch as the springtime crowds walked by. Their drinks and menus were dropped off, and Mike bit his lip and toyed with the corner of the paper, unsure of what to order.

"Hey," Ezio murmured as he leaned in. "What's going through that mind of yours?"

"Oh, um… Trying to figure out what to order." Mike flushed and turned away, his cheeks heating. He didn't want this date to just be a prelude to them getting into bed together, but it was all Mike had been able to think about since Robyn raised it with them. He was conflicted too though. Robyn knew they were together, and she'd given him her blessing to be physical with Ezio, but he was scared that things between them would change once it happened. If it happened.

"Mike, look at me." Ezio waited silently until Mike turned and their gazes met. "Are you nervous?" His lips twitched in a small teasing smile, and Mike elbowed him playfully. "It's just food."

"It's also something that I can completely overthink. Do I opt for a salad? In case, you know… Or should I just order the steak? I don't even know what you like to eat. It just occurred to me that you could be vegetarian, and I brought you to a steak restaurant."

Ezio's laugh was a soft chuckle, full of warmth and a little sadness too. "Not a vegetarian, although I do like my root vegetables. I really like my meat too." The smoulder in his eyes and the way Ezio's tongue darted out and licked his lip so purposefully took Mike's breath away. His body pulsed like a live wire, his cock twitching as desire ran rampant through him. "As for the rest, we can take things as slow or fast as we like. This time there's no use-by date on our relationship, and believe me, I'm going to take full advantage of that. I want to be here for the long-term, Mike. So, if you want steak, get it. But if you want salad, I won't object." Mike's breath left him in a rush. He didn't realize he'd been holding it while Ezio was talking. Anticipation danced along his veins, but he needed to be upfront with his doubts too.

"I'm scared, Ez, of what this might mean for Robyn and me, as well as for us. We're putting ourselves under so much pressure to make this work."

"So we wait. Like I said, we don't have an expiry date. I'm not going anywhere unless you want me to."

"In that case, I'm getting steak and salad." Mike smirked at Ezio's groan and his unsubtle readjustment of his jeans. When their eyes met, Mike couldn't help but eliminate the distance between them. He kissed his sexy doctor. Their tongues explored, caressing and tangling together before they broke apart long minutes later, gasping for breath.

Ezio motioned to the waiter and ordered two of what Mike had pointed out. When their food arrived, the air between them sparked, crackling as if it was electrified. Watching Ezio cut a piece of his steak and pass it between his lips—lips that Mike was almost desperate to have on his body—then swallow the morsel left him hard and wanting.

"You should taste this," Ezio rasped, clearly as affected as Mike, before he cut a sliver of the meat. It was the same cut Mike had on his plate, and both had the perfect amount of pink in their centre, but feeding each other was hot as hell. Ezio held the fork up to him, and Mike couldn't look away from those rich hazel eyes. Mike licked his lips and reached for Ezio's hand, closing his around it. He curled his lips around the tempting piece of meat and, letting the tines slip from his mouth, he moaned as he chewed. He rested his other hand on Ezio's waist, his little finger just touching the button on his jeans. Ezio sucked in a breath, and his dick twitched hard enough that Mike couldn't help but slip his hand lower and squeeze. Ezio's rigid shaft pulsed in his hand, and he moaned. The sound made Mike's insides squirm in anticipation.

There were few words spoken between them for the last bites of their dinners. Conversation wasn't necessary, especially when they had stretched out their date until they were the last two people in the restaurant. The waiters were flipping chairs onto the cleared tables to wash the floors when Mike finally tore his gaze away from Ezio's.

"Let's get out of here," he suggested. They were on the street only a few minutes later, Ezio's arms wrapped around him from behind as they wandered in the general direction of the light rail. The footpaths were nearly clear of people, and Mike looked in the direction of his building. He should go home, but he also didn't want the evening to end.

They laughed as they stumbled around together, Mike holding Ezio's hands around his waist when the other man went to pull away. "No, you stay there," he demanded, threading their fingers together. He'd never been one for public displays of affection, but this was exhilarating. Not because it was taboo, but because this was him refusing to deny Ezio. He wanted to be out and proud. Mike lifted Ezio's knuckles to his lips and kissed them, using his other hand to tighten Ezio's arm around him. There would be no doubt about who Ezio was to him for anyone looking, and that sent a thrill of acknowledgement through Mike.

"This is me," Ezio murmured as they reached the crossing lights.

"I should…" Mike motioned back in the direction he'd come, and Ezio stepped around him, drawing him close once more. He nuzzled their noses together, and Mike sighed happily, pressing his lips against Ezio's.

His phone vibrated in his back pocket, and Mike apologised, "Sorry, I need to check it in case it's Robyn. The kids—"

"It's okay."

Mike opened the message Robyn had sent and laughed before reading it out loud to Ezio.

If you're tossing up whether to come home, don't. I want this for you. See you sometime after dawn. ILY.

"I can see why you fell for her." Ezio grinned and nipped Mike's throat playfully. "She's pretty bloody amazing." Mike's words were more of a moan as he ran his hands up Ezio's arms and tangled his fingers into the coal-coloured strands of his hair, urging him to continue. More open-mouthed kisses landed on his skin, and he tilted his head back, giving Ezio more room to move, and groaned as his lover flicked his tongue along the column of his throat.

"She is," he moaned. "So, ah..." Mike lost track of his thoughts when Ezio hummed, waiting for him to continue. "You have coffee at your place?"

"No idea," Ezio mumbled as he sucked on the sensitive patch of skin near his pulse point. With Ezio's arms wrapped tightly around his waist as he tempted and teased him with his lips, Mike's knees went weak. He moaned, quietly grinding his hips against Ezio, seeking friction. "Need you," Ezio groaned, palming Mike's arse and squeezing hard.

"Now," Mike rasped.

TWENTY

Ezio

They stumbled through the door, and Ezio kicked it closed, barely registering the snick as it clicked into place. He was ravenous. He needed Mike with a desperation bordering on insanity. He knew he should slow down but having Mike there in his arms was a dream. Fear of losing him again had him frantically trying to pull him closer. He couldn't let him slip through his fingers again.

With trembling hands, Ezio undid the buttons on Mike's shirt and walked him backwards through the apartment. Mike's knees hit the back of the bed, and his shirt fluttered to the floor. Ezio dropped to his knees and tugged off Mike's shoes and socks before running his hands up Mike's long legs to the button on his jeans. He slid the soft material down his legs without fanfare until he spied the sexy navy blue jock framed in white elastic Mike was wearing. Ezio groaned, remembering their time together on the ship and how desperate he'd been to make love to Mike while he was wearing it. This time though, Ezio didn't want a single thing between them.

Still on his knees, he kissed a path up Mike's leg and pushed him gently onto the bed. He lifted Mike's feet, tugged the jeans off, and tossed them to the side. Crawling up his body, Ezio laid open-mouthed kisses over every ripple of muscle, every valley, and every piece of smooth skin he could reach. Mike writhed underneath him, desperate for friction in the places he needed it most.

"You're wearing too many clothes," Mike growled, scolding him. When Ezio yanked at his shirt, nearly tearing the buttons off, Mike brushed his hands away. He drew him down until their lips were pressed together and slowly undid each button. It was as if he was unwrapping a present, savouring each moment.

Finally, his shirttails lay open, brushing against Mike's skin, and Mike ran his hands up Ezio's sides and over his chest. Ezio wanted to shy away. The changes in his body since they'd last been together weren't flattering. His chest was softer and his belly bigger, but Mike's appreciative hum had warmth uncurling in his chest. He wasn't disgusted. He wasn't pushing him away. Instead, Mike wrapped a hand around Ezio's nape, urging him down again. He was inviting him to rest in the valley between Mike's legs. The warmth against him, the vitality in the man Ezio was pressing into the mattress was everything. He was living a dream.

Mike reached between them and undid Ezio's jeans, using his feet to push them down his legs. Their lips met and tongues tangled, and Ezio tasted that same vitality and uniqueness that was Mike. He sipped from his lips, tracing every contour in his mouth as he relearned it after so long apart. He never wanted this moment to end, and Mike didn't seem to be in any rush either, slowing down Ezio's frantic movements even more.

Hooking his ankle over Ezio's leg, Mike flipped them so he was straddling him. He pressed down, grinding their cocks together and Ezio gasped and chased the pressure, arching up into his hold. Mike did it again before threading their fingers together and lifting Ezio's hands above his head. He loved having Mike under him and wrapped around him. The intimacy of the position as they gazed into each other's eyes while they moved was undeniable. But this? Having Mike hover over him, his lips a hair's breadth away from Ezio's, was even more so. Need rushed through him, but that frantic clawing had subsided. Now his driving force was the need to reconnect. To get closer. To make love to the man he'd fallen for last summer.

Ezio arched into him, and Mike's chuckle was more of a rush of breath against his skin than noise. With whisper-soft kisses, Mike worked his way down Ezio's throat, licking and kissing him until Ezio was dazed from the high. He nuzzled every part of his chest that he could reach, burying his face in his armpit and inhaling deeply, all without separating their bodies. It was exactly the way Ezio needed it to be. Mike was making love to him with his mouth, and the words he'd longed to say teetered on the tip of his tongue. His lover's movements were slow, his body rocking against Ezio's in a sensual glide. Their erections were trapped be-tween them, still separated by their underwear, but the sensation had Ezio in a tailspin. Ezio trembled when Mike's fluid thrusts of his hips faltered and Mike re-joined their mouths, kissing him deeply.

"Need you," Mike murmured.

Ezio needed to touch him too. Needed to show Mike just how he'd held him in his heart too. He untangled his fingers from Mike's and ran them along Mike's arms, the coarse hairs of his forearms contrasting with the smoother skin over his biceps and triceps. Thick arms with muscles so clearly defined, Ezio mapped them with his fingertips like he'd done to his medical school anatomy textbooks. Except this time, he wasn't naming the muscle and exploring their joins. He was exploring Mike, discovering what differences a year had made to his physique. The changes were there— thicker muscle, less fat. Down his sides, he followed the line of his latissimus dorsi and moved down to his waist, feeling the divots in his back just above his arse. Wrapping his hands around each meaty cheek, framed like a piece of art- work by the jock, Ezio spread his cheeks and thrust upward. "Like this?" he asked as Mike cried out, doing it again for good measure before rolling them.

Mike was once more on his back, Ezio between his legs. He gathered his man in his arms and hitched Mike's leg higher. His lover tightened his limbs around Ezio's waist, trapping him. Ezio closed his eyes, memorizing the mo- ment. The way Mike was clinging to him, keeping him close. The way their bodies aligned. Mike's scent—the heady smell of sex in the air and the freshness of the ocean. The warmth and love between them. This was no fuck fest, no mad dash to orgasm so he could kick the man out of his bed and move on. No, this was the man Ezio wanted to grow old with. The man he wanted to love and laugh with for a lifetime. He'd found him. Then he'd found him again.

Ezio kissed him and instinct kicked in. His body moved with no conscious prompting, grinding down on Mike until his eyes rolled back his head and he arched his neck, seeking more.

"Or like this?" Mike's kiss and his blunt fingernails pressing into Ezio's back were all the answer he needed. Mike moved, trailing hands down his back until he reached the waistline of the black boxer briefs Ezio wore. He tugged at them, pushing the material down Ezio's arse. Ezio shoved them down to his knees, kicking them away and exposing himself to his man.

A pang of self-doubt reared its ugly head, and Ezio pulled back a fraction, but Mike's hold tightened. "You're perfect," he whispered, awe in his voice. Their eyes met, and Ezio didn't doubt for a second the truth in his statement. There was no hesitation, no lie in the brown eyes reflecting love and warmth back at him. He moved then, pressing himself against Mike's body once more, and kissed him, communicating with his body. Trying to show Mike what he didn't think the other man was ready to hear.

One-handed, Ezio opened the drawer next to the bed and searched blindly. His fingers closed around the cool plastic of the bottle he needed, and the foil wrapper was next to it. He dropped them on the bed within reach and went back to trailing open-mouthed kisses down Mike's body, tasting his man once more. He followed the line down the centre of his abs while he gripped the jock and tugged it down. The scrap of material sailed over his shoulder when Ezio tossed it, landing in some unknown place. He didn't care. All he could focus on, everything he needed, was in front of him. The man laid bare before Ezio, his legs spread open in invitation, his hard cock lying along his hip, a drip of pre-cum at its tip, was beautiful. But it wasn't just Mike's physical beauty that Ezio had connected with. It was his heart, his mind, and his generosity of spirit. Ezio poured all his emotion into his kisses. The soft brush of lips, the trail of his tongue and the caress of his fingers until Mike was trembling beneath him, open and waiting for Ezio to join with him.

"Come inside me, Ez." Those four words were like kindling to a match. An inferno of want and need roared over him as Ezio rolled the condom on his oversensitive dick and slicked himself with lube. He gritted his teeth and held his breath as he positioned his aching cock at Mike's opening, looking to his man for any sign of hesitation or doubt. There was none. It was as if Robyn's earlier encouragement had freed Mike from his lingering worry. For giving that to his man, Ezio fell a little bit in love with Mike's girlfriend himself.

He pressed forward, his crown breaching Mike's resistance, and held there on shaking arms, waiting for Mike to adjust. Tight, wet heat surrounded the most sensitive part of his dick, and Ezio fought the urge to thrust. To push forward and claim his man like he so desperately wanted.

Mike wrapped his hand around Ezio's nape and drew him down, delving in for a soul-deep kiss. When he pressed his heels against Ezio's arse, urging him deeper, he complied, sliding in one tiny thrust at a time until he was fully seated. His hips flush against Mike's arse, Ezio shivered. He was in heaven. Slick, tight heat surrounded him. He couldn't get any closer to his man. Couldn't bury himself any deeper. His cock throbbed, blissed out and happy. Mike must have felt it too. He moaned softly and urged him to move.

But Ezio couldn't bring himself to pull back. He never wanted to move, never wanted to lose the connection by separating them. He rolled his hips, pressing deeper and burying his face in the crook of Mike's neck.

With Mike's hands in his hair and the other man's lips on his, Ezio began to move. Slowly, he savoured every push and pull of their bodies. He touched whatever part of Mike he could reach. His face, arms, chest, arse, legs, and back up again. Slow kisses and sweet caresses. Time slowed, stretching out the seconds they were together. Like a bubble had formed between them, life outside could have been moving at warp speed, but inside nothing mattered more than this tender, intimate moment between them. The tether between them solidified, shoring itself deep in their psyches. Their connection blossomed into an unshakeable bastion of strength. Ezio had known Mike was different. He'd had an inkling the moment he'd laid eyes on him. It was why he'd broken all the rules to be with him.

Riding a euphoric high, Ezio moved. His breath mingled with Mike's, their bodies so close that they were breathing the same air. He'd never experienced anything like this before. No one had ever even come close to Mike. But there was a niggle in the back of his mind, the ghost of a whisper calling him a liar. Ezio brushed it aside, concentrating on the here and now.

He thrust again, and Mike arched into him. Every pump of his hips elicited a soft moan from Mike, and each twist of his wrist over Mike's slick cock made the other man gasp. Sweat dripped down his temple as he held back the tide threatening to wash over him, and Mike licked it, a shudder passing through Ezio as he did. He was edging, on the brink. Ezio moaned, nearing the point of no return as he tried wrestling his orgasm into submission. His body was in a state of confusion, millennia of instinct screaming at him to race to the finish line, but his heart and his head were telling him to slow down further. To never let this moment end.

Mike was hard and leaking in his hand, every one of the veins on his dick pronounced. Ezio knew he was riding the edge too. It was the only thing holding him back. Ezio needed Mike to come first. He needed to watch his man come undone. Ezio doubled down, tightening his grip and flicking his wrist over the head of Mike's cock over and over. Mike cried out, going rigid underneath him. He arched his back, bucking his hips into Ezio's hold and tightening his legs around Ezio's hips as cum shot from his cock in thick white ropes. Watching his man in the throes of ecstasy was too much. It catapulted Ezio over the edge and sent him flailing into an abyss from which he wasn't sure he ever wanted to return. He emptied himself into the thin latex barrier between them. He wanted that barrier gone, for there to be nothing between them again.

Aftershocks rocked through him, and his limbs turned to jelly. Letting his weight rest fully on Mike, Ezio nuzzled his nose against Mike's sweaty throat and pressed a kiss to his pulse point, the fluttering of his heart matching the *thud thud thud* behind Ezio's rib cage.

Ezio couldn't hold back anymore and whispered, "I love you, Mike. I think I've loved you all along."

Mike tilted his chin up and pressed their lips together in the sweetest of kisses. A gentle brush, then in a deeper caress before he whispered against Ezio's lips, "I love you too."

It was hours later, when they'd cleaned up and were lying wrapped in each other's arms, the moonlight streaming in from the open blinds, that Ezio felt him shift. Mike put a sliver of distance between them, and Ezio grumbled, protesting. He grasped at the air and found Mike's pillow instead. Pulling it to him, Ezio breathed in Mike's scent—the same scent mixed with his—and sighed. The bed dipped, and Mike pressed a kiss to his temple, whispering, "I need to get home."

"Love you." Even in his sleep-addled state, Ezio was compelled to tell Mike. Now that he'd said it, now that he knew Mike felt the same, he never wanted there to be a day that Mike didn't hear it. Ezio loved Mike, and Mike loved him. The thought made him smile, and Mike's responding chuckle and soft press of his lips made his heart soar.

"And I love you."

* * * * *

Ezio looked at the text he had received from Mike that morning after he left and smiled. I'm home. Love you. The nurses and other doctors were wondering what had gotten into him. He'd been smiling his whole shift, even though he'd been called into work on his day off. He smiled even more broadly when Mike's follow-up message had shown up on his phone: *Apparently, we smell good together. Like sex and man. Robyn said she loves that you looked after me last night.*

How was this real? How had he found his way back to the love of his life? He'd found him, and his buried dreams of happiness had been instantly unearthed and dusted off. Then that same hope had crashed and burned when Mike announced he was in a relationship. And yet, he'd been surprised again. Mike's partner was perhaps the one person in the world who understood what all three of them needed. He was amazed that there was zero jealousy between them. It was inexplicable. He could read the subtext of Mike's message—he and Robyn had slept together that morning too. The thought of it turned him on rather than making him rage at the injustice. Mike being buried inside her, his dick sliding between her soft silken folds as he took them both to the edge made him want to jack off. It made him want to watch.

"Hey, you," Robyn greeted him with a smile, shaking him out of his thoughts. They were meeting outside the gym, ready to surprise Mike with a late dinner.

"Hi," he greeted her with a kiss to her cheek. He had an instant kinship with Robyn—loving the same man apparently did that. "Why aren't we jealous of each other?" he blurted, not meaning to voice the question.

Robyn grinned. "I have no idea, but it makes me happy that you love Mike too." She linked her arm in his. "I'm ecstatic that he told you, and it was even better that you said it first. Mike's ex… she's an amazing woman, incredible with their kids, but she did a number on his confidence and his self-worth. He was on cloud nine this morning when he crawled into bed."

Ezio flushed. "I have been too."

Robyn knocked into his shoulder and grinned. "Good."

"Did you say anything to Mike?" Ezio asked as they waked into the gym's reception area.

"No, he thinks I'm working late today."

"I told him my shift ended at midnight. He was heading home to clean the house. It was good timing that his ex wanted the kids tonight. What's her name?"

"Wani, yeah." Robyn linked her arm with his and they walked into the gym. "Hi, Meiko. Is Mike in his office?"

"No, he's on the floor."

Ezio smiled politely and followed Robyn through into the gym. He'd been there once since his meeting with Mike—to be introduced to his personal trainer and do a training session—but Ezio was still a fish out of water entering the main part of the gym. Robyn had no such hesitation, stopping only to search for Mike. She greeted people like they were old friends and slid onto the weight bench that Mike was leaning over when she got close enough. Ezio wrapped his arm around her shoulder and grinned when Mike yelped in surprise and spun around. His face lit up like springtime sun emerging from behind rain clouds, a smile spreading swiftly over those kissable lips.

He stepped forward and kneeled on the bench, bending to press a kiss to Robyn's lips. "What are you two doing here? I thought you were both working."

"Surprising you, obviously." Robyn laughed when Mike rolled his eyes, and she squeezed the hand Ezio held on her shoulder when Mike reached up to kiss him.

"We thought we might take you out to a late dinner," Ezio said before stealing another kiss.

Mike grinned and motioned over his shoulder with his thumb. "Sounds great. You just caught me. I was about to leave. Gimme a minute, and I'll grab my things."

Mike was walking backward, a smile firmly in place as his gaze bounced between them. Ezio saw it in slow motion. The man stepping backwards with a bar loaded up with iron plates. The twist. The edge of the bar connecting with Mike's head. His man reaching for the sore spot. Grasping his chest. Falling to his knees.

He reached out, shouting to watch out as he hurdled the weight bench and skidded to a halt on his knees. Robyn reacted in a nanosecond as well, diving onto her knees and grasping Mike to stop him from falling forwards. An "oh fuck" sounded, and the clanging of metal rang out across the gym as Ezio checked that Mike was conscious and responsive. Checked his breathing.

Noise faded into the background, but the ragged breathing of the three of them shook through him. Mike's eyes were dilated. Shock and what looked like a healthy dose of fear was painted in Mike's eyes. "It's okay. You're okay," Ezio murmured soothingly as he checked Mike's head where the metal bar had connected. The blow looked minor. It hadn't even broken the skin. A small lump had formed, but it was on the thickest part of his skull. Mike likely wouldn't even feel it in the morning.

But that wasn't what worried Ezio.

It was Mike's heart.

"Ezio," Robyn called, the panic in her voice making it wobble. A sweat had broken out across Mike's brow. His face was deathly pale. His breathing short and sharp. It was as if all he could manage were little gasps of air. The fist he held pressed against his chest was white. He quaked.

"Mike, we need to lie you down." He turned to Robyn and nodded, reassuring her without words. She gritted her teeth, blinked back tears, and nodded back. "Hold his hand. Let him know he's okay."

To the man who'd been working with the weighted bar, he instructed, "Help me get him stretched out. I need some room around him. Move anything that can impede access." There was a commotion around them, and Robyn was breathing hard, barely repressing her panic. She held Mike's hand, brushing her thumb over his knuckles over and over, murmuring nonsense to him.

Ezio pressed his fingers to the pulse point in Mike's throat and the anvil in his gut dropped.

Fear ripped through him.

Mike's pulse was racing so fast that he couldn't make out individual beats. Barely holding onto his sanity himself, the years of training kicked in, instinctively protecting him so he could protect his love.

"Robyn, call triple zero. Ask for an ambulance and then put the operator on speaker. You"—he looked to the man who'd helped him lie Mike down—"I need you to find me a defibrillator."

With shaking hands, Robyn dialled, and Ezio comforted Mike. He ran his fingers through his hair and whispered his encouragement all while taking in Mike's symptoms and changes in his body. Mike's gaze bounced between him and Robyn, wide eyed and scared. He groaned in pain and sweat pooled on his skin, running down his face in rivulets.

Something was very wrong.

Ezio was jolted out of his spiralling worry when Robyn thrust the phone in front of him. "Ambulance, where is your emergency?" Robyn rattled off the address and gave the operator Mike's name and date of birth. "What's the emergency?"

"I'm Dr Ezio Dimitriades. I need a specialist ambulance officer, trained for heart attacks—" Robyn gasped but he ignored her, trying to reassure Mike with his steady gaze. He needed to get the right treatment for Mike. "—and a bus urgently. He's in tachycardia. I can't keep up to count the beats per minute. Airways are clear, and Mike's conscious, but he's slipping. Jesus Christ," he mumbled, pressing his fingers to Mike's throat again. "He's previously been diagnosed with anxiety, and prescribed medication, but the last I heard doesn't take it because it doesn't work. This is not an anxiety attack."

Mike's terrified eyes slipped closed, and Ezio gently shook him. "Eyes open, babe. Let me see those beautiful browns."

"He doesn't take any regular medication," Robyn confirmed, squeezing Mike's hand when his eyes fluttered open. His chest heaved, and sweat poured off him, drenching his hair and shirt. If he didn't get his heart rate down, and quickly, he was going to have a heart attack. Or stroke out.

Ezio gritted his teeth and forced himself to focus. He had never been a blubbering mess in an emergency.

But he'd never had the love of his life fighting for his own.

Ezio wasn't about to begin now and lose Mike. "I've seen these symptoms in him before. It's been present for at least twelve months, possibly longer. It's an undiagnosed heart condition, I'm sure of it."

"It's been getting worse, too," Robyn added. "I've seen this before too. Not as serious, but he's had a few of them when we've been together." *Fuck. Had he been to his doctor like Ezio suggested a year ago? Did Mike know what this was?*

"How far away is the ambulance?" Ezio's voice wobbled, fear strangling him.

He pressed his fingers against the spot where Mike's vagus nerve was in his abdomen. If he could stimulate it, it would help regulate Mike's heart.

"Six minutes," the operator replied. "Dr Dimitriades, I need you to check if you have access to a defibrillator and commence vagal manoeuvres. Continue to monitor his heart rate. The ambulance is on its way."

"Already doing it, and defib is right here next to me."

"Okay, have someone fetch some cold water."

"On it," a voice in the background responded, and Ezio continued the technique, trying to slow Mike's heart down. He shifted his hand slightly and pressed down, monitoring Mike's pulse with the other.

But it made no difference.

"Any change?"

"No. Trying pressure on the carotid artery." He shifted his hands and counted, still unable to keep up. His panic rose as Mike faded a little more, growing weaker with every passing moment. "Fuck, it's not working. Where are they?"

"Try the water, Dr Dimitriades," the calm voice of the operator ordered.

A drink bottle was thrust in front of him, and Robyn grasped it. He lifted Mike's face, to allow the water to run off without any getting into his airways. "Baby, we're going to wet your face."

Robyn tipped the water and the cold of it made Mike gasp deeper, drawing more oxygen into his lungs. But it had the opposite effect to what they'd hoped. His heart rate spiked higher. "Stop," he ordered, and Robyn cut the flow immediately.

Everything was spinning out of control. It was all a blur. As every second ticked by, he watched Mike's body speed toward the point of exhaustion. His heart could only beat at this level for so long. If it kept up, there would be a fatal ending.

Mike's eyes fluttered closed again.

It was now, or never.

"Commencing defib. Everyone back. Hands completely off. Robyn, help me with this. Cut his shirt off." He passed her the scissors in the defibrillator box and she cut it away, a line straight down the middle of his chest. "Okay back. No touching from this point." Ezio checked around them. "Move that bench. Make sure it's not touching him." He made short work of the pads, peeling the backing off and sticking them to his skin, waited for the defibrillator to analyse his heartbeat. He issued the charge when instructed.

Mike's chest muscles tightened, and Ezio held his breath.

TWENTY-ONE

Robyn

"**S**hock delivered." She expected the jolt, like she saw in Hollywood movies every time a person was shocked. But Mike didn't move. If anything, he was too still.

His eyes still didn't open.

Why didn't they open?

Robyn's own heart beat erratically in her chest, fear and adrenaline running through her to make her mind spin like a category five hurricane. What if? What if? What if? Her hands shook and she clenched them harder, her nails leaving bloodied half-moon indents in her palms when she unclenched after Ezio laid a hand over hers.

"Why isn't he waking up?" she whisper-cried.

Robyn lurched forward, needing to touch Mike again. But Ezio was quicker. His arm shot out, pulling her back, keeping her away from her man. She fought him, but instead of pushing her away, he drew her into his arms.

"It is now safe to touch the patient," the mechanical voice of the defibrillator said just as a commotion sounded at the doors. Two ambulance officers dressed in olive green coveralls, one a woman and the other a man, strode purposefully through the door.

Robyn grasped Mike's hand again, and the floodgates opened. Fear that had barely been kept at bay spilled out, and she couldn't stop shaking. "Wake up, please," she begged him, tears spilling over and running down her cheeks. Robyn curled forward, resting her head on his belly, and cried. "Please."

"His heart rate is nearly normal. That's good news, but we need to get him onto the gurney and into the hospital." Robyn looked up and watched Mike blink his eyes open. She sobbed again, squeezing his hand.

Mike lifted his other hand, reaching for her, but he dropped it quickly. Robyn choked out a cry, and her eyes shot to his. They fluttered, like he was struggling to stay awake.

"Rest, babe," Ezio cooed, brushing his fingers through Mike's caramel-coloured hair. "Your body is exhausted. Let us look after you."

There was a hand in her hair, smoothing it down. It wasn't Mike's, but it was comforting. Ezio spoke in a language Robyn didn't fully understand, throwing medical terms at the ambos, and she realized it was him calming her. He never stopped running his fingers through her hair, soothing her the whole time.

"Mmm," Mike groaned.

"Mike!" Robyn cried.

Ezio's breath left him in a rush, and he leaned on her. Robyn held him close, grateful that they were all together. "You want a drink, babe?" he asked. There was barely a nod from Mike in response. He didn't open his eyes again, but even that small flutter was enough for the moment. Robyn pressed the pop-top bottle Meiko passed her to his lips, letting a few drops wet them. His mouth opened a fraction and she let a few more drops slide past.

"Only a tiny amount," Ezio instructed her. The relief in his eyes and the tears tracking down his cheeks did Robyn in. She couldn't stop the wave of crying and leaned into Ezio, taking comfort in his embrace. He held her close, breathing deep, while they both held on to Mike.

"Mr Hayes, let's get you up here and we'll get you seen in hospital." The ambo patted the bed, and Ezio pulled back.

When he spied the man who'd helped them earlier, he nodded at the bed. "Can you give me a hand to help him up?" Ezio asked as he peeled off the defibrillator pads. "I doubt whether he's got the energy to even sit up."

"Let me lift him." Robyn had never met him before, but he hadn't hesitated to lend a hand. It was all Robyn needed to know; she liked him. He picked Mike up as if he weighed nothing and deposited him gently on the gurney. Ezio packed up the defibrillator while the ambulance officers made a fuss over Mike.

Ezio's hands shook, and Robyn watched as he squeezed his eyes shut. She clasped her hands over his, threading their fingers together, and held tight. "He's going to be okay." It was a promise she had no right to make, but Ezio was struggling and desperate for reassurance. The doctor in him had finally taken a backseat. Before her, vulnerable and scared, was Mike's boyfriend, the man who needed her just as much as she had needed him a moment ago.

He nodded and drew her into a hug. "Why don't you go with Mike in the ambulance? I'll catch the tram in. It'll be quicker than a ride share." Robyn nodded, incredibly grateful for his consideration. He was a good man, and Robyn understood why Mike had fallen head over heels in love with him so quickly.

She sat down in the seat and buckled her belt after Mike was loaded in through the rear doors of the ambulance. Ezio held up a hand in a wave as he closed the door, and Robyn smiled, nodding at him in encouragement. Mike was quiet and terribly still, except for his chest expanding and contracting as he breathed. "Is he okay?" she asked the ambo sitting across from her. His name tag read Toby.

"He's certainly had a workout. His heart rate is holding steady, but his blood pressure and oxygen are still very low. That's normal with tachycardia. I've got the oxygen mask on him to help with it," he answered, his voice calm and friendly.

"Is he unconscious?"

"No, just asleep. From what your doctor friend was telling us, this was a pretty severe attack. Think of it as if he's just run an entire marathon at the speed Usain Bolt would run the hundred metres. He's completely wiped out. But as I said, he's currently stable."

Robyn hung her head and rubbed her stinging eyes. This was not how the night was supposed to go. Not because their dinner was ruined—she didn't care about that—but because they'd come far too close to losing him. "What will happen now?"

"We'll take him to emergency, and he'll probably be admitted into the cardiac ward overnight. Unless they can figure out what caused the tachycardia immediately and treat it, the doctors will likely refer him to a specialist for testing. He may be given medication, but that's something the doctor or specialist will advise on."

"Is it serious?" Fear made her voice shake, but she needed to know.

He reached forward and patted her hand. "We don't muck around with anything to do with a person's heart. Yes, it's serious, but he's receiving excellent treatment. When we get to the hospital, he'll be in the best possible hands— aside from mine, of course." He winked, and Robyn huffed out a laugh at his attempt to lighten the mood.

The ambulance slowed and reversed into a parking spot. "Right, we're here. Follow me, and I'll make sure that the docs know you're with this handsome fella." He patted Mike's arm, and the doors opened, nurses and a doctor waiting patiently for the ambulance officers to wheel the stretcher out of the ambulance. Robyn followed them through two sets of doors into the ED, a large open room divided by dark blue curtains drawn across treatment hubs. A half wall closed off a central section where doctors and nurses milled around looking at screens and talking on phones. It was calm and quiet, but Robyn could see exactly how the space would be buzzing if there were multiple emergencies.

Robyn waited while Toby gave the treating doctor a run-down of Mike's condition and explained Ezio's care. "And this lovely lady is our patient's partner."

"Ma'am, if you'd like to take a seat." The nurse indicated to her. "We're going to do a workup of Mr Hayes's vitals and order some tests. Can you give us a rundown of his medical history?"

"I can do my best, but it won't be complete. His ex-wife will be able to fill in a few more of the blanks though."

"Let's see what information you can give us." For the next twenty minutes Robyn held Mike's hand and answered every question she could about his health. No, he didn't take drugs or any kind of stimulants, even coffee. He rarely drank alcohol. His diet was good and overall, his health was excellent. Apparently, except for his heart. When it came to Robyn giving them details of his episode, she wished Ezio was with them. *Where is he?*

"Where's Ezio? He took over when Mike's attack started. He was amazing. He should be here by now. Can he come through?"

"No, he has to be a relative to be back here."

"But he can help; he can give you the information you need." The nurse shook her head and apologized. With her nerves frayed, Robyn had to rein in her exasperation and bite her tongue. The nurse was only doing her job, even though it was frustrating as hell. Robyn pulled out her phone and noticed, for the first time, three missed calls from Ezio. Dialling him, she started to pace, but he picked up almost immediately. "Where are you?" she asked.

"They won't let me in. I'm not family." Ezio's words were resigned, as if he'd been having the same argument at his end.

"Can't you just badge your way in? You work here. You saved his life, for goodness' sake."

"I'm not supposed to." He sighed. "They aren't going to understand even if we try to explain it to them. You stay with Mike. Text me details as and when you can. I'll wait out here."

Mike stirred from beside her and reached out to take her hand. Robyn grasped it like he was a lifeline and kissed his knuckles. Relief hit her, nearly buckling her knees. "Hey," she greeted him breathlessly, her voice cracking with emotion. "It's good to see you awake." In her ear she heard Ezio let out a sob, and she put the phone on speaker. "Ezio, he can hear you."

"Mike, babe, I'm so sorry, but I can't come in there. I'll see you soon though, and I'll be waiting right here for up-dates."

"I want you in here," Mike rasped. "Both of you."

"Okay," the nurse responded, nodding and smiling at them. "Ezio, I'll come out to reception now."

When Ezio walked through the doors, he looked as if he'd aged a decade. But the light in his eyes when he saw Mike awake was breathtaking. He stepped around to the opposite side of the bed where Robyn was perched and grasped Mike's hand, folding his entire arm into his embrace. No words were exchanged, but the soft brush of lips against Mike's knuckles and look of utter love and devotion in Ezio's eyes filled her heart. Tears tracked down Ezio's face, and Robyn let Mike's hand go, giving them their moment together. He bushed his thumb over Ezio's cheek, and he fell forward, burying his face in the crook of Mike's neck. Mike held him close while Ezio's breath hitched.

"I thought I was going to lose you," Ezio mumbled, putting words to both their fears.

Mike cupped his face and drew his lips forward kissing him softly. "I'm not going anywhere." He held his arm out for Robyn, and she snuggled in closer. "I promise. I'll get checked out, figure out what the hell happened and get it fixed. I'm. Not. Going. Anywhere."

They waited there, Robyn and Ezio sitting on either side of their man, holding his hands and playing with his hair for what felt like half the night. In reality, it was probably only an hour. Ezio asked for a meal to be delivered to Mike, but the best they could do was a sandwich and juice. It barely made a difference to his energy levels. Mike was hooked up to monitors that beeped and buzzed, the background noise keeping him awake. He was weak. Far more tired than Robyn had ever seen him. Drifting in and out of sleep, he was woken up every time the doctors and nurses stopped by to check on him.

The doctor who walked in when Robyn stood to stretch her legs hadn't visited them before. Wearing navy blue scrubs and a white coat, a stethoscope around his neck, he smiled and pulled the curtain closed behind him. Mike stirred and slowly blinked open his eyes.

"Good evening, Mr Hayes, my name is Dr Christopher Knox. I'm one of the resident cardiac specialists here at the hospital." He chatted benignly with Mike, asking him questions about how he'd been feeling in the hours, days, weeks, and months leading up to the tachycardic attack. Both Ezio and Robyn added information for the doctor, and slowly a picture emerged of Mike's health deteriorating in the last few months. He'd been suffering from these episodes since he was a teenager, but they were getting progressively worse—longer and more frequent of late.

"Well, I think we should look further into what's going on. You need a diagnosis, but more importantly, we need to treat you. There are a few heart conditions that present similarly, and each has its own course of treatment. You're otherwise a healthy, active man in his mid-thirties. The tachycardia tells me there is something underlying that has been getting worse the longer it remains untreated, so we need to get to the bottom of what's going on. Without addressing it, you're at a much higher risk for heart attack and stroke."

"How do we figure out what it is, Doc?" Mike asked, his voice still raspy with exhaustion.

"We test for it. We're going to run an ultrasound to check the structure of your heart, as well as do a few other tests—blood tests and the like. Then, you'll get hooked up to a Holter monitor and we'll check the results after a week."

"I'm not seriously going to be stuck in here for that long, am I?"

He smiled. "No, I'm having you transferred to the cardiac ward now so you'll be there overnight, but I anticipate you'll be right to head home tomorrow arvo."

* * * * *

A week later, they sat in the doctor's office waiting to hear the results. Mike was agitated, unable to sit still, but lethargic at the same time. Dark circles marred the soft skin under his eyes, and they were a flat brown, missing the spark of life that usually burned within him. His skin was pale, and he sat hunched over, lacking the energy to sit up straight. It didn't surprise Robyn. They'd all been up most of the night, and Mike had suffered more than she and Ezio combined.

Another attack, the second since Mike had been in hospital.

They'd taken a toll on Mike. He wasn't bouncing back. His well of boundless energy had run dry, no longer refilling no matter how much he slept. Gone were his early morning surfs. Instead, whichever of Robyn or Ezio started work the latest would wake him and shuffle him into a shower to get him functioning. He'd missed work twice and slept for most of the day both times. Ezio had confided he'd been worried about Mike a year earlier, but Mike had dismissed it. Robyn was kicking herself for not noticing it earlier. She prayed that whatever was wrong was not a death sentence.

It was an anxious wait to see the doctor.

Robyn's head throbbed as she sat, holding hands with Mike. His other was in Ezio's. No words were spoken between the three of them as they watched the door. She hadn't been able to stomach breakfast that morning, the smell of the scrambled eggs, toast, and bacon Ezio cooked Mike making her want to puke. Mike had stared listlessly at the food until Ezio fed him. If it wasn't out of necessity—if he had the energy to feed himself—it would have been a beautifully intimate moment between the two of them. Instead, Robyn had cried silent tears in the kitchen watching as Mike curled into him, leaning heavily on Ezio as his boyfriend lifted a few forkfuls of food to his mouth.

She was at least glad that the kids hadn't seen their dad so weak. They'd protested when Robyn shipped them off to spend an extra week with their mum, but they'd be terrified seeing him like this. She was terrified. Mike had even missed some of their nightly telephone calls, unable to stay awake long enough to talk. When he did, he sounded winded; talking sapped his energy to the point of exhaustion.

Robyn was pinning her hopes on the heart monitor Mike had worn for the week. She needed it to give them some answers. Mike needed a diagnosis—they all did—but what could the best case scenario possibly be with a heart condition?

Dr Knox strode in, all business, shook their hands, and sat behind his desk, his gaze lingering on Mike. "How are you feeling?"

"Like shit," he mumbled and yawned. "I have zero energy. I just want to sleep. Even watching the telly is exhausting. I can't even fucking feed myself." A little of Mike's fire made a reappearance, but it was frustration not laughter that shone through.

"Did you have any attacks?"

"Two." Mike paused and sucked in a breath, his next words uttered on a whisper. "What if it's bad, Doc? I'm not ready to die. Not yet." Robyn's breath caught, and a sob hitched in her throat. Tears pooled in her eyes, and Mike let go of her hand to pull her to him. She went easily but hated that she couldn't be strong for him. The helplessness didn't sit well. She fixed things. It was what she did, and yet this time, she was powerless.

"Let's see what we can find, hey? Give you some answers." He turned his attention to the computer and opened what looked like a line graph on his screen and asked, "When did you have them?"

"Friday afternoon about four o'clock and last night."

"How bad were they compared to the one that landed you in hospital?"

"About thirty percent. I could talk during both. I got both under control pretty quickly, but the one last night was worse."

Dr Knox scrolled through the recordings of Mike's heartbeat, pausing to zoom in on certain sections. He furrowed his brow and tilted his head, humming thoughtfully, before moving on. When he reached the attack, his eyes widened. "About thirty percent? Holy shit."

"What?" Robyn and Ezio asked at the same time. What little colour was in Mike's cheeks had drained, turning him white as a sheet.

"It's Wolff-Parkinson-White Syndrome." The doctor smiled triumphantly and continued, "That's good news. It's eminently treatable." When Robyn tried to interrupt, he ploughed on, adding, "The Parkinson element has nothing to do with Parkinson's Disease. It's named after the three doctors who fully described WPW syndrome in the 1930s."

"What is it?" Mike asked.

The doctor reached for a plastic model of the heart, which he opened into three different sections. "Your heart operates with an electrical signal that fires in the upper chambers of the heart—the atria"—he pointed to the plastic heart and traced a path through what looked like a glob of tissue—"and goes through the atrioventricular node, where it pauses, then travels to the ventricles." He moved to the lower half of the heart and circled the chambers there before following a pathway out through the arteries at the bottom. "They contract, and blood is circulated where it needs to go." Dr Knox pointed his pen back at the top chamber of the heart and drew a line directly down to the bottom chamber. "WPW syndrome is an extra electrical pulse in your heart. You can see here"—he pointed at the computer screen to the point where Mike's heartrate visibly accelerated and seemed to vibrate on the screen, the lines separating—"where it kicks in. The second electrical pulse skips the atrioventricular node, and essentially, you end up with extra pulses accelerating your heart rate."

That made sense. Mike's heart rate climbed dramatically during an attack. From the outside, it looked as if he was doing high intensity exercises while standing still—he broke out in a sweat, became short of breath, and was exhausted afterward. That second electrical pulse, as tiny as it was, wreaked havoc on Mike's body.

"The normal resting rate for an adult is between seventy and eighty beats per minute. During an attack, WPW syndrome sufferers will have a significantly faster heartbeat, which slows when the extra electrical pulse deactivates. During this particular attack"—Dr Knox pointed to the screen—"your heart rate reached one hundred and seventy-five beats. If your other attack was far worse than this one, your heart was likely beating at well over two hundred beats per minute."

"What triggers the extra electrical pulse?" Robyn asked, swallowing hard. Maybe if they figured out what Mike's trigger was, they could avoid it like people did with migraines.

"We aren't sure what causes WPW syndrome. Anecdotally, I've heard stories from patients that their triggers are medication, stress, and in one case, mixtures of food combinations. However, we aren't one hundred percent sure. I don't know whether it's causation, or a simple correlation. In addition, the triggers may change over time, meaning that you won't be able to eliminate the attacks altogether without treatment. As I mentioned to you in the ED, it's important to treat you to reduce your risk of heart attack and stroke."

Mike looked at her, the naked fear in his eyes and the thin line of his lips obvious. Robyn held on to him, reassuring Mike as much as she was trying to ground herself. The doctor had said the condition was treatable. She had to hold onto that thought rather than let every worst case scenario run through her mind.

It had to be okay.

Mike had so much love to give. It wasn't fair that the very thing that made him so special was the one thing that could bring him to his knees. Robyn knew the ridiculousness of what she was saying, but everything was going so well. They were happy, all of them. Her lover had found the two pieces of his heart, and Robyn knew Ezio loved their man as much as she did. And what about Lexi and Jax? They needed their dad too. But he would be there to watch them grow up. He had to be.

Tears of both frustration and relief—a letting out of all the fear that had built up that long week—started again, and Robyn failed miserably to hide them. She wanted to be strong. Wanted it so much, but she was overwhelmed.

"Like I said, the good news is that it's eminently treatable."

"What's the treatment?" Ezio asked, his tone business-like.

"We have the option of a beta blocker like Bisoprolol—"

"No," Ezio refused adamantly, shaking his head and dismissing the doctor's suggestion immediately.

"I agree." Dr Knox nodded and explained, "The drugs slow the heart rate to reduce the severity of attacks, but they don't eliminate them. Beta blockers aren't the best option here. For someone as fit as you, and who leads such an active lifestyle, there is a risk that you'll overexert yourself without even being aware. It is, however, an option if you don't want surgery."

"An operation? As in open heart surgery?" The pitch in Mike's voice rose. Fear showed in the strain lines on his forehead and his hand was tight around Robyn's, squeezing her knuckles to an almost painful point.

TWENTY-TWO

Mike

Things were happening too fast. Surgery on his heart. Urgent surgery on his heart.

The next day, urgent.

He sat in the doctor's office, unable to take anything in. Dr Knox was talking, and Ezio was asking questions, but all Mike could do was stare. His brain had completely switched off. Got up and left the room.

He was numb.

"I need to see my kids," Mike whispered when they all looked at him, waiting for something—what, he had no clue. But any sort of reaction was beyond what he was capable of at that point. He tried to relax the grip he had on Robyn and Ezio, scared of hurting them, but he couldn't. He was terrified of his fucked-up heart sparking with another electrical charge and killing him. How many more would he survive? One? Two? Ten? How long did he have? Would he even get through the operation?

"I'll get Wani to bring them over," Robyn reassured him. "But, Mike, did you understand what Dr Knox said was involved with the surgery? Do you need him to explain it again? Or Ezio?"

"Um, no… I…" He rubbed his forehead. "I didn't really take any of it in."

The doctor explained everything again, and this time Mike listened harder. He understood more than before. The fear was still there—it had been growing exponentially for the last week, but now Mike was reassured. He needed the surgery, and he knew he was in capable hands. He just hated the rush—the fact that his condition was serious enough to warrant surgery so urgently terrified him. He hadn't had a chance to get his head around his diagnosis, never mind come to terms with the fact that he'd be under anaesthetic literally getting his heart zapped in less than twenty-four hours. How did he tell his kids what was going to happen? How did he explain that there were risks with every surgery, but the risks of doing nothing were far higher? Then another thought hit him like a Mack truck to the face. Was the condition hereditary? Did his kids have it? Could their hearts give out?

"Can they get sick too?" He had to force the words out, pushing them past the lump in his throat.

The doctor smiled gently. Mike supposed it was to reassure him, but it did nothing to ease the fear instilled in him with the words "syndrome" and "operation."

"Genetic factors don't seem to play a role, but there does seem to be a weak hereditary connection with some sufferers. In most people it resolves in childhood. It's only an unlucky few who need treatment as adults."

The ride home was quiet. Robyn drove, manoeuvring his big SUV into the car park, while Mike tried to keep his eyes open. Ezio's shift was starting soon, so they'd dropped him off on their way home, and Mike missed him terribly already. He hadn't wanted him to leave, but how did he ask him to stay? He was being ridiculous, but Mike was scared.

No, he was terrified. Of not being cured. Of not being able to be there for his kids. Of dying. The doctor had told him the statistics. He'd explained the risks and the success rates. Mike knew he had a good chance—a great chance—of making a full recovery, but the what-ifs still niggled.

The door opened, and Mike cracked open his eyes. The car was turned off, and Robyn was standing next to him, beckoning him out. "Hi," she whispered. "Let's get you upstairs for a nap."

She helped him out and he leaned heavily on her as they walked, needing sleep as much as he needed to breathe. When he stepped inside his apartment though, the last thing he wanted to do was sleep. His kids were there, watching the telly with a big bowl of popcorn between them. Wani was outside on the balcony talking on her phone, and she smiled and waved. Tears sprung to his eyes at the sight of his kids, and he sucked in a shuddery breath.

"It's okay," Robyn murmured, squeezing him around the waist as she helped him over to the couch. The kids dropped the popcorn onto the coffee table and patted the spot between them. He eased himself down, wishing he could be their climbing gym like he'd been months earlier, but exhaustion threatened to pull him under like the tide. Mike resisted, fighting his body so he could have this time with his kids.

He wanted to enjoy every moment with them. It would take a while for him to be back to normal—a couple of months until he was healed fully—so if he had to restrict himself on playtime then, he was going to get enough of it now.

Uncaring of what they were watching, Mike hugged them close. He breathed in the strawberry scent of Lexi's shampoo and smiled at how Jax squirmed because he couldn't sit still. They cuddled into him, and Mike's tears fell.

"Dad, what's wrong?" Lexi asked, alarmed.

"I'm okay, honey," he whispered. "Just happy to see you both. I missed you kiddos."

"Dad, I was practicing with nunchucks today," Jax announced, glowing with pride.

"You were?" he asked, his eyebrows rising in surprise. "Did you look like Bruce Lee?"

"Who's that?" Jax looked at him, confused, before shaking his head and waving him off, not waiting for an answer. "Anyway, I was really good. I hit myself in my testicles." Before he could ask for it, Robyn passed him Lexi's iPad and kissed his temple.

"Ah, buddy, you aren't supposed to do that." Mike couldn't help his wince.

"I know that now!" Jax crossed his eyes and gripped his groin, and Mike laughed. The lightness returned to his chest, and Mike grinned as his boy re-enacted his reaction to the no doubt painful discovery. "But now I know how to do it if there's ever a bad guy or a bully." Jax jumped up on the coffee table and feigned a karate pose, shouting, "Hiya." He did a karate chop and came far too close to kicking Lexi in the face.

"Jax," Mike cautioned, pointing to the floor. "Hey, take a look at this." He opened YouTube and pulled up old clips of Bruce Lee and the famous nunchuck scenes from his movies. Jax, like a ping pong ball, bounced onto the couch and stuck his head under Mike's arm so he could get a closer look. Before he could think better of it, he added, "Maybe we can get you started on karate lessons after…" Mike swallowed, knowing that he'd just created a monster of begging and cajoling until they took him.

"After what, Dad?" Jax squirmed excitedly, and Mike shook his head, kicking himself for opening his mouth. At least it gave him an opening.

"After my operation," he explained calmly, pausing the video. "Mum has you this week because I haven't been feeling too well. The doctor is going to do surgery to fix what's wrong with me."

"What's an operation?" Jax asked.

"It's where the doctor takes your tonsils out," Lexi explained. "Arabella had it. She got to have a week off school and eat ice cream."

"This is a little different to Arabella's operation. My heart is being fixed so I can run and surf again, and we can all go bike riding and stuff."

"When, Dad? Can we come and visit you in hospital?" Lexi asked at the same time as Jax blurted, "Can we eat your ice cream?"

"It's happening tomorrow. I'm not sure if I'll be able to have visitors at the hospital; it might only be when I get home. But as soon as I know, I'll ask your mum to bring you. And yes, I'll make sure you get ice cream."

"Will you have a big scar?" Jax asked, fascinated by gore.

"No, bud. No scar. I'll just have a few stiches in my leg."

"Your heart is here." Jax pointed to Mike's chest. "That doctor's dumb if he thinks it's in your leg."

Mike laughed. "He knows it's in my chest. There's an artery—like a pathway—in my leg that leads directly to my heart. He's going to use it to carry a laser into my heart and zap away the problem."

"Cool," a wide-eyed Jax exclaimed.

"No way," Lexi said, awed.

Mike wasn't brave like them. If he thought about it long enough, there was no way he'd be in that operating theatre the next day. But what choice did he have? So, he pulled them tighter, hugged them closer, and murmured that he loved them. While they watched movies, he slept, waking only when Jax shook him to do another Bruce Lee impersonation.

TWENTY-THREE

Ezio

"**W**hat the hell is taking so long?" Ezio mumbled as he paced the room. Mike had been in theatre for hours already, and he was a nervous wreck. Adrenaline raced through his system, his hands shaking from the overload.

There was a healthy dose of fear too.

The catheter ablation the surgeon was performing was a relatively low risk procedure with a high success rate, but it was an operation nonetheless. There were risks. And Mike couldn't live without his heart. If the doctor couldn't fix it, or there was the slightest complication, he could have another attack. He might not pull through the next one. Then there was the surgery itself. Using lasers on a long thin wire pushed through arteries up to an organ that was essential for a human being's survival to kill malfunctioning tissue was a procedure that had to be perfect, right down to the micrometre. Dr Knox was the best there was—Ezio had done his homework—so he knew Mike was in capable hands, but it didn't lessen the fear.

Robyn stood in front of him, halting his movements, and instinctively he curled an arm around her shoulders, drawing her close. She hadn't spoken much during their wait. It was as if she'd retreated into herself, taking solace from her thoughts. Ezio wished he could do the same—drown out the medical practitioner in him. He knew a surgeon clearing his schedule to operate on a patient the next day wasn't good. It meant the risk of leaving it longer was too great, and Mike was also at a higher risk of complications because of it. If his heart was already weakened or damaged by the countless times he'd been in tachycardia, would he be able to survive another attack? Or the operation to fix it?

Robyn grasped his hand and threaded their fingers together, and Ezio lifted her knuckles to his lips. He pulled her tighter and soaked in some of the innate strength that she displayed. "Why haven't we heard anything?" She looked up at him, her eyes bloodshot and raw from the sleepless nights and worry that had compounded itself into an unbearable weight over the past week.

"He'll be okay. He has to be."

"Ms Stevens, Dr Dimitriades," Dr Knox greeted them, still in scrubs with his surgical mask hanging from his ear. He was so grateful to have Robyn with him in that moment. They'd clung to each other the entire wait. The hours that Mike was under the knife had passed interminably slowly, and now time had sped up to warp speed, their fate tied to the next words out of the surgeon's mouth.

"Dr Knox," Robyn begged, her voice cracking. "Is he okay?"

"Mike is out of surgery and resting comfortably in recovery. He'll be transferred to the cardiac ward once he's awake. Surgery was a success, but it was lot more complicated than I initially thought. The ablation was performed successfully, but as we were withdrawing, Mike had another attack. We got it under control, and I performed a second ablation. He was under anaesthetic for a lot longer than what I would have liked, but we've been observing him very closely. He's coming out of it nicely. He has a strong heart."

"So is that it? Is he okay? Is it cured?" Robyn asked, the words rushing out of her. She was gripping the front of his shirt, keeping him close as if he gave her strength. He could have laughed at that—she'd been his rock since Mike's health deteriorated.

Dr Knox smiled broadly. "Yes, to all of it. He's going to be just fine."

The breath that whooshed out of him made Ezio dizzy. He hadn't realized he was holding his breath until his oxygen-starved lungs forced him to gasp for air. His hands shook, and the rush of relief was like a tidal wave crashing into him. He reached out to shake Dr Knox's hand and whispered on a sob, "Thank you."

"My pleasure. I'll see you again when I run through post-operative care with you. In the meantime, I'll have one of the nurses come down and let you know when he's on the ward so you can go and see him."

Ezio held Robyn tight as tears of pure relief fell. Just when he thought he had everything, it was almost yanked away from him, and it wasn't just him. Mike's kids, Robyn, all the people who loved Mike had come far too close to losing him. He'd never been so scared before. But now, knowing Mike was going to be okay? It was a relief like nothing else. Knowing his heart wasn't suddenly going to shut down any moment and he'd live to see his twilight years had joy unfurling in his chest.

He laughed, relief and love making him giddy. He hooked his finger under Robyn's chin and leaned down, brushing his lips against hers. They were soft, and it was so very different from kissing Mike. She was shorter, more petite. But just as sweet. The contrast made him want her more. It wasn't the first time he'd seen her as more than Mike's girlfriend. If he were being honest with himself, he'd instantly developed a kinship with Robyn. That first telephone call with her had lit his insides up. She wasn't the competition. She wasn't the woman who stood between the man he loved. She'd given him hope. Given him everything and was adamant she wasn't sacrificing anything to do it. When Ezio had laid eyes on her the first time, he was stunned. Her outer beauty matched her incredible mind and even bigger heart. Having her in his arms was as natural as holding Mike. Maybe it was because they both loved him. Maybe it was because they understood each other.

The night he'd had his first date with Mike came back to him. The whisper that he wasn't the only person who held his heart. He and Robyn had exchanged texts and bantered a lot since that date. Then they'd been together constantly since Mike's health went downhill. Ezio didn't believe in love at first sight—the concept was ridiculous as far as he was concerned—but he'd fallen fast and hard for Mike. It stood to reason that the same could happen with the other love of Mike's life.

But when Robyn kissed him back, he reconsidered the whole notion of love as he'd believed in it. She made him rethink everything.

Robyn opened to him when he licked her bottom lip. Their tongues tangled, slowly exploring and teasing each other. She brushed her hand over his chest, a zing of sensation passing through him straight to his dick. He was already half hard, and Ezio reached down to the small of her back and pulled her tight, letting her feel what she was doing to him. Robyn moaned and gripped his nape, taking over the kiss. Her other hand on his arse, she squeezed, and he bucked his hips, his breath catching as she sucked on his tongue.

"Whoa," a woman said, and Robyn pulled away from him like she'd been burned. He stood stock still, breathing hard, his head spinning from the instant shift from high gear to screeching brakes and especially because of the thoughts he'd been entertaining. He willed his cock into submission. The tent in his jeans was hardly appropriate for a hospital waiting room. Ezio discreetly adjusted himself, but the two newcomers' eyes were on him. The toddler the man was carrying was blissfully wrapped up in a small toy—a small mercy given his current state.

Robyn wrapped her arms around herself and rocked back on her heels when she looked at the other woman before flicking her gaze to Ezio. Wide-eyed shock and devastation were written all over her face. Realization hit him.

What had he done?

Had he just cheated on Mike? With Mike's girlfriend?

He opened his mouth, ready to explain. To apologize. But Robyn spoke instead. "Ah, Emma, Nick, this is Ezio, Mike's boyfriend. Ez, Mike's and my closest friends."

"Mike's boyfriend?" Nick hedged, his confusion obvious. The man's gaze bounced between him and Robyn, and Ezio watched as he adjusted the toddler with blonde curls and wearing a football jersey and a tutu on his hip. Brow furrowed and mouth open, he blinked and closed his mouth, only to open it wordlessly again before blowing out a breath. Ezio could see the questions forming in his mind, bouncing around like they were in a tumble dryer. They were almost the same questions Ezio had. His partner looked equally stunned, but a smile was slowly forming on her lips.

"I... had no idea. I'm sorry, Mike hasn't told me anything about what's going on. Robyn, what's going on?" the man, Nick, asked.

"It's pretty simple, actually," Wani answered with a smile. The relief he experienced at seeing Wani struck him as ridiculous. She was the only other person he knew in Mike's group of friends but was also another person Mike had been intimate with. She must have walked in behind Robyn's friends and heard the tail end of the conversation. Ezio certainly hadn't noticed her before, but he had been a little occupied. "Mike has a girlfriend and now a boyfriend too." Raising her eyebrow in a challenge to Nick, she added, "It doesn't matter if you understand or agree, Nick. All you need to know is that he has two people who love him."

"Um, yeah, no. I'm not…" Nick rubbed his forehead with his free hand and blew out a breath. "I'm sorry, I'm thrilled for him. If you're all happy, I'm absolutely thrilled." A smile spread across his face, and Ezio could see the genuine affection this man had for Mike. "It's great to meet you." Nick held out his hand, and Ezio gratefully took it. His handshake was firm and no-nonsense. Despite the smile, Ezio could see he was fiercely protective of both Robyn and Mike, and the seriousness in those blue eyes had Ezio nodding in understanding. *No, I won't hurt them. Either of them.*

"It's pretty new," Ezio explained as he turned to Emma. "We ran into each other again only a few weeks ago, and both of us wanted something more than friendship. We've got Robyn to thank for making it happen."

Emma ignored his outstretched hand and embraced him instead, pulling Robyn in for a one-armed hug too. "I'm so happy for you three."

Ezio awkwardly patted her back. "Thank you?" He had no idea where they now stood. He smiled, trying to act like their relationship was perfectly normal. He hadn't needed to explain it to anyone. Hadn't even thought of doing so—when he and Mike were together, they were a couple. Same with Robyn and Mike. But now, he'd muddied the waters and overstepped a boundary that none of them had agreed to.

God, what had he done?

Ezio cleared his throat, not letting his thoughts spiral, and added, "We just got word that Mike came through the op okay and he's resting in recovery. When he's awake, he'll be transferred to his room so we can see him. The surgeon said that it was a success, but more complicated than they thought."

"Thank goodness," Wani breathed, falling into the closest chair. Tears welled in her eyes, and Robyn went to her, wrapping an arm around her shoulders. They whispered something, their heads together, and Wani nodded, wiping her face. Ezio went to her and sat on her other side, silently supporting her like she'd helped them without hesitation. "I've been so scared," she whispered.

"Us too. Every worst-case scenario has run through my head," Robyn confided in her.

"Now we can focus on getting him healed," Ezio said with a smile. Mike would regain his strength over time, and his heart would operate normally for the first time in his life. Robyn looked at Ezio, determination in her eyes, and nodded before Wani exhaled, her head still down.

"I'm glad he has you both, you know? I was jealous and angry when you got together," she said to Robyn. He couldn't see Wani, but the sad smile Robyn gave her told Ezio that Wani had just admitted a hard truth. "I walked away from him when I shouldn't have, and I hurt him. But I'm glad that happened, because now I realize neither of us could be what the other needed. Please, both of you look after him and love him with everything you have."

"We will," Ezio answered, a promise he had no right to make. Especially because he might have screwed everything up.

"Dr Dimitriades and Ms Stevens?" a nurse asked, interrupting them.

"That's us." Robyn stood, and Ezio followed. When Robyn reached for him, threading their fingers together, he smiled. Her excitement at seeing their man was contagious, and Ezio put aside the swirling worry in his head about their future. He focused on the weight that had lifted off his shoulders with Dr Knox's announcement. It was indescribable. He was walking on air, almost giddy with the thrill of knowing Mike would get well.

The nurse led them up a level and across the vast hospital building and eventually into Mike's darkened room. He lay prone, his chest rising and falling slowly, the monitors silently watching over him. Instinctually, Ezio checked them, and they looked good. He was resting peacefully, the anaesthetic working its way out of his system. There was a pillow under his leg, propping the uncovered limb up. Long surgical socks were pulled up to his knees. In the white paper gown and dim light, Mike looked so pale his skin was almost ashen. Robyn went to his side, and Ezio automatically stepped around the bed to his other.

Reaching out to touch him, Ezio held his breath. Despite the pallid tone to his skin, he was warm. Life buzzed inside him, and Ezio gently gripped his forearm, grounding himself. Robyn brushed her fingers through his hair, tenderly pulling away the strands stuck to his forehead. Mike's attack during the op must have been bad if his hair was drenched in sweat.

He stirred, and a small smile appeared on his lips before he nuzzled his face into her hand. Ezio leaned in, pressing a kiss to his forehead, and thanked the universe for steering the man in front of him into his path once more. "We're here, babe."

Robyn stayed like that, standing sentinel over Mike and waiting for him to wake up properly as Ezio studied his chart. "His colour is coming back," Robyn whispered. "That's good, right?"

"It is." Ezio went to him and brushed the backs of his fingers over his cheek. "The grogginess is a side effect of the anaesthesia. He'll wake up soon."

Robyn's phone buzzed. She didn't even reach for it, ignoring it completely, but when it vibrated again, Ezio motioned to the table it was sitting on. "You should answer it."

She flipped it over and swiped at the screen, a wistful smile appearing on her lips. "It's from Jacob, my landlord." She responded, typing something before she turned her attention back to Mike.

"Everything okay?"

"Yeah, he was checking how Mike is and sent me a photo of a listing he's signing up. It's lovely."

"You thinking about moving?" Ezio enquired, genuinely curious about what Robyn's long-term plans were.

"No. Kind of? I was thinking about us living together one day. But our apartments are too small. Jacob suggested we buy something together."

Ezio nodded, a gaping hole yawning open in his chest. Never mind he and Mike being a couple or him muddying the waters by kissing Robyn. Mike and Robyn were the couple. The family. He couldn't forget that. Robyn wanted to make plans for their future. It wasn't fair to hold them back either. He needed to be satisfied with always being the boyfriend. Mike's piece on the side, albeit one Robyn knew about. Knowing Mike would have his happy family filled him with joy, but damn, it hurt too. He looked away and swallowed hard, devastation clouding the high he was riding a moment earlier.

A groan sounded from beside them, and Ezio shook off his morbid thoughts. This was about Mike. He needed them both. No matter what his future with Mike held, Ezio would be there for him. He would support Mike and help him heal because he loved him. He smiled at Mike when his lover opened his eyes.

TWENTY-FOUR

Mike

He stretched, blinking his eyes open after his nap on the couch. It was a week after the operation, and all he'd done in that time was sleep, watch movies, and snuggle, but he was regaining his strength. He'd gone for a walk across the road down to the point where sand met the concrete path and he could watch the waves up close rather than from fourteen storeys up. He'd loved every minute of peace there, but the exercise had sapped all his energy.

He could hear talking in the background—Robyn on a call for work. She was using her professional voice, schooling whoever was on the other end of the phone on the way things were going to work. Ezio sat on the armchair opposite him, working quietly on his laptop. Mike wanted to go to him, to squeeze onto the armchair with him and kiss him stupid. He wanted Robyn there too, but he'd have to wait until she was able to be interrupted. He shifted, swinging his leg off the couch, and the stitches in his leg pulled sharply. Mike hissed, "Shit." Ezio's eyes snapped up, and he tossed his computer aside. "It's okay," Mike grated out through clenched teeth.

"Hush, let me look after you." Ezio was on his knees at Mike's side, helping to sit him up and swing the other leg off the couch. Ezio's gaze met his, and Mike's heart did cartwheels in his chest at the love shining there. Ezio's smile... he was smitten. Just as much as Mike was.

When he had both feet on the floor, Ezio crawled between his legs and shifted his boxer shorts up, checking the waterproof bandage on his leg. No new blood spots had appeared, and Ezio gave him a satisfied smile. Ezio adjusted his shorts back, innocently brushing against his inner thighs. Mike's breath caught and his dick lengthened, thickening at having the man of his dreams between his legs. He moaned quietly, his libido finally making a reappearance after a few weeks of it being completely uninterested. Ezio's breath rushed out when Mike hooked his hand around his nape and drew the man to him. He crashed his lips to Ezio's, kissing him with all the longing and desperation inside him. He pulled Ezio close, letting his man feel just how much he needed him. Pressed against him, Ezio rocked his hips slowly, sending delicious sparks of energy down Mike's spine straight to his balls. Their tongues tangled, and Ezio ran his hands down Mike's sides, his touch tender. He hooked his hands under Mike's legs, manoeuvring him so his semi-healed leg wasn't jostled too much and the stitches weren't pulling.

"I need you," Mike gasped, arching into Ezio's touch. But Ezio stilled and pulled back.

"We need to talk."

For the first time since the operation, Mike's heart stuttered in his chest. He hadn't understood what it was like to have a normal heartbeat before, but since his surgery, it was as if there was a new, stronger organ beating in his chest. Until that moment. His erection instantly deflated.

Ezio sucked in a breath and the couch dipped next to him. Robyn.

"We do."

He looked to her, fear now tinging the blood running through his veins.

"What did the doc say that you aren't telling me?" he asked, his voice wobbling with untold dread.

"No, it's nothing like that," Ezio explained. "You're healthy. Your heart is fixed. You're cured from the WPW, okay?" Mike nodded, unable to put words to the simultaneous relief and worry coursing through him. Ezio sucked in a breath and, on the rush of an exhale, said, "I cheated on you."

Mike blinked. The words lodged in his ears, playing on a loop. Mike tried to make sense of them, but there was nothing. Ezio met his gaze, and the distress there gutted him. Ezio squeezed his hands, and Mike swallowed, unsure if he wanted to hear more. "I kissed Robyn. When we got news that you were okay, I kissed her—"

Wait, what? They'd kissed? The two of them? Together? Not someone else? Not some random person? Mike looked between the two of them, shock rendering him mute.

"This isn't on you, Ez. I kissed you back. It was both of us."

It was as if time had frozen. Like everything went still. He could imagine looking down on the scene before them, then panning out to the world below. The frisbee being thrown in the park between the holidaymakers pausing mid-throw. The dolphins riding the swell—the waves too—stopping. Mike opened his mouth, but no words came. His gaze bounced between them, and he saw it. Every one of their interactions in the last couple of weeks sharpened into focus. The lingering gaze from Ezio and blush from Robyn the first time they'd met. The instant friendship that had struck up between them. The way each of the three of them had slotted seamlessly into their roles. Robyn and Ezio laughing together. The instant draw between the three of them.

"How?" Mike asked. It was a completely random question, but one he needed to know the answer to.

"It was just the once. It was spur of the moment. I… I promise, it won't—"

"Stop." Mike held up his hand before reaching for Robyn without letting go of Ezio. He kissed her, letting his lips linger against hers until she kissed him back. Their tongues touched softly, and Mike palmed the back of her head, sliding his fingers into her silky hair. When she relaxed into his embrace, losing her tentativeness, he pulled back and silently moved his lips to Ezio's. He kissed his man, trying to communicate everything that he'd shown to Robyn too. He loved them both without limitation. Without reservation. He pulled back, kiss drunk and indecent with his semi poking out from the leg of his loose boxer shorts. "Do it again," he whispered. "Kiss each other again. Let me see."

Ezio moaned, and Robyn shivered. Each with a hand on him, they reached for each other too, joining them together. Ezio ran the backs of his fingers over Robyn's cheek. Mike bit his lip. He knew how soft her skin was, the shape of her jaw and the taste of her lips. Robyn slid her hand against Ezio's hip, her thumb reaching under his white polo. They gazed at each other, a million emotions crossing their faces. Surprise. Desire. Love. They were falling for each other too.

Ezio dipped his head and gently tugged Robyn closer. His fingers brushed Mike's as they curled into her hair, and he pressed his lips to hers. One, then two brushes of their lips before they opened, and their tongues touched. Mike sucked in a breath at the beauty of what he saw between them. The need. The restrained urgency. He shifted his hand, letting it trail down Robyn's side until he reached her hip. He nudged her, and she shifted instantly, moving off the couch until she was on her knees before Ezio. The other man eased back and turned to Mike, his gaze searching.

Mike bit down on his lip, closed his fist around his cock, and barely muffled his moan. He stroked, his rough hand giving him some much-needed friction on his aching dick. Using his pre-cum to slick his hand, he ran it down his length. His eyes closed, and his head fell back as sensation shot down to his balls. "Show me how much you want each other," he gasped, his mind's eye replaying his dreams of the three of them together.

"Show us too," Robyn ordered, her voice husky. "Get undressed."

Mike stood, his head spinning with the thrill of it. Light-headed, he reached out, and two hands landed on his arse, steadying him. His boxers were lowered before Mike's vision cleared, and his cock slapped against his belly. Simultaneous moans had his gaze snapping back into focus, and Mike watched as Ezio pulled Robyn closer to him, one hand reaching around her back, curling over the swell of her arse and slipping underneath the short hem of her summer dress to palm her. Mike wanted to reach for her breast. Slip his hand under the thin material and brush his thumb over her nipple. He wanted to watch Ezio do it. He moved to sit again, but the two hands on his arse tightened, keeping him exactly where he was. Too unsteady on his feet to reach anywhere else, he kept his hands threaded in their hair and watched as Robyn arched into Ezio's touch.

Their gazes never broke, the silent conversation passing between them just as hot as being naked in front of them and watching their hands wander.

Mike closed his fist around his cock and stroked slowly as Robyn reached for Ezio's shirt. She nodded, and Ezio took his hand off Mike's arse to tug it off and toss it aside. She ran her fingertips down the swell of his belly to his linen shorts and yanked them open, before Ezio took her cue and pushed them over his hips. The two of them were naked, and Robyn had far too many clothes on. Desire raced up his spine as Ezio shimmied Robyn's dress up her curvaceous body, exposing centimetre after centimetre of tanned skin. Mike gripped one side of it and helped slip it over her shoulders, leaving her in only a black satiny-looking G-string. Ezio stared, shamelessly gazing at her from head to toe. Her nipples hardened, and she shivered under their attention.

"Jesus Christ, you're beautiful," Ezio murmured. "Flawless."

Robyn blushed, a shy smile tilting her lips up before she reached for him again. Running her hands over his body, Robyn bit down on her lip and moaned softly. "I..." she shook her head and didn't bother finishing what she'd started, kissing his cheek, then his throat. She pressed herself against him and sucked a mark into his collarbone while she gripped his shaft and worked him slowly. Mike could only see the movement of her arm, not her hand wrapped around Ezio's thick cock. The man's girth was his best asset, and Robyn was hopefully going to enjoy it as much as Mike did.

Ezio's hand on Mike's arse made him jump, the fingers sliding down his crack gentle and teasing. Mike adjusted his stance, giving more room for Ezio to play, and the man didn't disappoint, fluttering his fingertip over Mike's tight hole. Robyn pulled back, and she and Ezio had a silent conversation in the wordless moments that passed between them. Their kiss was sensuous, tongues tangling and hands roaming. Mike worked his cock, watching as his two lovers came together.

Then they shifted, their kiss enveloping his cockhead. Two tongues, two sets of lips working their way down his rigid shaft. Making love to his cock. The finger tapping against his hole wasn't enough. Robyn's hand cradled his balls, rolling them. Her finger teased his taint. He wanted more. Wanted it all.

It was a feast for his senses. A visual banquet that he couldn't look away from even if he tried. His lovers on their knees for him. Loving each other as well as him. The three of them, together.

Mike shot to the edge of bliss.

It was stimulation overload. Heaven at the end of his dick. He needed something buried in him, and Mike didn't care whether it was a cock, fingers, or a dildo. The emptiness had become too much to bear. "Please," he begged, his words probably incomprehensible.

But Ezio knew what he needed. He spat on his fingers and brought them back up to Mike's arse, wetting his hole and pressing two inside before Mike could form the words to beg again. The stretch and burn, the fullness, set him off, his orgasm crashing into him with the force of a tsunami. Cum shot from his slit, painting his lovers' faces with every pulse of his dick. His heart beat hard in his chest, but the flutter that had happened every time an attack was about to kick in wasn't there. Instead, in its place was ecstasy. Painless fire burned through his body, leaving him quaking and breathless.

Ezio licked his cock clean, sucking the oversensitive head and down his shaft until Ezio's nose was buried in the wiry pubic hairs at its base. Then he turned to Robyn, sucking the viscous liquid off her cheek. She did the same to Ezio, and Mike's cock twitched, already wanting to start round two. He panted, his legs turning gelatinous, and Mike slumped down onto the couch, dislodging Ezio's fingers. "Fuck me," he breathed.

Robyn whimpered, and he opened his eyes, watching as she let her head fall back while Ezio sucked on her breast and slipped his fingers between her legs. She blindly reached for him, but he was too far away to grasp his cock. Mike didn't have the energy to help though, unable to move, even to lift his hand and jack off his lover. "Mike," Robyn gasped. "I need to—"

"Fuck, yes," he moaned, his hole clenching and his balls tingling as his cock flexed. "Bedroom. Now."

Ezio pulled him up off the couch and guided him into the bedroom. Mike was limping. He'd pulled his leg, tensing it for too long as his lovers had worked him. Ezio eased him onto the mattress and held the weight of Mike's leg as he shifted to his side, hitching his knee up. "Like this?" he asked Robyn. She shivered and nodded.

"Does Ezio know?" Robyn asked, and Mike shook his head, drawing her in for a deep kiss.

"No, but I think he's going to love watching, and maybe joining in if you'd want that." Robyn smiled, desire sparking in her eyes. She rubbed her legs together and nodded. "Good. Get set up then."

When Mike reached for the lube, Ezio looked at him questioningly.

"Help me prep?" He immediately nodded, and Mike held his arse cheeks open, his hole clenching under Ezio's scrutiny.

"Is what's happening here what I think?"

"If it's Robyn with a strap-on fucking me into next week, then yes. This is us, Ez. I bottom for you. I do the same for her."

Ezio's eyes widened. "So when you leave my place and come home to Robyn, she slides inside of you where I've been? That's why you never let me wipe the lube off you?" Mike nodded, and Ezio gripped the base of his dick. He closed his eyes and sucked in a breath through his nose, his nostrils flaring. Every muscle in his upper body was tensed, vibrating with the strain. "Fuck. Oh fuck," he hissed, wrapping his hand around his sac and pulling the tightened skin away from his body.

Robyn clipped the last leg strap on and rubbed her body along Ezio's side, her hand falling to his arse. "If you want me to top you too, I can. But right now, I need to be inside Mike. I need to come, and I want you inside me when that happens."

Ezio groaned, Mike sympathizing with the pained sound burbling from his chest. He exhaled on a rush and shuddered as he let go of his dick. Mike could see the veins throbbing in his shaft, his balls instantly retracting to their position snug against his body. Mike knew it wouldn't take much to set his man off. It never did when he was edging like this.

Cool, lubed-up fingers landed on his arse, and Ezio coated his hole liberally before slipping inside him. Two fingers, scissoring to loosen him up, before Ezio added a third. Mike moaned, his cock lengthening again as Ezio tagged his prostate. Fireworks lit up behind his closed eyelids before Robyn pressed her mouth to his. When he blinked open his eyes, she was hovering above him, kneeling on all fours. Ezio was behind them, his fingers inside each of them. His cock bobbed with the movement, and his eyes were bouncing between both their bodies where he was buried deep.

But then Ezio pulled out of him, and Mike cried out. He hated the emptiness, but Robyn's moan had Mike straining to see what was happening. He couldn't see, but Robyn's pant gave him an idea. She shuddered and reached for the dildo, stroking herself and rubbing the nubs against her clit. The noises they made were a turn-on, and Mike wished for a mirror so he could see them. He reached between his legs and stroked his reawakening cock, tilting his hips in invitation. Once more, wet fingers were at his opening, coating the skin there as he moaned.

"Show me, Robyn. Make him scream."

Robyn didn't waste time, but she was gentle as she climbed over him and positioned herself at his opening. Holding herself up one-handed, she pressed forward, letting the dildo slowly stretch his hole around her. The vibrations started, a low hum that was too weak to get him off, but strong enough to create a Pavlovian reaction in him.

Mike moaned as the widest part of the strap-on breached him, and Robyn stilled, swivelling her hips and lighting up his nervous system.

"So sexy," Ezio murmured. Mike looked over his shoulder but couldn't see Ezio. Heated breath wafted over Mike's sac, and he closed his eyes, imagining Ezio kneeling on his haunches to get the best view of them. Ezio licked Mike's balls, bathing them in heat, and Mike moaned, pressing back into the sensation and seating Robyn fully within him, tagging his prostate the whole way in.

"So thick. Fuck," he groaned. "So good."

Robyn moved, dragging her hips back before gliding forward again, setting a slow and steady pace. He was stuffed full, stretched around the dildo in his arse. Hands on him, tongues and cocks, and Mike was in heaven. Robyn dropped lower, grinding her body against his, and Mike cried out. Her hardened nipples dragged against his skin, and her hips pressed against his arse, the dildo lodged deep inside him. The bed shifted, and he groaned as Robyn adjusted her weight, opening her legs wider and pressing further inside him. At her gasp, Mike's eyes flew open again and he craned his neck to see Ezio's eyes roll back in his head and his muscles straining. He was holding himself back, but Mike wanted it all.

"Need to roll onto my belly," Mike moaned. He needed the friction against his dick and, even more, needed Ezio to fuck both of them into the mattress.

Robyn pulled out, and Mike shuddered at the sudden emptiness. He shifted and canted his hips, holding open his arse cheeks in invitation as Robyn crawled back over him. She notched herself inside and paused there, teasing him. Making him whimper with need. It wasn't enough. He wasn't full enough or stretched enough. He needed more. He needed everything they could give him. Mike's cry of desperation grew, and Robyn petted his sweaty skin, running her fingertips down his tense back as he waited.

Neither of his lovers left him hanging for long. Ezio's feet landed beside Robyn's knees, and his hands braced his weight against the padded headboard of the bed. Robyn cried out when Ezio buried himself inside her, pushing Robyn deep into Mike. The dildo ground down against his prostate, the vibrations from its core sending him wild. Mike shouted out at the instant sensory overload. There were a few awkward strokes until they found their rhythm, but once they did, their bodies moved as one.

His cock rubbed against the sheets as his two lovers moved, Ezio thrusting fluidly into Robyn as she pulled back and let their man drive her back into him. Robyn cried out, shaking through an intense orgasm, and Ezio groaned, picking up the pace. It was all Mike needed. He shot to the edge of bliss and flew over, his voice hoarse from his shout as his balls emptied his load in long pulses onto the sheets below. He lay there panting as Robyn slumped down onto him and Ezio rocked his hips again, pressing hard into Robyn as he cried out. Mike could feel the twitches of his hips as Ezio shot deep into the condom surrounded by Robyn's still-clenching core, constantly renewed by the buzz of the vibrator against her clit.

They'd come together flawlessly. The next time though would be different. Next time, Mike wanted to feel both of them inside him. He wanted to be stretched around their cocks as they chased their orgasms and sent him into a frenzy of ecstasy.

TWENTY-FIVE

Robyn

It was the first night that the kids had been home after Mike's operation. It was also the first night they hadn't crammed into Mike's queen bed. Robyn offered to take the couch and was woken up by Lexi and Jax tiptoeing past her toward the master bedroom. Mike and Ezio were in there, and with the door open she knew they wouldn't be getting up to anything. So she'd joined them, creeping into the bed, giggling as they slipped under the covers. Ezio had woken up with a start, but Mike's reaction showed just how accustomed to it he was. He'd lifted his arms, so the kids could snuggle into each side of him and reached for the re-mote on his bedside table. Robyn was the last in, squeezing in next to Ezio. They'd watched early morning cartoons until Jax started to get antsy and hungry.

The pancakes had gone down well, but Robyn could see where Jax got his restlessness from. Mike was climbing out of his own skin, needing to do something that would burn off his excess energy. The only thing he was capable of just over a week post-operation was walking. Robyn instructed the kids to put on their hats and lather up with sunscreen.

"Let's go," Robyn announced as the excitement at getting out lit up Mike's face. Robyn grinned, happiness lighting her up.

The beachside park across from Mike's apartment building ran the full length of the Broadbeach beachfront. With wide lawns and clusters of trees, as well as play and exercise equipment dotted along the concrete pathways, it was easily accessible and flat enough that Mike could exercise without the terrain overtaxing his energy.

Their walk under the cerulean sky was more of a meander. The summer heat was starting to kick in—their 5:30 AM wakeup call had given them an early start—but the ocean breeze and speckled shade over the path kept the heat from becoming unbearable. Lexi and Jax rode their scooters, racing forward and turning back when they saw they were too far ahead.

"How are you doing, babe?" Ezio asked when Mike's limp became more pronounced. Aside from the burning in his chest—which he described a bit like heartburn—Mike's main complaint was the deep bruising and healing incision point on his leg.

"My leg's aching a bit, but I'm good. Finally feel well enough to walk without feeling like I've had the wind knocked out of me."

"Should we head back and sit in the park for a while? I can run upstairs and get a blanket and some pillows. The kids can burn off some more energy before we go inside." Mike nodded a response to her question and called out to the kids. They circled back to the park in front of Mike's building, and Robyn spotted a cluster of sprawling pandanus palms. The shady canopy they cast was broad enough to sit under and play kick to kick. "Wait here." She kissed Mike and furrowed her brow at the exhaustion she read on his features.

"Sit with me, babe." Ezio patted the bench seat after he'd straddled it, holding out a hand to Mike. The pained groan Mike let out when he sat worried her, but his smile when Ezio pulled him close had Robyn smiling.

"Hey, kids, can you help me bring some things from home?" Home. It was such an innocuous word. Four letters, two vowels and two consonants, but it held such a loaded meaning. Robyn hadn't been back to her flat other than to get fresh changes of clothes, and as much as she loved the little space, it was no longer home. That was with Mike and Ezio. With Lexi and Jax. Since Jacob had suggested the house to her, she hadn't been able to get it out of her head, but Ezio hadn't been keen to talk about it. She understood. Buying a place with another person was a big commitment, but with two? Especially when he'd only just met that second person—her—it was a big ask. But every time she drove out of her way to go past the weatherboard cottage next door to Jacob and Cassie's house she paused. She could imagine just what it would look like if given the love and attention it needed. With a fresh coat of paint and a new roof, the house would come alive. The yard would be transformed into an oasis with flower gardens and a sitting area with a fire pit. The canopy of the jacaranda trees would provide just enough shade without making it dark. She could imagine sitting on the veranda drinking a cuppa in the mornings or working from the screened-in porch on days she didn't feel like commuting to Brisbane. There was a big backyard too. It was overgrown with knee-length grass, from the peek she'd taken from Cassie and Jacob's kitchen, but it would be the perfect open grassy area for the kids to play in with a dog or two. It needed work. A lot of it. But between them, they could do it.

If only.

"Ow, Jax, stop!" Lexi cried, and Robyn snapped back to attention, immediately lunging for Jax. He had a handful of Lexi's hair, pulling it until tears sprang to her eyes.

"Jax, no. Stop," Robyn ordered as the lift doors opened. "Inside, please." She motioned to the apartment and shook her head. "Go to your room. You're in there for five minutes. You can come back out after I've heard your apology to Lexi, so think about what you're going to say."

She sat Lexi down and touched her head where Jax had been pulling her hair. "Does that hurt, honey? Do you need an ice pack?"

"No, I'm okay. He's a poo head." Lexi rolled her eyes, and Robyn had to bite her lip to stop her smile.

"It's not really nice to call him names." Robyn sat next to her and smoothed down Lexi's ponytail.

Jax coughed, and it sounded as if he was heaving. "Robyn, I just farted," he yelled, far louder than he needed to. "It stinks. I gassed myself. Can I go to the toilet? I need to pee too."

"TMI, Jax," she muttered, then to him she called out, "Yes, you can go."

"He probably farted on my bed," Lexi grumbled, reaching for the TV remote and flicking it on. "Is he stressing you out as much as he is me? Geez."

This time Robyn couldn't hold back her smirk. "He's okay." Robyn lowered her voice to a whisper. "But he is pretty gross."

"He's only doing it because he's an attention seeker." Her huff was one of pure annoyance.

"Why do you think that?" Robyn couldn't help the concern lacing through her. Jax was a good kid at heart, but he was boisterous and often too full of energy. He rarely played up though.

"He's silly. He thinks that if he's naughty, you'll stay. But I keep telling him that if he's too bad you won't want to come back."

"I… but I'm not going anywhere." Then she thought better and amended her comment. "I mean, when your dad's well again, I'll move back home, but I'll keep coming over like I normally do. Same with Ezio." Lexi went quiet and crossed her legs at her ankles, playing with the battery cover on the remote. Robyn eased it from her hands and noticed Jax standing at the doorway to the lounge room. She held out her hand and motioned to her lap. When Jax was seated there, she prompted, "Lexi?"

"Are you and Dad breaking up? We know Ezio is Dad's new boyfriend, but we don't want you to leave so he can stay. We love you."

"Yeah, we do," Jax added sadly.

"Oh, kids, I love you too. Your dad and I aren't breaking up. He's an incredibly special man. He's got such a big heart that he's fallen in love with both Ezio and me, and we love him back."

"Nan said you would probably break up. She said that Dad can't make up his mind."

"Your dad can and has made up his mind. Your nan was wrong to say that, especially to you. She doesn't understand." Robyn paused, contemplating how wise speaking her next words was. Bugger it, Mike deserved more than his parents gave him. "But she hasn't tried to understand either. We definitely aren't breaking up, okay? In fact, instead of there being four of us in our little family and your mum, there's now five of us."

Lexi nodded slowly, and Jax eyed her. He was like a lie detector, assessing how truthful Robyn was being. "Your dad having a boyfriend and a girlfriend isn't what most people are used to, but you've seen it happen before. It's just like Katy, Levi, and Connor. They're happy together, aren't they?" Robyn didn't wait for them to answer her rhetorical question. Instead, she ploughed on ahead. "We're happy together too."

"Do you love Ezio like Dad does?" Jax asked, looking up at her with big brown eyes. Heat flooded to Robyn's cheeks, and she laughed self-consciously.

"Can you keep a secret?" The kids nodded furiously, and Robyn tucked her hair behind her ear, stalling. "Between us, I think I might."

"Okay." Jax hopped off her lap. "Can we go back to the beach now?" With Robyn's nod, he turned and added without missing a beat, "Hi, Dad."

Robyn's gaze snapped up, and she stilled. Ezio and Mike were standing in the doorway. She'd been so focussed on Lexi and Jax that she hadn't heard them arrive. "Ah... what are you doing back?"

"Thought we'd suggest picking up fish and chips for lunch."

"Yes, please," Lexi responded. "Can we swim, Dad?"

"It'll have to be in the pool, but sure. Why don't you and Jax get ready?"

Ezio made his way over to sit on the couch, turning sideways so he was facing her. Mike eased himself onto the coffee table so they sat in a triangle. Ezio slipped his hand into hers, threading their fingers together, and Mike brushed her hair back off her shoulders. "Did you mean it?" Ezio asked. Robyn looked at him through lowered lashes, scared to voice the words.

"It's okay," Mike encouraged, and Robyn nodded.

"I can't explain it, but I'm falling for you too. I mean, I know... God, I'm fifteen again." Mike laughed, and Ezio looked between them. "We've had sex, yeah, but I don't really know how serious it was between us. I mean, you're supposed to be Mike's boyfriend, but..."

Ezio grinned and brought her knuckles to his lips while Mike pressed a lingering kiss to her lips. When Mike pulled back, Ezio was there, kissing her too. "I kinda want to be your boyfriend too."

"We need a bigger bed," Mike added, kissing a line up her throat and across her cheek until he and Ezio were kissing. "And a bigger place." Ezio pulled back and looked down. He nodded slowly, his shoulders hunching over. "I want to wake up between the two of you every morning."

Ezio's gaze snapped up, uncertainty mingling with hope. "All three of us and the kids?" Ezio asked. The puzzle pieces slotted into place, and Robyn understood why he'd been reluctant to speak about the house. It wasn't because it was a big commitment. It was because he didn't know if he was even invited.

"Yeah." Mike nodded, adjusting himself without any discretion. "Robyn, you, and me. One bed. Every night." Ezio's smile was radiant, and Robyn's belly flip-flopped, excitement and love coursing through her.

With a smile she added, "I know just the place."

EPILOGUE

Mike

SIX MONTHS LATER

Jax held Helena's hand as they walked down the stairs of their new-to-them house and ran for the back gate. Mike remembered walking up those stairs the first time. It gave him a thrill every time he thought about it. He was the last of them to hit the top step. Robyn and Ezio were already standing there when Mike joined them, turning to survey the dilapidated front yard in disdain. But as his gaze roamed over the space, the vision Robyn was painting came to life before his eyes. The most uncanny feeling had washed over him. *Home.* From Robyn and Ezio's expressions, they'd known too. The three of them had explored the dilapidated house with childlike wonder in their eyes, excitedly moving from room to room, earmarking spaces for their family to use, and with every step taken, the picture became increasingly vivid. Not one of them hesitated when it came to signing on the dotted line. Mike knew without a doubt that all their dreams could come true.

The renovations on the old Queenslander were coming along slowly but surely. The latest achievement was finishing the front garden. The week before, the backyard had been overhauled, the fences rebuilt, and new turf laid. To celebrate, Ezio had taken the kids to pick out two dogs from the pound. The look on their faces had been priceless; totally worth the constant filling-in of holes and the house training that, so far, was hit and miss. Storm and Zeus, the two motley mixed breed dogs they'd brought home, were attached at the hip to the kids, and Mike loved being able to give them the gift of pets.

Mike looked around from his spot on the semi-circular stone lounge, Robyn curled into his side, and Ezio resting his head on Mike's leg. The man was exhausted, having come home from a long shift at the hospital only half an hour earlier. He could hear the kids' happy laughs ringing out from the back yard as they played with the dogs.

Their three sets of parents were gathered around the table chatting with Katy's parents. Their first meeting was going well, all things considered. None of them really understood the dynamics of their relationship when he, Robyn, and Ezio had explained it, but they'd been far more accepting than Mike anticipated. He had Wani to thank for that when it came to his parents, but Katy, Connor, and Levi had done them a solid too. They'd been a godsend, spending time talking to each of them and answering their questions until they came around.

Their friends were there too. At one end of the stone seating area was Will, with Eddie on his lap. Eddie was dressed in a gauzy blouse paired with jeans that revealed just enough ankle to be sexy and high heels that made Mike's feet ache just looking at them, while Will shared Ezio's style—chinos and a polo shirt. Mike couldn't believe what a small world it was when Ezio had introduced them and Robyn recognized Will. There really were six degrees of separation on the Gold Coast, but the fact that Will had been Ezio's boss, and he'd even lived with the captain and his boyfriend for a few months when he finished working on the very ship Mike had cruised on, was insane.

Katy, Connor, and Levi were laughing from the loungers across the fire pit from them, and they'd brought a friend too—a pink-haired lady named Adelaide. She was intriguing, and Mike's first impression was that she'd fit right into their group, not even blinking when she'd seen Ezio devour him in a long kiss before doing the same to Robyn when he'd arrived home from work.

"It's looking great, mate," Nick said as he slid onto the padded cushion beside Robyn. His gaze moved around the yard before lingering on the three of them curled up together. He knew his oldest friend wasn't just talking about the house, but their families too.

"It is, isn't it?" Mike responded, smiling. Warmth filled him, and it wasn't just the winter late afternoon sun shining down on them that did it. "I had no idea it could be like this."

"I'm happy for you. All of you." Nick clapped him on the knee before shifting so that Emma could sit next to him.

Mike caught Jacob's gaze from across the firepit. He and Cassie were sharing a lounger, drinks in hand. But while Cassie looked content to spend a lazy afternoon planted in the shade, Jacob's look of raw longing had Mike wanting to do something crazy and try to get him set up. He had no idea if the man was out—whether he'd even admitted his desires to himself—but Mike didn't want his new friend to go any longer without experiencing what it was like to be with another man, even if he was married to a beautiful woman.

"How do you guys know each other?" Nick asked the other trio and Adelaide.

"Connor and I have been friends for years, and I met Katy and Levi through him." Connor snorted out a laugh, and Katy elbowed him while Levi blushed to the roots of his hair.

"Oh, now there's a story." Eddie laughed.

"I helped Levi see what he was missing, that's all," Adelaide said, all prim and proper. "He just needed a nudge."

"In the form of a butt plug," Connor teased.

"You love it." Levi's voice was husky, and when he bit Connor playfully on his shoulder, the other man's breath audibly hitched. But Mike was more interested in Jacob's reaction than Connor's. The other man had his hands fisted in Cassie's white linen shirt and his eyes squeezed closed as if he couldn't bear to see the two men showing affection to each other. But Mike suspected that wasn't the case at all.

"Mate, you got an issue with this?" Will asked, pointing between Connor and Levi, himself and Eddie, and Mike and Ezio.

"He doesn't," Cassie answered instantly. Jacob slowly uncurled his fingers and straightened the loose linen. When he met each of their eyes, Mike gave him an encouraging nod.

"I don't have a problem. I'm one of you—I'm pan—but it's been a while since I've been with a man. Last time didn't end well. It ruined everything—"

"No, it didn't," Cassie interjected, spinning to sit sideways on the lounger. Waving her hand in the direction of their house, then their friends, she added, "Look at everything we have because of it."

"But we don't have him, do we?" Jacob's words were quiet, but the impact silenced them all. Cassie shook her head and cupped his face, leaning her forehead against his cheek. Whatever she said was for his ears alone. He nodded and hugged her close. After a moment he smiled, the professional-looking one he had on his real estate marketing material, and added, "Might just have to get back into it though, if you guys are anything to go by. Anyone know a good swingers' club?"

Adelaide cleared her throat. "Actually, I do." She reached into her purse by her feet and slipped Cassie a dark business card. The other woman looked at it with raised eyebrows and nodded before passing it to Jacob. He read it, slipped it into his shirt pocket and nodded his thanks.

"So... how good was the State of Origin?" Jacob asked, and there was a round of collective moans and a few choice words.

* * * * *

It was much later that night, when everyone had gone home and after he'd checked on the kids sound asleep in their bedrooms with their respective dogs curled up on the ends of their beds, that Mike stopped in the doorway to their bedroom. Their oversized king bed had three pillows, with his in the middle. Robyn was reading from her tablet, and Ezio was applying moisturiser to his hands, waiting for him to join them.

Mike smiled. This was home. His kids and their pets and being loved and cherished by the two people who made his heart whole. He hadn't believed in happily ever afters before them. He never imagined finding someone, never mind two people, who completed him. Who understood and loved Mike for who he was. But his heart had known. He suspected it had beaten for his two lovers—a triple beat— for as long as he'd been alive. It reminded him to keep looking until he'd found his way home to them. Robyn and Ezio had pieced together the parts of himself Mike had held separate, ashamed of what he needed. But they'd not only accepted it, they'd encouraged him. They'd shown Mike exactly what unconditional love and acceptance really was.

If that's what it was—if fate had dealt him that defect in his heart so that he could find his happily ever after on the way to finding a cure—it was a fate he'd treasure for the rest of his life. Life's happiest moments were the little ones. The quiet ones. The ones where he crawled onto their big bed and slipped under the covers with the two people who he wanted to share the rest of his life with. Mike closed and locked the bedroom door and dropped his shorts to reveal his brand-new hot-pink jock and crawled up the bed. As Robyn slid her e-reader on the table and Ezio shifted under the covers, kicking off his underwear, Mike grinned at them before palming himself. "I'm in need of a reminder."

"Oh yeah?" Robyn asked as she leaned into him and kissed him, their tongues tangling together. "Of what?"

"Of how perfectly we fit together."

Ezio licked up his throat and bit down on his earlobe before sucking away the sting. Mike turned, kissing Ezio too as Robyn pushed the covers down the bed. "And how do you think we should do that?" Ezio asked, humming as he palmed Mike's hard cock. Sensation rocketed through him, making every nerve ending tingle in anticipation.

"I'm sure you can come up with something."

And, boy, did he. When Mike's muffled shout as he came rent the air, while both his lovers moved inside him, worshipping his body and chasing their own orgasms, Mike sent up a silent thanks to the universe for double penetration. For strap-ons. For women who loved using them, especially when they were the love of his life.

For men who loved topping, especially when they were the other love of his life.

For problem-solvers and doctors who never forgot.

For his lovers.

For this perfect life he was living, full of love and lust and fun and more love. For the laughter they all shared every day.

And especially for Dr Knox healing his heart so he could live every moment of this magical life to the fullest with the loves of his life until he was an old, old man.

And they lived happily ever after.

Thank you for coming along on Mike, Ezio and Robyn's journey. I hope you fell in love with their story as much as I adored writing it. If you did, please leave a review. It doesn't need to be anything crazy-long, just a sentence or two about how they made you feel.
Leaving a short review helps readers like yourself find stories to swoon over and indie authors like me get the word out.
Thank you!
Ann xx

Want to see how Katy, Connor and Levi got together?

Three Hearts

He wants his best friend's girl. How can he want his best friend too?

When Connor met Katy, he knew she was the one. But it wasn't meant to be. Six years later, with PTSD and an honourable discharge from the army, he has nowhere else to go except home—back to the only two people who can help him heal.

Connor should leave, but he can't seem to stay away.

Falling for Katy again isn't supposed to happen.

Neither is falling for his best friend, Levi. His very straight best friend.

He's fought for his country, and now he's fighting for love. This is one battle Connor cannot afford to lose.

Three Hearts is a slow-burn, emotionally charged, friends to lovers, bi-awakening MMF romance that will leave you breathless. Previously published as *Delectable*, it is the first story in the Rule of Three series and can be read as a standalone.

Available on Amazon and in audio:
https://books2read.com/u/barEY6

Want to read Will and Eddie's story?

Yes, Captain

A cruise ship captain with an unbreakable rule. A dancer who tempts him to toss the rulebook overboard...

Will Preston lives by one edict: don't date staff.

But the new dancer onboard has the silver fox sailing into unchartered waters. Young, sexy, and with a penchant for lipstick and heels, the man pushes all Will's buttons.

It's not just the tropical sun that's heating things up; their chemistry is sizzling.

Will's been burned before. Can he throw caution to the wind and chart a new course with Eddie by his side? Or will an interfering crew-member steer them into stormy seas?

Yes, Captain is a stand-alone, steamy age-gap MM romance set on a cruise ship in the South Pacific, with a flirty dancer who loves pole dancing and his shy captain. Yes, Captain was previously published as *Dance With Me*. This re-release includes over 30,000 words of never-before-seen bonus content.

Available on Amazon:
https://books2read.com/u/bxePPo

About Ann Grech

By day Ann Grech lives in the corporate world and can be found sitting behind a desk typing away at reports and papers or lecturing to a room full of students. She graduated with a PhD in 2016 and is now an over-qualified nerd. Glasses, briefcase, high heels and a pencil skirt, she's got the librarian look nailed too. If only they knew! She swears like a sailor, so that's got to be a hint. The other one was "the look" from her tattoo artist when she told him that she wanted her kids initials "B" and "J" tattooed on her foot. It took a second to register that it might be a bad idea.

She's never entirely fit in and loves escaping into a book—whether it's reading or writing one. But she's found her tribe now and loves her MM book world family. She dislikes cooking, but loves eating, can't figure out technology, but is addicted to it, and her guilty pleasure is Byron Bay Cookies. Oh and shoes. And lingerie. And maybe handbags too. Well, if we're being honest, we'd probably have to add her library too given the state of her credit card every month (what can she say, she's a bookworm at heart)!

In 2019 she was an Award-Winning Finalist in the Fiction: LGBTQ category of the 2019 Best Book Awards sponsored by American Book Fest for her story In Safe Arms.

She also publishes her raunchier short stories under her pen name, Olive Hiscock.

Ann loves chatting to people online, so if you'd like to keep up with what she's got going on:
Join her newsletter (you'll get two free books!):
https://landing.mailerlite.com/webforms/landing/d8m4r2
Like her on Facebook:
https://www.facebook.com/pages/Ann-Grech/458420227655212
Join her reader group:
https://www.facebook.com/groups/1871698189780535/
Follow her on Twitter and Instagram: @anngrechauthor
Follow her on Goodreads:
https://www.goodreads.com/author/show/7536397.Ann_Grech
Follow her on BookBub:
https://www.bookbub.com/authors/ann-grech
Follow her on Amazon:
https://www.amazon.com/~/e/B00IJPO3EM
Visit her website for her current booklist:
http://www.anngrech.com/

She'd love to hear from you directly, too. Please feel free to e-mail her at ann@anngrech.com or check out her website for updates.

ANN GRECH'S BOOKS

RULE OF THREE

Gift Unwrapped (MMF) part of the Holiday Kisses
Anthology – coming December 2021
Three Hearts (MMF) (Also available in audio)
Yes, Captain (MM)
Triple Beat (MMF)
Threepeat (MMF) – coming 2022

UNEXPECTED

Whiteout (MM)
White Noise (MM)
Whitewash (MM)

MY TRUTH

All He Needs (MMM)
In Safe Arms (MM)

PEARCE STATION DUET

Outback Treasure I (MM)
Outback Treasure II (MM)

SPINOFF FROM PEARCE STATION

Three of Us (MMF)

STANDALONES

Home For Christmas (MM)
The Gift (FMMM - free for newsletter subscribers)
Take Two (MM – free for newsletter subscribers)

M/F TITLES

One night in Daytona
Ink'd